Wolf Moon

Lesley Smith

The LICHFIELD PRESS

Wolf Moon
Lesley Smith
First published 2021 by
The LICHFIELD PRESS

ISBN 9780905985954

Cover design by Alena Plevey

The LICHFIELD PRESS
www.lichfieldpress.moonfruit.com
lichfieldppress@hushmail.com

Author's notes

This book is set over the short period of just seven months from July 1568 to February 1569. These dates are not, however, how they would be described in the mid-sixteenth century, as until 1752 New Year's Day was March 25th, known as Lady Day. This is arguably a more logical calendar in some ways than our modern version, as Lady Day usually shows the clear signs of Spring. This means all the action in this story would be recorded at the time as happening in the same year of 1568.

In the narrative I use modern language and spelling for accessibility. Spelling at the time was not standardised, and was usually phonetic, which meant that the same word might be spelled in different ways, even within the same document.

I write in some detail about the interiors of three important properties on the borders of Derbyshire and Staffordshire. These are Somersal Hall, Woodroffe's and Tutbury Castle. Of these, only Tutbury Castle is open to the public, and at the time of writing I have been its curator and lessee for the last twenty years. Descriptions of the castle are based on research carried out during that period as part of a research project led by Dr Gareth Williams of the British Museum. The other two properties I previously owned with my late husband, and my memories of having lived in them informs the details which I provide about the interiors and grounds of both houses.

Some of the characters are based on real people, not necessarily from the same period in which this book is set. The leather-bound medical book mentioned in this novel is based on a genuine surviving example from the period, which was the subject of my MPhil dissertation. The book remains in private hands, preserved and protected for future generations.

Wolf Moon contains much discussion about English country traditions and belief structures. Some of these are found across the whole country, while others vary from region to region, and not all can be dated with absolute accuracy, as many are only attested in oral tradition. I have borrowed those which I feel lend colour to the story, but their inclusion does not mean that they are necessarily accurate for the precise time and place.

It has been such a pleasure writing this book and I do hope you enjoy reading it.

Lesley Smith
Tutbury Castle
November 2020

Dedicated to
My husband Gareth and son Henry,
with love

and to
Elizabeth Marshall, brilliant mind and kindest heart
RIP

How poor remembrances are statues, tombs,
And other monuments that men erect
To princes, which remain in closèd rooms
Where but a few behold them, in respect
Of Books, that to the universal eye
Show how they lived; the other where they lie!

Concerning the Honour of Books

John Florio (1533-1625)

Chapter 1

A two-headed calf was born in the long barn, the night the summer rains came.

Just a mile from the barn, a small group of riders were braving the storm, cantering through the tight lanes whilst above them an ominous pale green sky cracked open, and sheets of water poured from the heavens. The three men and one woman drove their horses onwards determinedly, with their riding habits and hooded cloaks soaked through to their flesh beneath. For all of them, whether horses or humans, it was a matter of head down and fly, just half a mile to go and then home.

The young woman who led the group heard a shout from one of the riders behind, but the noise of the thunder, pouring rain and horses' hooves made it impossible to hear clearly the warning, as overhead a black branch snapped and fell in front of her. It was only with immense skill that she kept her seat, as her usually steady chestnut leapt like a dancer in a masque. The other horses in turn were alarmed at the sudden rearing of their stable-mate, and the lady's companions struggled valiantly to remain in their saddles. There were hoots of laughter behind the young woman, both of relief and pleasure at having stood up to the challenges of the ride in such appalling conditions.

The rain beat relentlessly on the cracked, dried earth, at first like a drumbeat and then forming great pools before being drunk eagerly by the parched land. Two whole months with hardly a drop of rain throughout the kingdom, and London had become dangerous as a yellow miasma rose as a mist off the river Thames. Plague stalked the streets, striking down both rich and poor. It was the same, messengers said, as far away as York in the north, and Plymouth down on the south-west coast.

The female rider was Mary Dudley, a member of the famous Dudley family, but from a minor branch. She was always keen to point out that the glittering Robert Dudley was merely a 'cousin of my father' and that was because she didn't want to have to put up with a rush of enquiries for an introduction to her esteemed relative. People always looked either pained or irritated and drifted away upon receiving the news that she had no influence with the earl.

One or two occasionally would cling on to hope with questions such as 'You must have met him – surely?' or even worse, 'Well, as a special favour to me' - Mary had no idea who the enquirer was - '...do you think you might try and see him for me, as I have such an interesting claim?'

That came from a short round woman being nudged by her husband, but the ingratiating smiles and eager onion breath both disappeared when their request was refused gently, but firmly, by Mary. 'I am so sorry, I really do not know my distant cousin Lord Robert Dudley. My father is at court, but I really would have no more hope of seeing him than you.'

It was all very embarrassing when they flounced off, muttering and glaring over their shoulders, no doubt sure she was lying, which is why Mary tended to move away smartly when her name was given to ensure she was not hijacked again. Well, not often anyway. When she told her father of people pressing her in such a way he would smile cynically and say 'Ah, the excesses of human conduct when ambition calls.' Mary knew he was teasing her for complaining, as such occasions only came about because they were perceived as influential, and she could make the most of enjoying the moment instead. She didn't enjoy it and, knowing what a modest man her father was, had her suspicions that he didn't enjoy such attention either!

She had never even met Robert Dudley, now Lord Leicester these past four years, although her father had met him often, and Mary herself had seen him from afar. It was almost impossible to miss the Queen's favourite, as he cut a swathe through the court. Everyone knew in the halls of power when someone of great importance was arriving, as a murmur started like a buzz and then a group would surge forward, waving papers or calling a name. It could equally well be Dudley or Sir William Cecil, or indeed Lord Paget, as they were all men of immense influence for different reasons, and each with close personal contact with the queen.

Mary's father Edmund Dudley had been a widower for many years, and Mary was his only child. He was a quiet, thoughtful and studious man, but he had a sense of humour that was intensely dry, and could be rather wicked in its own way. Her father had just one living sibling, a sister, Mary's Aunt Phoebe. Aunt Phoebe was a relative to avoid at all costs, as she was an intimidating giant of a woman who struck fear into those that knew her. It was not her considerable size in every sense that terrified the fleeing relatives, but her obsessive desire to order people about and interfere constantly, giving her unwanted opinion on everything from medicine and clothes to furniture arrangements. Her voice was mostly on a pitch with a shriek, as she told cringing acquaintances that 'I say this for your own good' or 'You know I have your best interests foremost in my mind'. Her husband had died young: Mary's father said he didn't blame him.

Mary had first seen Robert Dudley in a great parade when she was ten years of age and the glittering red-haired new queen was riding alongside him. She had been placed safely on a raised platform on the route of the procession with her father's steward, Thomas Ashbourne, who was holding her hand tightly as the platform swayed when the massive crowd below surged like the sea coming in. Even as a child she recognized the intimacy between Robert Dudley and the queen, as he pulled her reins towards him to whisper to her, causing Elizabeth to smile. It was not inappropriate for him to be close to the queen, as her newly appointed Master of the Horse, but it still seemed slightly shocking for him to show such familiarity with an anointed queen.

Mary had been elated to see her father in the parade riding alongside other courtiers some way behind the queen. He had raised his bonnet to her which made her clasp her hands to her face in sheer joy. She remembered vividly that scented rose petals had poured in showers from the looming balconies on either side, and Mary had lifted her young face to feel them fall upon her skin, blinking and laughing under a bright blue London sky.

There were no parades now in London, no feathers or bright silks, as those who could afford to had fled the capital with its quietly dark, sulky streets, leaving behind the sweating poor who did not have the means or were too ill to escape.

The Dudley house was on the outskirts of London, where the Thames was sweeter and the air less foetid than in the heart of town. Their grounds had formal gardens, and a few steps to a gateway on the river Thames, where beyond the water were green fields and trees as far as the eye could see, with only the odd cottage dotted on the horizon. Its rural glamour meant it didn't look like a risky place to live in plague times, but the chance of some disease in the hot months was always a danger either in or near London. Like many other large towns or cities, any delivery of food or goods upon cart or boat could also bear an unexpected and fatal parcel of death, as indeed could the carrier. Both Edmund Dudley and Mary always left London in the summer each year escaping to their Derbyshire country home to which she now rode that stormy afternoon.

Mary's father continued his work wherever he was, reporting on events in the Midlands or North, and relying on the large number of messengers who raced backwards and forwards across the roads and lanes of England and Wales in all weathers. When Mary was little, she had dreamed of being a messenger dressed as a boy, and of the drama of racing around the country with important letters in her leather bag, changing foaming horses every thirty miles and seeing off footpads with her brilliant sword-play.

Mary loved to think of those joyful, heroic dreams of her childhood but now she thought of the present truth. As Mary was cantering her last few hundred yards to home, her thoughts turned to the queen, who was on progress across the land in the summer months. Whitehall Palace had been left if not entirely, then almost empty, as the buildings echoed to the sound of the footsteps of palace servants who had little to do except a perfunctory sweep, or wipe of furniture and then drink the cellar wines.

A few busy civil servants could still be seen, as well as the elderly courtiers like drifting ghosts, who stayed behind to administer matters of state and make decisions about an almost deserted capital. Most of the elderly and infirm just couldn't face the royal progress, with months on the road grinding along at up to twelve miles on a good day. They had done it before, and with monarchs before this queen, but were now excused duty. It was a massive exercise to plan how to move many hundreds of people on progress, both courtiers and in turn, their servants, as they all had to be fed and cared for. Her father had told her all about it. Arriving at their destination, one of many, they would invariably be greeted by a row of trembling parish councillors and a mayor who would stumble through dull speeches of welcome. This was about the last straw for many who had to continue to sit in their saddles and bear it. Restraining yawns had become an art form and silently (so as not to creak saddles) shifting buttocks from one cheek to another in an attempt to ease weary muscles.

The queen, Edmund Dudley had told his daughter, had always been wonderfully gracious, ultimately patient and kind to those who greeted her in these towns and cities. This was a rather different queen, apparently, from the one an hour later shut away in her private lodgings, who would shout and throw shoes at members of her retinue who annoyed her in the smallest way when she was tired. Of course, Mary had observed upon hearing of this change of character, the generous gifts of gilt objects or gold coins that those welcoming groups would usually present the queen to demonstrate their loyalty might help Elizabeth to bear the speeches more gracefully. Her father had tutted that she might think such a thing, but smiled at the corner of his mouth, as he did looking down at his papers.

Over the years, she had come to appreciate that the queen was a woman of great intellectual and political skill who understood that staying in London without going out to eat meat and press hands with her people as far across her kingdom as she could reasonably manage, was asking for trouble. She was not going to risk leaving a door open for an uppity earl claiming Plantagenet blood to start an uprising against the relatively new Tudor dynasty. One way of developing loyalty amongst the masses was to allow them to see their queen and to wonder at the air of majesty which she wore heavy as a cloak around her shoulders. Those who saw her were awed by her almost unearthly presence, Mary's father said. Mary knew this was true, for she had seen it for herself and people falling on their knees if she looked straight at them. Elizabeth had looked straight at a breathless Mary, and a tiny frown of attempted recognition had appeared on the white brow and then passed as she moved on. No wonder, perhaps, as Mary had something of Robert Dudley about her looks and colouring.

The queen displayed a carefully manufactured style, as she often included elements in her parades that suggested an intimate knowledge of the area she was in.This gave a sense that wherever she visited, the people were not strangers to her and she valued them and their loyal history. When Her Majesty rode through Stamford in Lincolnshire, she had had in her parade two magnificent camels in jewelled collars led through the streets and by doing so she was giving public recognition of the brave crusaders who set off from Stamford, with its beautiful river and many churches. Locals would talk about both the exotic camels and the queen for generations afterwards. While her subjects generally had the chance to admire the queen in all her majesty, a select few had the even greater honour of providing the queen and her entourage with accommodation, all at their own considerable expense. Elizabeth was a shrewd and thrifty businesswoman, and like her grandfather Henry VII, the first Tudor to take the throne, she had a reputation for counting the pennies. Many great landowners were left almost, and in some cases actually, bankrupt as they waved off the vast progress, wondering desperately if they could borrow money from relatives.

On this inclement summer afternoon, Mary Dudley was now on her own more modest progress to one of the most beautiful places in her heart, that family home in Derbyshire: Somersal Hall. Small in comparison to some of the great buildings in which the queen lodged on her travels, as it had only twenty-eight rooms and a labyrinth of out-houses, it was nevertheless one of the finest houses in that part of the shire, and Mary loved it. Soon she would be there once more. Shaking the rain from her eyes, and thoughts of the queen from her mind, she touched a spur to her horse and pressed onwards towards the shelter of home.

Chapter 2

Thomas Ashbourne stood in the long barn looking down sadly on the pitiful scene of the dead calf. His wide-brimmed leather hat and cloak were dripping with rain, as he held up his lantern trying to adjust his eyes to see better in the steamy gloom of the hot barn.

The tiny calf had two perfect heads locked at the neck and its coat was wet from the birthing: it was golden red in colour. He was not alone in this silent vigil, for the herdsman Edward Loxley and his son, Will, were also looking down at the creature, hands on hips and shaking their heads in disbelief. Two more lanterns hung from the overhead beam, flickering yellow in the darkness and throwing strange shadows on the walls and roof. The rain continued to drum loudly outside.

'Didn't even draw a breath, poor creature' said Edward in his broad Derbyshire accent. He was not a brutal man, but a countryman who had compassion as well as hard work in his bones, and an immense respect for nature. He and his forefathers before him had worked for the Dudley family for as many generations as any could remember, and beyond. His son Will was also quiet and steady. All of them felt uneasy just to be standing, staring at the calf, as if it were an abomination of God's design, and therefore shameful in some way.

Thomas Ashbourne seemed to rouse himself and said, 'We'll have to get it out of here. Make sure you bury it deep, so foxes don't try to dig it up . Burning it will just draw attention to the corpse, with nosy types drifting over to see what is burning, and I can't risk it being seen.' He sighed, taking off his hat and wiping his sweating brow with the back of his hand. The barn smelt of sweet hay, cows and rain. It was strange, he thought, that you could smell rain but couldn't hope to describe it. His mind was wandering again so he pulled himself into action.

'Back to the job in hand, Edward.' He looked directly at both men, making sure they got on with what was needed, instead of the numb inactivity, spiralling into more gloom. He added, 'There is enough to contend with, with this thunder and lightning, as the country maids run around, covering anything up that might reflect the flashes. If they see this poor creature, they will believe there is a curse upon the house, and flap about shrieking, with their hands over their ears with panic. You know what they can be like.'

Aye,' murmured Edward, who was watching his son Will already dragging the corpse out of the back door of the barn covered in a bit of sacking. 'I am afraid it will be hot work digging a deep pit in this clammy heat, Will, but it must be done.' His father and Ashbourne both knew that Will would do it without complaint or question.

'Thank you, Edward,' said Ashbourne, as he absent-mindedly patted the cow gently on the rump. She was looking round with eyes rolling dolefully, looking for her sad issue, now gone.

'Give her some grain from the brewing shed as a treat, and let's see how she is in the morning,' instructed Ashbourne.

Edward nodded, and placed a large slopping, pitch-sealed wooden bucket of fresh water in front of the cow, before beginning to rub her down with wisps of straw twisted in his gnarled brown hands. Ashbourne walked away and stood with his hand on the door frame, looking out over the yard at the magnificent half-timbered hall on his left. It was three stories high, and was heavily decorated with trefoils and carved figures. Through the driving rain it looked like a ghostly apparition, and the roof seemed to groan and bulge under the weight of the sky as it pressed down on the hall.

The steward was the third generation of the Ashbournes to hold that position under the Dudley family. As a widower in his mid-forties, he had come to terms with the likelihood of having no child to follow him and would therefore break the line of service. There was still time, as his friends would tell him, for according to them, there were many pretty and eager women who would be pleased to marry such a respectable man attached to a great family.

Ashbourne told himself that that he was too busy to make time for an eager young wife. Or perhaps not too busy, if he was truthful with himself, but simply not prepared to take on another marriage. His late wife had been a pleasant but demanding creature and her short life and their brief marriage had not made much impact on her widower. He felt guilty about that on the rare occasions when he considered it, but it was the truth of the matter. Before and since his marriage he had enjoyed the occasional tryst, but they tended to be brief affairs, as he was not at all keen on commitment. He would be loyal to his master's family until death, but not to another woman.

Like all his stock he was dark, with a pleasant face and always neat and smartly dressed. His hair, much to his irritation, was thinning rapidly, with a monk-like tonsure appearing on top of his head like that of his father and grandfather before him. Thomas Cromwell might have closed all the priories and monasteries casting out the monks and nuns but it seemed that God made his own monks, he told himself, as he touched his bald pate and frowned. He was not a vain man, but reluctant to give up the abundance of youthful curls and firm stomach that he once had. Those had gone to the wall too, he told himself ruefully.

He was different in other ways from his father and grandfather with their settled marriages, as he was fortunate enough to have been the only Ashbourne who had lived and worked at court with his master. He was also highly educated compared to his forebears. The Dudleys were a successful, if at times a fatally over-ambitious family, but many believed that Edmund Dudley was the best of all of them, being modest, hardworking and intellectual. He treated his servants with compassion and dignity, if not a rather soft hand. He was not a man who cared much for conflict, encouraging others to deal with such matters. People like Thomas Ashbourne, in fact, who with tactful skill could deal with most tricky situations both at court and at home.

Ashbourne spent much of his time with his master,

wherever he was, including accompanying him on his travels. However, over the years it had become customary for Ashbourne to open the Hall each summer, in preparation for the arrival of the family from London. Somersal always had a full complement of servants, both inside and out working on the estate, but standards could slip a little when the family was away, so Ashbourne was on hand to ensure all was well in advance of their summer return.

The grounds and the animals were always wonderfully cared for, and the fresh water wells were clean and sweet upon inspection. This diligent household management at the Hall was largely due to the efficient housekeeper, Alice Goodrich, whose job it was to crack the whip. Alice had held that role for some eleven years and lived in a grace and favour cottage by the Hall that came with the job. With her in the cottage lived her grandson Warwick, who was a sly ne'er-do-well.

'He'll never do well, that lad,' Ashbourne said out loud, but Edward did not comment even if he had heard, as he believed in privacy, so he just carried on with his duties in the barn.

Ashbourne's train of thought was interrupted as he was startled by a great slam of thunder which broke open the heavens as a silver bolt of fork lightning struck the oak tree in the next field. The tree split open with a great wrenching noise and, wreathed in white smoke, a massive branch fell to the ground. Edward came to the side of Ashbourne and was joined by his son, who also came to the crowded barn door to see what the dramatic noise was all about.

In the distance, women's voices could be heard screaming. It would be the servants huddled together no doubt, except Alice Goodrich. She would be busy jeering at them for their fears.

'So there's the oak gone then.' Edward was not a man, nor was his son, to be of many words and they both turned away into the barn. Ashbourne was hoping that if Lady Mary and her outriders were travelling today as planned, they would all have the sense to stay at Tutbury Castle, five miles away, instead of risking the storm by pushing on to Somersal. The rain was now hammering so hard, it was deafening and any speech, even in close proximity, would need to be overwhelmed by shouting.

Unusually this year, Ashbourne would stay at Somersal, rather than accompany Sir Edmund, who was about the queen's business in some unstated place. He had been taught over the years not to ask too many questions, as some of his master's work was secret and protected state interests. His master would just gently ignore such questions and with a brief, distracted smile, carry on with what he was doing at the time.

Although Ashbourne was not to travel this year, he was given clear instructions that he was to take care of Mary instead. He had been surprised but tried not to let his face show his disappointment. Looking after the young mistress was hardly an onerous task, as she was an engaging, and educated young woman, but Ashbourne would have preferred to be with Sir Edmund where his real skills as a confidential assistant lay. Working alongside the skilful professional secretaries at court, there was always much to do and anyway he felt in the thick of everything worth knowing about. It was exciting if demanding work and Ashbourne thrived on it but was well aware that his duties stretched into the family and properties. So, like a good steward he did what he was told to do and prepared to carry out his duties to his best ability (and try not to complain about it too much even to himself.

There was a noise behind him as Edward appeared again back in the barn, having helped Will half-carry the calf to a suitable spot for deep burial. Leaving his son to finish the job, he carried with him in one hand a bucket of grain mash taken from the brewing shed. A 'cushing' sound at the cow produced favourable results, as she dipped her head into the bucket and started to munch the grainy treat. Edward commented that there was 'nowt much wrong with any creature that could eat.' So the cow was saved, and there would be more bulling ahead for this cow and, hopefully, another live calf so her creamy milk could continue to flow.

Ashbourne then suddenly heard the dogs barking frenziedly, so knew that they had heard something worth commenting on. Four small rough-haired terrier noses appeared sniffing under the stable door in a row. The wood was chewed away at the bottom as evidence of the frustration of the dogs when they were unable to get out and take part in any excitement in the yard. Their acute ears could indeed hear something approaching and, despite their considerable fear of thunder, this had not stopped them being on duty as riders approached.

'Lady Mary,' whistled Ashbourne through his clenched teeth and set jaw, irritated at this rashness. 'What a wild creature, to attempt this weather!' He stamped across the yard in his long brown leather boots, still swinging his yellow lantern, and opened the porched front door, shouting for the servants to be on hand.

Anne Compson, Mary's personal maid, only carried out that duty when Mary was at Somersal. The rest of the time she helped her husband on their nearby small farm, which formed part of the large Somersal estate made up of many tenanted properties, which unsurprisingly were mostly involved in farming.

She had everything in readiness now for her young mistress, from aired bed to a night shift laid across a chair. Ashbourne knew that he could depend on Anne Compson, so was content that Lady Mary would be well received and her private apartments properly arranged, including a bright fire in a clean grate to fight off the dampness despite the summer heat.

No more than seconds after the barking began, Thomas Ashbourne could also hear the approaching horses and as if by some saintly intervention, the rain slowed up to almost a halt. The dogs somehow squeezed out from under the door, leaping about and fighting with each other like idiots, and rushed immediately to the hall porch to see who was arriving.

Everyone, it seemed, had turned out to greet the young mistress. Even Ashbourne, despite his misgivings, could not resist a grim smile as the group of riders came round the bend and clattered through the great gates at a tremendous lick. They were all chattering, puffing and blowing as they reined in, clearly delighted at their safe arrival. here, at the front of the riders, under a dark hood on a fine chestnut, was Mary Dudley. For about the hundredth time, he told himself that the chestnut was far too big for Mary to manage. It was a man's horse, but he also knew that Mary would vigorously resist having her much-loved horse taken from her, as she considered herself equal to any man as a rider. Ashbourne also knew her father wouldn't dream of trying to challenge her, as he liked a quiet domestic, as well as professional life, and anyway Mary probably was equal to most men when on a horse. She had always been a bit boyish after her mother died, and spent spare time out of lessons climbing trees, playing with the dogs and riding horses - far too big for her.

Ashbourne was resigned to her personality, for despite his misgivings, if anyone would ride in this storm it would be Mary, as she would love the excitement of it all. The summoned scruffy gang of stable boys arrived at the big stone mounting block to help.

Meanwhile, the riders were swinging their legs from their saddles assisted by the stable boys and one went to help Mary dismount, but Ashbourne beat him to it, as he stood open-armed to help his young mistress from her horse that was madly champing its bit. She looked down at him from the saddle, smiling with pleasure at the sight of him. Mary was still in many ways that little girl he remembered who loved to lie on the grass and watch rabbits. Ashbourne smiled in return at this incorrigible maid, handing his lantern backwards to the stable boy so he could catch her, whilst the other lads were leading the rest of the group's exhausted horses to the stables. No doubt Mary's particular favourite terrier Porky would lead the way, head high and tail wagging.

'What a wild night, Thomas Ashbourne.' She knew he would be annoyed at the risk she had taken, but gave him her winning smile which worked every time, adding 'But I could not wait!' The many days on the road from London, either in the rickety carriage or on horseback to Tutbury Castle, was never very comfortable.

She added, 'They have made good the lodgings at the castle on the orders of the queen, who has decided to invest gold there for some reason.'

Tutbury Castle was the centre of one of the great estates within the Duchy of Lancaster, effectively the private estates of the king or queen since Henry Bolingbroke had taken the throne in 1399. The decades that followed had been the high point of the castle's history, with grand new tower houses and a fine curtain wall, and a new great hall built at the southern end. The castle had still been in a grand state when Elizabeth's father Henry VIII had visited as a young man and established the royal stud there. More recently though, the castle had been sadly neglected by the Duchy, and the repairs had become matters of desperate need, with great cracks in some of the curtain walls and parts of some of the buildings actually tumbled down. It was only with the personal intervention of the queen that restoration work had begun in the last few years, in recognition of the castle's history and importance as the centre of one of her greatest estates in the region.

As Mary and Thomas Ashbourne made their way through the porch, Mary admitted her wild behaviour by stopping and looking up into Ashbourne's face with a tinge of guilt. 'It's true we would have been warm and dry at the castle, but after a couple of hours there, I had had enough and was restless to be home. How are you, Thomas Ashbourne?' That question was a deft move to change the subject, as she dripped her way through the porch and then into the Great Hall, looking at him briefly over her shoulder.

'I am of great good cheer that you are here, and not least because you have arrived safely in one of the greatest summer storms anyone has ever seen.' There was a pause as he added, 'But still you ride!' He wasn't exactly scolding her for taking the risk, as it was not his place. Even so, she knew he had worried at the thought of the risk, and appreciated only too well that there are many forms of family. She didn't reply, but simply nodded at him with laughter in her eyes, accepting the criticism but knowing very well that she would do it again. Pulling off her leather gauntlets, she saw clear raindrops were falling from them, like jewels glistening in the light of the candles. The servants took the wet clothes and hurried them to the kitchen to dry out, leaving her to run eagerly up the great staircase with its wide low treads to her room where her Anne was waiting with dry linen and a rubbing cloth.

Chapter 3

In the warmth of her chamber, Mary chatted about London, as she was rubbed down like a horse, and her hair loosened and squeezed. She talked of court, the great processions, how horrible and cruel bear-baiting was ('and they should stop it', and the latest fashions, in a tumble of information for Anne to tut and wonder at, until Mary was warm and dry. Mary Dudley was always enthusiastic, which she was aware made her unpopular at breakfast time, so frequently took a tray in her room. That was what grown up ladies did, so she did too, but Mary was not at all sure she would ever grow up if that meant sitting about moaning, as she had seen too many do, with far too much spare time on their hands and a petulant desire for attention through imagined illnesses.

Over Mary's head went the soft light shift edged with black-work, then on her feet a pair of buskins lined with fur, and finally a summer dressing robe of pale green, tied at the waist with a cord and tassels. The buskins were a bit tight now and Mary frowned as she was sure she hadn't got bigger feet since last year. Still, after a few minutes they gave way as she wiggled her toes in them.

Mary was intensely happy to be at the Hall. There she was free and could relax, away from the prying eyes of the court and packed, noisy streets of London. She ran her finger at the edge of her supper-plate, feeling a tiny dent on one side of the pewter. Smiling to herself, she remembered having caused that dent by playing cook when little, working alongside Eleanor, the real cook, who was still working at Somersal after all these years. Mary's little five-year-old fingers could not work at such a fast pace as the cook's and her eagerness to keep up had resulted in her accidently knocking the plate on the floor, denting it as it landed on the stone flags, scattering little red moulded marzipan mice, tinted with red sanders. She remembered that hot, brimming tears had quickly dried as Loxley had produced a little hammer, and knocked most of the dent out, leaving just a hint of the past accident.

Loxley had been happier then, he smiled more, but then his much loved wife was alive and it seemed he had been mourning all these years. As she felt the dent, she liked to trace that moment of her past under her finger, for it reminded her of the continuity of her life here where so many faces had watched her grow up and many were still part of the staff. She liked to feel safe, which was a foolish notion, for didn't everyone?

Mary was also bright enough to know that her mother's death had affected them all and she wondered if her father had been more noisy and enthusiastic about life, like Loxley had been before the death of his wife. Nostalgia for Mary was the happiest of pastimes, and she would listen for hours to tales of how high spirited she had been as a young child, and how she had come downstairs when she was four to a grand dinner party in London in her night shift, appearing like a little ghost in the doorway. The guests had pretended to be frightened of her, which made her laugh, before her previously sleeping nursemaid appeared in a flurry of apologies and taken her back to her bed.

Mary was always 'saving' animals, bringing home everything from baby ducks to an adder. On one memorable occasion she had produced the snake from a sack, with its beautiful green and black diamond back, the sight of which sent everyone flying when she shook it hissing out on the kitchen table. It was trapped by the usual hero, Loxley, using a forked stick hanging on the wall in the kitchen and Mary was in some trouble for that. She pointed out that she had caught the devil in a bag and that everyone should be happy – she was only eight at the time.

'Is Alice in this evening?' asked Mary, shaking off the past.

'Not this evening, my lady,' Anne replied stiffly, as Mary leaned back into her seat. 'She is in early in the morning, as usual, for fires and bread, as well as getting the house staff moving'. She sniffed, which meant she didn't approve of Alice. Well, no one did really.

'Alice is getting a bit keen to be in control these days, again!'

Mary looked up sharply, recognising that there was more to this than met the eye from that one, small, comment. Anne didn't want to burden her with domestic strife the moment she got off her horse, but at the same time a troubled brew was in the cauldron.

'I thought she had learned after Warwick.' Mary frowned at Anne as an invitation that she was concerned and wanted to hear more, which she was taking seriously. They shared confidences and Mary was content that her lady's maid would not breach their private conversations.

The housekeeper's grandson Warwick Goodrich would be about thirteen now, Mary thought. The boy could be charming when he wished, and had been a good worker as a young child, but a year earlier it had finally been recognised that Warwick had become a sly, cunning, manipulative creature who did as little as possible, but made others do his tasks for him. It had also become apparent that he was a thief, as despite his denials he had stolen both small amounts of money and food. The boy was poisonous, and it was decided that he could continue to live in the cottage with his grandmother, but would have to find work elsewhere, and he was forbidden to come to the Hall itself, or grounds.

Alice had pretended at first that the other servants were just jealous of Warwick, and had built up a story to damage his reputation, insisting that she would never allow him to behave in such a way. It was true that Alice was a hard-working, capable woman, but she would hear no criticism of her grandson. She also had a serious problem with wanting to know everything that was going on, and if there was trouble, you could be sure that Alice was in the middle of it, either as the direct cause of the trouble, or goading other members of staff against someone to whom she had taken one of her illogical dislikes.

Evidence was slim on that account but Mary, Anne and Cook all knew it was true. Nevertheless, Edmund Dudley was loyal to his servants despite the disloyalty of one or two, and had not wished to punish Alice for her grandson's misdeeds. It was only for her sake that he had been so lenient towards Warwick. Edmund had even encouraged, at his own expense, those who wished to have the chance to learn to read and write, believing that education was the greatest gift of all. He was disappointed that few took him up on this kind offer, and most of them did not stand the strict local schoolteacher for long.

Anne and Mary talked a little more, until the candles had burned low. 'What moon is it then, Anne?' the young mistress asked, always fascinated by Anne's broad knowledge of traditional beliefs. The question, asked each month when they were together, would give Mary a sense of what influence one could expect on earth, for as Anne would say, 'The moon be a feminine creature and sings to us especially, changing our moods and ideas.' Anne was convinced of this, as had many other generations been before her, and as no doubt many would be in generations yet to come.

'This be the Mead Moon, although it now bc waning and soon will wax again for August with a red moon.'

'That always sounds ominous, Anne. Some call it the Blood Moon, don't they?' said Mary.

'True, some do, so we have been warned by the heavens and should be watchful of any rising feelings that may go on to do harm. There is blood of the spirit as well as the flesh.' Anne spoke with the certainty of belief in country tales that was bred into her bones.

'Does that moon really mean, Anne, that some will be called to murder or cause blood to flow? Is that true? Really?'

Anne looked up. 'Some say it happens in one form or another to us all, but that is talk for a winter's night by the fire. I do know though that some, who are already known by the Devil (she crossed herself, have urges at full moons, and they be different each time.' Anne was still carefully unpacking her mistress's bag.

Mary never wanted to stop her maid when she spoke of such things and she sat back watching her affectionately as drowsiness started to fall on her. She could feel her back and legs were stiffening a little from the days in the saddle, but she was an experienced rider and strong of limb, so knew it wouldn't last long.

Eventually, Mary made her way to bed. The light summer cover was turned down and the windows shuttered against a violet sky which filled the heavens, as the storm had subsided and moved away to torment another place. Mary lay back and closed her eyes, savouring the familiar sounds and smells of the Hall. She was tired from her journey, so all thoughts quickly melted into dreams.

Chapter 4

That night, high in the heavens about Somersal Hall, there was Anne's waning moon nestling amongst the stars which was calling the tides of all on earth: from the oceans to every woman of child-bearing age.

When midnight arrived after just three hours' sleep, Mary got up. She didn't have insomnia, nor was she worrying about anything. It was a common practice for her to do so, even if she didn't really know when it all started, for it formed part of her earliest memories. Walking about in her nightgown, robe and slippers at a secret time was her way of making sure everything was as it should be. It was a chance to examine her home, without interruption or distraction. All these years she had gone starlight rambling and no one, as yet, had discovered her moving about, as sleep sat heavily upon the Hall.

She walked her usual walk along the highly polished oak floor of the beam-lined corridor, passing one, two, three diamond-paned windows on the right overlooking the lawn and rose gardens. Counting softly to herself as she drifted along, all indeed seemed well. The moon was so bright that the corridor was well illuminated in that odd silver blue a bright moon brings.

Her movements were so practised and familiar, she felt she could do it with her eyes closed. She whispered to herself 'Down the two steps and turn left to the next corridor', whilst padding almost silently past the doors of those at slumber.

The young mistress of the Hall knew each floorboard, every creak to avoid and every diamond window pane. On the lower corridor, her name had been scratched in the glass when she was ten summers old: she squatted down, holding her knees and, squinting, could still see her name, white in the moonlight. There it was. She knew it would be, but liked to see it all the same.

Now down the back staircase generally for the servants' use, and onto the flagged kitchen corridor, she ducked into the drying room under the gathered bunches of lavender, bay and sage hanging from the ceiling. The air in the room was pungent and spicy, making her want to sneeze. Peas and beans ready to be podded were piled into baskets on the table and, in the far corner, a carefully locked ancient cupboard.

This cupboard in many ways represented the new worlds that were being discovered in a recent wave of exploration: nutmeg, mace, pepper and glittering cones of sugar sat in tight jars, whilst clove pushed its way forward and tried hard to overwhelm all the other smells. The cupboard also contained jars and bottles of medicines for coughs, chills, and burns amongst others, all made up according to receipts passed down from one generation to the next.

There was a leather-bound handwritten book around somewhere that had been added to over the years by the Dudleys, usually the women of the family. Mary could just remember her mother writing receipts in it, which she had carefully gathered wherever she could, from neighbours, relations and even some of the grand figures with whom her husband had contact at court. She had taken great pride in including a receipt passed on from the marquis of Dorset, later duke of Suffolk, whose daughter Lady Jane Grey had married another Dudley cousin, Lord Robert's brother Guilford. Unfortunately their story hadn't ended well, and even Lord Marquis Dorset didn't know a cure for a decapitated body! Mary reminded herself to look at the book again and store this treasure of time more carefully. She was proud of the tradition that the Dudley women should be educated enough to write as well as read, and she too planned to add to it eventually.

The Dudley family could afford the finest physicians,

but grandmother's cough elixir was somehow more trusted. Mary knew there would also be a box of moss and bandages. She must look through the cupboard again, it had been such a long time. To others she would pretend this exercise would be to ensure that it was well-stocked and to clean it out but in truth, it would be a happy hour of fun for her and would draw her for a short amount of time to her mother's side.

Mary felt sad at the thought of her mother and so moved on to look in the cool wooden barred store room, where the best raised pastry meat pies sat proudly on plates and a little row of possets, candied nuts and jumble biscuits - sharp with the taste of honey and lemon – lay in their tight little knots on a cool stone bench, covered in muslin. Below, on the floor, stood a large, lidded wooden flour bin.

The dairy stores such as milk, cream, and cheese were kept still further down the corridor in the cold room beyond a separate door. Raw meat was kept far from the milk for it was believed that the milk could smell the blood, and be turned sour.

Mary considered country ways, which were found across most of England, as so few lived in the cities compared to the countryside. Superstitions permeated rural society, such as the belief that women who were menstruating should not handle milk or cream – even milking cows was frowned upon. That was a difficult superstition to manage amongst the poor, with perhaps one cow, for they did not have the luxury of choice, as the men were usually busy in the fields, leaving the milking to the women. It was also well known, but not spoken of, except in whispers, that women who worked together, eventually changed their cycle so that all would menstruate at the same time. Now, that was awkward to manage with one dairymaid per six cows so it was just as well not every monthly moon brought 'flowers' to all the women.

The heart of domestic life came next - the kitchen, with its scent of fresh bread and sweet almonds, and she observed with pleasure the old black and white spaniel, which her father had brought back from a rare trip to France. The dog, named Foxglove, thumped a happy tail at the sight of her and rolled over to be tickled, whilst sighing in front of the embers of the great fireplace used for cooking. Mary knew as she crouched down that only she and the old dog had knowledge of her night-time strolls.

As she looked around, Mary took in the detail of the room. The black rack fireplace with handled spit still had a slight glow. Even in the hottest summer, such as this one, the fires had to be lit to cook, and to boil water in the great lead-lined inset bowl for washing and cleaning. In the middle of the room, as one might expect, there was a vast, well-scrubbed table which was the pride and joy of the cook, Eleanor. Neatly lined up were clean bowls and a pile of wooden spoons, with more bowls, plates and flagons, some of pewter, which were neatly stacked on the many shelves. The gilt vessels for grand occasions were locked away for safekeeping in the house's treasury box. Also on the table, great bouquets of fresh herbs collected from the Hall herb garden flopped in jugs. The dried herbs hanging from the drying room beams were for the winter months. A couple of chairs stood by the fire, and benches were arranged around the room for the outside workers to come in and eat in stockinged or bare feet.

Mary remembered in that moment that the vast red brick kitchens in Hampton Court were so cavernous and high that when the pots released their steam in deep winter, the steam cooled so much in the roof space that it fell as snow on the servants below. Such tales passed amongst the aspiring middling classes in London, keen to show that they knew of the wonders of aristocratic and royal life. Mary reminded herself to tell Cook this extraordinary fact, so that she could see her stand, hands clasped in front of her ample bosom, and cry out with pleasure to hear such wonders.

Onwards she ventured, back through the drying room, then the laundry room with its barrels of lye soap and pressing stones, and past one of the garden doors leading to the kitchen garden. Through the window she could see in the semi-darkness the fruit nets pinned in neat rows, and beyond them the brook with its tiny bridge of stone. Close by, mirroring the moonlight, was the round fish-pond, always stocked fresh for the table. She knew the brewing place, dairy and a myriad of other outside sections followed each other, but she was not worried about these places, just the immediate core of the house. Having seen that all was well, she retraced her steps to the bottom of the servants'stairs and went into the body of the Hall.

The studded great hall door swung back silently, and the scent of floral polish filled the air, with the floor gleaming in the moonlight. There were no shutters closed in the Great Hall and the bright moon splashed the panelling with light and shadows. There was always some new way of looking at her home and she kept it all locked in her heart as tightly as the pantry. Passing the magnificent carved oak table and matching chairs, trailing her fingertips lightly over their carved backs, she thought about all the faces of the household over the years who had entertained guests in this room, and imagined all the family dramas that had been discussed going back for longer than anyone could reasonably remember, elbows on this very table and feet resting on the stretchers below.

Another door beyond led to her father's study door and on her left, the grand main stairs winding their wide treads up to the top corridor from an inner hallway. As she looked up the stairs, above her, deep-set in the corridor wall there was a tiny door beyond which were steep stairs leading to a maze of the minor female servants' rooms.

Mary then craned her neck back, and took in the sight of the long window and saw the tapestry of smudged colours hanging on the facing wall. Satisfied it looked as was expected, she stepped through the door into her father's study to soak up something of him. As she looked around the room, she was struck by the sensation that she was at home, and yet homesick. It made no sense, except that her father was part of what made home feel like home, and he was still absent.

It was just as well that her betrothal to a distant cousin had fallen through two years earlier, as she wasn't ready to leave her father. There was time yet, as most of her contemporaries married at around the age of twenty-four. In royal marriages, and in the old days, people of her class married much younger, as the official age for marriage was twelve for girls and fourteen for boys. Now, the average age was early twenties for women and even later for young men, many of whom had to complete apprenticeships and end indentures to start out as their own masters. Mary was glad the age of marriage had crept so high as it seemed a brutality, a denying of opportunity, to be married so young and possibly die in childbirth or soon after. So many, too many, did so before twenty years of age surrounded by 'godsiblings' who were female relatives or neighbours who came to offer advice and it was a tradition to let them. The same tradition also allowed for them to have free food and drink while they were interfering as some, like Mary, would say. The poorest houses could not offer free food and drink so were more likely to have fewer nosy relatives clustered round the bed.

Maybe that was it, she wondered - deep inside she was fearful of marriage and that dangerous childbed, as she loved life. Standing in the silver light of the great window, tipping like a waterfall down the stairs, she decided it was too much thinking for the middle of the night. Everything could seem exaggerated.

There was a little sadness in her heart as she opened the door to her father's study for the first time in almost a year and went in like a hesitant child. Standing quietly, enjoying the stillness, she looked all around and then surprisingly she heard a creak. Then another.

One of the unshuttered windows was swinging open with a little repetitive squeak, although the sill was dry under her fingers despite the early evening rain. Frowning, she closed it with its little pewter catch then rattled it to make sure that it was truly shut tight. Satisfied, she pulled her robe around her comfortingly and perched on the small sloping sill. All else in the well-ordered room seemed as it should, and closing the door carefully behind her, she went slowly up the great stairs.

At the top of the stairs, she turned away from her own room and looked into the little panelled room on her left. Some said it had once been a tiny chapel as one or two members of the family had resisted the Reformation and held secret masses in this once-sacred space.

There were no adventures in the room any more, as the family now firmly formed part of the establishment, so Mary left and, crossing the corridor went into the fine main guest room. It was a room that astonished visitors when they saw it for the first time, as it was full of diamond paned windows, including a great curved oriel. She had always particularly liked this room, and the many aspects of the lovely Somersal gardens and indeed church that could be seen clearly in the grounds nearby. Part of her had wanted this to be her bed chamber, but it seemed flippant to ask, as hers was lovely with its fine panelling. By contrast, the oriel room had exposed beams and creamy plaster, making it really light with all the windows.

Moving on now and turning towards her own room, down two steps and up two steps, with the start of her moonlight route laid out in front of her again. The subtleties of light and temperature and indeed time itself, changed everything – a little. It was dark in her shuttered room, but her eyes adjusted quickly.

Taking off her robe and laying it in the same place as before on the press at the foot of the bed, she then kicked off her buskins, which slid together on the shining floor. That made her smile because they stopped sliding together at precisely the same time, next to each other, in a tidy manner.

As she bent her knee and climbed back into her soft, welcome bed she heard a creak from above, where the minor female servants slept in a series of small rooms in the loft space, along with a constant scampering of squirrels who shared the space too. Single male servants mostly slept above the stables in warm, hay-scented rooms. Ashbourne, as he was steward, had a fine room along the main corridor. She would always creep past that particular door! Married staff usually lived in cottages on the estate, and the fact that Alice Goodrich had one for her and her grandson, showed special favour at some point in the past, as she didn't have a husband.

Mary thought of all those sleeping souls with coverlets rising and falling. She was slipping into dreams and gave up trying to fight. All indeed was well, she told her long feather-filled bolster. Mary Dudley, young mistress of the Hall, was home and her mind at rest: real rest.

Chapter 5

Mary awoke for the second time that night from a deep sleep, but this time with a start. She realised she was on a soft bed, spread out in its warm curves and folds, but for just a moment she blinked and frowned for as much as she tried, she could not place herself. Screwing up her face, she tried to recognise the green and gold bed canopy above her. There was something wrong, for everything was quiet, too quiet. Where was the noise? Had a terrible disaster silenced London completely?

Then she remembered that she was in her own bed, in Somersal and had that lovely feeling when you are not quite asleep and not quite awake and you don't have to do anything but simply lie there and enjoy it. Dream upon dream had come to her in full vivid colour and she had been so deeply asleep that at first she couldn't think where she was, despite the fact she had been walking about the place a few hours earlier.

In the house in London, it was different at dawn from Somersal, for the chorus had little to do with birds. In all seasons and all weathers there would be a great rumbling mass of carts, horses and beasts of burden being driven to market in the smoky capital. Traders called brightly to friends and argued vigorously with enemies, their livestock and vehicles causing a great jam in the road, through which none could pass, resulting in yet more shouting and more often than not, a vigorous scuffle would break out.

Geese, sheep and other animals driven into the London markets invariably became more and more raucous as the morning developed. It was the same every day. London was rarely quiet, including in the deepest part of the night, when often a drunk or two could be heard singing in the distance, sometimes followed by irate shouting and then silence. Even on the very edge of the outskirts of London in Chelsea where they lived, it was terribly noisy along the roads and lanes. In fact they had the crowds massing earlier at the beginning of the day and later in the evening as they were a full five miles from Saint Paul's Cathedral.

Chelsea had been particularly fashionable when the Lord Chancellor, Sir Thomas More and his family lived there thirty-five years earlier. She would ride past their house occasionally with its grey aspects and overgrown grounds. A sad place she always felt, full of broken promises and death. No one could believe it could be possible when the King's friend and Chancellor of all England had refused to accept Anne Boleyn. He had so much to lose, but lose it all he did, including his head and 'That', as her father had put it, 'was that'. Despite this family tragedy, Mary continued to be inspired by Cecily Heron, one of Sir Thomas More's clever daughters, who had started a small hospital of her own.

The Dudleys' London house was a pleasant place, and although smaller than Somersal had lovely formal gardens with green lawns, which in the spring and summer were spattered bright with flowers. The busy River Thames could be reached from their land via a short stone alley and past a decorated metal gate to two steps (sometimes three, dependent upon the water level. Large rivers tended to be busy and therefore exciting, but the Thames was on another scale as it was a massive living thoroughfare of boats, ships and wherries jostling along the water lanes and sometimes banging into each other.

Mary remembered seeing some fool in a coracle of all things trying to weave through the boat-crammed waters. Coracles are notoriously difficult to paddle, being circular, and with just one oar but this young chap was pretty good, for a while anyway, and then even he was defeated and tipped up. Mary had been watching from her bedroom window and called down for one of the staff to run and help the fellow to their bank. She could do with Ashbourne on such occasions, but he was often staying away at court with her father so she made do with Whitworth, the London house 'do everything' person.

The happy news was that the wet chap and his coracle were both saved. After some ale and a piece of pie he was sent away when dry with his coracle on his back, looking remarkably like a tortoise walking away from the house on the Chelsea lane, as the rip in the tarred leather from the accident meant that walking was definitely safer until it was repaired. Mary had seen pictures of tortoises with one of her tutors, who was attempting to show her drawings of far-off places and wondrous beasties.

When she was in London and missing Somersal, she would make a point of opening the window in her room, in all weathers, and looking out over the river, wondering whether if she sat in one of those boats she could sail up to Derbyshire. Even as a small child standing on a stool Mary had discovered that the boats and ships on the great river were romantic, and some of them might even have been going to places that had tortoises.

Now she was grown up and in Somersal, in the beautiful middle of the country known as 'The Beauties' with good reason. Mary turned her head towards the two large diamond-paned windows. They were shuttered but still the insistent light streaked in through cracks and holes. Tiny shafts of bright light evolving with sparkling dust particles marked the floor in little white circles. She felt calm, her body as light as the feathers she lay upon.

After a while, she got up, and this time didn't bother with buskins but went barefoot on tiptoes, to minimise the risk of splinters from the polished planked floor, to the window on the right. Carefully folding back the shutters so as not to make a noise, she stood blinking in the bright sunshine of the new day.

Eager to enjoy more of the moment, she returned to her bed and carried the still warm feather bolster to the padded window-seat, prodding and punching the bolster for comfort. Climbing up the seat, she settled into the cushion, pulling her long white shift over her bent knees and toes. She found her hair was trapped tightly against the wall, so she tugged it free, letting it fall down to her waist in great curls. Sighing with relaxed pleasure, she looked out over the garden so that she could really soak up the view.

She leaned forward and opened the window slightly. The day ahead promised to be very hot, following the storm, as the rain evaporating from the ground would make it seem even hotter. Now, however, it was a cool and scented morning as the gardens were covered in drifting white fog. The ornate knot garden of herbs across on the left of her windows could hardly be seen. Fronds of white mist broke away and floated up, then melted like snowflakes in a river. As they disappeared, they released sweet, herby scents of rosemary, mint and lavender. It was intoxicating and she breathed in pure English air.

Then something caught her attention: a sudden movement in the churchyard, just beyond the Christening Gate.

'There, by the yew tree,' breathed Mary to herself. She was intrigued, watching, suddenly wide awake. Directly below her window was a noise, the sound of footsteps crunching on the path below. This drew her attention, and from her vantage point above she could see a woman with grey, frizzled hair tied tightly, wearing a sage-green linen working gown which sat over her broad hips.

The figure underneath her window pressed itself furtively against the house wall and in doing so, revealed a basket over one arm, with a cloth over it. There was no doubt it was the housekeeper, Alice Goodrich. Also, unless Mary was very much mistaken, that dark-haired figure skulking stealthily through the mist by the Christening Gate was Alice's wayward grandson, Warwick. His grimy reputation was still firmly in place by the looks of things. Alice was beckoning him over to her with real urgency, looking around to see whether anyone was near.

Mary was absolutely gripped, and she swiftly pressed tightly back into the bolster, so she couldn't be seen by Warwick, which could have been a risk if he had looked up. However, he was far too engaged, grinning at his grandmother, knowing very well he must not enter the Hall grounds. He was taller and considerably fatter, Mary decided, but she hadn't seen him for over a year and then only glimpses at the boundaries of the Hall, as he was usually dodging about keeping out of the way after being dismissed. However, on this summer morning he had his usual smirk on his face, and that conceited swagger as he made his way up to his grandmother.

Everyone knew he was forbidden to enter the hall grounds, having been banned by Ashbourne the summer earlier. Mary remembered that not only was he a thief and a liar, despite him being only about twelve years of age at the time of his dismissal, but his taste for indecently touching the young kitchen maids had also made him deeply unpopular. Mary had always thought he had got away with too many liberties because he threatened people with his grandmother, so they would deny any knowledge of his wrongdoing when questioned.

Mary thought about the detail that had been reported to her of Warwick's final misdemeanour that had cost him his job. He and a small maid had been in her father's study. Warwick shouldn't be in there anyway, but the room was tucked away so it would be unlikely he could be caught out, or so he thought. 'One word from me; and you'll be out and I'll make sure you are,' he was overheard hissing to the weeping young maid, who had the shoulder of her linen gown torn, and she was trying to hold it up for decency.

Unfortunately for Warwick, the person who had heard him was Thomas Ashbourne, and he had described to Mary how Warwick had responsed when his substantial shape had filled the doorway, startling the pair in the room. The girl was grateful to be sent out, and ran like a frightened rabbit.

However, Warwick this time had completely overrated his grandmother's power. Indeed, he went on to make the grave mistake of threatening Thomas Ashbourne with the wrath and revenge of Alice if Ashbourne reported him. Mary wished that she had seen Warwick having his collar grabbed by Ashbourne, who ran him from the study, squealing like a pig, out into the grounds, finally driving him through the great gates with a firm boot on his backside. Apparently he had fallen in the muddy road and, getting up, had given a look of sheer hate to Ashbourne, before shuffling off to the Goodrich cottage, swearing and muttering curses under his breath. He was warned never to enter the house or gardens again, and Ashbourne had made sure that Alice and all the staff, both inside and out, were aware of this ban.

Mary remembered how Alice had tried wheedling, and made excuses to attempt to have him return, not least because she did not want to lose face with the other servants. Away from the eyes of other servants, she stood modestly with bent head and hands clasped in front of her, begging for Warwick to be given his job back, and saying how he had been beaten by her as punishment, which Ashbourne and Mary very much doubted.

Alice, however, wanted to have him back as a public show of her considerable influence and yet suddenly it appeared to count for nothing. If they had allowed the return of Warwick, Alice and Warwick would have boasted how they had stood up to - and defeated - Ashbourne, which would have been complete nonsense but that is how the Goodrich family worked. Mary had seen her muttering and glaring at Ashbourne behind his back, cursing him further no doubt.

Warwick had now entered the grounds 'cheeky as you like' as Cook would say. Mary wanted to know what on earth he was doing, as he was clearly involved in some intrigue: his whole demeanour was criminal - it was the same for both of them.

Alice leaned forward, catching his jerkin and pulled him to her sharply in an irritated manner, then he and his grandmother muttered together under the window, but Mary, straining her neck as far as she dare to hear, was not quite able to catch the conversation, as much as she tried, just her own name. She did witness Alice pull back the cloth on the basket, and inside were two large raised pies, heavily decorated with glossy pastry leaves. There was a bundle of what looked like jumble biscuits, some wafers and a quarter of a wheel of cheese. Not everything was clear to see, but what was clear was that that basket was full of expensive food from the Hall kitchens that was being stolen in front of her eyes.

With a gasp, Mary had to pull back sharply again as Warwick turned away. He might look back and wave at his grandmother. Actually no, he was off, and Mary was pretty sure she knew where he was going, which was to Uttoxeter Market.

Alice watched him for a while, then turned away after a moment to the kitchen door to be about the business of breakfast and to instruct staff to clean and fetch fresh water from the well, as if nothing extraordinary had happened. It seemed that it hadn't been extraordinary to them, as this appeared to be a frequent event and a well-planned habit.

The peace of the perfumed dawn had been shattered for Mary, as she found real anger and personal hurt burning inside her. It was also the certain and irritating knowledge that she knew she should not be surprised by this scene, as Warwick was ghastly - but Alice's involvement was the shock. It was evident that Alice's attitude was more than just doting refusal to accept her grandson was rotten to the core. Alice was just as bad, worse in some ways, as she was in a position of trust. What other revelations would be discovered over the next months at the Hall? Mary intended to find out.

She remained in the window seat for a few minutes, working to control her emotions, and telling herself sharply not to be upset by the revelation of Alice's dishonesty. She must grow up and make sure justice and loyalty came back to the Hall.

Gradually she became calmer but it was horrible that she had been made to feel unclean watching this crime played out before her, like finding a man in a room getting undressed and feeling ashamed, although she was not at fault, as the witnessing had merely been an accident.

Chapter 6

A noise awoke Mary and she turned towards it. Anne Compson was tidying the room and asking herself out loud why the shutters were open already. The maid was always talking to herself, but sometimes Mary suspected it was Anne's way of asking a question she knew she shouldn't.

Mary had no memory of going back to bed after her dawn vigil, but she must have been in a deep sleep as dreams still crowded in trying to seduce her to return. Mary sat up rustling and on hearing her, Anne came over and plumped her bolster behind her so she could eat breakfast.

'Good morning, Lady Mary, and a fine morning it is after such a storm. You have slept heavily, and no wonder after such a journey. Here is breakfast,.You must be hungry.'

'I am, Anne. Ravenous and thirsty too. My first breakfast at the Hall is always my favourite.'

There was a tray near the bed on a little table with warm wheaten-bread, golden butter and milk and honey in a small jug as well as some cold sliced ham. Mary had never cared for small beer which was the traditional drink for most people at breakfast time –

too bitter. The sun was high and it was much later than she had thought. Anne patted her young mistress on the hand in an affectionate manner. She wouldn't dream of being critical of her mistress, believing she had been exhausted upon arrival at the Hall. Little did she know that Mary had been up and about for much of the night.

'What is the time please, Anne?' Anne could tell the time, which was a matter of pride to her, and so she went to the round silver object standing in its usual place on the oak press, and opening it declared, 'Nearly eleven of the clock.'

Mary smiled, and clapped her hands, 'Well done, Anne.' This ritual happened regularly, so that Anne could have the chance to show she had not forgotten this skill as she smoothed down her gown, knowing it was a rare thing to see a pouch-clock, never mind be able to tell what time it told. Her family, like most others in the kingdom, told the time from a sundial, or the insistent rumbling in the stomach signalling a particular meal was due.

Anne's husband was a shepherd, and had a hand-sized portable wooden sundial with markings down its tubular shape and a little pewter arm that was pulled out to cast shadows on the tube as it hung from a tree. It was understandably a family treasure. When Anne was first shown a clock she had twisted it about to try and see the shadow, making Mary laugh as she had understood why Anne did that, but she showed her the new way with a portable clock from the clockmaker, Urseau of London. Now that really was a treasure.

After some happy munching Mary jumped out of bed and then regretted it for a moment as her lower back was indeed aching from so much riding. If the ride was difficult, as last night's had been, she ached even more, as every muscle had been tense in the saddle during the worst of the storm.

'Ouch! I am not sure I have ridden a horse so much as had it kick me!' Mary winced as she arched her back.

Anne was sympathetic. 'I am much afeared watching you ride sometimes, in case you do have a fall.'

'Don't tell me it'll have my eye out,' teased Mary, as this was one of Anne's favourite sayings.

Anne shook her head. 'Well, I can worry, mistress. I can worry!'

Mary made her way to the washing bowl and, using a soft cloth, rubbed on Castile herb soap, whilst asking Anne to fetch two pots from a small leather bag. Anne went to the bag excitedly, as there was usually a gift from

Mary brought from London as a treat. Anne started to rummage, taking out a wooden double sided comb, a square of muslin cloth and some green gloves.

'The two blue glass pots, please, Anne. Do open one. and smell the roses.'

Anne did so, and cried out with pleasure. 'It is like a miracle, mistress, for the sweetest red roses are in this cream.' Her enthusiasm was delightful.

'I bought them on London Bridge from an Italian apothecary, who has a mirrored and gilded shop full of lit candles, so that is always crowded out with people trying to buy his extraordinary beauty creams and flowered waters. Beneath the counter, for discretion, were cosmetics.' Mary enjoyed telling Anne that, knowing she would be shocked.

'Not face paint, madam? Changing what God has given a woman, t'isn't right.'

'Careful if the Queen comes into your path, Anne, as she wears white lead on her face, neck and breast and crushed beetles in wax on her lips and cheeks.'

'Beetles – do it not poison her?'

'No,' laughed Mary. 'It all makes her look extraordinary though, and plenty of women at court and beyond copy her in the hope of looking like a relative.'

‘Fancy,’ was the unsure answer, as Anne folded cloths. Mary had had enough fun teasing, and during dressing smiled at her maid.

‘Anne, one of those jars of rose cream is a present from me to you, for you have always been such a loyal and good servant and friend to me .’

Anne’s eyes brimmed with tears of pleasure as she flung herself on Mary and kissed her cheek.

Mary was absolutely thrilled to see Anne so happy, and then remembered sadly that she had once given such gifts to Alice, and yet Alice had betrayed her and her family.

‘Anne, fetch my pale blue gown and a light shift, please.’

As it was summer and in the country, Mary was always relaxed on ordinary days when no visitors were expected, and avoided the formal highly structured gowns of court when at Somersal, as it was so much easier living in the country.

There was nothing comfortable about Mary at this precise moment though, for as Anne helped her finish dressing she felt a wave of irritation move up her body. All was ruined, she thought, as these moments should be full of joy, but they fluctuated with resentment against Alice and Warwick and the fact that she was going to have to tackle it herself for once, and not depend upon Ashbourne all the time. She could have lived without the prospect though.

She finished dressing, 'girding her loins' as warriors were supposed to do according to something she had read, but couldn't remember what book it was. She also had no idea what 'girding' meant, but she was going to be her version of a warrior, peradventure!

Determinedly, having gone over in her head how she was going to address Alice, Mary went down the great stairs to the kitchen with a firmness of purpose, for now she was prepared to be judge and jury and more to the point, had a sentence to pass.

As she came over the main kitchen threshold there were cries of welcome all around, especially from Eleanor the cook, and two of the maids. Four of the outside men were sitting on one of the kitchen benches eating bread and drinking cider, for it was yet another hot sweaty day and they had been working for the past eight hours - it was lunchtime.

They jumped to their feet out of respect when she came in, but Mary quickly signalled for them to carry on with their food sitting down, and smiled around the room at everyone else. Inside, she was terribly worked up, but determined not to show it.

'Stay calm' she told herself.

Eleanor came forward, her round red face delighted and wiping her hands on her voluminous apron which fitted her voluminous shape. She clapped her hands crying out 'Welcome mistress! You were so brave, coming in last night in the storm. We have all been talking about it.'

There was much nodding, including from Alice, who was wearing the green gown that Mary had seen in the dawn. She was standing,hands on hips as usual, by a table laden with food in various stages of preparation. After joining in with the welcome, she then pushed everyone back so she could walk unhindered to Mary and take centre stage, for she was Alice Goodrich.

Cook threw Alice a venomous look of pure hatred. In all these years, Mary had never noticed the animosity appear so bitterly between them before. Then again, she hadn't been looking for it, and for much of that time had not been grown up enough to see the nuances between adults that said so much without the need for words.

Mary kept her composure as Alice approached her. Inwardly, Mary was furious, but continued to stare steadily at Alice in what she hoped was an unnerving manner and she said nothing.

Mary was taking her time and Alice had started to

look a little uncomfortable, her eyes looking shifty as she was trying to work out what was happening and a silence fell on the whole kitchen. The staff present could tell something was seriously wrong and were watchful of Mary, as she was not her usual self - full of affection and good humour – to everyone else in the kitchen , but silent and staring at Alice.

Alice Goodrich had a really nasty habit when embarrassed, which was rare, of laughing loudly and harshly. The inference was that the situation was just a joke. As usual with Alice, this was all about her saving face and the laughter a sign to onlookers that she didn't care.

Her hollow laugh rang out but Mary did not join in, or even flicker, as she was expecting it. Instead, she remained quiet and did not drop her eyes. Alice then fell quiet too as a brown onion rolled off the table with a thump, and bounced on the flag floor, but no one moved.

Mary spoke softly to Alice. 'Ah, Alice, laughing again, and there is much to smile about, for you will be pleased to learn, I am sure, that I have grown up at last.' Alice looked around with eyebrows raised and rolling eyes, as if Mary had lost her head. Nobody laughed and Alice looked back at Mary questioningly.

'Here is the news, Alice, fresh from London - I'm

ready to take the house keys off you now, to wear at my own waist'.

There was a hardly audible gasp from someone. Mary lifted one eyebrow at Alice and smiled pleasantly but dangerously, as there was a challenging undertone in her voice, and she looked directly into Alice's eyes, still without a flicker.

The greeny-yellow flecked eyes of Alice's, which had a snake-like quality, beneath a fuzz of grey hair, at first looked slightly alarmed and then narrowed ever so briefly as she tried to regain lost ground

'Ooh, Mistress Mary, I will make sure I have you a set cut in Uttoxeter by the end of the week. Now then, tell us poor country folk all about London!' She spoke breezily, her lack of sincerity showing through.

She was trying to change the subject, of course, and make Mary feel so embarrassed and uncomfortable that she would comply. Meanwhile, the servants were watching this ball of trouble as it was thrown backwards and forwards by the two combatants. Fascinated, they all stood stock-still taking in every word of the exchange.

Mary shook her head, still smiling, which made Alice throw her chin up obstinately and blow down her thin hooked nose. Out of the corner of her eye, Mary could see Eleanor cross her arms in an angry movement aimed at Alice. She also nodded approvingly at Mary.

'No, Alice.' Mary carried on quietly, not rising like a fish to the bait. 'Thomas Ashbourne and Cook have a set of keys as well as you, so I want yours, because you won't need them any more, not even when we go back to London.'

For a moment there was a spasm of fear in Alice's face, as she wondered if she was losing her job and that would mean her home too. Then she changed her mind, having decided in her usual arrogant way that the Dudleys needed her too much. Instead of giving way, Alice's sharp features flushed anger for a moment at this public insult, and then she contained herself, for if nothing else she was manipulative and fully intended to win this challenge, and if she managed to do so, was capable of raising her authority even higher amongst the other servants and Cook who was, Mary realised, now Alice's enemy.

Again, without changing the direction of her gaze, Mary saw one of the outside men draw his finger across his withered brown throat indicating that Alice was finished.

Mary was glad, as she felt she needed as many people as possible to support her against Alice, and it gave her extra strength to continue this particular battle, which was not quite over. Alice stepped a half-step nearer Mary and put her head to one side. It was a subtle move, intended to intimidate. 'Well, my goodness, Mistress Mary, of course. Although I really do think I should keep a set, because you never know when I might need to have access if no one else is around.'

Mary saw Alice was not giving up her crown and sceptre easily, and was still trying to press her ownership of the keys. Alice was belligerent and determined, but so was Mary, both of those things.

'No thank you, Alice. Give me the keys now, please.' She made it perfectly clear it was not a request, but an order. Alice hesitated for as long as she dared and then reluctantly unhooked them from her leather belt and gave them over to Mary, who victoriously hooked them onto her pale blue belt patting them in place. Alice's jaw was working backwards and forwards furiously with temper and her face was livid, with her neck blotched scarlet. She had lost, and everyone knew she had.

To avoid further humiliation, she gave Mary the smallest of bobs and didn't look around the rest of the kitchen, but turned on her heels and left at speed, disappearing off into the grounds.

Chapter 7

For a moment, everyone in the kitchen stayed frozen to the spot except Mary, who beamed and said, 'Carry on.'

So everyone did carry on with their duties, with much giggling and nudging at the spectacle they had just witnessed. The outside man who had made the cut-throat movement was pulling on his boots and had the widest grin on his face. He pulled his forelock and went with the other men wafting his shirt in the heat. Mary saw his legs were thin and really bandy.

'Couldn't catch a pig up an alley, that one,' nodded Eleanor at his departing shape, making Mary laugh.

Eleanor was humming as she returned to her task of beating rose water into a bowl of batter, singing a bright country song. Mary knew what Cook was up to, which was hoping Alice could hear her loud singing, glad she had to endure her come-uppance in public. Of course, what this really meant was that Cook could keep her house keys and therefore was trusted and Alice was not and this was a powerful victory in front of the servants for Eleanor – and Mary.

'That's grand, Lady Mary,' said Cook. 'Reet grand.'

'What is, Cook?' asked Mary, with devilment in the question.

'You coming in here and putting that madam in her place. She's much worse of late and loathed by all.' Cook started to melt butter in a black skillet and when foaming, poured little rounds of batter in to make rose pancakes. 'Your favourites.' She nodded to the pan contents, which were golden brown and sizzling.

'Indeed, thank you,' and just touching Eleanor on the shoulder, Mary asked her to leave one of the kitchen maids to finish them and to join her for a moment.

Eleanor followed immediately, calling for one of the other youngsters to peel some apples.

The young mistress and Cook made her way down to the store room and unlocked the door, going in to check the contents. Foxglove the spaniel had followed them, and sat at the door wagging her tail gently, making a soft, swishing noise on the flagstones.

'Now, I want to show you what this morning is all about, Cook, and you must not breath a word to anyone or all will be lost, do you understand?'

Eleanor nodded vigorously, listening intently.

'Now, I want you to look here in the store-room and tell me what is missing from yesterday, please.'

Cook looked astonished. 'What's missing?'

'Yes, missing, and not to be confused with what someone may have eaten in the household. You must be sure.'

Eleanor started to count and then went back into the main kitchen briefly showing Mary with a finger to her lips she wouldn't give anything away and then returned.

'Yes, Lady Mary, as I thought. Two of the raised pies are gone, all fine decorated with leaves,' she moved a few items on plates about and opened a wooden container,'… and the lemon jumbles.' She then stood on tiptoe and looked on a shelf shaking her head '... and blow me down with a feather, an uncut quarter wheel of cheese has also disappeared… and the batch of almond frangipane tarts made special for you coming back.'

She seemed mystified how Mary could have known, That, she said, was like magic. The tarts, too, must have also been in the basket over Alice's arm, but Mary remembered she had not been able to see everything under the cloth.

She observed grimly 'Nothing magic about this, Cook, just plain and simple theft at the hands of humans, not fairies.' Cook crossed herself. Everyone in the country, it seemed, was frightened of fairies and witches, and some cunning folk, not to mention saints as well as demons.

'Well, who could be taking it Lady Mary? And I must

say I am ashamed that I haven't seen these things have gone. We make so much you see. I just checked with the maid Jennet, and all is as I say. '

Mary held up a dismissive hand. 'Don't blame yourself, Cook. This food has been stolen by experts. Please don't ask any more questions now: all will be revealed in time, and don't forget.'

Cook nodded fiercely 'Aye, I'll be quiet until you tell me otherwise.' She turned back towards the kitchen and Mary took the opposite direction to the Great Hall.

Cook was no fool, and knew from the scene over the keys and the missing food that Mary knew Alice had taken it. She was also very much aware that Mary had used the plural 'thieves'. It had not been missed by Eleanor. No doubt, she would spend a happy rest of the day trying to work out who else was involved but Mary trusted her to say nothing. It was a relief to Mary that Alice had not rocked her own faith of the good in human nature and trust still existed in her heart - for others.

'Is it market day today in Uttoxeter?' she asked Eleanor, for she had lost track of the days with so much travelling. Eleanor nodded and said, 'Aye, mistress'. Mary noticed that Cook had a small red bowl on a ledge near her hand that Mary hadn't seen before and the sight of it drew her with its bright glaze.

Cook saw her and surreptitiously pushed it behind a jar, before carrying on with her work. Mary thought that behaviour was a little odd, but having thanked everyone for their kind welcome, Mary went across the Hall and into her father's study to think. She had much to think about.

On market days in Uttoxeter, the roads, including the one at the end of Somersal Lane, were crowded with carts and animals from dawn until dusk – a bit like Chelsea – whatever the season. Farmers and traders came in from the immediate countryside and further afield to sell their goods and to buy some too. She was sure she had been right about Warwick going to the end of the lane with the basket. Then all he had to do was simply hitch a ride with one of the passing carts, perhaps in exchange for a melting, buttery jumble for the driver to munch on for the three miles ahead of them to market.

The whole episode in the dawn was so well practised, it was likely that Warwick was picked up by a regular driver looking out for him - one of Alice's contacts perhaps. Mary could see how the morning would then develop as once at market, Warwick would spread out his wares on the basket cloth on the pavement, as so many did, or perhaps just locked into his usual spot (wherever that was) showing the content of his basket to regular customers. When sold out, he would then bring back the money to share between Alice and himself.

Mary wondered, knowing they were as bad as each other, if Warwick pocketed some of it, and claimed he had to sell some things underpriced as time was running out, or a similar excuse. Even if this was the case, they had formed a nice little business, and no doubt Alice would have justified these actions to herself, because Warwick had been dismissed. There was revenge as well as greed for money present in these plans. That all made perfect sense, and Mary hoped that by standing up to Alice and putting a stop to the food pilfering by taking her keys, she would learn a lesson and consider herself fortunate still to have a cottage and employment at all. There was also a possibility that Alice would realise that she might have been spotted, and if she had any sense she would keep quiet and start behaving herself.

Going to one of the long windows, Mary could see a little group of people in the next meadow. They were chopping up something vigorously and then she remembered the great oak had been struck by lightning the evening before, and people were gathering up the branches for firewood. Many believed that the wood from such a tree would bring good fortune and others wouldn't touch it, saying that the devil would use that blasted oak as a way in and out of hell on his fiery chariot. She watched the busy country folk for a minute or two arguing over the wood and a heavily laden cart tipped over sideways as a wheel broke. 'That will be the Devil's doing then,' Mary said to herself, shaking her head as the man threw his hat on the dusty ground in frustration.

At that moment, with a little tap on the door, Thomas Ashbourne joined her, and she invited him to sit down as she wanted to talk to him. This was a surprisingly formal invitation for his young mistress to make, he thought, indicating that whatever it was, it was serious. He sat down when invited, and put his head to one side as he was wont to do, listening intently. He was also hoping whatever it was, that it was not too much of a drama for him to deal with as Edmund Dudley was away. Summer tended to be a bit of a holiday in Somersal for Ashbourne, and he liked it that way. If he was missing out on court life, at least he could take it easy.

Mary sat down too and clasped her hands in her lap saying, 'There is something going on with Alice Goodrich and Warwick here – do you know of any rumours?' The steward was completely taken aback, as it was a question that was unexpected.

'Please tell me,' he said earnestly as he leaned forward, frowning at the name of Warwick which he didn't think would be on his horizon again.

With a steady voice she told what she had seen and done and, as the story unfolded of her dawn observations, Thomas Ashbourne flushed red. Mary could not make up her mind whether it was embarrassment that he did not know of this theft, or perhaps the thought of her wanderings in her night shift - or was he was just angry? 'I am aghast to hear this, mistress,' he said with gritted teeth (so he was angry, then).

Mary shrugged. 'We should have known really. Alice is such a bad influence in this house in terms of her pushy, trouble-making nature and Warwick has shown the makings of a criminal for years. We shouldn't be surprised.' Ashbourne leaned back in his chair 'You are right, and it is not fair to complain others have not prompted us.'

'Of course it's not,' Mary interrupted sharply. 'Alice is a bully. They were probably afraid to say anything, making their position impossible.'

'Well, she must go, of course,' said Thomas Ashbourne. 'Clear them out, and their version of poison can go with them.'

Mary had been waiting for her chance to reveal to Ashbourne what steps she had taken already, it was her small triumph.

'Well, Thomas Ashbourne, you may be surprised to learn that I have started to take matters in hand already.'

His eyebrows shot up as rightly it should be his task as steward, but he was a wise creature and did not comment in a critical or smart manner: he was too respectful and too well trained in his job. He was wondering what on earth the climax of this tale would be. Then, when Mary told him victoriously of the actions she had taken with the keys, he gave her a warm look of admiration, for he too recognized in that brief moment that she, indeed, was no longer a child.

'Remarkable, if I may say so, Lady Mary, for in that action you were able to show other servants publicly that bad behaviour does not pay in the end.'

No doubt everyone else in the house would be reaching the same conclusion, Mary was quick to point out to him, as the scene with Alice would be much enjoyed as common gossip. At twenty-two, she had not been a child for some years, but it wasn't always easy to acknowledge the subtle changes from girl to woman.

After he had thought a moment he looked directly at Mary and gave verdict on what he had heard

'Well, Mistress, despite the key battle being won, I urge you, they really must go – both of them. Really, I would like to have them arrested by the magistrate, but I know that your tender heart would not be keen, so allow me to dismiss them at least.' His voice was showing that beneath the calm professional surface, he was very angry indeed – more so by the minute, as the information he had heard fully sank in. Mary could also see a vein on his temple pulsing slightly, something which she had observed before on the rare occasions when he had shown that he was agitated.

Mary looked down at her hands before replying firmly 'No, Thomas Ashbourne.' It was an answer that was surprising. Looking up she went on, 'I want the length and breadth of this treachery, Ashbourne, and I want to see who else might be involved, so please don't take any action for the moment, so I can discreetly make enquiries.' Mary could tell that he was not keen on this plan.

'Mistress, people who are thieves can also be dangerous when cornered. I do think you have been remarkable this morning but I am fearful that you might be hurt in some way if they think the hangman's noose is lined up for them.'

Mary held up her hands. 'I know, and I expected you to be concerned, but I give you my solemn promise that I won't take any risks.'

Ashbourne shook his head sadly. 'Like riding in a dangerous storm, mistress?'

She had the decency to draw in her cheeks guiltily at this comment and said again solemnly 'I promise.'

So, he had no option but to go, but with a determination in his heart that he would discreetly guard her and at the same time, try to control himself from not going over to the Goodrich cottage and flinging them out on the streets with another firm boot on Warwick's even more substantial backside.

As Mary stood, she reached forward and touched Thomas Ashbourne on the arm saying, 'On another matter, Thomas. I do know that my father is about the queen's business at the moment, and I am sure that it is important, but he has never been away from my side before, here at Somersal in the summer, so there must be something extraordinary afoot. Have you any idea what it is?'

'No, Lady' he answered simply. 'All I know is that he is dealing directly with matters for Sir William Cecil, and that means ultimately for Her Majesty, but I am afraid that is all I know, Lady'. She looked beyond his shoulder at the bright green lawns and wonderful roses, before looking at his face again and said, 'I miss him'.

Thomas Ashbourne nodded and then after standing a little while quietly and respectfully, he left the room. Mary went over to a window and, opening it, let a butterfly loose into the summer air.

Over the following few days, Alice kept a low profile, and there wasn't even a hint of Warwick in the grounds or indeed the churchyard. Further night-time walks revealed that pilfering, certainly of food, seemed to have come to a halt. However, now knowing Alice had such a dark side to her personality, she fully expected other things to go missing from the Hall, both to make up for unexpected lost revenue, and for revenge!

Chapter 8

In the first part of the week that followed, Mary spent much of her time at her father's desk in the mornings busily writing letters to him and her friends in London, taking advantage of the regular messengers who passed between Tutbury Castle and the offices of the Duchy of Lancaster in the Savoy.

The old Savoy Palace had been the greatest private house in England, but it had been destroyed by fire in the Great Uprising during the reign of Richard II. The rebels, who had included those of the middling classes as well as the peasant, had tired of high taxes to pay for unsuccessful military campaigns, mostly in France. Rather than blame the boy king himself, they had blamed his advisors, including his wealthy and powerful uncle John of Gaunt, the duke of Lancaster, who was thought to be plotting to take the throne on his own account. They had targeted his Savoy estate in London, and other rebels had marched on Leicester, and there had even been rumours of a planned attack on John's castle at Tutbury, although that had come to nothing in the end.

Despite the rumours, John had remained loyal to the king until the end, but when Richard attempted to seize the Lancaster estates for himself on John's death,

John's son Henry had responded by taking the throne, and throwing Richard in prison. Since then, the Duchy estates had always been held by the ruling monarch, but were kept separate from the Crown estate, with offices and officials separate from the main court. Even so, many of the great offices of the Duchy were held by royal favourites, and the Duchy officials worked closely with those of the royal household, and many of them knew Mary's father. The court might be a vast arrangement of ranks and duties but those in, or close to, the real power- brokers were small in number.

Her father was one who was close to the great, but unusually lacking in ambition, not at all like most people of his time. Knowing he would appreciate that it was not for her own personal ambition, she plucked up the courage one day to ask him why he didn't crave to be in the Privy Council. He had responded by telling her the tale of Icarus, who had lived in ancient Greece and had flown too close to the sun with waxen wings because he was ambitious to do so. The wings had melted, and he had plunged to his death.

'I, daughter,' he had told her 'have wings of wax, not steel, and will survive because I recognise that is so. My life is about service to the queen in defence of this realm, but it is also to you, and I fly quite high enough, thank you.' She knew enough of his nature not to press further. He had been unusually animated in his reply and had patted her hand affectionately before returning to his papers. In time she would come to realise how dangerous that world could be and that her father had no intention of diminishing his height by a head! As the years passed, she would understand only too well how fragile the Tudor dynasty had been when it first ascended the throne, which was not so long ago. The court was a dangerous place of shifting sand where your friend in a moment could become an enemy and an enemy just as quickly, a friend.

That conversation with her father had stayed in her mind and she so admired him for his philosophy of survival. Mary could only imagine the grinding anxiety of receiving a letter stating that a member of her family had been arrested, or was being investigated. This was quite often because the people who received such letters moved in circles that had suddenly fallen from favour, often for some spurious reason. She thought grimly that this would be a situation very well-known indeed by many at the time of her queen's father, King Henry VIII. Then there were many days of terror for families such as the Boleyns, Seymours and Howards, as well as a multiplicity of others.

She had heard about old Lord Lisle, Deputy Governor of Calais at the time of the old king, Henry VIII. Lord Lisle had committed the sin of being born a Plantagenet (even if bastard), the old royal line. As a result, the suspicions of the king, who had become increasingly violent and unstable as he grew older, caused Lord Lisle to be arrested and sent to the Tower. This loyal man might have been found not guilty in the end, but died suddenly in the Tower after all, despite having heard he was about to be released. What a tragedy and waste of a good man. Perhaps Mary's father was right. Find a high level and then hover round the edge to be sure of survival in the changing seasons of kings and queens.

Back in Derbyshire, as the midday meal approached, after writing a positive shower of brief letters, she stopped and examined closely the second finger on her right hand, which had a bump stained blue, where she had gripped the inky quill for hours. It would take precious lemon juice and salt to shift it and she would scrub away, trying to avoid the really sore side of her finger, where she had a habit of chewing the skin away from the nail until it bled. She tore at her fingers particularly if she was anxious and although she didn't feel stressed on the surface, she knew she was lying awake too often for too long. It was starting to worry her, as unease sat on her spirit, although she couldn't work out why.

When not at her letters, she would play her small virginal in the cool great hall where its plucking harp-like sounds would fill the house. Out of practice, she was clumsy at first, slipping onto the wrong keys and making her mutter angrily to herself. Eventually however, with her usual persistence, out came the tunes, some stately, some jolly. She particularly loved to play the English country dances as they were bursting with a foot-tapping, heart-racing joy. The servants who could hear, both in and out of the house, would smile and some would sing or hum along, with heads weaving happily to the melodies.

In London, her education had been taken very seriously by her father as from as young as five, when she had to rise at six to wash and dress and then to prayers and her first lesson of the day when her letters tutor arrived. Writing and reading was followed by Music and Dance and twice a week Mathematics and French taught oddly, in every sense, by the same Tutor who was really her French teacher but offered mathematics. It would be a cheaper option her father had decided and as he put it, 'It avoided me having to interview another bore!'

Mathematics taught in a French accent was a double jeopardy, but it was clear after a few weeks, that the tutor didn't know much about the subject. They settled down and picked through it all as best they could. He would read letters with his feet on the table and she would usually fiddle with a ladybird in a box. If they heard someone coming they would leap to the books and look interested. She wouldn't tell on him, if he didn't tell on her. That was the first time she appreciated that adults that appeared to be honourable were not necessarily anything of the sort. That appealed to her. Naughtiness sometimes did. When small, she had learned to write on wax tablets with a sharp stick-like pen. Her wax book was made of two pieces of wood held by leather thongs with buttery yellow wax on each 'page'. Each practice session ended with a hot iron being passed over the scribbled-on wax to produce a clean flat sheet to use again.

Every Monday, her real bête noire - lessons in the dreaded sewing. She particularly hated sewing; constantly pricking her fingers and bleeding on the cloth - always frustrated. Once, when about ten years of age and carefully embroidering a small blue flower for hours on a kerchief corner she discovered she had sewn it directly to her over gown and it all had to be unpicked again, much to her fury. She had gone to her bed with bitter tears trickling hot in her ears as she lay on her back and emerged later that evening with a shiny swollen red face and a headache. Mary had planned to surprise her father with that marvellous little kerchief and now it was unsalvageable, a wreck of a kerchief. She hated it.

Her father, sitting back in his chair looked up and on seeing her puffy pink cheeks had risen and taken her hand and sitting by the fire pulled her to him with one arm round her waist and told her he loved her and that cheered her up. In just the past year, Mary had come upon her little kerchief-disaster at the back of the linen press where it had slept forgotten for years. She was surprised it hadn't been thrown away or used as a rag but someone had kept it, and hidden it affectionately so it would not be lost. Looking at it, Mary had smiled to herself, as she smoothed it out on her hand for it was indeed terribly badly sewn, not slightly neat, but had been what kinder tutors called 'A good effort'.

This was annoying, but not as irritating as charcoal drawing a fine picture on a smooth piece of wood and people saying 'Lovely, Mary' and then a quizzical pause as the picture was rotated followed by 'what is it meant to be?' Now, that really was annoying.

So her childhood, without a mother or siblings, had been full of lessons, most of which she didn't enjoy much, and instructions to make her fit to be a daughter of a fine house, and make a good marriage. She had been allowed a great deal more rein than most children of her family's rank and an unheard of amount for a girl. She was told by disapproving female relatives that children should be quiet and pious and in public never burp or sneeze (sneezing was considered the worst social sin, or blow their nose and also to be utterly obedient. Mary wondered how true that really was as an ideal for a child. She was indulged,her relatives said, and if she wasn't careful she would grow up 'no better than she should be'. That always sounded like a conundrum but her father seemed to enjoy it as a saying and kept repeating it and laughing.

Thank goodness her planned betrothal had fallen through. She hardly knew Peter Grey, and didn't care for what little she saw of him. A thin, dark wispy-bearded creature, a year younger than her, with the added bonus of spots and spindly legs.

'And he smells odd, like old fish. Please don't make me marry him, Father.' Her father shook his head in an exasperated manner, so she knew she had won. That head shake was a sign he had given up the argument, and although she had lied about the smell of fish, her intended was indeed deeply unpleasant and yet remarkably could hardly pass a reflection of himself without stopping to admire the handsome creature he thought he was. The thought of sharing his bed was enough, Mary decided, to finish anybody off.

Father was trying to do the best he could for her but although Peter Grey was from a rich and influential family linked to court, she felt she simply wasn't ready to be married and certainly not to him. She had gathered the Grey family were not at all happy about the betrothal withdrawal, but she was very grateful.

Edmund Dudley had taken his revenge on her by offering her a suitor in the form of an elderly, fat merchant from Cheapside, with a great monster of a nose: the thought of which made her run away, with the sound of her father's laughter chasing her up the stairs.

The family humour was based on teasing and it wasn't always kind or funny. Mary had sulked for a while but at the same time knew her father was reminding her that children, particularly girls, had to follow their parents' wishes without argument, and although he would do all he could accommodate his wayward daughter, one day she must be married. She wasn't really wayward, she told herself but she knew her own mind and sought ways to move away from situations if she didn't like them. Like almost everyone else.

Mary knew friends who had married horrid men, some of whom were drunken and violent or gambling the family fortune away and pestering their new wives to beg more money from their families beyond the dowry to get rid of violent and dangerous debtors. The danger of childbirth pressed heavily on her. Mary wanted freedom, not marriage, not yet.

Her Majesty claimed the same desire, to remain a virgin and be unmarried. Mary wondered if both of them would be able to keep up that position, before having to yield to pressure, she from her father and tutting relatives, and the queen from the Privy Council.

She was dwelling on these thoughts when she made her way into the quiet scented garden, as the sun was too hot and so she could sit on a bench in the shade and enjoy the stillness of the countryside. There was always something to look at. In the next field just beyond the remains of the blasted oak was a small coppice with the light filtering through for the trees that were so close grown even in a bright summer's day it was quite dark. For a moment, she saw a movement that reminded her of Warwick in the churchyard, but this was a much more slight figure that seemed to melt into the dark bark of the trees. Then nothing, so she must have imagined it, she decided. A trick of the light, she told herself, but still kept looking back at that spot.

These past days, she had enjoyed the yielding of the greatest heat of the day, often sinking into a rose-pink twilight, and she would take the chance to ride out across the parched fields, away from the crops, and feel her spirit free and bright. There was a sense of a burgeoning self-awareness in her, in that she felt much more in charge of her own destiny. There was little to disturb her quiet waters. Alice Goodrich, thankfully, continued to keep herself to herself. No more could be heard that strident cackle that could only come from her, but still most of the servants were creeping about whispering as if expecting an explosion of some sort, and they didn't want to be the one who started it, or indeed to get caught in the crossfire in any way.

Mary had a horrible feeling that they were probably right and that Alice would strike like a snake when she had the chance, so Mary was on her guard. She was glad when riding out to get away from all this domestic intrigue. Her chestnut was highly responsive and soft-mouthed, an effortless creature to ride, biddable and careful of foot.

Meanwhile, as the days ticked by, Thomas Ashbourne was constantly busy on estate business away from the Hall, usually visiting tenants, but he and the whole household made their way through the

Christening Gate without fail on Sunday mornings for church, with Mary taking her place in the carved family pew. Consequently, there was a rhythm to the hours of the days and the days of the week that lulled her into a sense of security. It would turn out, as she discovered later, to be a false sense of security.

Chapter 9

Just when she thought nothing exciting would happen ever again, she received an invitation to a formal dinner at Tutbury Castle from the Deputy Constable, William Agard. The Earl of Shrewsbury, an important landowner in Derbyshire and a figure at court, held the positions of Constable of the castle and Steward of the lordship that surrounded it, but he took little interest in what were essentially sinecures, and simply enjoyed the revenue that went with the posts. Agard, a local man whose family had long held Duchy offices associated with Tutbury, was the real power in the area, and Mary knew that her father considered it important to maintain cordial relations with him. She was to represent her father, accompanied by Thomas Ashbourne and her maid Anne, so they would travel there together in the carriage. Anne was beside herself with excitement, and Ashbourne sighed and frowned a little at this news, for he was busy.

Mary, however, felt it was about time she had a little more company and she resented his frown.

The Thursday came quickly, and Mary was dressed carefully in scarlet and clashing bright blue silk for maximum London impact. She sat before the glass in her chamber with just one candle, as the sun had not set and would not for some hours, struggling to fix her pearl-drop earrings whilst Anne in her festival gown (as she called it stood behind Mary, deftly dressing her young mistress's brown hair high on her head, fixing. pearl-ended pins to hold the curls in place.

Mary was aware of a chattering noise, but she had been miles away in her thoughts. Coming back to reality she hoped she had not missed a question from Anne as she hadn't been really listening. Anne was often a background noise for Mary, who had been thinking when looking in the glass whether she might be a little tanned, which was not at all fashionable. She wondered if she should use some chalk powder, but decided against it as it could look as if she'd had her face in the flour bin.

Mary tried to pick up the end of what Anne was saying, which was something to do with outsiders who had come to the area over at Marchington village.

'Quite a surprise, I must say, having clever folk take Woodroffe's. It's usually for yeomen having all that land around it, I mean I was surprised and so was Mistress Chatting (who has just had her twelfth child, and all alive, that cottage of hers must be rammed.' Mary had no idea who Mistress Chatting was or why she might be surprised. It struck Mary that anyone who had endured birthing twelve children would not be surprised by much.

Still, her ears had pricked up at the sound of the yeoman's house at Marchington, as she had been enchanted by that house since she was a child. Maybe over dinner at the castle she might find out more. She was sure that the local magistrate, the lecherous Roger Bartholomew, who lived nearby, would know something, as might his terribly dull but worthy wife. Mary told herself how insulted she would be if anyone thought her 'worthy'. It felt like the last present from the barrel on Twelfth Night, a compensation title from society for being plain. She remembered having drummed into her that chastity for a high born woman was to be valued above all other things. Irritated by this comment from an aunt with a 'homely' face, she had pointed out that it was easy to be chaste with a face like a boot. That evening had not been a happy one.

Back in the present, Anne was continuing to talk in her garrulous, fussy way. No wonder her small round husband was quiet, Mary thought. He might not really be a quiet person but couldn't find a word small enough to slide into pause when near Anne. Sometimes in a musing moment, Mary wondered if Master Compson had a glamorous mistress somewhere in a cottage where he would visit, talk non-stop, and get drunk. She felt guilty thinking of that passionately wild scene as she watched her maid carefully folding clothes and tidying the room in her usual efficient manner. Then Mary was aware her maid was still talking, and began to register what she was saying.

'So, I am really looking forward to meeting them at the castle if I can as he is a rum lot, I hear, although she, the sister, is a pretty thing and not at all like him.' Anne's voice had broken into Mary's thoughts, so she put up her hand to stop her.

'What was that, Anne?' She turned in her chair. 'Forgive me, but who are you talking about? Tell me properly and by that I mean slowly. Are we meeting them tonight do you know?'

''Tis fine, mistress. I was talking about the new folks who have taken up Woodroffe's at Marchington. You know, the place that looks like a galleon tied up.' Mary nodded. She was really interested now, as new neighbours offered variety of company and news in the small local community. Anne told her what she knew, which was that a man who was a stargazer from Oxford University had taken Woodroffe's with his sister.

'Because he wants time to write his book or something.' Anne's voice faded at the end because she wasn't entirely sure, as she would put it, 'saying it right for clever folks'. After some careful prompting from Mary, the tale came out in full, or as near to full as it could be, as it would be made up entirely from hearsay.

According to Anne, one of the castle messengers had told her when resting (lolling in the kitchen, (and enjoying a large piece of pie, no doubt that before he had delivered the invitation to Mary for dinner at the castle, he had dropped off an invitation to them at Woodroffe's too. The messenger had added that they had accepted, and he knew that because they had replied immediately asking him to wait.

Then Anne added 'And they seemed pleased, apparently.' She was holding up a forefinger and looking at the ceiling to aid her memory. She often did that, but Mary had no idea why, as neither the ceiling nor the finger seemed to have anything to do with whatever particular tale she was telling at the time.

'And he read their answer?' added Mary cynically. Anne looked shifty and Mary suspected that married Anne quite liked that particular messenger from Tutbury Castle. She was watching Anne's face in the looking glass, but she had turned away, as if she hadn't heard, and started rattling bottles unnecessarily.

Mary considered the news of these new neighbours.

The man sounded a little strange, but the younger sister sounded more hopeful, as no doubt she would want to escape the clutches of star charts now and again.

Mary had seen star charts, as their compilation formed part of a new child's birth amongst the rich and aspirational. Charts would be rolled out at the christening or similar family gathering for everyone to admire and pretend they saw signs on the parchment too. No one did, including the stargazer, Mary suspected, but kudos and fashion was all about high society. Stargazers trained for years, Mary was told, but she was not convinced. Neither was her father, she could tell, because when they were with other guests somewhere boring and they began to examine a chart, he would look at her and raise his eyebrows. They could go really high and even one at a time, which was a real skill and that made her want to laugh out loud, which was why he did it.

It would be good not only to get out and meet the new residents in the area but to enjoy a fine evening meal at the castle. The food was always good and there was always a pinch of court gossip to chew over along with the sticky sweetmeats. Perhaps everyone would be more discreet this evening with the newcomers – outsiders as they were - being present.

Chapter 10

The castle had been through a ten-month period of repairs and rebuilding, which Mary had seen when she arrived the night of the storm, but it was all a bit hectic and she hadn't had a chance in the rain to take it all in. However, the changes were obvious later that night as the carriage clattered through the great gatehouse, built some two hundred and fifty years before.

Even though she had known Tutbury Castle all her life, riding up that steep green hill to the vast ancient grey fortress ahead of them was exciting. To discover a complete town nestled inside the walls was always a revelation, always remarkable.

This night was no exception as the three of them looked out of the coach windows. Spread before them were lots of tight cobbled alleys of half-timbered houses filling the innermost of the three baileys. A small army of servants lived in them. Laundry women, dairy maids and cooks all rubbed shoulders with armed guards and archers, some of whom they were married to. Everyone seemed busy, always. Stablemen ran forward and took the heads of the carriage horses as the party climbed down and made their way to the Great Hall, rebuilt just before the queen's grandfather, the wily Henry Tudor, had taken the throne, and with it control of the Duchy of Lancaster and its castles and manors.

Close to the Great Hall, below the state apartments in the South Tower, was a little garden, a rose-filled, jasmine-scented oasis away from the smoke-pumping bowels of the castle. Horses and smoke were what the castle smelled of, Mary had always thought, with the added spice of the sharpness of burned black powder that she could almost taste on her tongue.

Tutbury Castle had always been important because of its strategic position in the very heart of England, not to mention the sweeping estate that surrounded it, on the borders of Derbyshire, Staffordshire and Leicestershire. The Castle had been visited by a glittering array of monarchs and princes, including Henry VIII, who had stayed within her walls sizing up his property and deciding which of the surrounding fields would be used to house the royal stud, known as the Tutbury Race. Henry had come to Tutbury early in his reign, as a golden young king, described by the Venetian ambassador as 'the most perfect man God had ever made'. Mary liked the thought of the young handsome king, taller than a vast majority of men, striding in, having just been married to Katherine of Aragon, and not knowing the dramas his life and loves would bring him during the years ahead.

Mary, as a child, heard her father and other guests of advanced years in the London house talking about 'the old king'. 'Unbelievable brutality in that man in the end,' puffed one from behind a large cup of wine. They were talking discreetly, they thought, but Mary was nearby. King Henry VIII might be dead, but treasonous talk of the dead can reflect on the royalty living, especially if they are direct relatives, and the quickest route to disgrace and even death was such talk. Her father was younger than the other men but listened carefully with rather less wine in his cup. Her father was a watchful man, taking advantage of learning whenever he could and ensuring he was sober enough to absorb it all.

'Just such a brilliant mind, was Hal,' said another. 'All lost in greed and the belief that all were working against him. The old boy lost his mind in anxiety and lashed out like a wounded lion.' All the men had nodded together, and moved onto another subject linked to finances and Mary had lost interest and gone into the garden to play with a ball. If she had been caught listening at doors, she would have been in terrible trouble, as her father told her that it was a sinful and deceitful thing to do. In those days, Mary had been frightened of sin and Hell, with all those flames and red demons poking people with pitchforks, so when she did wrong she prayed until her knees ached and then she felt she had suffered for her sins. It was her form of penance, but nobody else knew that she went in for this form of self-cleansing, as although her father believed in many things he did not approve of self-mortification. 'Too papist,' he said, 'and there's something wrong with a person who does that to his - or her - own body'. Mary had listened, and over time had stopped doing it.

She did love to listen to stories about the famous who had visited the castle in the past and often when she was staying at Somersal and was reminded of the castle, she would ask her father to tell her more. She could hear her father's voice: 'Before Henry VIII, the last Plantagenet king, Richard III, stayed for five nights just ten months before his death at the battle of Bosworth field, which is only about twenty-five miles from the castle.' She had been aghast at that name, as she remembered being told that he was the one who had murdered the young princes in the Tower. 'Wasn't he the wicked one?' she whispered to her father, fearing that the name would cause the king to be resurrected before her and drag her to Hell.

'Some would say so,' her father had answered, 'whilst others would say he played the game of ambition, and played it hard after the Cousins' War. Power draws men to do many things in its name.'

'How old was he when he died?' she asked, knowing her mother had been only 24 when she had died. 'He was thirty-two years of age,' said her father.

'As old as that!', which made her father laugh. 'Yes, my daughter, as old as that and when you reach it, it will not seem so old, my love'. When she grew older she had discovered that some people believed King Henry VII had slaughtered the princes, rather than Richard, and no one would ever know the truth of it all, as the bodies had not been found nor a single witness to vouch for events. All Mary knew was that as the Tudors were now firmly on the throne of England it would be a good idea to continue to think that it was King Richard III after all.

Mary had always been interested to find out more about Tutbury Castle, gathering information wherever she found it. One of her tutors who had an interest in history was a valuable source, as she discovered that although he lived in London, his mother had as a child lived near

Tutbury. Mary remembered him telling her that in the 1360s the magnificent John of Gaunt had often visited Tutbury Castle, which he had inherited along with enormous wealth through his beautiful snow-white wife, Blanche. After a number of living and dead children she had tragically died within the walls of Tutbury Castle, days after giving birth. Blanche had been much loved, and Geoffrey Chaucer, a clerk in Gaunt's household who had later become famous as a poet, had written a book in memory of Blanche called 'The Boke of the Duchess'. When Gaunt married his second wife, the Spanish princess Constance, he gave her Tutbury as one of her main residences. To make her feel more at home, her husband had apparently revived the ancient custom of bull-running through the streets of Tutbury, that still continued once a year at Lammastide in August.

Mary had never been allowed to witness the bull-running at Tutbury, although huge crowds travelled to the area just for this sight. She hadn't appreciated when her father refused his permission that this was to protect her, both physically and mentally from this horribly brutal spectacle.

Gaunt's line had become kings of England, and many of the finest buildings at the Castle dated from the period when the house of Lancaster held the throne.

Tutbury had been given as a wedding present to another foreign princess, Margaret of Anjou, the wife of Henry VI, who had built a beautiful tower overlooking the slope at the entrance to the Castle. Later under the Yorkists it had become the court of the Duke of Clarence, while Richard III himself had been responsible for rebuilding the Great Hall and Great Chamber in which Mary would dine that night. So Tutbury, perched high on the hill above the beautiful green Dove Valley below, was a castle visited by many of the great and good in English history. The drama and romance of it all captured her imagination.

A woman's voice from behind Mary broke into her thoughts, startling her. 'Forgive me for imposing myself upon you, when we haven't even been introduced, but I have been so keen to meet you.'

Mary turned to the light feminine voice and saw an open-faced, pretty young woman beside her, with bright blue eyes and a mass of blonde curls. Lost in her thoughts, Mary hadn't even heard her approach. The woman was dressed neatly and quite smartly but her dress was worn, and the plush on the cloth was rubbed almost bare in places.

'Forgive me,' said Mary courteously. 'I am very pleased to meet you too.' They took hands and broke into easy conversation together. Her name, she told Mary hesitantly, was Margaret Rich and she pointed out her brother Gregory. Apparently he was a scholar, and without Margaret saying so, within a few sentences Mary could tell that she was bored - bored to death by her brother and by being shut away in the nearby village of Marchington, with no close neighbours. The move had taken her away from established friends so she was desperate for the company of someone of similar age.

Mary was delighted that the very person she had come to the event with the intention of meeting was here in front of her and keen to make her acquaintance too. Although they had only just met they sat in a corner of the Great Hall companionably, and chatted like chirping birds in a nest. Anyone looking at the two young women together might have thought they had known each other for many years.

Mary saw Thomas Ashbourne dart looks over in her direction now and again as he was talking to Margaret's brother, a glass of wine in his hand. Margaret told her new friend, when asked why she was in the area, that she and her brother had recently come to Woodroffe's cottage because he had wanted peace and quiet to write.

'And the last thing you want is quiet?' observed Mary perspicaciously and Margaret nodded enthusiastically, obviously seeing Mary as her new friend in a much-needed social desert. 'A kindred soul and someone to share secrets with', thought Mary, and they chatted in a relaxed way throughout the evening, even though manners sometimes took them away to make conversation with other guests. From long practice, Mary took care to avoid the magistrate, Roger Bartholomew, but she saw that Margaret needed rescuing as she pulled imploring faces to her over his shoulder. Bartholomew was addressing her bosom, as he always did to personable young women, sometimes making circular hand movements in an alarming fashion as if he would like to do more than just address them.

Mary disappointed the magistrate by intervening with a 'Forgive me sir, but I must introduce my new friend to ….someone else.' She just couldn't think who for a moment, but it didn't seem to matter to the magistrate as he nodded affably, and headed off to another bosom or two, elsewhere.

Margaret, after such a shared joke, felt able to talk openly to Mary, and said that she was seeking to get time away from her brother. 'I don't want to be disloyal, and I know you and I have only just met, but I do find his work dull. Like a caged bird wherever we are, he wants quiet and has the fiercest of tempers if he doesn't have his own way.'

Margaret was also quick to point out that Gregory and she were only half-brother and sister, sharing the same father, which was why there was such a large gap in age between them. It rather sounded as though what she was keen to stress was that her nature was not at all like her half-brother's, or as Mary put it, 'You are not made of exactly the same stuff,' which Margaret thought was a marvellous comment.

Then she suddenly looked troubled and frowned, saying, 'Oh dear, here I am chattering on. What must you think of me?'

She caught Mary's hand. 'I am just so desperate for female company – I am run wild.' Margaret had a charming and utterly disarming manner, and it felt impossible not to like her. Mary put her head to one side and smiled for in that moment she realised she had found a true friend. Perhaps, one never knew, a friend for life.

Chapter 11

After the dinner, as the girls perched on a deep window sill, Mary saw Margaret's brother weaving his way towards them. He was a squat, grey-haired, red-faced man and looked as though he had drunk far too much. Ignoring Mary, he slurred, 'We're going, Margaret.'

Mary took an instant dislike to him because of his appalling manners, as he hadn't even glanced at her, never mind a proper acknowledgement of her presence. He had blue eyes, that were red hot with drink.

Margaret blushed, looking down. 'Of course, Gregory.' She opened her hand towards her new friend. 'This is Mary Dudley.' He merely glanced at Mary and nodded curtly, before turning away and making his way to the door. Quite a number of the gentry from the surrounding area were at the dinner in the Great Chamber. By the look of them, pretty well all of them had also been drinking heavily, so hardly anyone noticed them leave. He hadn't even bothered to thank his host.

The next moment, brother and sister were hurriedly bustled back into the room by a group of armed men, who had barred their way in their urgency to enter the Great Chamber. Everybody looked rather shocked as the captain made his way to William Agard, the Deputy

Constable of the Castle, who was having an animated conversation with the magistrate. The men bought with them the smell of burning wood on their cloaks, and an atmosphere of great tension.

The captain reported in a low voice, Agard and Bartholomew listening carefully, but in the silence most could hear the tragic news he brought with him. Agard turned and addressed the room, repeating what many had already heard.

'I am afraid I am the bearer of bad news, after such a pleasant evening. I hope the ladies will not be too shocked, but I have to tell you that not one but two bodies have been found within a few miles of the castle, and I am afraid that both poor souls appear to have been murdered'.

A cry of horror went up in the room, and hands flew to mouths, while eyes opened wide. One old lady sat down sharply and was attended in her faint by two other ladies. The guests looked at each other, clutching their glasses, and there was much muttering, before one of the party asked, 'Are they both men?'

The magistrate answered, 'The good captain here reports that one is a woman, found just outside of Yoxall, not eight miles from here, in a ditch. The other, a man, was found by charcoal burners in their fire heap in the woodlands of Hoar Cross.'

'How do you know it isn't just an accident or old age in each case?' asked another man's voice. Mary couldn't see who asked it.

The captain replied, 'Unfortunately, it seems that the murderer or murderers of these two people are not very good at hiding their identity, as they have left a mark. In both cases, the hands and feet are bound with frayed cord.'

'That is surely not so unusual?' asked Agard. 'Yes it is, because the cord has a thread of blue running through it, most peculiar. I haven't seen anything like it before'.

Mary impulsively caught hold of Margaret's arm, as she could tell that she was quite distressed. In that moment she looked up, and saw that Gregory Rich showed no reaction to the news, merely glaring pop-eyed at his sister, no doubt because they had not left earlier when he had insisted they should.

Mary whispered to Margaret, 'You'd better go, my dear, as your brother is blowing up a storm of a temper.' Margaret nodded, looking anxious, and rapidly left the room with Gregory, who had caught hold of her arm harshly. Mary thought she heard her new friend cry out slightly as if in pain. and felt a flash of anger at this, suspicious that violence from Gregory towards his sister was quite usual. A disgusting state of affairs, and bad enough between husband and wife, but most unusual between brother and sister unless youngsters, when sibling rivalry was quite normal, and sneaky pinching and arm-twisting common. To see a grown man, who was highly educated, prepared to be violent in a public place, made Mary wonder what else was going on in private. She felt deeply offended at this brutality and determined to help Margaret if she could, even if just as a supportive friend.

Open interference in domestic conflict could make matters worse, she knew. It had been pointed out to her by her father once when attempting to explain elements of human nature. 'Break up two dogs fighting in the street, and unless you are careful then both will turn and chase you.' Father, as usual, was taking the less challenging route to survival, but she knew he had a point.

Within moments of the announcement, as was to be expected, the whole party broke up, with much muttering about how sad it was, and how everyone should be locking their doors. Agard was thanked for an otherwise wonderful evening. Cloaks and carriages were called for at speed, and in a very short amount of time, the Great Chamber was almost empty, except for the servants now busy clearing up quietly so as not to disturb those left in the room. William Agard swung around and snapped at them. 'Leave all this. Leave it, I say, until we have left the room.' The servants left at cannon-ball speed, and only then did Agard return to the intensely focussed discussion about the murders.

'That's better, I can't have alarmist gossip flying around the area. It's going to be bad enough as it is, suppressing it.'

Now the room had cleared, all that was left of the men were Thomas Ashbourne, William Agard, the magistrate and the captain, who stood in a small masculine knot and discussed what should happen next in muted and respectful tones. Mary sat quietly nearby, hands folded demurely in her lap and looking straight ahead so as not to appear an eavesdropper.

The officer reported that the bodies had been brought to the church of St Mary the Virgin, which stood just below the castle. It was agreed that to get a clear picture, Bartholomew and Agard would visit together with the captain to view and consider the fatal injuries.

One body, the man, had been found burned terribly next to a charcoal burners 'clamp' in Hoar Cross. The woman had been found in Yoxall, with her head and face smashed in, tied up like the man had been, and dumped in a ditch. The captain explained that Agard and Bartholomew would be able to take full statements from the witnesses who had found the bodies at the church, as they had been brought from the murder scenes by the soldiers. He added that in both cases the condition of the bodies meant that they could not be recognised from their faces alone.

Further enquiries about missing locals might prove helpful, but if not, an examination might offer all that was ascertainable from the type of death, clothes or goods still on the corpses, perhaps in pockets. The magistrate pointed out that the burned corpse was not likely to offer much of that.

'Except sir, the rope with the blue thread still in the middle, which was only partly burned.'

Mary supposed as she heard this that it was a great thing to keep one's spirits up with optimism, if there was nothing else.

'They'll be lucky to find anything in pockets,' she thought. Surely any clues are likely to be removed, unless the murderer was an amateur or disturbed and ran off in panic. It would be a tricky task trying to pin anyone down for such a crime, but it would fall upon the representatives of the law in the area to hunt down, arrest, charge, and carry out the harshest of justice on such a brutal killer. Strong authority and the obvious secure rule of law in action were essential at such times, so confidence could be present in society and ensure mob rule did not take over instead. It happened occasionally, she knew, but thankfully was not common.

Ashbourne came over to Mary and bent down slightly as she looked up at him. 'I am afraid I will have to go with them too, as I have an obligation to report all this to your father. He always insists on detailed information about any crime in the area, particularly matters surrounding the castle.'

At the mention of her father and suddenly acutely aware of his absence, she did feel a little vulnerable and a flicker of her unease must have crossed her face, for Ashbourne picked it up.

'Don't be concerned Lady Mary, I have your care in mind always, so I will arrange for two of the Castle guards to escort your carriage safely home.' Mary nodded to show her appreciation for his thoughtfulness and then he left with a couple of the men. Only a few minutes later a man-servant dressed in respectable Castle livery of dark blue and red arrived, to tell her with a small bow that the carriage was ready to take her and Anne, who had been eating in the Castle kitchens, back to Somersal.

In the carriage on the way home, the two of them bumped along in the dark, talking of the murders in voices as hushed as they could be, as it was difficult to be heard above the rattling of the wheels on the hard rutted roads and the voices of the grooms and soldiers who were riding alongside. The murderous news had apparently reached the castle servants almost as quickly as it had reached upstairs. Anne knew as much as the magistrate, which was half irritating and half amusing. Stopping gossip, particularly of dark matters, was a lost cause. Mary smiled grimly.

Despite her earlier misgivings, Mary Dudley was not the sort of woman who thought that if there was a murderer in the area, he had picked her out as the next victim and was just waiting at the next corner. She did feel secure though, in the knowledge that she was protected by not one, but two guards on horseback carrying flares, as well as the coachman and groom. Father did not need to hold her hand at all times, she told herself, firmly bolstering up her self-confidence.

Mary thought about Thomas Ashbourne as she looked out of the carriage window into blackness. A ghostly white owl flew by and startled her for a moment, but she was pleased to have seen this dramatic bird of the night. Its paleness reminded her how she had seen the colour drain from Ashbourne's face when he heard of the murders that evening.

Only she and Anne had returned to the Hall in the carriage: he would be given a horse from the Castle to return home, perhaps in the early hours, depending upon how complicated all the evidence was. 'Or even tomorrow morning,' she unintentionally muttered out loud.

'What is that, mistress?' asked Anne, who thought for a ghastly moment that she might have missed something.

'Nothing, Anne, I am just thinking out loud about Thomas Ashbourne getting back home.'

'Do you not think it will be tonight?'

'No. I really don't, as there will be so much to see and talk about while the trail is fresh.' Mary sounded distracted, because she was thinking things through.

Anne decided to be quiet, just adding, 'Makes me shudder,' into the collar of her cloak.

'Me too, Anne. Me too.'

The night bore down on the carriage and their outriders, and dawn was far away.

Chapter 12

Thomas Ashbourne had already returned from the Castle when Mary came downstairs from her room. She raised her eyebrows when she saw him standing by the great hall windows, looking out over the rose-gardens. 'He is up early', she said to herself, for he had been working virtually all night. A grim task too.

He quickly span around when he heard her movement. Actually, he jumped as if startled, and it was most unusual for Thomas to be jumpy about anything. He was a steady individual with a strong sense of logic and plenty of common sense. These murders had clearly seriously upset him. His face was swollen and his eyes red-rimmed with exhaustion, and by his actions he appeared very unsettled. Leaning backwards against the wall, he told her what they knew so far, knowing she would be eager for news. His young mistress was her father's daughter, intelligent, educated, and interested in many things and murder was definitely one of them. She wasn't fascinated by the gory violence itself, but what drove people to deliberately take the life of another with all the ramifications, both body, and soul.

His master had warned his steward to treat his daughter as a boy from when she was small, and that instruction had paid off, as she coped very well. Sometimes she could even be helpful in breaking puzzles with her natural insight into human nature, unusual for one so young.

Not looking directly at Mary but staring off into the distance, Ashbourne recalled the detail. He told Mary that first the man had been found, yesterday morning at first light. The charcoal burners usually started work at dawn or before in deep winter. She had seen these work-blackened creatures in equally black-smoked clearings when riding through the woods.

Charcoal burners could be found all over England, shovelling away, talking loudly together in thick clouds of smoke with white cracks around their eyes. They usually worked in gangs of about eight men, supplying an ever-increasing demand for charcoal. Part of the process was that they would bake loads of wood at very high temperatures for days on end in massive built-up dome-shaped ovens, piled over with earth that would bake and crack in the intense heat. While a bake was on, they would cut down and sort more wood ready for the next batch.

Early yesterday morning, the foreman had seen when he arrived that something large was on top of the charcoal bake-pile and had gone over to investigate, half expecting a dead animal. A large, dead animal. Earth had been piled on whatever it was in an attempt to hide it, but that plan had failed as the packed soil had fallen away revealing the smouldering object underneath.

Upon closer inspection, the foreman was aghast to see it was the blackened corpse of a man. To add to the horror of the discovery, the foreman had seen that the corpse had its wrists and ankles tied cruelly with only partially burned rope. Unfortunately for those that put him on the heap, the fire was dying down and not banked up for a new load. There had been a short but heavy burst of rain in the night, which had pretty well put out the fire as well as washing the earth off the body. However the body was still badly burned with little stubbles of grey hair that could be seen on the blackened skull. The tied wrists were drawn up to the chest and the hands clenched into fists.

Mary interrupted this grim tale, 'Why? Why were his hands pulled up like that? Was he fighting when he died and rigor mortis had set in before they dumped the corpse, or was it in agony that caused the fighting-style fists?'

'Neither' said Ashbourne, wincing. 'A physician staying at the Castle has already seen the body, and says the intense heat at the beginning of the corpse being on the fire caused the muscles in his arms to contract, causing the clenched fists and the arms pulled up.' He sighed at the sadness of such an appalling act. Mary was quiet for a moment before asking, 'Was he dead before he was dumped on the fire?'

'Let us hope so, Mistress,' muttered Ashbourne, looking down at his riding boots.

'Have you seen the body?'

The steward nodded. 'Only briefly, both of them. Both the murdered bodies are in St. Mary's church in front of the high altar.'

'And the woman? Were they found almost at the same time?'

Ashbourne shook his head. 'The man at dawn, and the woman…' - he hesitated, and Mary saw a flash of horror across his face - '… was found by a farmer late in the afternoon on his land.'

It struck Mary that what Ashbourne had seen must have been bad, for both in London and the country, death was always on show, whether for the morbid who liked attending public executions, or from the many accidents of life under carriage wheels or falling drunk from balconies. Despite a life-time of experience, Ashbourne was still clearly moved and disgusted by the murders, both of them, but particularly the woman, she could tell, as his manner had dipped to deep, dark depression. Mary could also tell Ashbourne was reluctant to tell her of the woman's body but she insisted on hearing all, and braced herself.

All her young life, she had been fascinated by medicine and the workings of the human body, with all its mysteries and the wonders of healing. It was an enduring longing in her to be able to heal. Not kitchen-magic or as a 'cunning woman', although they had their place in society, but as a real physician. She knew it was impossible for her to study the liberal arts at university and then to travel to the continent to study medicine in places such as Montpellier or Salerno. Women were just not accepted in such academic society, in England or abroad. There had been a nun called Hildegard of Bingen some centuries earlier, who was one of the greatest medical scholars and healers the world had seen, but most thought her work involved divine intervention.

Mary had decided such healing didn't really count on the human scale, as Heaven proved an unfair advantage. Then she said a quick prayer, for she didn't want to anger anyone in Heaven, just in case. Over the years, she had wondered if some women did more than wash bodies, mix cough medicines or deliver babies. Perhaps there were women tucked away who had been trained for higher medical professions privately, by forward-thinking tutors or physicians. Maybe, she could be the first – she told herself on optimistic days.

Now she was discussing with Ashbourne not the living but the dead, beyond help on Earth at least. She also knew their bodies might give up the secrets of who had murdered them, where, and even possibly, why. They would be frozen in the moment of death, and, if not entirely destroyed, might provide clues. It was the clues from the silent and still who lay in the former priory of Tutbury that really interested her.

Ashbourne knew his mistress well enough to understand that she was not just being voyeuristic, but making her way on a journey of understanding that might always remain unfulfilled, at least in terms of gaining formal qualifications. Ashbourne always encouraged her, as indeed her father did. Edmund Dudley privately did not think it was an inappropriate interest for his only child, never mind a girl. He was a man with a broad philosophy and he was also a polymath with great curiosity.

Ashbourne shared what he knew so far of the dead woman. It was merely a coincidence that her body had been found in the evening on the same day as the man. It was found in the village of Yoxall, about three miles from where the man had been found, near Hoar Cross.

'How was she found?'

'The flies had gathered in a great cloud over a dry ditch by an overhanging tree, and a group of foxes had been seen slinking away, so the farmer was concerned about his stock, thinking perhaps a dead calf lay nearby'.

Ashbourne continued speaking in his usual steady, low tone, 'It was horrible for the farmer. He was badly shaken. I met him when a statement was being given to the magistrate. You see she was…' - he stumbled over his words - 'partly eaten by some animal, presumably the fox, and her face had been brutally smashed in'.

'I hope she was dead too,by then.' Mary thought for a moment of what it might feel like to know someone was murdering you. That tree canopy was probably the last thing she saw.

'Was she forced?' Mary hardly dared ask, but it might help to find the killer if the woman had also been raped.

Ashbourne looked up at her. 'Because of the summer heat and fox-damage her body is in a poor condition, so it is difficult to tell. Dr Caius, the great physician from London, was at the Castle anyway, and is with the body now. Agnes, the apothecary from Uttoxeter, is assisting him along with a local surgeon of good reputation.'

Mary did not know Dr.Caius, but had heard of him at Court. It was surprising the number of great names that had arrived at Tutbury Castle, as the heyday of the Castle had now passed, but it was still grand and very important in terms of its position. A large number of people moved around the country, which often took them through the Midlands.

Mary was pleased that Agnes was with the bodies, as she was a well-known and much respected medical practitioner in the local area. Not a physician, as Mary craved to be, but a practitioner all the same. Agnes was a widow who had worked at her apothecary husband's side for many years, and had taken over his successful business upon his death. Actually, it was very much their shared business in fact, but could not be claimed as such until she formally inherited. Mary understood she had a strong young son with bright red hair, called Giles, but had never met him and had only seen Agnes at a distance. Her considerable reputation meant that the people of Uttoxeter were fortunate to have her in their midst.

'How do you know the deaths are connected?' Doxies are found dead in ditches, and men are killed in fights all the time from drink and high tempers.'

Thomas Ashbourne looked her in the eyes, steadily and quietly. 'We know, because both bodies had the faces smashed in, with similar damage to the skulls, as if a large metal ball had hit them. The damage was so similar, it looks as though the same weapon has been used on both. More importantly, you may remember that the captain said that both corpses had wrists and ankles tied with fine rope and some of the thread in the rope was blue for some reason.

Mary was astonished and then narrowed her eyes. 'But the man was burnt black, and so presumably was the rope.'

It was a good point, and Ashbourne acknowledged it, before producing a small frizzled length of black rope from a leather pouch at his side and a six-inch knife from a leather sheath tied to his belt.

The rope was clearly from the remains of the man and if the sight of it wasn't enough, there was a bonfire smell and a hint of cooked pork from it that was surprisingly intense. It made her feel nauseous when she thought about where the rope had been not so long ago, and the horrors it had enabled the murderer or murderers to commit.

Mary watched Ashbourne intently as he cut the black rope in half, then beckoned her to join him by the window and showed her the cut portions at the ends, moving them backwards and forwards to throw more light on them.

The core of both pieces had traces of blue surrounded by black where the fire had burnt through the outside of the rope. Mary gasped, pulling back from the rope, and stared up at Ashbourne.

'It was the same rope used to restrain the woman, I suppose? And no doubt it was even easier to see because no fire had damaged the rope.'

Ashbourne nodded. 'It was bloodstained on the feet and hands, but yes, you are right, Lady, it was easier to see.' There was silence for a couple of minutes before Mary asked, 'What now?'

'I am going back to St. Mary's church, but first a wash and change of clothes, if you will forgive me, Madam.' He was still incongruously dressed in his evening finery, which was now dishevelled, and his eyes looked even more sore and swollen than earlier.

As he walked towards the door, he stopped and turned, saying, 'I am afraid I cannot allow you to accompany me. There is a limit as to what you should see, and I am sure your father would agree in denying you this.'

Chapter 13

An hour later two horses were trotting towards Tutbury Castle from Somersal Lane. One was mounted by a thin-lipped steward and the other a smart young woman with a smug look on her face.

As they turned into Draycott Lane, two horses came across their path on the right, unexpectedly. One was a broad cob and the other an elegant bay that Mary had seen before, and there sat her new friend, Margaret Rich.

Margaret cried out with pleasure at the sight of Mary, tumbling out words breathlessly, 'Oh, my dear Mary, what a pleasure to see you,' and then she apparently remembered the murders and perhaps felt she was being irreverent, so added more quietly, '… and how sadly our evening at the Castle ended. We were so joyous, and then this shocking and horrible news was thrust upon us. Do you have any idea what had happened yet, and are you on your way there now?' She was dressed demurely in dark green.

A tactful little cough from Thomas Ashbourne was enough to suggest that Margaret Rich would not be a useful companion for such a serious investigation. Mary took the hint, and as much as she would like to spend time with her friend, she silently agreed, offering an excuse. 'I am just collecting some letters from, and for, my absent father rather than wait for the messenger.'

Mary spoke breezily, as if the small matter of the announcement of the murders had passed her mind already. She could feel alongside her that Ashbourne approved of this method of escape from the chattering blonde.

'I doubt we shall hear much about these deaths for some time, Margaret, and even then, everyone will have moved on, I am afraid.' Mary didn't believe any of this statement but was rather enjoying shocking Ashbourne next to her as she wove a web of deceit. She didn't need to add all this detail, and believed that by now he had moved from approval to exasperation. She was teasing him.

Then Mary noticed for the first time that the man on the grey cob, who sat silently alongside Margaret, was a stranger. On reflection, she realised it was perfectly likely he would be a stranger to her and the area, as the Rich siblings might well have brought their own servants with them.

Mary acknowledged him with a courteous nod, at which he took off his bonnet and dropped his chin deferentially. He was a grey-haired man in his early fifties or perhaps late forties with a broad, ruddy face. Mary noted there was something indefinable about him that reminded her of Alice Goodrich – or was it Warwick he reminded her of? She just couldn't put her finger on it but would try to find out more about him from Margaret when they were alone. She was half-intrigued and half-certain that she didn't like this servant of Margaret's. He was short but stocky, and the veins showed on his neck. His pale grey eyes had a cold stare. There was nothing modest about that stare, and the man must have registered her concern and immediately dropped his eyes and fiddled with his reins.

That drew Mary's attention to his saddle and in front of him Mary noticed a thick club in a leather pouch held by a loop on the saddle. It was not unusual for a servant to be armed in some way while escorting his mistress, especially in the light of the murders, but something made Mary feel uneasy.

'Who is this, Margaret?' asked Mary pleasantly, ignoring the impatience of Ashbourne at her side, who must have thought she was wasting time. She had her own ideas, and was sure she was doing nothing of the sort, for with killers about she wanted to know more about this stranger who unsettled her.

'This is James, our stockman and helper at Woodroffe's. We can afford few servants, I am afraid.'

James never moved, or even flickered his eyes, but just looked up blankly at his name and turning to his young mistress waited for instructions for the horses to walk on. After farewells (and noticeable silence from James, both sets of horses set off in different directions: Mary and Ashbourne towards Tutbury Castle, and Margaret and James towards Draycott.

There was a silence between Ashbourne and Mary as they rode on, but it was not born of irritation, for the steward revealed that he too had been uneasy about James.

'I don't care at all for him, Thomas. Did you see that monstrous club he had across his saddle?'

Thomas Ashbourne looked at her. 'I quite agree, Lady Mary. That man has the stink of blood about him, and the saddle club! Most men carry a dagger or those fortunate enough to have one, a sword, but not a club like that. All very odd.'

Mary was particularly concerned about her friend having such a watchful, odd man around. She decided not to mention that James reminded her of Alice and Warwick Goodrich. Maybe that was just fanciful, she decided, and guarded her tongue.

The rest of the journey was uneventful as they arrived at the Castle for the sober task ahead. The horses were taken off them at the mounting blocks inside the outer gatehouse, where stable boys were called down to assist. The stables were among a number of wooden buildings inside the two enclosures outside the stone walls of the inner Castle. Silently they made their way down through the churchyard, where before them a small huddled crowd of village gossips had gathered at the west door of the church, with its wonderfully decorated alabaster arch. She could also see that the doors were guarded by the magistrate's men to fend off the nosy locals, which Mary knew would be a full-time job. Perhaps it was a little unfair of her to be critical, as they were obviously keen to have news of the murders, whispering and muttering amongst themselves.

Mary looked to her right and could see two new graves were being dug by sweaty young men with wide brimmed hats.

At the sight of Ashbourne and Mary the crowd parted, looking them up and down, and the guards immediately opened the doors for them. There was shuffling as the crowds tried to look beyond the guards as they went in. Mary saw one of the soldiers frown at the sight of her, no doubt disapproving of her being allowed entrance to where the murder victims lay. She wondered if he thought she might have a fainting fit or something equally suitably feminine.

The magnificent, dark cavernous church, formerly a priory until the monasteries had been suppressed by the old king Henry, had a veil of blue smoke reaching right up into the darkness above and swirling around the great Norman pillars with scented curls. There were streams of light from the high windows illuminating patches of the tiled floor, but not enough to fully break the gloom. The smell of incense was a common smell in any church, but there were burners dotted around everywhere and it took Mary just a few minutes to realise why, as she snatched a kerchief to her mouth and nose.

The stench of death hung sickly sweet in the air like early lilac. Mary made a promise to herself never to have lilac in the house again, not any house, anywhere. There was an arresting blaze of light near the altar where candles were mounted around two tables where the figures of Dr. Caius, a surgeon and Agnes were busy about their business of justice.

Mary sensibly stayed back by one of the pillars, observing while Ashbourne strode forward, hat in hand out of respect for this place of prayer and the dead. He bowed his head towards the altar. Agnes must have heard him and looked up at his approach. Mary saw she was wearing an unusual garment of natural linen, that covered her body to the ground, her hair tied back and sleeves rolled up. She nodded at Ashbourne, who she obviously knew better than Mary previously realised. Dr Caius raised his head, frowning impatiently at this interruption as he was discussing something about the body with Agnes and the surgeon. Agnes lifted her hand to Dr. Caius, signalling that it was appropriate for Ashbourne to approach them, and necessary that she should talk to him. The physician gave a curt nod to Ashbourne before returning to the blackened corpse.

The physician was famous for his brilliance. He was a tall, thin angular man, with a long, grey beard and hair reaching down to his shoulders from under his black scholar's cap. Even from a distance she could see he had a remarkable face, with eyes close together, thick eyebrows, and high, jutting cheek-bones. He too had his sleeves rolled up. 'No wonder at this disgusting duty' thought Mary.

The surgeon at his side looked a big, strong man in his forties. She muttered to herself, 'Like a farmer. I must ask Ashbourne who he is.' Surgeons needed strength for bone-setting, and pulling teeth, and returning unwilling dislocations to sockets.

Thomas Ashbourne was talking quietly and, irritatingly to Mary, it wasn't clear what he was saying before he turned away, and returned to her. He took her arm gently, guiding her to where the monks had once prayed and there they sat, side by side in the carved pew and waited.

There were three elderly women, all dressed similarly to Agnes, also in attendance. Mary had not seen them at first, as they were in the shadow of one of the pillars, waiting to be called forward.

One held a bowl of water and had a cloth over her shoulder as if dinner was just about to be served, and another a large linen cloth over one arm. The third just had her hands folded in front of her, patiently. The dark-haired woman on the left, Mary recognised as a local midwife and she thought the others probably were too. Midwives carried out more than one duty in many villages and towns, including in some cases laying out the dead. It was a perk of the job, as the church or local council paid a small fee for the service. The women all looked quite grim, even from where Mary was sitting, and Mary told herself that the duty was no perk today.

Mary saw Agnes ask for a cloth to be lifted so as to make a screen across the remains of the woman, so that no prying eyes could see her work behind it. Shaking her head slightly she disappeared behind it and after a few minutes Mary saw her rise again from behind the cloth, and ask for the water-bowl to wash her hands and a cloth to dry them.

After this ablution, the third woman took off Agnes's gown and folded it, and placed it on the floor. Agnes said something to Dr. Caius, who looked up at her and then she made her way across the priory to join Ashbourne and Mary.

Her face looked drawn and she was clearly strained from the task she had performed, but was able to give a small smile to Mary and nod kindly to her. She looked at both of them and said, 'Well, she was a virgin, and has suffered most terribly – her identity hidden by the smashing-in of her face. At least she did not have the indignity of rape. Dr Caius has also nearly finished his work, and both of us will produce a report for you, Thomas Ashbourne, to pass to Sir Edmund, and of course to the local magistrate and the Deputy Constable at the Castle. There are scribes a-plenty up at the castle and we shall make use of them.'

She looked over her shoulder at the two corpses and said, 'Both murdered, both disfigured, and only God at this point knows their identity, but I do hope you get whoever did this. For they need stopping,' she said, with anger in her voice. She looked again at Ashbourne, adding sharply, 'I shall release the bodies for burial now, with your permission. We have no idea if they knew each other but they were both killed by the same person using the same method, so they are linked in some way, which might merely be the desire of a madman. We shall not put them in the same grave for we know not their relationship'.

She looked at Mary. 'Now I have to go and find a virgin's crown of paper and some leather gloves, that they may be carried before her, as a dignity at her funeral later today, before being brought back here and lodged in this church as a reminder of the death of a virgin. I have one last duty to perform, if you'll excuse me.'

Ashbourne and Mary watched her walk slowly back to the altar, deep in thought. She knelt down before the altar rails, and prayed for these people who had once lived, and would now be received into the earth.

'One does miss the dead,' thought Mary, which she knew was foolish, for she did not know these people, but would have liked to have known what this woman had looked like in life, how she filled her days and whether God was kind enough to allow her profound unconsciousness before her murder and disfigurement. She didn't feel this about the man, although it was tragic, but the woman, a sister in God, yes, she cared.

Mary knew about the crown and gloves for dead virgins. There were always one or two spare of each in case of sudden death; the vestry would have them carefully stored upon a shelf, for they were delicate. These beautifully made pieces of art were much appreciated and this old tradition lingered on. Out of the corner of her eye she could see other virgin's crowns suspended from the walls, some with gloves too, and she suddenly realised with a bit of a jolt, that if she died now she too would have the virgin's crown and gloves.

Chapter 14

Their time together in the church had been almost unreal, with the curtain of incense, the strange light, and the sense of quiet dignity and respect. To see Agnes kneeling at the altar steps and praying for a man and woman she had never met made Mary's eyes prick with tears.

As they reached the doors, the guards inside opened them onto the sunlight which lit up the surging, goggle-eyed crowd. She quickly dashed away her tears, and with impassive face moved through them, past the grave-diggers and towards the Castle.

Lost in thoughts, she was startled by a strange bird-like cry. She and Ashbourne looked around and saw a young man break away from the crowd and run towards them clumsily with that same strange cry. He was closely followed by a young man chasing after him. As the first man arrived by them Mary could see he was an innocent, with eyes very far apart and his tongue almost too big for this mouth. He was still crying out and then stopped, looking nonplussed and confused that Mary and Ashbourne were staring at him. The younger man caught his arm, but gently, saying, 'Sorry, if you will, forgive my brother. He is simple.'

'Yes,' said his brother happily. 'I am simple. Simple!'

'What is his name, please?' asked Mary.

'Toby,' his brother answered, looking surprised that Mary would even give him the time of day. Toby tapped his own chest. 'Toby,' he repeated, excited that the lady was smiling at him and not pushing him away. Mary took a silver sixpence out of the leather purse at her waist and gave it to Toby, who gave his odd cry again with sheer joy, looking at the coin. Then he frowned, trying to look at the detail.

'That's the queen, Toby.' Mary told him gently. Toby smiled happily, and then opening his hand with the coin in the palm, asked earnestly, 'Will she whip me?'

Mary was aghast but saw he put his other hand up to his cheek, where there was a sore red weal she hadn't noticed previously.

'No Toby, she won't whip you. Who did this to you? Was it a lady?'

Toby just cowered. His brother meanwhile was gently comforting him and thanked Mary profusely for her time and kindness. The brother was definitely changing the subject, no doubt fearful for their jobs.

'Do you live at the Castle, both of you?'

'Yes,' said the brother, 'We work in the stables'.

'We help,' agreed Toby who was now a lot more cheerful. They parted, Toby absorbed in his coin, and his brother with his arm around him walked back to the crowd, and Mary and Thomas Ashbourne made their way to collect their horses.

'That was a great kindness, Lady.' Ashbourne's voice sounded gruff, as if he was moved by what he had just seen. Mary looked at him sharply, but he looked away in the opposite direction.

'I am appalled that someone would whip the face of an innocent like that.' She was angry at the thought.

'Life can be disappointing, Madam, and there is good on one corner and wickedness on the next.'

'Isn't it true that if a child be born innocent in such a way, then they are under the queen's care?'

'Yes, that's right,' agreed Ashbourne. 'By long tradition, all property that is theirs by inheritance passes to the monarch, and in turn they are given protection.'

'Does it happen in reality?'

Thomas Ashbourne shrugged. 'I doubt it, Lady. Sadly, I doubt it, don't you? However, I am equally sure that if a fortune were involved then suddenly the Crown would take an interest in such as Toby.'

She didn't answer, looking at her gloves, the gloves of a virgin.

'What about people who become ill, possessed in some way of a malady that attacks the mind and spirit?'

Ashbourne gave that some thought as they walked 'I know little about medicine of the mind, but of course Christ cast out demons from a mad man on the opposite shore of the Sea of Galilee. Do you remember in the Bible it said that the evil spirits were driven from the man and sent instead into the bodies of a herd of pigs who spoke, saying they were 'legion' in number before drowning themselves in the water?'

Mary shuddered 'How horribly frightening. Do priests still cast out demons, Thomas?'

He looked pained. 'I should think, if I may say so, Lady, that we have had enough darkness this day without searching for more elsewhere.'

Deep down Mary agreed, but was still upset, not only about the appalling murders but also about Toby being struck across the face with a whip, and she asked herself again who would do such a thing.

They went back up the hill to the Castle for Thomas Ashbourne to give further instructions for the reports to be drawn up. These would later be brought to him to approve that night, prior to being sent by messenger, on a dash to London, or wherever Edmund Dudley was at this moment.

Later, on the ride home, knowing a load of bent-backed clerks would be busy copying faithfully the documents for her father, the magistrate, Dr.Caius and goodness knew who else, Mary decided to ask Thomas Ashbourne a question.

Leaning towards him, Mary asked, 'Where is my father?'

He looked at her and frowned, for it was an unexpected question that threw him from his quiet thoughts, and said, 'I know very little, mistress, and keep nothing from you that you hunger for, but I have to say I am sure all will be right, and all will be made clear'.

She was not giving up. 'How do you know where to send the messenger then, Thomas Ashbourne? You must know where.'

Ashbourne winced, but replied that the messengers went to an office in Sheffield Castle, to be ferried elsewhere as instructed.

'North!' said Mary, astonished. 'I thought Father would be in London.'

Thomas Ashbourne looked pained and Mary realised she was making him very uncomfortable, as he was just following orders. She was peeved, but there was nothing more to be said. The quiet and reflective mood continued for both on the ride back to Somersal, where

Mary looked forward to a simple supper. She hoped it wasn't roasted meat.

Alice Goodrich had kept out of Mary's way since she had taken the keys from her, but now she was sly-eyed and eager for gossip about the murders. Mary was cool with her. She realized that Alice was using this gruesome pair of murders as a chance to relax tensions between herself and her mistress, and trying hard to engage in conversation with her. Mary was not going to be drawn and remained private in her thoughts, unwilling to discuss such darkness even with Anne Compson, who also could not resist questioning her about the murders, albeit more discreetly.

Mary was pleased, however, to see that a note with quite neat, but not very educated, handwriting had arrived during the course of the afternoon. It was from Margaret Rich, asking if she might visit Somersal the following morning, as she was keen to be out of the company of her brother, and to be with her new friend. Of course, the note didn't say that directly, but its meaning was clear. Mary asked who had delivered it and was told that it was just a young boy with a cheeky face who had already left. Mary dashed off her response and had it given to Will Loxley, asking him to ride over to Woodroffe's, happy in the knowledge her friend would be with her after breakfast for a few hours at least. She also wanted to ask about James, but would have to do so carefully.

Her prayers were full that night and she thought of the two bodies now planted in the earth, with all the ritual that the Church could offer, and the gift of blossoms from the villagers to these anonymous souls. She didn't wander that night, but dreamed she saw a motionless dark figure by the gates.

Chapter 15

The following morning, Mary looked again at the note that had been sent by Margaret the afternoon before. It not only said that Margaret wished to visit Mary at the Hall, but apologised for her brother's behaviour, and begged that it should not put Mary off meeting again, as they had enjoyed each other's company so much.

Margaret arrived at eleven of the clock, a vision in blue which showed off perfectly her tightly-curled blonde hair. Mary knew that her fashionable friends in London spent a great deal of time and effort with hot goffering irons to achieve such curls, often with disastrous results like burnt bald patches and sore scalps. It was a common accident amongst the young and fashionable, including some men who were just as vain.

Margaret, it seemed, was blessed with curls naturally.

The two girls were thrilled to see each other, the only sour note being that had Margaret was accompanied by the shifty James. Mary understood she could not have ridden alone - it was unseemly and unsafe - but she was still unhappy to see him, although Margaret quickly dismissed him, telling him to come to collect her later in the day.

Mary first showed Margaret the lovely verdant gardens and cool tree-lined walks as they moved around the grounds arm-in-arm. The roses were in full bloom, carefully watered each day and sparkling with colour against the green lawns and blue skies. Creamy jasmine tangled with scented woodbine and daisies sprang everywhere.

Margaret was entranced by the gardens and the outside of the house as they made their way round the back of the Hall and through the long doors to the great hall. It was so dark inside that they couldn't see a thing for a moment after the bright sunshine, and stood blinking like owls.

Mary waited for her friend to adjust her vision, as she had an idea what she would do when she fully appreciated the great hall. Sure enough, Margaret cried out in wonder, putting her hands over her mouth at the sight of the glamorous panelled room with its huge fireplace and bowl upon bowl of flowers everywhere, filling the huge space with scent. The great table, court cupboard and chairs with tapestry cushions were rather marvellous, even by London standards. She was so happy to share all this with Margaret, joyful at her pleasure just being there - away from Gregory, and from James for that matter.

'My dear Mary!' exclaimed Margaret. 'I am overwhelmed by this lovely house. It does suit you, my dear friend, and I am glad of your good fortune. I have never seen such a place.' She looked around in wonder, taking in all the detail, going to each long diamond-paned window in turn.

'What about Oxford, Margaret?' laughed Mary. 'You have all those wonderful, grand honey-stone colleges and such wealth. We must be small change in comparison.'

Margaret was leaning on the window sill, looking out over the front turning circle and was so absorbed, Mary had to say it again as she drew close to her friend who span round, 'Yes, of course, there are wonderful buildings there, but Gregory is low down the ladder compared to almost all the other academics, many of whom have a great deal of private income. We very rarely have a chance to attend any formal functions, so I have seen very little indeed. Gregory is not well-off, and it is a constant irritation to him that his work is not better recognised. Poor Gregory,' she added sadly, shaking her head a little.

Mary restrained herself from saying that she thought Gregory deserved all the ignoring that Oxford could offer and a sharp kick into the bargain. It was a happy thought, kicking Gregory on the shin. Not ladylike but fun…

Over the next few hours on that late summer's day, Margaret Rich fell in love with Somersal Hall, rushing everywhere like a bouncy puppy. Mary trotted behind her gathering up her skirts, crying, 'Wait for me!You are dashing ahead! She was breathless and laughing at the same time.

Margaret demanded to know from Mary, in such excitement, what was in every room, looked out of each window so she could see another view, and asked where doors led to.

She wasn't so interested in climbing the steep stairs to the female servants' rooms but enjoyed immensely the grandeur of the Oriel Room, with its massive curtained bed – she had jumped up and down on it like a small child falling backwards with her arms out wide.

'This is bliss Mary: such comfort, and all in an atmosphere of freedom and lack of censure.'

As if by magic, the very person who could put paid to this idea came into the room without knocking. It was Alice Goodrich who, seeing both of them, said in false humility, 'Forgive me, Lady Mary, and you, Mistress. I thought some of the servants' children had come in here and were playing where they shouldn't be, and I was going to send them out and beat them for making such a noise.'

Margaret had sat up on the bed looking rather pink and no doubt feeling foolish. Alice's comments were designed to make Mary feel uncomfortable, embarrassed in front of her guest. All Alice's comments were loaded and she knew it. She had made it her business to find out who was in the room, for if there was one thing Alice was good at, it was listening at doors and she knew only too well there were no children's voices in the room. Alice had a half-smirk on her face which was infuriating.

In the past Mary would have replied, 'You are quite right, we were acting rather wildly, Alice.' This was not the past, however, and Mary looked directly at Alice. 'Kindly knock when you come into a room - or scratch.' That was what the lower order of servants did, as knocking was too intrusive. Alice looked hard at Mary, aware of the insult to her position in the household.

Mary continued, 'I am sure, as you miss nothing in this house, Alice, that you knew very well I was entertaining a guest, and knowing your unpleasant habits, no doubt you were listening at the door before you burst in. Go away and be about your tasks, Alice Goodrich, and you would do well to mind your own business, please.'

Margaret was still sitting up on the bed like a doll with mouth open looking backwards and forwards to each woman for reaction. Alice, despite the twitching of contained rage in her face, knew she was beaten, so she bowed, apologised and withdrew.

Mary waited a moment and with a finger to her mouth tiptoed to the door and opened it quickly. No, Alice had gone, the half-beamed corridor lay empty, so she had enjoyed enough victory for one day.

'Well, Mary Dudley, I had no idea you had a lioness in you.' Margaret was full of admiration. 'I wish I could be strong like that, and then I might stand up more to my brother and anyone else for that matter, but I am too weak of spirit and mind to think quickly enough.'

She had swung her legs off the bed and came to Mary, putting her hands on her shoulders. 'Please Mary, teach me to be like you, strong and able, and then my confidence might grow and I could achieve many things like you.' Her voice faltered uncertainly.

Mary caught her hand. 'Margaret, your faith in me is misplaced, for I am not particularly fair of face, unmarried, with no queue for my hand and trying to take my place in the world whilst attempting to avoid the great game of childbirth. I am a disappointment, and you - look at your personal beauty, and knowing that your work with your brother is helping with academic achievements.'

'Is that really important though, Mary?'

'Furthering knowledge! That is the great drive within our nation at the moment, these are times of exploration, discovery and learning. You take your place well enough and if I took you to court with me one day, I am sure you would have great men clamouring for your hand.'

'I doubt it,' Margaret retorted sadly. 'No fortune, no hope. Anyway you help your father greatly, I am sure. You told me he is at court and with your name, you must have access to all sorts of exciting people and places. Does he write to you a great deal? I am sure he does and tells you what he is doing. He is bound to trust you.'

Mary nodded 'Sometimes, in fact some letters arrived this morning. I am glad, for sometimes, as he is terribly busy doing I don't know what, I do miss my father terribly.' She lowered her eyes, wishing she could take back the words, for Margaret had lost her mother as she had, and her father too, just left with the ghastly brother.

Her friend seemed to understand and smiled kindly. They went downstairs still arm-in-arm, with Margaret pointing with wonder at things she saw for the first time. Finally, at the foot of the stairs they went into Edmund

Dudley's study and that, surprisingly to Mary, was the room Margaret enthused over most, by far. 'The books! So many books, even more than my brother,' and 'That desk is the biggest desk I have seen in my life, and so neat and ordered. Does it have little cupboards? I shall sit at your father's chair and pretend I am a great person, like your father.'

As Margaret sat back in her father's great chair and moved things around the desk, opening the leather message bag and looking inside, Mary felt uncomfortable. This was an imposition. Only she and her father sat at her father's desk, and Margaret's little-girl way of presenting herself was suddenly starting to grate on her nerves. She had seen grown women speak like little children to their husbands, wheedling out of them a trinket or in an attempt to get their own way. That was what Margaret was doing, she was treating Mary like a man to be manipulated and managed for some reason. Was she really so naive?

'Come to dinner now, Margaret. My father is rather fussy about his desk, I am afraid.'

'Oh I am so terribly sorry!' Margaret jumped up, looking horrified. 'I have completely taken for granted your hospitality and run around like an excited child in your family home. Forgive me, for I am desperate for a friend here, and would hate to think I did anything to offend you. Please say you forgive me. I am so sorry.'

Mary smiled kindly at Margaret who gave her a grateful half-smile in return with watery eyes, looking ashamed of herself. Mary wondered whether she had been over-hasty. She spent so much time with people very much older than herself, it was easy to forget that maturity is not always a matter of age. She wondered if she had become a little staid in her ways, not enough patience or fun in her life. 'No, Margaret it is for you to forgive me for being so sharp. You intended no harm.' Mary was starting to wonder if her guest was so needy because she was brutalised by her half-brother in some way.

She had seen for herself that he was not above violence. Albeit in a small way, it was there. Worse still, was the girl put under sexual pressure by him? Nothing would have surprised Mary, as he seemed a thoroughly bad lot, and no wonder Margaret needed a friend. 'Here', she said to Margaret, 'Teach me how to laugh again.' Taking her arm, she steered her guest to the Great Hall for the noon meal which they shared alone, as Ashbourne was about the business of reporting on the murders.

The difficult moment in the study was forgotten and the long doors open over the gardens let in a sweet breeze of calm. Then both girls were startled by a strange sound, and turning towards it at first saw nothing and then a small black kitten wandered in from the garden, mewing loudly. When the servants clearing the table tried to chase it out, both Mary and Margaret rescued it, even if it was arching its back and spitting.

'Look at it. It is so small and yet it be fierce.' Margaret stood back as Mary fearlessly scooped it up and immediately it settled tight against her warm neck and purred loudly. Its eyes had not been open long, still clouded with blue. 'Probably a new batch born in the barn. There are cats everywhere but we need them to keep the rats and mice down like everywhere else.' Mary understood running a great house, and the ranks of servants were not always human.

Whilst engaged with the kitten, Mary had noticed out of the corner of her eye that Alice Goodrich was standing in the shadows, no doubt listening and still stinging from the scene in the Oriel room earlier. The pride of that woman and her arrogance were breathtaking. Mary looked at Alice sharply, saying 'Did you want something, Alice, or are you just standing there eavesdropping? Haven't you got a job to do?'

Alice probably hadn't realised she had been seen. Startled, she just nodded and slipped out of the room by the servant door, shutting it with a respectful click.

'Goodness me, Mary, never mind the kitten, how fierce you are today! You quite frightened me.' Mary put her hand on Margaret's arm saying, 'No need. Alice Goodrich has had control in this place for far too long, treating me like a puppet and making the lives of those who work with her a misery, and now I have taken the crown-jewels back - which are the house keys -Alice resents it.'

Margaret was turning over a kerchief in her hands and hesitatingly asked, 'The murders - I know you know about them - what has happened? Do they know who has done it? Are they two separate murders? Or will other bodies be found? Forgive me sounding morbid, but I am afeared of these matters, and feel if I know a little more, I can cope. My imagination is running riot, you see.'

In that moment, Mary instinctively knew that she must be discreet. She had carried out private secretarial work for her father, including reporting court papers, and had been held in the highest confidence. Even this kind, innocent young woman, who would do no harm, and who obviously asked as she was nervous about her own safety, could not be given the details of the investigation, so was told hardly anything.

Ashbourne had warned Mary not to mention the blue threads in the rope fibre at any costs as this was their greatest clue, but might have been forgotten by those who had initially heard the news at the Castle. She did not want to lie to her friend but it was important that she should, so as not to risk the work done so far, so she answered brightly, 'You know what it is like being a woman. We are told next to nothing, and kept away from the darker sides of life, so I know no more than you do.'

Margaret listened and nodded in agreement, before blurting out, 'Oh! I quite forgot, I have sweetmeats for you.' She opened a little embroidered bag at her waist, and looking up at Mary, produced a handful of delicate little succets. 'Oh, how lovely,' said Mary, pretending she did not have them regularly in London, for she knew this great treat would be considered by Margaret a rare and expensive gift.

She put one in Mary's open palm, and said, 'Close your eyes tightly and taste it, and then open them and see if you can guess what flavour they are. Go on, close your eyes.' Laughing, Mary played along with the game and closed her eyes tightly before putting the sweetmeat into her mouth. The sugar paste was flavoured with lemon and then the next an intense orange and finally the last, nutmeg. She got them all right. ‘Oh well,’ she said, 'It just proves I am greedy!’ One of the men servants came in discreetly, telling them that James had arrived. Margaret had fallen silent and seemed tense.

‘What is the matter?’ Mary asked gently, encouraging her to speak while there was time. Margaret shook her head but then desperately caught hold of Mary’s wrist almost shaking the black kitten, which was still resident against her neck, out of its perch, and it hissed.

‘It’s Gregory. ‘she whispered ‘There is something wicked about him.... I am frightened of him, you know.’ She wrung her hands in distress. ‘We only started to live together after our parents both died and then, only then, did I get a sense of darkness about him. In time, I would come to see such wanton cruelty, with a kind of bloodlust and then these storms would pass and be replaced by a sullen gloom.’

Her face was twisted with anxiety as she liberated herself from this dreadful secret.’ She saw Mary blanch, and suddenly apparently felt guilty about sharing the secret. ‘It’s all right, I manage as I am used to it, but sometimes it can be overwhelming.’

Her eyes were darting backwards and forwards over Mary's face. She looked over her shoulder as if Gregory was there. was it because she was fearful that James was there for he was, without doubt, Gregory's creature?

Mary spoke quietly and firmly. 'I shall come to Woodroffe's, soon. I can't see you every day but there are days and hours we can spend together. I will help you as much as I can and if you need shelter, if things' - that was said in a pointed way - 'become unbearable, please, please, come here and I shall give you refuge.' Margaret nodded earnestly and then was away. Mary didn't want to go out to see her off because she didn't want to acknowledge James. Then Mary said to herself, or perhaps the kitten, 'Maybe, Mary Dudley, you are frightened of him yourself, and perhaps, just perhaps, you have good reason to be.'

Chapter 16

The next day, Mary was in the garden, which was particularly beautiful in the mid-afternoon sunshine when the heat of noon had passed. Her shoulders had started to ache so she stood and stretched a little. Closing her book, she put it behind her on the garden bench where she had been sitting by the tall waterfall of pink roses that fell down the back of the house.

As she stretched her neck with her hands behind her head, she admired the high cascade of scented blooms. She stood, smoothed out her skirts, picked up her book and made her way through the herb garden towards the great hall door.

She was suddenly aware of excited chatter and turned her head towards it. She had heard it before on occasions but this was loud, unusually loud, and coming, she thought, from the drying room off the kitchen area.

Setting off to investigate, she was aware that there was something about this particular noise that made her feel uncomfortable. Once, two years earlier, when in a carriage in a part of London she didn't know well, she was unfortunate enough to hear similar noises coming from a bear-baiting ring and had closed her hands over her ears and shut her eyes tight.

She wanted no part in the crowd's enjoyment of the brutal agony and fear of a creature tormented. Poor bruin, with four dogs jaw-clamped as they probably were, hanging from it, and knowing that it could not hope to win this desperate battle to the death. She had asked herself what darkness was in the souls of men that were entertained by such brutality, and kept asking herself over the years.

As she arrived unseen at the kitchen doorway, she took in the scene in a flash. Cook was sitting hunched by the low fire, glowering and furiously podding peas out into a basket in her lap. Meanwhile the younger servants, both boys and girls from the house and grounds, stood by the table laughing and pointing, or with hands on hips. Anne was not there, and neither were the Loxleys. Alice Goodrich was there, though, and the focus of the laughter, for she was providing the entertainment with relish. One of Mary's ruffs was tied round her neck and she was parading up and down the room, waving one hand in an exaggerated manner, whilst swinging her hips and fluttering her eyelids at the admiring audience.

'Oh yes, your majesty,' she crowed with an affected voice, pouting her lips. 'Are you not lucky to be in my company? For I am queen of Somersal, and a very important person with a very important father. Unlike your father, your majesty, he was only the king!'

Alice expected a further jeering roar of laughter at this gem. Instead, cold silence fell on the room because the mistress had now been seen standing in the doorway, and hands went over mouths in horror. Alice still had her back to Mary, but swung round on her heels to face her when she saw the reaction from her now wide-eyed silent audience. At first she looked alarmed, and then her eyes narrowed in temper because she had been on the receiving end of two run-ins with Mary over the past week, and this one could be dangerous as she was caught red-handed, mocking her mistress to undermine her authority.

Instead of apologising humbly, she was irritated to be caught out and had to act quickly to save face in front of the other servants. Thinking on her feet, she did what she always did when caught doing something wrong, by shrieking loudly with false laughter. She was inviting Mary and everyone else in the room to join in with the joke as if the young mistress didn't mind, thereby proving Alice Goodrich ran everything in the house on her terms, including the Dudley family itself.

Alice had gone too far this time. In fact, Alice was long overdue to be dismissed. Mary's heart was racing with anger, for it was clear to her in that moment that the family had allowed this woman to get away with too much for too long. The stealing was bad enough but there was a lot more going on than just theft. Years of mourning mother and being away at court or other places on state business meant it was easier to let Alice get on with running the Hall. Stones were left unturned and if Father had noticed them, Mary had a horrible feeling he would just have turned away. It was all too much trouble, and surely Eleanor the cook would alert Thomas Ashbourne if there was anything too serious. Apparently not.

Mary realised in that moment that by her inaction she had been complicit in Alice's dreadful behaviour, and was aghast that this should be the case. She now fully saw Alice Goodrich for what she really was, a vicious, manipulative woman with no loyalty and without, it seemed, a shred of decency at any level.

Mary turned to the young staff, raising her voice for the first time to any servant that anyone could remember.

'Go back to work. Haven't you something better to do than stand here watching this woman make a fool of herself by being treacherous to me. You shall all be without jobs.' Mary's eyes flashed. 'Now get out!' she shouted, as she flung her arm out pointing to the door.

The staff scattered like frightened rabbits, all except the kitchen maids who were meant to be there, and who huddled together around the silent cook. They had never seen the young mistress seriously angry, never mind furious. They didn't know what to do and some who had joined in the laughter were now in tears, both ashamed and frightened in equal measure.

Now the energy had changed in the room, and Alice had a look of shock on her face. Her usual recipe to make Mary buckle to her will had failed, again. This was a different Mary, one she did not recognise. The small child who had grown up at the Hall, often at Alice's side, really had left, forever.

'Goodrich,' said Mary calmly, 'I would like you to come to my father's study. Now, please.' Mary stared at her steadily with one eyebrow raised. Alice's eyelids fell in submission. Throwing down the ruff on the kitchen table, she followed Mary out of the room, past the newly reinforced pantry door (Mary had ensured she would not get in without keys), and in silence to Sir Edmund's study. Once there, Alice was told to stand whilst Mary made sure she sat herself with the light of the window behind her so her face could not be easily read. Mary felt her heart fluttering as if in her very throat.

Alice had stumbled into the study. She was so conniving, Mary wasn't sure she hadn't done that deliberately to gain sympathy. Well, if it was, it hadn't worked. Alice's green and yellow-flecked eyes were darting about, and it was clear from the workings of her face that she was desperately thinking of some way to get out of this situation. Now she was in a new territory, as her relationship with Mary had collapsed as she had felt until recently that she had her mistress just where she wanted her and was horrified to see her realm crumble before her.

Mary waited for some time before speaking, until Alice's nerves were jumping. 'What in God's name do you think you were doing in the kitchen, mocking me in front of the younger servants, Alice?' she asked softly, but with a threatening edge to her voice. Alice was twisting her dress like a dairymaid and looked near to tears. Could this be possible?

'Little Mary' she coaxed 'You know I wouldn't do that to you.' That was the great emotional blackmail statement, 'You know I wouldn't do that to you,' spoken with a sincere and saddened face so that Mary would be sorry she had accused her, and accept that it was all just a joke. When Mary didn't respond but sat silently, Alice put her hands over her face and wept. She had never been seen to weep before, not in all the years she had been at the Hall, but she and Warwick had caused many tears, so Mary remained completely unmoved.

'You forget yourself, Alice.' Mary replied 'I am mistress of this house and I am also not a child any more for you to manipulate. I see through you now, and I see all the damage you have done here to many people.' Her voice was hard-edged, an ability she didn't know she possessed.

The housekeeper had soon turned off the tears, as she saw the pathetic and misjudged act simply wasn't working. It was strange to see this feisty creature brought low but Mary did not give way. She knew this familiar face knew a great deal about her, and had helped at times as lady's maid, and she also realised with a blush that Alice would have told all her body secrets to anyone who would listen, of either sex, if it diminished the standing of Mary or anyone else in the family.

Alice always had to win in her way, she had to be cleverer than anyone else as she plotted and planned her revenge for being a servant, plain of face, who would never own such a house. Mary also realised that whatever anyone else had from beauty to brains to husbands, Alice had to get one over on them, somehow. She was envy personified.

Mary's answer was cool. 'Alice, this is your last chance. For the sake of the years we have known each other, I will forgive you this time, but not again. You forget you not only have wages for your work, you also have a fine cottage and good food for you and your family, and the pickings of discarded clothes. You risk all of this. By the way, keep Warwick on a tighter lead.' Alice baulked at the mention of Warwick, for members of her family were never at fault or up for criticism, whatever they did. 'Don't ever try to rule this house again. Never again, do you hear? Or you will be out, or worse.'

Alice frowned at this speech, perhaps wondering if Mary knew more than she realised. A creeping alarm was showing on her face, but she left, closing the door behind her without noise in a respectful manner. Then Mary started to tremble violently, catching her left hand by the wrist to try and steady herself. She felt exhausted suddenly by the violence of the exchange and the tug of two wills at war.

A flask of red wine stood on a tray with a glass nearby. Mary drank some and the sharp, hot flavour brought her into some semblance of normality as she sat at her father's desk. Touching each thing on the desk in turn she was making contact with her father. There was the silver-lidded pot, alongside a small basket of quills sharpened ready. A small knife for the sharpening and there, blocks of dark red beeswax with a bundle of red ribbons each, for a seal. The paper was on the right-hand side of the desk, a small pile with cross hatching on the surface that she could feel as she ran her fingertips over it. The yellow wax candle in the holder was new, with a creamy woollen wick waiting patiently for a flame to bring it to life. Cupboards in the polished desk were locked, but Mary knew where the keys were, and opened each in turn. It was a happy half hour at her father's desk, a small space of time had calmed her nerves after that unpleasant scene. Pushing back the chair, with its floppy red velvet cushion, she went to the long diamond-paned windows and leant against the warm wooden shutters, looking out over the garden.

She squinted, bringing one hand to her forehead to shadow her eyes so she could focus against the bright light, because she could see beyond the waving blossoms, two figures by the Christening Gate. Unless she was very much mistaken, it looked as though there was a confrontation of some form taking place. The figures moved aggressively backwards and forwards on heel and toe, with poking hand movements towards each other's chests, and heads thrown back in temper. This was a heated argument and far enough from the Hall not to be overheard. Who on earth were these two tucked away from everyone else, and speaking in such an angry and animated manner? They both moved forward, and in that movement Mary could now see that it was Edward Loxley and Alice Goodrich.

'Not more trouble, Alice? You ghastly woman!' Mary said out loud. She bit her bottom lip and made a promise to herself that she would get to the bottom of all this. Alice had just been warned about her behaviour, and here she was yet again stirring up trouble with one of the best of men. Mary had something to do first though so she got up and rapidly went through to the kitchen to sit with Eleanor, who was still furiously podding peas into a basket.

There was silence in the kitchen from the other women, cowed by what had happened earlier. The pile of pods at Cook's side was enormous. She was muttering under her breath and on the ledge by her was the usual small glazed red pot. Mary signalled to her not to get up and sat down on a stool beside her. Cook tried to smile, but was clearly upset about the scene that had been enacted, and Mary sought to comfort this loyal and kind woman.

‘I am sorry if that upset you, I know you have worked with Alice for a long time but I am afraid I wasn’t going to allow her to be so insolent.’

Cook looked up furiously. ‘It’s not for you to apologise, Lady Mary, if I may say so!’ she railed. ‘It’s for her to get on her knees for once in her life, and ask for forgiveness, if you don’t mind me saying.’ She took a drink from the little red pot and carried on podding.

‘What is that, Eleanor?’ Mary asked, nodding at the red pot. The cook looked a little surprised Mary was interested in such a small matter. ‘Don’t know’ she said simply. ‘Alice gets it for me, I think she makes it.'

Cook handed over the pot when her mistress stretched out her arm. She sat back and smelt it. It was a clear, coarse alcohol, eau de vie that was distilled in the back room over a charcoal burner. Eau de vie was the basis of fruit cordials and an important cleansing agent, as the fiery spirit took out greasy stains. The draught that Eleanor was drinking was stronger than most, and loaded with a range of herbs in such a potent mix it was not possible to determine one herb from another. Knowing her as she did, Mary had a feeling that Eleanor had absolutely no idea how strong this drink was, or indeed that it could be the type of drinking habit one could get dependent on.

'Why did Alice brew this for you, Cook?' she asked gently, still swilling the potion round in the pot in her hand.

'I had trouble sleeping, so she made this up for me and told me to have it often through the day, and then at night I would sleep. It's medicine,' she added, nodding innocently. 'I do want to say, though, if you will forgive my blunt ways, although she does some good things, do not be fooled, Mistress Mary. She is a bad woman, who makes many lives a misery. Worse still, they are held captive, and no one dare say anything until this day, which is a day that many will bless.'

To Mary, who was looking at Cook with a mixture of affection and sadness, it was obvious why Alice wanted her to drink her 'sleeping potion' regularly, because not only would she come to depend on it, if she drank it as often as Alice said, then she would sleep in the kitchen for hours at a time. That meant Alice could do as she pleased including stealing, and ensuring that other servants came to depend on her and not Cook. In a planned and deliberate way Alice had undermined Mary's authority both that morning and probably for years, and now Mary had discovered in a disturbing way that Cook was under her control too.

'Can I ask you something, Cook?'

‘Of course, Lady Mary.’ Cook had at last finished her work, and wiped her hands before leaning on the vast, scrubbed table to listen.

‘Why would Alice and Edward Loxley be hidden up the garden arguing just now? Any ideas?’

Cook put her neat grey head on one side and thought for a moment before answering. ‘They were friends once, you know, when Edward’s wife died. Alice comforted him and was kind to him. She can be at times, as I said earlier.’ She thought for a while then added, ‘It didn’t last long.’

Mary was sure she knew why the friendship hadn’t lasted long, as when Alice was apparently kind, she was doing it for personal benefit or to cover her tracks following some misdemeanour. Alice was able to comfort someone weeping with distress over a theft, knowing she herself was the thief. It was extraordinary that this woman seemed to have no conscience, almost less than human.

Mary was determined to root this cancerous business out of her home and family and by family, she was including the servants. By listening to Cook, and getting a much clearer sense of who the woman called Alice really was, she could see a plan of action was inevitable. This stranger called Alice, who had lived and worked alongside them for years, was not the woman they had thought she was. Warwick, when caught doing wrong had given way quickly, but Alice wasn't going to do anything of the sort. She was going to fight.

Unfortunately for Alice, so was Mary.

Chapter 17

Mary took her leave of Cook, and on the way to the study called to a passing servant to fetch Thomas Ashbourne urgently. The girl bobbed, and obediently hurried away. He arrived at the study door within a couple of minutes, looking concerned, which was hardly surprising, as this was the first time his young mistress had sent for him in such a way.

Mary invited him in, and offered him a glass of wine. With an inclination of his head, he sat down and they talked and considered matters together. Anyone watching the two figures seated in the study would have seen the natural sight of the young mistress apparently discussing some usual estate business, except that on closer observation there was a crackling tension in the air.

It was far from usual businccss and Ashbournc, who was an understated person by nature, showed that even he could also be agitated when given a certain type of news.

He sat silently with his chin deep on his chest with that tell-tale vein twitching in his temple as he thought about what he had been told. A dark story and one that needed to end, they both agreed.

'Of course it is disgraceful, Lady Mary, that this witch was able to steal in such a way, and she has obviously made quite a little business out of it. The treachery to a family that had cared for her and Warwick for many years, as well as giving her trust, makes the whole thing worse.'

Ashbourne now stood tapping his hand against his leg in a distracted manner before continuing, 'I mean, if a stranger comes into your house and steals, there is nothing personal about such an attack – it's just a matter of greed. There is a darkness about Alice's crimes here that is compounded because of the relationship, not despite it.'

It was the first time Mary had heard the use of the word 'witch' as a description of Alice Goodrich, although she had used it herself when considering Eleanor's red pot brew, but it was in many ways accurate. Alice secretly wove spells of malice and humiliated all round her, if she could. No doubt the parish priest would ask Mary to pray for this poor woman, but Mary decided that she would leave forgiveness to God where Alice was concerned, and she could tell from his responses that Ashbourne felt the same.

Mary leaned forward, asking a difficult question of Ashbourne. 'She is not going to change, is she? I think she is so entrenched in this behaviour that she is only going to get worse.'

Thomas looked directly at her steady brown eyes and nodded. He was flushed. 'As you know, Mistress, I am very used to handling staff and if you would be so kind, please allow me to deal with this woman.' He waited quietly for her response. Mary realised he wasn't simply telling her what he was going to do, or indeed that he wanted to write to Father. Instead, he was accepting that Mary was the mistress, and he wanted to serve her.

Mary simply said, 'What are you going to do, Thomas?'

'I shall take action fast, so she can do no further damage. It is crucial that we do so - if you will allow me leave, Lady?'

Mary stood up, feeling resolute, as Ashbourne leapt to his feet. 'Very well, do what you must.' He turned away before she called him back. 'And Thomas,' she said softly, 'Thank you for your wise counsel and good offices.' He stopped and bowed respectfully before leaving the study at speed. Mary felt a rush of relief as she knew he was absolutely right in wanting to settle this matter with Alice, and anyway she wanted to get to the bottom of what on earth was going on during that heated conversation by the Christening Gate.

Now it was all likely to be revealed.

Chapter 18

Ashbourne left the room, leaving Mary to tug skin off the side of her thumb until it was sore. It was a destructive habit of hers when she was tense and she had done it since she was little. It was an undesirable habit, as well-groomed hands, without blemish, were the sign of a lady, not someone working in the fields. She didn't feel very ladylike at this moment, for despite all her determination to be the mistress of the house and act like an educated woman, her heart had sunk at the thought of the scene that would happen when Ashbourne found Alice Goodridge and Warwick. Mary really disliked change, and since her mother's death she had wanted everything to be secure and have around her the things and people she was used to.

'Even if those people were lying thieves?' she asked herself, and in a way she wanted to say, 'Yes, I am prepared to put up with that,' avoiding change, for a new housekeeper might be even worse. Then she realised that it was all very well for her to think in such a way, but the other staff were having the most miserable time with Alice and, to some degree, Warwick, and yet the other staff were hard working, loyal and more to the point – honest.

She fidgeted about Father's desk, looking round the window now and again and then sat on a cushioned chair and tried to doze but failed.

Just over an hour later, Thomas Ashbourne came into the study with a strained face and deep frown.

'Please would you come with me to Alice's cottage. All is well, mistress. She has gone.'

'And Warwick?' asked Mary anxiously, as she got up slowly from the chair.

'Yes, mistress, and Warwick, They will not be back on your father's land and neither may have any communication with you. Please would you come and see for yourself what was her cottage. There is much I want you to see, for I made sure they had no warning, and therefore no time to hide anything.'

Mary raised her eyebrows, and crossed silently to the door which Ashbourne was holding open.

There was a determined wind blowing outside, catching up the first of the falling leaves as they swirled about. Mary looked up at the canopy of the Somersal oaks waving gently high above them. She had always thought of them as guardians but in many ways, Thomas Ashbourne was the true guardian.

Through the gates and turning left, they crossed the dried-out lane to the end property, which had the neatest garden out of all of the six servants' cottages. Edward Loxley was waiting for them both at the door. Mary saw he looked pinched and angry. He touched his forelock and said simply 'Lady Mary,' in greeting as she went through the door.

It had been years since she had visited Alice's cottage and it had been virtually impossible after the removal of Warwick from the servants, as it would be uncomfortable for her and them. Anyway, she had had no reason to. Usually patrons went to visit servants only when they were ill, with baskets of food and medicine. That was a tradition and duty unless the illness was contagious, in which case the goodwill basket was left at the door.

Inside, the cottage looked like a scene from a ghost story. Alice and her grandson had obviously been surprised by their visitor, as the remains of an unfinished lunch was still on the table with knives askew. Another knife was on the floor and a pot of flowers in the middle of the table was turned over, with the water still dripping. Mary corrected the pot, and picked up the knife from the floor and put it on the table.

When she looked more closely at the plates she saw lunch was made up of the same content as the supper she had enjoyed the night before, which had obviously been taken from the kitchen without permission. The servants were allowed some left-overs in addition to the food specially prepared for them, but not venison pie and spiced pippin tart which could be served another day.

Mary shook her head, and looked around the cottage where Alice and Warwick had lived rent-free for twelve years since they had first arrived, he in a woollen bundle in her arms, and she with a pitiful tale.

The one room had a neat pile of wooden logs by the fire and a range of expensive pans and skillets that belonged to the Hall. A large and highly decorated majolica bowl was on the table, and a cone of sugar stored carefully in a carved wooden cupboard. There were also expensive spices, wine, brandy and eau de vie. There were soft rugs over the chairs, two of them that Mary recognized from two of the guest bedrooms. She had wondered where on earth they had gone, and not thought to order a search, expecting them to turn up forgotten in an unused room or behind a chest somewhere in the main house.

Mary just glanced at Ashbourne and Loxley before going up the narrow stairs to the bedroom where the fine feather mattress had a bright coloured cover on. Mary didn't recognise it at all and turned to look at

Ashbourne, who alone had followed her upstairs with that very same question on his lips.

He answered,'Mistress, she is a born thief, so we are not the only ones to have had things taken by her.'

'But surely someone must have come to this cottage and seen all this - the other servants for instance. How could she possibly explain all this, which means she was living like a gentlewoman?'

Ashbourne frowned, and nodded. 'I quite agree, mistress, but she had her secret life tuned to a fine art. Somehow she overcame any revelations about what was in this cottage.'

'Until today' added Mary.

'Indeed, until today,' agreed Ashbourne.

At that point, Loxley joined them from downstairs, where they had heard him dragging things about, presumably to take back to the Hall, where they belonged. Loxley stood by the upstairs window, leaning against the wall and looking out towards the big house. He seemed tense.

Mary started to investigate the contents of the bedroom and went over to a small box on top of the decorated linen press. She opened it and saw it was full of beads, but then she had a horrible shock for amongst the beads was a little, creamy ivory comb, decorated with faded blue forget-me-knots.

Mary cried out in horror, startling both the men as she took out the comb, staring at it wide-eyed. Then she sat on the bed and started to cry silently, with the tears pouring unchecked down her face and dripping onto her neck. The men were deeply uncomfortable to see their young mistress so distraught.

She looked at them both. 'It's mine,' she said. 'It was my mother's.'

Mary was devastated, not only because this comb had once belonged to her late mother, but also because it was particularly left in her will to her 'beloved daughter', who had absolutely treasured it. Within a few months of her mother's death it had gone missing and Mary had looked for it desperately. In fact, the whole house had looked for it, upset to see this young girl who had recently lost her mother, distraught at this little pretty comb going missing.

'She sat with me!' choked Mary. 'Alice sat with me, comforting me with an arm around my shoulder, telling me how she was sure it would turn up one day and how very sad she was for my sake, but was sure my mother in Heaven would not want me to be so upset.'

Loxley blew out his cheeks and stamped one foot in temper. Ashbourne had his arms folded and was looking down at his feet. 'She is capable of anything, so you must prepare yourself as there may be worse.'

'Worse than this?' cried Mary, 'I doubt it, Ashbourne, I very much doubt it!'

Mary remembered how upset she had been. She had looked up to Alice then, and was grateful for her comfort. It had taken months for her to stop looking feverishly day in and day out when at Somersal, as she was sure it had never travelled to London in one of her bags.

All in the room remembered how Alice had made a big show to the other servants to express how sorry for Mary she was, and how she would play games with her in an attempt to distract her. Mary, Ashbourne and even Loxley had remembered all of this. They had been dark days for the mourning child, but this was a darker day - the appalling betrayal made it so. Her mother could not help dying, but Alice did not have to steal from a child.

'Why?', asked Mary again.

'Lady,' Ashbourne replied gently. 'Alice Goodrich believes she is cleverer than anyone else in this world. She is sly and calculating and in many ways she is clever, but cunning is a better description. Look around you. She has a large amount of success in her life - but as a thief.

Mary looked at both men 'Surely, one of the servants would come to one of us, or indeed Father. They didn't all like Alice. Eleanor certainly didn't.'

Thomas Ashbourne folded his arms, adding, 'She dominates, or, rather, dominated the servants with an iron hand, to make sure that she had them under her control, and to prove the point of how invincible she was to impress the younger servants. Based on what you told me of the last days, mistress, she spent time mocking you in one way or another, which the other servants wouldn't dream of doing. Entitlement is her philosophy. If she doesn't have something, according to her, she is entitled to take it and without a trace of guilt. She and Warwick are entitled – they think.'

Ashbourne cleared his throat, and reluctantly continued, 'There's worse, I am afraid, Lady Mary.'

Mary looked at him. 'Surely there can't be. What wickedness now?'

Ashbourne looked embarrassed, but Mary said impatiently, 'Tell me now, please. Let's get the horror of all this out in the open.'

He nodded. 'Have you noticed how much Loxley here hates the company of Alice?' Loxley, with his honest, open face was looking at Mary, but now dropped his eyes. Ashbourne continued, 'How he would walk out of a room when she came in?'

Mary nodded.

Then the whole sorry tale came out, which Loxley had previously told to Ashbourne, for he trusted the steward and knew he would protect information given confidentially, but on the understanding that the Dudley family should know. The story had begun five years earlier, when Loxley's wife had died, leaving only him and his young son. Ashbourne's steady voice filled the small bedroom.

'Alice had apparently comforted Loxley - much as she comforted you - and that had led to an affair.' Ashbourne was quick to add his own comment at this point. 'Just a brief affair, and strong drink had been involved. Almost immediately, Loxley was distressed about what he saw as letting down the memory of his late wife, and put an end to their meetings.'

Mary had been trying not to look at Loxley, knowing how difficult this conversation would be, but a brief glance was enough to see saw how mortified he was to have this all played out in front of the young mistress.

She decided to take the proverbial bull by the horns for all their sakes, as the atmosphere was getting oppressive. 'Oh, my goodness. This is horrible for you, Loxley, and I can quite understand how this affair came about in the circumstances.'

Loxley looked surprised, and Mary turned towards Ashbourne, who also looked a little shocked at her response. Mary wasn't too sure whether she wasn't meant to know at all of such matters between men and women, as if she had lived in some kind of gilded cage all her life. She might not know all the dark desires of men, but she knew enough.

She asked, 'So what happened next?'

Ashbourne continued, mindful that Loxley was still standing there with them. 'Alice was waiting for her chance, and used the affair to blackmail Loxley in return for her silence. If Loxley's son, so young at the time, had found out about the affair, having lost his mother so recently, he would have been devastated, and Loxley's reputation as a decent man would be lost at the Hall and in the district. So Edward paid her, as he couldn't see any other way out. She got a large chunk of his wages in the end because, like all blackmailers, she got greedy, and the price went up steadily until Edward was beside himself with anxiety.'

Mary looked at Loxley with sympathy, knowing how embarrassing and indeed humiliating this all must be. She was also more angry than she could remember in her whole life. Loxley was crimson so she kept her questions for Ashbourne.

'How long has Loxley here been paying her and suffering this appalling anxiety?'

'This has been going on for five long years. It has been a living death for Edward here. Blackmailers take away people's lives, and feed off fear'.

Mary's hand went to her mouth in horror. 'So when I saw you, Loxley, having that heated row over at the Christening Gate and wondered what on earth it could be about… this all makes sense now.' Loxley looked at her and then dropped his eyes again. He looked utterly defeated, as if the spirit had gone out of that strong, sun-tanned man.

'Ashbourne, did he tell you about the blackmail and everything this afternoon?'

'Yes.' Ashbourne smiled kindly at Loxley. 'He was ashamed, naturally, but I told him not to be and gave him my word that other than you and your father, there was no need for this to go any further. I hope you will excuse me, Lady, for making that assumption, but I did so believing that you would want to protect the Loxleys, both of them, as much as I do.'

Mary could tell Loxley wanted to say something, but he just couldn't find the words, so stood shifting from one foot to the other and twisting his battered hat in his hands. Mary did not hesitate to face him so the matter could be closed.

'Please don't feel you have to say anything, Loxley. I just want you to know that no one will hear of the very distressing time you have had with Alice Goodrich. It must make you shudder to hear her name, but it is all over now. I do mean all over, Loxley, and the slightest hint that she is causing trouble for you in the area, she will have the Dudley lawyers to contend with, so you really must try and forget it all and look to the future instead.'

Ashbourne raised his eyebrows at the mention of lawyers but it was obvious he liked the sound of this new incarnation of his young mistress as she explored the very real power her family held.

Loxley's relief was palpable as the colour flushed back into his pale cheeks. 'Thank you so much, mistress, it's good of you. I have been so upset about all this, and am reet grateful for all you have said.' He added 'So, perhaps I can start living again.'

Mary stood and took Loxley's brown and sinewy hand and gripped it firmly, looking him in the eyes with a kind smile. Loxley seemed surprised and grateful all at once, as the mistress had never done such a thing before.

Ashbourne then leaned forward still slightly bending his head under the low beams and also shook Loxley's hand vigorously.

This afternoon of revelations ended with the considerable amount of stacked-up furnishings and foodstuffs being carried across from the cottage to the Hall by a small army of servants. Warwick's neat little bedroom with its tiny window, beyond his grandmother's room, revealed not much more: just gewgaws and an expensive looking white shirt.

'What do you want to do, mistress, with the items that did not come from the Hall?' asked Ashbourne.

'Give them all to the Loxleys please. After all,' she added dryly, 'he has paid for them.'

Ashbourne smiled. 'Justice. Time for a bit of justice for Loxley, at last.' Mary agreed gently and, as she pointed out to her steward, as they walked companionably back to the Hall, all these revelations about Alice and Warwick, meant that she was able to let go of them both without a hint of regret. In fact, she could do it with a light heart.

Ashbourne wanted to call the magistrate and have them arrested, but as Mary pointed out, she didn't want all the servants to be caught up in this mire of unpleasantness.

'For they might well have to give evidence, and I certainly don't want Loxley called, as Alice would enjoy letting news of their affair come out, to humiliate him in public.'

'You are right, of course,' Ashbourne agreed regretfully. 'If I may say so, your father's mind and logic are starting to show themselves. Impressive too.'

'I do believe that is a compliment, Thomas Ashbourne.' He bowed his head a little. 'I hope you are right about my mind, for I am a great deal more than fine gowns and court gossip, I hope!'

'Whatever you say, of course. It is what I expect from you, mistress. However, I have known you a long time and seen you grow.'

Now he pressed his lips together tightly, a sign he didn't want to say anything else. Rightly so, for he had decided that he had said quite enough, some of which probably should not have been said. It was not for him to make personal comments about a member of the family. Always diplomatic was Ashbourne, the consummate professional. He did however feel that the time they had spent together that afternoon with Loxley had bound them closer together in some way.

That night, Mary was able to put the forget-me-knot comb back in her jewellery box.

'You've found it!' cried Anne with pleasure, standing at Mary's side. 'Your saintly mother's comb. How lovely!'

Mary decided that Anne probably knew already where the comb had been found, for the servants having supper together were chattering like rooks.

That night, Mary heard a noise that she hadn't heard for a very long time. It came from the stables.

Loxley was singing…

Chapter 20

A few days after the removal of Alice, Mary suddenly started to feel rather ill. It had been coming on for days, if she was honest with herself, and at first, hardly noticeable, so she tried to ignore it, putting it down to a summer chill.

Anne had been solicitous as usual and arranged for Cook to make up some broths and lemon possets to tempt Mary's loss of appetite, but she wasn't really interested. That was unusual for Mary, for despite being a slight creature she was always eager for meal-times.

'You will have to eat something, mistress.' Anne was looking down sadly at the quarter-emptied bowls. All Mary wanted to do was drink water, lots of cold water.

'Don't worry Anne, I am sure it will pass. These ailments come and go in life, and I am sure this will go.'

Anne shook her head, looking worried.

Mary added, 'Tell Cook please that the dishes she is preparing for me are delicious. I just don't feel well enough to enjoy them. It isn't her fault. Do tell her that, Anne.'

'I will mistress. I think she knows, as I do, that you are just ill, but we would like you to eat a little more.'

Mary sat up in her bed 'You haven't told Ashbourne or anyone else have you? I don't want people to fuss about me.'

Anne told her that her privacy was assured, and went out of the room closing the door gently. Mary had her doubts about that assurance, as she knew that Ashbourne would see she was not about the house and enquire as to her whereabouts. With luck, Anne would say it was 'women's matters' - enough to shut up any man, especially if said in that usual dark and secretive tone.

Mary tried to read a medical book by her bed, 'The Rose Garden of Women', written by a physician in Germany earlier in the century, and now translated for all to buy and read. It was a work on female ailments most particularly aimed at midwives, but anyone could access its secrets now. Usually she would be engrossed for hours, picking over the symptoms and possible diagnosis, but now she just ended up feeling queasy after about ten minutes of reading, so she gave up and lay back in her pillows waiting for the feeling to pass.

It didn't pass.

The next day she started to deteriorate rapidly until she was feeling unable to cope with the smallest task before nausea set in. Two days later, she fully took to her bed and then the horrible nightmares began.

Mary knew enough about medicine to appreciate that a fever can bring on bad dreams but she was wasn't particularly feverish at first and these were not like any nightmare she had ridden before. These dark horses came from Hell itself. They were so real, she couldn't tell if they were actually happening or not. Sometimes in dreams it is possible to recognise it is a dream and shake oneself out of it, but not always. She endured some terrifying images. In some, she was being chased in a state of dread, but didn't know who was pursuing her except it was a threatening, tall, dark-cloaked figure. Everywhere she looked, it was relentlessly pursuing her and no matter what she did or where she turned, she just couldn't get away. It kept repeating itself: the same theme of the dark-cloaked figure following her. She would run in her dreams in a blind panic across great empty moors with vast skies, or befogged beaches with fist-like grey seas smashing on the shore, and she would frantically seek shelter, but there was the figure again, looming nearby, its pace unbroken.

On other nights, she would go to one of the bedroom windows and see hideous faces appear, grinning or screaming in her face through the glass. The worst was when she would lie in her bed hearing a slow and ominous knocking on the door. She could have sworn she was wide awake.

She would often start with her eyes open in a terrible sweat with her heart beating so fast and loudly it was banging in her ears like a drum. Breathless, she would try desperately to calm herself from the rising panic. The feeling that she couldn't breathe, like a drowning woman, made her plunge in the bed or thump her chest to catch her breath and then she would cry helplessly and, strangely, after the weeping, feel better. The tears, she discovered, were cathartic.

Anne had, at the start of all this drama, moved away from her jolly farmer husband and into the Hall, sleeping in a truckle bed that slid out from under Mary's bed, so she could look after her day and night. The maid would wake, hearing Mary's fearful cries, and would be at her side trying to rouse her. This was risky for Anne, as it could make Mary fight her like a wildcat, thinking she had been caught by the dark figure, as the reality of someone catching hold of her penetrated the nightmare and gave it a different form.

In the early hours of one morning she had scratched Anne terribly as she struggled and clawed her. After some minutes of her storm passing, she was still breathless, and her hair wet with sweat.

Mary had been mortified to discover that she had

hurt Anne. 'So sorry, so terribly sorry,' Mary wept, trembling with her hands over her face, but Anne realised, of course, that something was terribly wrong with Mary, causing these horrors.

Mary confided in Margaret when she came visiting. That unburdening to a gentle and sympathetic Margaret helped her to cope with the terrible dreams and anxieties that were now merging with real life.

'Some nights I dread trying to sleep, Margaret. I just can't stand what I might see or feel and have no control over it.'

Margaret was deeply sympathetic. 'It must be so dreadful for you, my dear friend, although none of us have control over our dreams. I have nightmares too, Mary, sometimes about Gregory.'

As ill as Mary was, she realised that there was a good chance her illness, whatever it was, would eventually pass, whereas poor Margaret had no such hope of escape and was stuck with Gregory. In a way, that made Mary feel ashamed of complaining and the young women fell silent together. Before Margaret left, she took Mary's hand and kissed it, a simple, sweet gesture of affection, so needed by Mary.

On the next visit to Mary's room, Margaret found Mary so ill she told her visitor, 'I feel weak and listless in the

the day, with hardly any interest in food. That is bad enough, Margaret, but then as the evening closes in, I start to feel desperate. I dare not go to sleep.'

Margaret sat frowning sympathetically, shushing Mary and stroking her hand, telling her friend how she would do anything to make her better and comforting her as best she could.

Margaret became deeply protective of her friend and when they were together and someone came to the door she would leap up and get between whoever was at the door and Mary, so she could have some peace and did not have to deal with anything.

Margaret's interventions caused much resentment from some of the servants, particularly, and unsurprisingly, Anne Compson who would stalk about thin-lipped when Margaret was at the Hall. On one occasion Anne told her mistress that she had discovered Margaret in the study, having heard a noise within, and that Margaret gave a weak excuse that she had been told Mary was in there.

'A likely tale' sniffed Anne. 'She is stealing more like it'. Mary felt sure this was nonsense, but felt too weak to deal with some kind of territorial feud and so left them to it.

Margaret did all she could to comfort Mary, sometimes tempting her with sweetmeats that Mary really didn't want, so she would ask Margaret if she would oblige by cooling her forehead with a wet cloth. After this she would drop off into a deep sleep without effort, and then wake up surprised she felt a little better, and that Margaret was gone.

The two of them had become so close Margaret would be at the Hall most days, and seemed to read Mary's mind.

'I know you think you are going mad in the grip of some misbalance of your humours, for whatever reason,'she said, and Mary nodded, sobbing into her hands, hair dishevelled. Margaret gently pulled her hair away.

'Don't you think we should write to your father and tell him what is happening? Where is he?'

Mary shook her head 'Please, I don't know what I want'. Mary rolled backwards onto her bed, and saw Margaret leave the room telling her to try to rest. looking really concerned as she looked over her shoulder at Mary.

At this point Mary did not know what she would have done without Margaret. Anne was helpful, of course, but Margaret had become like a sister.

Ashbourne also saw the change in her in the very first days of her illness, and particularly how nervous and jumpy she had become - quite out of character for the spirited young woman he knew. 'I am going to have to write to your father. He has the right to know how these terrors are assailing you.'

Mary at one time would have refused to allow this, valuing her independence, and not wishing to have her father troubled over some ailment as if she were a child, but she too was now so alarmed by her condition she would do anything to feel better.

Understandably she started to lose weight and grew uninterested not just in food but other things she used to love, even turning her face away from music. She asked for her looking glass. Anne was reluctant to give it.

'Why, mistress, you are ill, so don't ask to look at yourself until you are a little better.'

'Give me the glass, Anne,' she almost snapped. So Anne did, reluctantly.

Then Mary saw why her maid had not wanted her to see herself. The image looking back was almost unrecognisable. Gaunt, yellowing skin and great purple shadows under her eyes. Her lips were cracked and her hands were shaking, as she pulled back a curtain of hair, only to have some come out in her fingers. The shock of her own image was appalling.

'I need help now, Anne' she said weakly. 'Go and get help, please.' Anne fled from the room calling for Ashbourne, and he relayed back through Anne that he was seeking the help of a physician.

Mary started to fight back that day, asking for broth and wheaten bread and small amounts of fruit and coddled eggs so she could pick at it - even if she rarely did so. Cook was thrilled as well as Anne, and the tray had a tiny bowl of fresh flowers on it.

Mary started to take note of the things that disturbed her equilibrium such as discovering that she wanted neither the smell of strong perfume near her, nor spicy foods. She started to take care of her appearance, asking that twice a day she could have warm water to wash her face and hands, and had Anne comb her hair, gently, so that not too much hair would fall out in the teeth of the comb. She couldn't stand visitors, not even Margaret, although she heard she had called at the Hall, but was told Mary was too ill to see her. What Mary didn't know was that any gifts that Margaret left for her were put on the fire or thrown away by Anne.

After a few days, she started to try and gain strength through exercise, and took to walking round and round her room. Although it made her breathless and her legs were wobbly she was determined, catching at furniture in the beginning but then managing to get round her chamber on her own. The more she walked, the deeper she slept, mercifully without dreams, in deep exhaustion from the effort.

Hope, the cat, who was getting blacker and sleeker by the day, gave her additional comfort, snuggling and purring into her neck. The cat had been put off this for a few days in the early part of Mary's illness, as she would sometimes be driven away startled and yowling as Mary cried out in her sleep.

As Mary recovered, she found the strength to walk in the garden. She even climbed on her horse and with Porky the terrier at her heels, rode at a gentle stroll up and down the lane she knew so well.

Chapter 21

The next day after her ride, when she was feeling so much better, she shared this good news in a letter to Margaret, sent over to Woodroffe's by young Loxley. Margaret's reply was swift, returning with Loxley. Mary smiled as she read the letter.

'Come to Woodroffe's as soon as you feel strong enough,' wrote Margaret. 'Just for the day, for a change. It may do you good. If you only stay an hour it will be wonderful. I have missed seeing you.'

Ashbourne was less pleased at this idea when it was mentioned to him, as he had seen and heard Gregory Rich in action. 'I am not your keeper, Lady Mary, but as your father cannot come here for weeks, and a physician not for days yet, I want to be sure you are safe and I really don't want you to stay at Woodroffe's. You are too fragile at the moment, if I may say so.'

Mary noticed for the first time how terribly worried about her he looked, his face lined with the strain and eyes shadowed. Mary was inclined to be rather sharp about this comment, but deep down she agreed and so said it would just be a visit, and she would take Edward Loxley with her.

So, after a couple of days of feeling better, and not having seen Margaret for a while she decided to clear her head and test her strength. She would gently ride over to Woodroffe's on the chestnut, accompanied by Loxley, who was a quiet riding companion, and very capable and strong if there were any problems.

'Only a few miles, Lady Mary,' he said. 'I think this horse could go on his own anywhere you chose without much encouragement'.

Loxley had said this to comfort her when she asked him if he thought she could manage it. Loxley was of the farming 'fresh air can cure anything' type, so it was agreed.

After a few miles of gentle riding, Mary had to be helped down by Loxley, and she vomited violently on the side of the road, crying out with the force of it. She lay on the grass, as her legs had given way. Her legs were kicking like a fish tail as her body convulsed.

Of course, to be seen in such a state by Edward Loxley was mortifying for her, but she couldn't help it. He made sure he was busy getting a cloth and a drink of sweet water from his saddle bag and brought it to her.

'Thank you Loxley' she said weakly as he propped her up.

'Lady Mary, 'tis a sad thing to have you brought so low. Come now, the purge is over, shall you go back to the Hall or on to Woodroffe's, which is just over the hill?' Mary allowed Loxley to help her to her feet and, staggering a little, looked at the bright green hill ahead with a cool breeze blowing, and realised that suddenly she felt very much better so maybe Loxley was right, the purge had helped.

In fact, she felt better than she had in weeks, although she really should feel worse in view of the violence of what had just happened. She rolled up her summer cloak and gave it to Loxley to take back to the Hall for cleaning and rode happily in her short jacket towards Woodroffe's.

'You know, Loxley, I feel so much better now.'

'It may be all the poison has gone now Lady Mary.'

'Poison?' said Mary sharply. 'Why do you say poison?'

'Poison of your humours, Lady, that's what I mean. Or maybe a dirty star has tumbled dust on you.' Mary nodded as, whatever it was, she felt intensely happy to feel so much brighter, both physically and mentally.

'Loxley, when you get back to Somersal, please bring the carriage, and cushion it out for the return journey. We can tie the chestnut to the back and she can trot behind, but do give me some time with Margaret as she will cheer me. I know she will.'

They agreed a time for his return and if it was too soon, he would go down the hill to his brother's farm, just a lane along.

By now they had reached the ornate metal gate of Woodroffe's. It was a romantic half-timbered building surrounded by carefully tended gardens. The roof and floors bent this way and that, giving a wonderful shape that was slightly twisted one floor to the next.

'Looks as if it's having an argument with itself,' observed Loxley, which Mary thought was a brilliant comment to describe the shape of the house.

She laughed. 'It does, Loxley, and I intend to look at all its twists and turns. How marvellous to be here.' She was, apparently, her old self.

Many people in the area described the house as looking like a galleon tied up in the middle of the countryside. It had a large ornate lantern swinging on the end beam, creaking in the wind, which gave a further impression of a ship. Some people in London would turn their noses up at the thought of living in such a place, for it was considered a poor choice compared to stone, but Mary thought it heavenly.

The garden was laid out as a fashionable clock shape with white roses, green box bays and blue lavender hedging at the front of the house, which blended into a soft, muted haze. Then next on the clock face, an ornate pond followed by a flower garden, an orchard, bursting with the promise of fruit and finally, like every other such garden in the country, a large vegetable and herb kitchen-garden. The fish pond was big enough to put a small boat in and was situated across the road in a gated, hedged enclosure, which Mary had previously seen from the saddle of her horse. It was a decent-sized yeoman's house, surrounded by a glamorous garden and glorious countryside, all tiny in proportions compared to Somersal, but in many ways more desirable, as it was compact and not overwhelming in terms of upkeep. All around were green meadows with grazing sheep and cattle. Above her birds sang, and Mary felt like singing too.

A cry splintered the peace. It was Margaret, of course, rushing out, her arms outstretched with excitement.

Once Loxley had helped Mary to dismount, she sent him away, telling him not to return for at least two hours, leaving her own horse contentedly eating some hay from a rope net and drinking from a bucket.

Loxley nodded, although of course he had previously received his instructions from his mistress and, unbeknown to Mary, from someone else too.

The two young women listened with cupped hands over ears in a joking manner until the hooves no longer rang out on the dry lane, before laughing together and embracing. Mary looked at her friend's wide-set blue eyes, and with a lift in her heart felt new energy flowing in her body in a burst, like a spring rising from the earth.

'It's enchanting, Margaret,' Mary cried, looking about her with hands clasped in front of her with pleasure. Margaret took her arm companiably as they strolled around the gardens in the fresh air, just as they had the first time Margaret came to visit Mary at the Hall.

Somersal was situated in a small valley enclosed by low hills, but this cottage seemed to be on top of the world with views of pastureland and tiny shapes of cottages and smoking chimneys on the horizon all around.

'You look better, my dear,' Margaret smiled, gazing into Mary's face.

'I am, Margaret, and it is all down to seeing you.'

'Oh, I am glad! Come into the house now, and let me make you more comfortable. I have been so terribly worried about you, and the way some days you are so much better than others.'

'Where are your staff, Margaret?' asked Mary, changing the subject. She really wanted a break from the endless talk of illness that surrounded her.

'Ah, we are not grand enough to have them with us all the time, I am afraid, Mary. As well as the 'job-all' James, whom you have met of course, a local lad comes each morning to deal with the horses and dogs. He is also the one who brings notes from me to you. Finally, a gardener comes once a week, who is so decrepit I keep expecting to find him floating in the fish pond. The house is cleaned each morning by the stable boy's mother - whose name escapes me.'

Margaret looked vague and slightly concerned that she couldn't remember and then continued, 'Otherwise I prepare all the food, and everything else that needs doing. James lays the fires and does the heavy-duty work, so it's not so hard on me.'

This happy domestic report was only broken by one name, 'James,' and Mary tried not to let a flicker go across her face. If Mary disliked Gregory, she disliked and distrusted James even more, with his sinister, watchful air. That evil-looking club across his saddle was unforgettable. He seemed an odd choice of man to have near Margaret, and Mary was determined she would try to find out more about James, in time.

'What about the farm animals?' Mary nodded at the field of cattle nearby.

'We only lease the house, not the farm, Mary, with the exception of a golden cow, two pigs round the back and some chickens, of course.' The brown chickens were fat, and pecking around the yard contentedly.

'Well, it's lovely and it suits you, Margaret.'

Her friend hugged Mary's arm tightly in affection as they went into the neat and tidy kitchen. The fire was bright for cooking and the shelves were lined with cleanly wiped jars and pots, all labelled. There were two large windows made up of smallish green glass panes set in lead, and a blue pot of flowers on the scrubbed table. 'It looks as if fairies live here,' exclaimed Mary. Margaret looked pleased.

Mary suddenly had the oddest thought that perhaps if neither of them married, then they could live in this place together and just laugh and have fun and spend evenings by the fire. This would never happen, but the concept of the freedom was so attractive in that moment to Mary, reluctant to marry as she was. Margaret poured out two long cups of perry from a great earthenware jug, and rummaged for a cold raised pie and other treats for lunch in the small larder. Meanwhile, Mary took an interest in the jars and pots and started to lift them down. 'This one is in Spanish, Margaret,' Mary called out. 'I didn't know you spoke Spanish.'

There was silence for a moment, and then the response, 'I don't,' Margaret laughed. 'My dear brother has all sorts of bits and pieces in the house, from all over urope, as he likes to pretend he has travelled a great deal.' Then she appeared from the back of the larder door and stage whispered behind the back of her hand, 'But he hasn't.'

Before the meal they went through the house, room by room, admiring the flowerengraved panelling and carefully embroidered cushions, that Margaret admitted modestly were her own work. 'every bit as fine as the ones at Somersal,' Mary observed, as she sat back in a comfortable chair. She crumbled pastry with her hand on its pewter plate and having lost her sense of taste for some time, found she had it back as if by magic while eating Margaret's fine spiced pork pie.

After the noonday meal, Mary asked if she could see regory's study, which had been missed off the tour earlier, the door left firmly shut. 'I don't want to pry, Margaret, but I would so love to see the study here, as the study in Somersal is the most important room in the house, for me.' That was not entirely truthful. Mary wanted to find out more about Gregory too, and the shut door made her want to look all the more.

Margaret looked doubtful. 'If we are really quick.' She opened the door on a room which was rather bleak, with an astrolabe and handful of books and piles of papers on the desk, as well as some rolled-up maps. It was a disappointment. Mary also couldn't help noticing that the ink pot needed re-filling, and that the rather scruffy quills needed sharpening. It seemed that Gregory did not have his sister's trait for neatness. Nor was it much like an academic's study, well, not the one that she had imagined anyway. It lacked discipline and preparation for extensive writing. No, this study was not at all like her father's orderly book-lined library. Mary felt rather sad that perhaps they were just terribly hard up - it seemed such an effort to be an academic with little money. She disliked the brother but, in a way, felt in that moment that perhaps if they had been richer, he would be less resentful of life and those around him. The star charts looked interesting though, so Mary turned one round to see it better, when a dark voice came from the door that made her jump.

'Don't touch that please, Mistress Dudley,' said Gregory Rich, who stood just outside the room with the most irritating smirk on his face, but behind that smirk he was purple with temper.

Mary had been told he was not due back for hours and she could tell Margaret was as surprised as she was to see him. She put down the chart down straightaway. 'I am sorry, I was merely interested and shouldn't have touched it. You are quite right'.

Rich took no notice of her apology, but snatched it away from the table with unnecessary aggression and rolling it up, put it on a bookcase, wedged in with a pile of others and then turned with an icy cold stare to Mary. She was embarrassed and angered by his rudeness. There was something about him that made her want to argue with him, and she struggled to control herself, hardly trusting herself not to flare up at him bitterly.

Mary went out of the room quickly, followed by a downcast Margaret, who whispered to her, frightened of being overheard. 'I am so terribly sorry, Mary. It was quite unnecessary for Gregory to be so unpleasant after you had asked pardon. You are a guest and I can only say…well,I can't say anything, I just can't do anything about it. He is always a bully to everyone.' She added quietly, 'Including me.'

Mary felt a rush of sympathy for this gentle, feminine woman - the thought of being trapped with that horrible man was ghastly. To make matters worse, Margaret had told her she only had a tiny allowance, so had no opportunity until married to escape his clutches. Mary wondered if she could find a place for Margaret in London. Doing what, she had no idea, but she could think about it.

'You can't save everyone, Mary,' her father had said to her over the years, and her response was always the same - 'I can try!'

The timely clipclop of horses in the yard gave the signal for Mary to leave, for Loxley had arrived with a padded out open cart, that was not the Somersal carriage. With him was a giant of a man, with a bright red face and who looked vaguely familiar. 'My brother, William,' called out Loxley, by way of an introduction. 'My boy Will is named after him.' That was why he was familiar, as he had the ghost of the Loxley face, but about four sacks heavier than either the father or son at Somersal.

Mary remembered that Loxley had said on the ride he was going to his brother's farm nearby, and had obviously stayed and decided he would use his brother's cart, rather than go back to Somersal for the carriage. That explained why William Loxley was along for the ride - he would bring back his cart.

Their two horses were being tied to the back of the cart. Edward could have ridden one of them, but he seemed fine in the cart, and no doubt it was a chance to talk more to his brother. It must be rare, for Loxley hardly ever left Somersal. She didn't know how happy she was aboutt his arrangement, until she saw the pile of cushions and a great feather mattress had been propped in the back.

They had gone to a great deal of trouble to make her comfortable, so Mary must show good manners and be grateful. She turned to Margaret and caught her shoulders, looking fervently into her face. 'You have made me well with this visit, after these weeks of being ill. Thank you my friend, and don't worry about me, I am improving by the hour.'

'How touching.' Rich's voice from the doorway cut through her words. His tone was as sarcastic and unpleasant as usual. Behind him was James, also watching her from inside the door. He stepped back into the shadows when he saw her looking at him.

Mary ignored both and walked hand in hand with Margaret towards the cart, which had been stopped by the mounting block, then stopped to kiss Margaret on the cheek fondly. The urge to snatch Margaret away to save her was overwhelming.

Her friend must have read her mind as she spoke quietly. 'All is well, Mary, I promise. I can tell he will be fine now, having had a bite out of you and me.'

'You will come to Somersal, won't you, if he is violent towards you? And I will help, you know I will.'

'Thank you, Mary, with all my heart, for now I no longer feel trapped,' Margaret whispered, with a light in those pale blue eyes.

Meanwhile, Edward Loxley was standing with a fresh cloak to wrap around Mary, which was lovely and clean, if a bit voluminous. It must be William's wife's cloak she decided, as both Loxleys helped the young mistress into the back. She almost fell rather than climbed in, with rather an ungainly manner, but laughing partly at how ludicrous her transport was, landed on to a cloud of softness.

They set off with Margaret waving. Mary craned her neck to wave back, and glimpsed the silent, still figure of Rich in the doorway. The look on his face was not friendly.

Despite that parting, Mary enjoyed the journey home to Somersal, propped up in the back of the cart on her improvised seat with people in the fields stopping work to look at them. She wasn't at all sure that some members of her august family would approve of such undignified transport, but she didn't care. She felt happy and well.

Meanwhile at the front of the cart the two brothers were yelling at each other like a pair of drunks. William Loxley was obviously a bit deaf, and his brother was forced to raise his voice above the noise of the cart and clopping of the horse. The whole journey felt like an adventure to Mary after weeks of captivity, and she had to admit the cart would not be ideal if it rained, but on a warm evening, it was splendidly comfortable.

The sunlight hit the green valley of Somersal Herbert in great patches as the clouds parted above. The water meadows glowed bright yellow, bursting with flowers, while birds were taking off in a rush of sound, and circling above. Mary, entranced with the scene, told herself she should go and look closer at the water meadows soon and take the time to trace the boundaries of the Hall, as she wasn't sure she knew them all.

Once back in the familiar yard, Mary discovered that getting out of the cart was far more difficult than getting in. It was all a matter of angle, but the problem was 'What angle? All very awkward, so in the end she allowed William Loxley to grab her and lift her to the ground, all the while apologising under his breath with cheeks as scarlet as a robin's breast. She thanked him formally for the use of his cart, and returned the borrowed cloak, remembering to send good wishes to his wife. After some odd bowing from both brothers, she went into the Hall, wanting to laugh out loud at what had just happened.

Chapter 22

That night she went to her bed early, chatting all the while to Anne about the day. Anne didn't like Margaret and made that perfectly clear with a cool expression, but was obviously pleased and relieved to see her mistress so bright again. Out came the comb, the tooth powder of salt and sage, with her black frieze cloth to rub it on with, the bowl of warm water and herb soap with finally a dip into the rose cream before jumping into bed in her shift. It felt a lot like the cart had felt - without the views, she told herself - as she slipped into dreams.

A fox startled her awake with its haunting, murderous, cry. She wasn't frightened, realising immediately what it was. There, it came again, and then a third time but moving away from the main building. What was interesting was that when a fox was about, the reaction of the canine inhabitants of the Hall was non-existent. The usually excitable dogs never barked, or even went to the door. Instead they always curled up tightly and kept perfectly still, as if they knew that this cousin of theirs was a wild and dangerous creature. She had seen this often in the country and in London too, where the usually rangy creatures would move through the rubbish piles, with ribs showing.

Mary wondered if maybe Loxley would get up with a lantern and a club. Or maybe he would be his usual sensible self and know that the chickens were all locked up and he should go back to sleep, for death could not claim prizes at the Hall this night.

So, Mary sat up and, as usual, hugged her knees and then told herself that it was time to set off again on one of her moonlight walks in buskins and robe. This time she would take a different route, by turning right and going down the main stairs and then left into her father's study at the bottom. Down she went, and as she pushed the study door and peered inside, she saw that the windows were unshuttered. Mary wondered why, but enjoyed the sense of moonlight in the room contrasting with the dark shadows. Then, one of the shadows moved. She caught her breath, and felt sharp pin-pricks of shock in her cheeks and her heart raced. She wanted to cry out but the sound froze in her throat in fear. 'It's one of my nightmares,' she told herself out loud. She then pinched her left hand hard and it hurt, which told her it wasn't a dream.

She could now make out it looked like a boy, all in black, stepping out of the shadows, and he had one hand splayed over his face and was looking at Mary through his fingers. The sense of danger coming from the boy was overwhelming.

'Wake up, Mary!' she muttered out loud through gritted teeth. 'Please wake up, I'm asleep, I know I'm asleep.' She rubbed her eyes and then looked again, and he was still there, motionless. She was trembling violently and caught the back of one of the chairs to steady herself. She then dared to look again – determined not to run.

The boy was gone; a soundless vision that had disappeared. Mary gasped, clutching her hand to her throat and saw that one of the long windows was creaking backwards and forwards in a light moon wind.

'I must still be unwell,' she told herself, and the stairs seemed to tip up as she ran back to her bed, catching at the walls for balance, with panic rising in her as she desperately tried to breathe normally. Throwing down her robe and kicking off her buskins she leapt into bed and huddled, bemoaning the fact that Anne was back with her husband. She felt so unsafe she dared to creep back to the door and bolted it. Then to be extra sure, she put a chair in front of it.

Closing her eyes, she hid beneath the cover, buryingher face in the bolster and waiting for her heart to stop racing. When she woke still tired and drained, she decided the vision of the boy, and the moonlight walk down the stairs, was no more than a dream. She hoped so - or was she going mad after all? Was the whispering amongst the servants that she had lost her mind justified? Why hadn't the dogs barked, if a stranger was abroad in the grounds?

Anne knocked on the door and in that moment Mary had the evidence that she had not been dreaming, as the door was bolted. She jumped from the bed, moving the chair quietly so Anne wouldn't hear and let in Anne, who looked bewildered at not being able to get into the room, and asked if Mary was quite well. Mary nodded, so Anne put down the tray of breakfast and came and took Mary's hand.

Her mistress's thumb on her left hand was bleeding, and the blood had seeped onto the linen. That was where she had torn the skin in her teeth in her anxiety in the night.

In that moment Mary saw sadly that Anne did indeed wonder if her mistress was going mad, as she was wary in the way she spoke to Mary and kept flashing glances at her, trying to read signs from her of something, anything, even if she did not know what it might be herself.

Then Anne seemed to relax and carried on with her usual morning duties, tidying round as Mary half-heartedly poked at her breakfast as if she was eating it. In truth, she only managed a tiny bit.

Anne told Mary the news that the magistrate's men had been at the Hall yesterday, questioning people about their movements in and around the time of the murders, and whether anyone had been in the areas where the corpses had been found.

'They were here hours, mistress. Asking questions they were, over and over again, and they said they would be back and none of us was to leave the area. My husband says they are going everywhere, doing the same.' She sniffed, rolling a wrap of creamy linen. 'I told them, no one here hardly goes anywhere, except the family and Master Ashbourne, and, oh yes, the magistrate and his wife.'

She looked hard at Mary before telling her secretively in a low voice all the while checking to see no one was listening, 'I keep seeing the magistrate here, in the gardens and I caught him sitting in the kitchen the other day. He looked guilty, so I don't know what he has been up to.'

Mary looked up from her plate with a piece of buttered bread in one hand. She wondered what it could mean, as it was so odd to have the local magistrate sitting in the kitchen downstairs, as Anne would put it 'cheeky as you like!' She put down the bread. 'Why Anne, that is rather astonishing. Does anyone know why he comes here without being announced to me or Thomas Ashbourne? Could he be doing more investigating into the murders as well as his men, from a different angle perhaps?'

Anne was clearly bursting with some news. 'I don't know, but when he is asked, he just makes a weak excuse about wanting to see Thomas Ashbourne, and odd I call it, because Master Ashbourne seems as confused as we are as to why he keeps coming here at the moment and…'

'Yes Anne, and…what?' Anne looked around her again, to see if anyone was near which was a fruitless exercise as the door was closed on the corridor and even Anne couldn't see through the wall. She leaned in conspiratorially towards Mary. 'He looks as if he had been up to no good – or thinking about being up to no good! There!' This was expressed in tones of revelation, but Mary was none the wiser and just shrugged her shoulders and made amental note to ask Thomas Ashbourne about it.

Having finished what breakfast she fancied, she decided to fight the night's experience and push it away from her with a long finger. She rebuffed her mind's desire to go over it over and over again. Over-thinking was one of her greatest weaknesses, and Father had wisely said once, 'Let your imagination be your slave and not your master, Mary, or you will find no peace thinking of all the things that might happen. If you must, though, think the worst, and then forget it!' Mary knew this was sage advice but was still inclined to pick over facts and twist them round to new angles if she was perplexed by some mystery. With her father's calmness in her head she decided to be practical, as she had felt better the day before and so she would again today. Just a small set-back last night, she told herself.

Mary washed, dressed and went out for a brief walk alone, along the ravishing flower-laced lane, and then turned back and forced herself to go into her father's study. It had been an ordeal opening the door after the night before, but a maid passed, carrying a tray, and looked oddly at her, so she went in and then sat for some time, writing a cheerful letter to her father about the tenants of Woodroffe's. Then she gathered flowers in the garden with a small sharp knife, and filled bowls and jugs with cheerful displays. The water made her hand sting where the thumb was sore but she ignored it.

The servants kept away from her, but the kitten Hope was like a little person following her about, but with the added feline benefit of not constantly watching her or asking questions. Some of the household were a bit nervous of little Hope, because black cats featured so often in witchcraft trials as familiars. These trials were meat and drink for those who enjoyed gossiping, particularly about dark matters. The content of such trials would be repeated and re-repeated for the delectation of the horrified listeners who always wanted more.

During the morning, she also made enquiries - apparently relaxed - as to why the shutters in her father's study were open and indeed, more ominously, a window. Nobody seemed to have a satisfactory answer, except one of the maids in an unguarded moment said, 'Maybe it's the murderer,' and somebody, not very discreetly, kicked the girl sharply on the ankle, to shut her up.

This had the opposite effect, as she yowled, drawing attention to the kick. It was in that moment, as she stood in the garden, that Mary understood that the Hall servants were in the grip of some kind of idea about the murders and linking them to Somersal in some way. She took a firm grip of the situation by saying, 'Of course it isn't a murderer, it is a careless maid, more like it'. She then stopped on her way out of the kitchen, and looking back over her shoulder added, 'It won't be Alice Goodrich, or Warwick either, they will not be back here, I promise.' One or two crossed themselves in the old way at the sound of Alice's name.

'Superstitious nonsense, now get on with your work,' snapped Mary, but not before she saw one maid flick a cloth at Hope to shoo her away. Hope didn't care and just sauntered alongside Mary with tail and nose in the air.

Just as she was settling down in the Great Hall to read, there was a commotion, and looking out of the window she saw a rider come in at great speed on a lathered horse, dismounting almost before the horse had come to a halt.

She saw Thomas Ashbourne run out to him, quickly reading a letter that the messenger gave him. Mary watched Ashbourne speaking urgently to the messenger, guiding him to the house, and Mary overheard Ashbourne telling him to take a quick drink while he could, as a fresh horse was already being saddled for him. Only minutes later, as the sound of hooves announced the messenger's departure, Thomas

Ashbourne came to Mary, having seen her at the window.

'What is it, Thomas?' urged Mary. 'What has happened?' He looked at her solemnly, and said, 'There is a great deal of interest in London in our murders, and messengers are backwards and forwards. I'm afraid I don't know, and therefore can't tell you, why there is such an interest in our small murders far from the capital.'

Ashbourne was only too well aware of the morbidity that Mary had often suffered in recent days, so did not want to dwell on that violence, or remind her of the worrying point that the murderer or murderers were still unknown and more to the point, still at large. Mary wasn't sure that she believed his protestations of ignorance, but she accepted them with good grace, and returned to her book.

Chapter 23

Mary was feeling very much better the following morning, and still elated at having been able to ride out to her friend's charming home. It had been a bit of a victory managing that journey. Things changed in the afternoon, as she started to feel nauseous again and weak, which made her want her bed and the quiet comfort of her room.

She did not expect privacy, however, as Anne had resumed sleeping on the truckle-bed in her room. In the day, Anne would go back to her farm and clean and cook for her long-suffering husband. Her eldest daughter - unmarried and still at home - helped with these tasks too.

Mary had mixed feelings about continuing this arrangement, as she really did prefer privacy and less talking in the dark. Worst of all, she discovered that Anne clicked her teeth in her sleep, which jarred her senses. Mary expected to get used to it, but didn't, and like many irritating habits of others, would listen out for 'that infernal teeth-clicking' as she put it. She would feel aggrieved, instead of trying to ignore it and would growl into her bolster in frustration.

Hope was, as usual, curled up in a sleek half-moon at the end of the bed. Sometimes the cat would stagger up the bed half-asleep, bunt Mary affectionately on the forehead and then flop down against Mary's neck, purring loudly. Unlike the teeth clicking, the purring was soporific, and calmed her.

Nausea was still a constant and unwanted companion and Mary lay in her bed in her shift, waiting to feel better. Her skin was sore all over, and her body was so sensitive she could feel the ropes beneath her mattress had been tightened, so she could 'sleep tight' and not slump like a sack, as it could give her lower-back a terrible ache if the ropes were not tightened properly. At least she felt safe in her own bed.

Then she started to feel much worse and groaned. Pins and needles developed in her finger-tips, and she had a headache starting. The headache was really concerning, as she had had only about four in her whole life, and so was not usually susceptible to them.

She could hear the steady plod of Anne as she came up the stairs, no doubt with yet more cold water, as Mary wanted nothing else to drink. Sure enough it was her and she sat by her mistress, feeling her cold, damp hands, and started to rub them with a cloth to warm them as best she could. As the evening light dropped, Mary started to feel a sharp pricking on the crown of her head, and reached up to touch it but in doing so, pulled out a great clump of hair – which was clearly not attached. Her hair had been thinning at the start of her illness but now it was shocking, much, much worse.

'No! No!' she gasped, and as she pulled out more of her hair, it came out in her fingers, in long, shiny brown tresses. Anne caught her wrist to stop her pulling any more, and Mary noticed Anne was terribly upset too. Behind her was even more hair on the pillow. The window was open and the hair moved in the breeze as if it wished to escape.

'Your beautiful hair,' whimpered Anne. 'It is all over your pillow. There's lots of it. By the saints, what is happening to you?'

Mary started to cry weakly, and the sickness had become overwhelming. Anne sensibly fetched a decorated night-cap and, putting what was left of Mary's hair in it, tied it under her chin with a bow. Mary asked for water and then spat it out.

'Anne, why have you given me sea-water?' she asked, wiping her lips with the back of her hand. 'It is disgusting. Am I not distressed enough without this quack cure you have thrust upon me without warning?'

Anne looked absolutely bewildered and, taking the glass tasted it herself. Anne's eyebrows shot up in astonishment. 'But, mistress, there is no salt in this water. It was just drawn from the well, sweet as usual. I don't understand why to you it tastes of salt.' Mary was dismayed, as she knew Anne well enough to know she was not lying.

'Please, Anne, go and fetch me a tiny portion of cheese, a slice of roast beef and a beaker of fresh milk.' Anne scuttled off and soon returned. She sat by the bed with a platter and watched Mary taste these things in turn with some trepidation. Mary had to spit out the beef, as this tasted to her like burnt fish. The cheese seemed to have no taste, but she could stand the milk – at least it wasn't offensive.

'Anne, there is something terribly wrong with my taste. Please take all this away, as I do feel so terribly sick.' Sure enough she started to vomit, taking away the last of her strength.

'But you must eat, mistress, and drink plenty or you will surely die'. Anne started to weep, as she was so overcome with anxiety for her young mistress.

'Milk,' said Mary, wiping her mouth. 'I am sure that hasn't made me sick. I can stand milk. As for this illness, I am sure it will pass but I will need some help, as I don't seem to be recovering completely. Some hours I am ill and other times I am fine – it is the oddest thing that grips me.'

As the night drew in, Mary fell into a semi-conscious state and was rambling incoherently. At one moment in the night she woke and felt burning across her breasts. Although barely able to lift her head, she saw in the candlelight red blood-drops appearing across her chest: they looked like little red blisters.

In the morning Anne saw the red blisters where Mary's shift fell open, and was aghast at this new development, saying she had only seen the like 'such as when you pinch your finger in something tight.'

Mary's health continued to deteriorate, fast. Her mother had endured the sweating sickness and was dead in four hours. Mary wondered if she would be seeing her mother soon. 'They say the dead come to collect you, those you love do,' mumbled Mary to Anne, who put her hands to her mouth and shushed Mary, passing a cool sponge across her forehead. From time to time Mary drank a little milk, but that was all she could cope with.

The next morning, Mary awoke seeing Ashbourne and Anne by her bed. Now she knew something was terribly wrong, for Thomas Ashbourne would never come into her chamber without invitation and certainly not to her bedside when she was in it. It was just not appropriate or decent in polite society for this to happen. Ashbourne was looking down at her, with a deep frown on his forehead, and she saw him bite his lip so hard, a drop of blood appeared.

Without a word he was gone, and Mary could hear that the horse-yard was full of clattering, followed by the sound of fast hoof-beats leaving the hall.

'I am going mad,' she told herself, 'like mad Joanna.' Joanna was the sister of Katherine of Aragon, that tragic rejected lady. Joanna had been married to Philip the Handsome, and borne him six children. When he died, Joanna went mad, and although pregnant, moved around Spain, with a vast moving entourage and her dead husband carried in a box beside her. After a while, her son, who would go on to become Charles V – the Holy Roman Emperor – gently took his bewildered mother to a convent for the rest of her days, and he buried his father with dignity.

It was the type of frightening tale for a winter's night, when a wide-eyed family would all gather around the fire to hear the story. Afterwards the children would all go to bed at the same time, where most would hide under the covers for the rest of the night, as Mary had done two, or was it three nights before. The time, the day of the week, were lost to her.

Some noise woke Mary in the dark. She was desperately weak and trying to focus, with only the dim light of the dying fire in her chamber. A piercing chill struck her heart, when she saw in the corner of the room where blackest, a pair of eyes looking at her. They were wild eyes and then the pale face of a woman appeared from the gloom, hair dishevelled, and finally, her swollen, pregnant body came into view.

'Mad Joanna!' whimpered Mary, appalled and absolutely rigid with fear. She tried to call out for Anne and could not make her voice heard. She was terrified that Joanna would come and touch her. Then the door handle of her room rattled slightly and Mary was relieved to see Joanna had disappeared. The door opened half its width and in the moonlight from the landing windows stood the dark boy, with his hand over his face. Hope got up beside Mary, and then Mary let out a scream which was thin and piercing, making the cat leap from her in alarm.

Anne leapt up beside her from the truckle bed and caught Mary's wrist. Other servants could be heard calling out and running towards Mary's chamber. They arrived at Mary's bedchamber, crowded in the doorway, wide-eyed and nervous.

Thomas Ashbourne was amongst them, so he had obviously returned overnight from some mission. He was still in riding clothes and hadn't even had time to wash, so was splattered with mud. He pushed his way through the servants, sending them with a bark back to their beds, and turned to Mary with his candle lifted high.

'God's breath, mistress, what has happened?' Mary stammered, 'The dark boy, the dark boy, he was standing there in the moonlight, a minute ago, and before him – there in the corner – I saw mad Joanna, she was here is this room, I saw them, I tell you. I did!' She had talked of seeing him in the study and at the gate all those weeks ago. Anne and Ashbourne looked at each other in dismay.

The servants were moving away to their own rooms but some had lingered, trying to hear what had happened. One voice, it wasn't clear whose, said ''Tis Alice Goodrich. The mistress is cursed with madness for sending her and Warwick away.' Thomas Ashbourne also heard that comment and, spinning on his heels in anger and hanging onto the door frame, shouted down the corridor to the disappearing heels, 'Get away, all of you. The mistress has had a ride on the night mare – she is sick – that is all'.

Anne had meanwhile thrown a wrap around Mary's trembling shoulders. 'Here, Mistress Mary, you are all of a shake, come hold my hand if you please, and let us together be calm again. I am here beside you.' Mary nodded.

Silence fell on the room, but it was the silence of fear. It took time to calm Mary, but she eventually fell back against the pillow, secure in the knowledge that Ashbourne was sleeping in a chair outside her chamber.

She remembered almost nothing the following day of the previous night's horror, except for the appalling spectre of Joanna, which she had seen three times in the course of the night. During these visitations, Mary felt so terrified she thought she might die, and then was terrified she might not. That night she prayed for Heaven to take her soul, as she had endured enough and could take no more.

Chapter 24

Two mornings later, Mary woke feeling a little less sick, but still terribly weak. So weak she couldn't speak or lift her head, as if weights were attached to her body.

In the yard outside, she could tell that someone had arrived. There was the usual fuss from the dogs and then shouting, and a man's voice she did not recognize, giving instructions. At first she had hoped against hope that it was her father, but it was not her father's voice, so her heart sank.

'Where is she?' demanded a cultured man's voice, and Mary heard Thomas Ashbourne answering, 'This way, sir,' in an urgent tone. Through the door of her chamber came a dark figure in a riding cloak, bringing the smell of the outside air with him in the folds as he tore at the clasp at his neck and threw the cloak from him. Behind him was Ashbourne, looking anxiously over the man's shoulder.

The stranger came over to the bed immediately, and peered down at Mary without introduction. His gauntlets had followed the cloak, thrown down on her linen chest, along with a large leather bag. Mary was too weak to ask questions, but could see behind him a woman had arrived, whom she also did not recognize, dressed in clean homespun, an apron and with a thick belt at her waist.

The man turned, seeing Mary look beyond him. 'Who are you?' he demanded. The woman was so nervous of him, she just wrung her hands nervously with her mouth open silently, clearly overwhelmend by this simple questionfrom a man of such authority.

He walked around her and looked at her belt, which held instruments for easy reach.

'A midwife!' He was clearly astonished. 'Why? The lady is not giving birth. This is a mad-house indeed! There is a midwife in here, and when I arrived a boy was staring at me from up a tree. What the hell is going on here?' He tutted, and blew out his cheeks in frustration.

Mary made a mental note to ask when she was better, who was up a tree.

Anne Compson's voice cut across Mary's thoughts and explained in a nervous tone, 'If you please, sir, as Agnes Pickard is away and unable to tend Lady Mary, I asked the midwife to come, as she has some medical learning and has a book. She can read.'

The stranger shook his head in disbelief and then, thinking for a moment, said to both of the women, 'On second thoughts, you can stay. You might be useful. Step outside the room for now, though, and you too please

Ashbourne, and close the door!' He added, 'If you have a lithotomist or tooth puller arrive, you can send them away.'

He came back muttering under his breath. He was not happy, Mary decided through the mist of her mind.

Everyone had left the room quickly, as the tall stranger drew up a chair, nodding curtly at Mary, but before sitting down apparently changed his mind and suddenly left the room without warning. Mary could hear him giving instructions in a firm tone, and then could just about hear his footsteps disappearing. She sighed to herself, wondering who he was, and what was going to happen next. The stranger's voice could be heard again nearby, demanding information.

'Tell me about this end room with three windows in it and a privy.'

Ashbourne's voice answered 'It's the best guestroom, and has a great deal of light and a good fireplace, with indeed its own privy and drop drain. It is a much-admired room, and Lady Mary particularly likes it.'

'I couldn't care less if it's much admired. I am just interested in its function, man. Facilities, security and function, that's all I am interested in, and so should you be!'

'Indeed, Dr. Ince, of course, I quite understand.' Ashbourne had a strained politeness in his voice. Mary guessed that Ashbourne was blaming himself that her condition had deteriorated too far before he sought help.

Two things struck Mary in that moment. This man Ince was a physician, which was hardly a surprise, except that they were rare creatures. The other matter of interest was the word 'security' that he had used.

She moaned slightly to herself in anguish - did that mean they were considering ways to lock her in and guard her? Was he at Somersal to make her some kind of prisoner? Was there to be a punishment for being mad, and shut away from the world, with the family not mentioning her again like a shameful secret? She had never felt so distressed.

There was more talking in the gallery hall outside, and some discussion over the little, panelled bed chamber that had once been a chapel. That was directly opposite the oriel room that was apparently planned for her.

Although Mary could not say much, she could hear well. She was right in that she was definitely being moved out of her own chamber and into the guestroom, which was hurriedly being cleaned and prepared to receive her.

Everyone had been called to clean – walls, floors, windows open, and a low fire lit were the loud instructions from the physician. All the bedding had to be replaced and aired, he said. The Hall was gripped with activity and there was much running about in the corridors. Mary felt that even if she was to endure some form of imprisonment there was, at last, some action. Some strength had come to the Hall.

The midwife came back into Mary's chamber, and with Anne closing the door quietly behind them, they set to work. They carefully took off her shift, somehow managing while she was still mostly lying down, as she was so floppy and her limbs heavy. Then, with some warm water from a jug that had been sent up, and no soap, creams or perfumes, gently washed her body in sections with a soft cloth, drying each part of her as they finished so Mary would not become cold, and then put her in a clean shift taken from the press. Mary noticed how respectfully they moved the cloak, gloves and bag of the stranger when opening the lid of the press, replacing them carefully afterwards. All the time they worked silently, and Mary had to be supported throughout the process, as she was as limp as a new born baby and still could not even summon the energy to speak. Outside her room, the servants were still moving about rapidly in the top corridor, talking in low voices.

The stranger came back into the room. He looked down at her, frowning a little, and wrapping a large, clean linen cloth around Mary without a single word to her, he lifted her up in his arms as if she were a child and caried her to the oriel room next door. One of the maids scurrying with a bowl came out of the panelled room as Dr. Ince approached the chamber door. 'Get out of the way, you idiot!' he snarled at the maid, who stepped back, and then when he had passed clattered down the main stairs as fast as her legs could carry her.

Mary and Dr. Ince were followed in a procession by Ashbourne, Anne and the midwife. Ashbourne looked desperately worried still, as he watched Mary being placed gently on the bed and quickly covered over. His hand had reached out to support her instinctively as she was lowered into bed.

'I know what I'm doing!' was all Ince said to him.

'Thank you, sir,' answered Ashbourne, which was an odd answer, and it was certain that Ashbourne was so anxious he hardly knew what he was saying. The doctor then thanked the midwife, and told her that the household would pay her, so she dropped a curtsy and left. He then examined what had been brought into the oriel room from Mary's own chamber.

On the table beside Mary had been placed a little tray, and on it the forget-me-not comb and a jar of the rose cream. He spoke to Anne without even looking at her. 'That comb can stay, but only if it is washed in hot water and lye soap that I will give you from my bag, and rinsed four times.' He then opened the jar, examined it in the light of the window, and sniffed it. 'What is this?'

Anne had been watching his every move intently, and was ready to answer him. 'Rose cream,' she murmured respectfully, adding, 'Lady Mary bought it herself,, in London.' As an afterthought, she added 'From an Italian apothecary on London Bridge, I believe,' as if that was helpful in some way.

The man ignored her, and sniffed the contents again cautiously.

'No,' he said simply. 'Throw it away'. Anne looked shocked at the order, 'But...'. she said weakly. His voice was as hard and cold as frost.

'I have said 'no' and I mean ' no'. Get it out of here and I mean throw it away – don't be stupid and give it to someone else, if you think it a waste'. Anne looked guilty as if he had read her mind. He decided to clarify any doubts by adding '...because I think it may be poisoned'. Mary's heart leapt at the prospect that she might be ill because of poison, and not because she was going mad. Not many people, she thought to herself, are pleased they are being poisoned, but she was.

Meanwhile, the mention that the rose cream might be poisoned was enough to send Anne scuttling away without argument. He called after her, 'I don't want anything coming into this room unless I check it first, and I mean anything.' Anne stopped in the doorway, and bobbed before leaving. A bit of Mary wanted to laugh. It was so odd to see Anne compliant, she never was with strangers as a rule, always wanting her money's worth out of every potential disagreement.

She saw Thomas Ashbourne take the hand of the stranger firmly.

'I am profoundly grateful you came so quickly, sir'.

The man answered simply. 'I am needed, I can see that straight away. You did the right thing, Ashbourne, sending for me, and now let me attend to the Lady Mary, if you will leave us'.

He drew up a stool by the bed and Ashbourne withdrew. Mary thought how very unusual this was that a chaperone was not present, not even her personal maid, but there must have been a good reason for it.

Alone with Mary, this man of action was less fierce and gently taking her hand, looked into her face. 'I have taken some liberties, madam, in lifting your body and apparently taking over your home – but I am here with a great purpose, which is, in short, to save you.'

Mary absolutely believed that to be true and gave a weak smile of gratitude. Imprisonment at the hands of this man was no longer even an idea, he was a healer.

'My name is John Ince, as you may have heard. I am a Salerno-trained English physician, soon to be listed at the Royal College of Physicians. Do you understand? Don't try to speak if you can't, just lift a finger if you can understand me.' She signalled that she did.

'Good.' He smiled just a flicker, this man who was tall, dark and not slightly handsome. He stood up and moved around the room, closing the windows and moving things around, looking all around him, including in the privy. After inspecting the room thoroughly, he came back to Mary. 'Now I know that this room and its contents are safe, I shall make you more comfortable'.

He washed his hands in a bowl of water, and taking off her nightcap looked at her lost hair, and then put the cap back on, tying it loosely. Then he took her hand again, but this time smelled her skin. Finally he opened the throat of her shift, looking at the red blisters on her throat and breast bone. He made no comment but produced some lavender-scented oil from his leather bag, and with his fingertips very gently rubbed the oil on the red blisters, and then put some on her hands.

'Lavender is both cooling and cleansing, so will soothe and calm you.' He then carefully propped her up on the bolsters, poured out a light cordial into a small beaker and lifting her head, poured it into her mouth. It tasted quite pleasant, and she took it like a little bird, nodding she had swallowed it.

After a few more minutes he spoke to her more gently than she had heard him speak since his dramatic arrival. 'You have trusted me after treachery has been at your door, Lady. I greatly respect you for that, as you have been very ill indeed, but I am pleased to assure you that you are not going mad, nor in my opinion are you ever likely to be. You see, I have been told of your visions and nightmares by Thomas Ashbourne and your maid Anne, or whatever her name is.'

Mary moaned a little, and silent tears of relief started to pour down her face as she looked at him. He picked up a light cloth and dabbed them away, being careful not to drag at her sore and sensitive skin. Then he spoke again.

'Now you should know more of me. I work with your father,' at which news Mary gave out a little cry and lifted her hand. 'Yes,' he said, 'That's right. I am here at your father's instruction, and as well as your esteemed father, I also work alongside Sir William Cecil. With this news, Lady, you can be assured I will use every drop of training and experience that I have in my bones, and I shall heal you by God's good will, and your working alongside me. I need you to fight for me.' She raised her hand a little again as a signal that she understood.

'There now, you know more, and I am going to call Ashbourne back to join us. Listen to what I tell him, and that will be enough for you to think about.' He then went to the door, where Ashbourne was already waiting outside, anxious for news.

Inviting him into the room, Ince told the steward what he was about, pointing out that Mary could hear it all, and that she should. His instructions were crystal clear.

'Every morsel of food or drink for Lady Mary I will check and examine, from ingredients arriving at this house to preparation, cooking, and serving. Now, where does the water come from here, Ashbourne?'

The steward told him about the covered well in the herb garden, but this was clearly not good enough. John Ince asked, 'Is there a small, clean spring in the grounds, that is not well known?'

'Oh yes,' said Ashbourne. 'It feeds the brook, and is little known by most of the staff or anyone else, as they tend not to go to that end of the grounds. The water cascades down from the Derbyshire hills of Dovedale until it becomes a light flow here on the lowlands.'

‘We shall use that,’ was the pleased response from Ince. The conversation went into more and more careful details. Milk should be collected each day in clean, rinsed containers. Eggs must be obtained for Lady Mary from the home farm. No ready-made food to be brought in, not even luxury goods as gifts, and particular care was to be taken in refusing guests. ‘All these matters to remain secret between ourselves and the cook, who I understand is to be trusted.’

Thomas Ashbourne raised his eyebrows questioningly at this comment, so Ince added, ‘From Sir Edmund.’

‘Oh yes, of course,’ nodded Ashbourne. There were further instructions from the good doctor, who paced up and down the room, prodding his finger in the air when a point was particularly important. Mary understood it all.

The Loxley men would take turns to sit on a stool outside the oriel room on watch, all day and all night. John Ince pointed out he and Ashbourne should also take a turn.

Mary could see on Ashbourne’s face the relief that at last he felt he could do something useful for her, as he had felt so helpless, when usually such a practical, able man.

'Finally,’ Dr. Ince looked down at Mary, ‘The lady is to be afforded complete privacy, and her maid can sleep in the room opposite, but not on a truckle bed here as previously. I was going to take that room but her maid can have it. Quiet and privacy is vital for her to relax properly. Tomorrow we shall begin a regime for good health and I shall explain more then.'

They both then started to leave the room, but not before the doctor had put a small brass bell in her hand, telling her that the keepers of her safety would be listening out for her. 'Lift it,' he said, smiling grimly, 'For if you cannot make a sound with it, you will have no privacy, for I must know if you need help.' It was a small bell, and Mary practised with some effort, and managed to ring it enough to be heard just outside the door. The men left - the doctor promising he would be back within the hour.

Mary, now alone, realised how very comfortable she was in the lovely oriel room, and started to doze gently in the clean scented sheets, with the soft feather bolster supporting her neck. There were three windows in the room, so it was full of light and air, and there were no ghosts, she decided. Mary was content when she thought of this extraordinary physician, John Ince. With his strength of spirit and professional confidence, combined with that vicarious link with her father, she felt sure she would survive. A deep sleep, restful and dreamless, took over and she didn't fight it, so for the first time in what felt like months, but had only been a week, she had a sense she was safe.

Chapter 25

Mary soon started to grow in strength and confidence. She was frequently brought dainty little dishes of hot whisked eggs, and cups of milk with honey melted in it. Not much more was attractive to her anyway, but her palate started to work again and food tasted as it should. The water no longer tasted of salt and she knew it would be carefully boiled before she was given it, which would not affect the flavour, but it was at least safe.

John Ince came into her room in the early morning, summoning Anne to take Mary to the privy and instructing that her urine should be collected for him to see and smell. Mary would have been mortified once at even the thought of that, but knew it was an important function of diagnosis and her interest in practical medicine helped her with her embarrassment.

The physician spent time each day checking on the red blisters, looking at her nails and asking her to put out her tongue and looking in her mouth before nodding and moving out of the room. Sometimes he would clasp his hands behind him and go to the window and stare out. He said little, and Mary wanted to pluck up the courage to ask, 'Are you looking at the heavens to help with diagnosis?' but could only make a rather pathetic squeak that turned into a cough. The noise must have startled him from his thoughts as he turned towards her voice quickly. He looked at her and narrowed his eyes, before turning back to the window, saying, 'I am looking to see if it is raining again.' Not the scholarly comment she was half-expecting of the great physician. Not a man for idle talk, and certainly not a man for idle gossip. He then just left the room, nodding briefly in her direction.

'Well!' thought Mary. 'Not the best companion I ever met, he is hardly here on earth with us mere mortals.' She was rather offended that he couldn't even be bothered with the basic niceties of civilized conversation. He could have tried with the invalid, she decided, as it would encourage her.

Then she realised she hardly had the strength to have a conversation if she wanted to. The rest of the day felt like some kind of sleepy Limbo. King Henry VIII had banned reference to Purgatory but not Limbo, so she floated between Heaven and Earth, sometimes clear in her thoughts and sometimes not.

Two days into her new regime, Dr Ince had arranged for her hands and face to be washed carefully again, and made sure that she had a clout of clean wet linen in her hand to cool herself down if she felt hot. He also had the windows in her room open most of the time. Mary thought she might be cold, but actually prospered in the cool air, which battled with the fire in the hearth.

At one point, after a small breakfast, as John Ince sat reading in a chair nearby or writing in his small leather-bound book, she heard a horse, probably a messenger arriving ,and the dogs carrying on as if they had never seen a trotting horse before. John Ince raised his head, listening out and left the room. Mary decided that the messenger would understandably have a letter of enquiry from her father, and that John Ince would make the messenger wait, so he could respond with an update on her condition and her progress. She called out to the physician, 'Please tell father I am improving - thanks to the physician he has sent me - and that he is in my prayers.'

He returned to the room looking down on her with a half-smile. 'Ah,'he said. 'So, now you have a stronger voice, and strength to take part in life again. I am glad. We have a long way to go, though, so don't be too enthusiastic, and try to get up or to do anything stupid without help.' Mary would have bristled at one time, but she had got used to the sharp, hard ways of this man whom she now trusted with her life.

Letting her father know that she was improving in strength was on her mind these last hours, and much of her wanted to protect him from the concept that she might be being poisoned, but she knew there was little she could do but let others take decisions for her in her weakened state.

Another horse arrived just after the messenger, and the dogs had an exciting time of it yet again. This time the horse left within minutes. She wondered who it was but decided she didn't care enough to ask. So, she fell asleep again, now sleeping most of the time. She wondered if that sweet cordial the doctor gave her every few hours was something to do with it, but she had noticed she was being given it less frequently, and yet still slept.

On the third day in the oriel room she was invited to walk unaided, but with John Ince holding out his hands to catch her, and although she was definitely wobbly and her heart was racing, she managed well.

'Good,' he grunted. 'Now I shall arrange for you to have some more varied food, that you must chew thoroughly and take your time over.'

Mary had no idea that chicken could taste so good, or tansy pudding and even half a glass of sweet white wine. Everything tasted intense after such a bland palate, but it tasted right, not strange. All was eaten with relish, and although she had acute stomach ache after her first really solid meal, she was able to recover both her strength and desire to do more.

'I have a friend called Margaret whom I would dearly like to come to visit,' Mary cheerfully told Ince one afternoon. He remained quiet.

'It would lift my spirits to see her,' she cajoled.

'No,' he said simply, and carried on writing in his small book, dipping into the little portable ink-pot he had placed carefully alongside the sander.

'What is that book, please?' John Ince looked up, a little surprised that she might be interested, but put down the quill on a side table next to the ink-pot and handed the book to her. She was not expecting him to give up his treasure so easily, and could it be possible that he seemed half-amused? It was far too difficult to tell what he was thinking: he gave nothing away.

The book fitted comfortably in Mary's hand but was quite thick, with the strong hand-made paper folded quarto inside. She knew something about books because she liked them ,and had asked questions over the years about how they were made. The cover was plain brown suede leather and there was a simple leather thong attached that wove round the book to close it, and then hang it from a belt, which is how John Ince wore it when not reading or adding to it. Not uncommon, and usually for the purpose of recording important matters or interesting ideas.

Inside the book, in tiny neat handwriting, she saw page after page of medical receipts. Each receipt was clearly topped with a rubricated title. The red ink stood out strongly, shouting out that this book was the work of a university-trained man, with a fine secretary hand and the usual abbreviations 'ye' instead of 'the' and numbers shown in small 'i' with a 'j' to show it was the last to be counted which meant that the number four was shown as 'iiij'.

Mary knew this system well, and was proud that she knew more about the little book and its content than her observer realised when he handed it to her. He was sitting back with the light behind him as a black shape, just watching her absorbed by his composition. Mary knew instinctively that he was continuing to observe her, to ensure that all her faculties were returning and her responses normal. He had not known Mary prior to the illness, so he could only guess at her normal range of response. That was empiric observational medicine at work.

'In English, not Latin?' she questioned. He merely gave a brief nod. Mary had never held anything in her life that she desired more. This wonderful little book was absolutely packed with treatments and therapies for anything from swollen testicles to thread worms, to leprosy.

Many of the receipts, unusually, gave instructions on measurements of the ingredients, and when the potions should be taken. Some had vast amounts of ingredients, up to a hundred in one case, and included not only plants and animal products but traces of minerals.

'So many ingredients in some,' she whispered to herself. He had heard her, and responded.

'Polypharmacology. It is understood that the body will recognize what it needs if the physician is unable to tightly pinpoint the problem with a patient. So he has draughts or pills made up at a reliable apothecary, consisting of a really wide range of *materia medica,* allowing the human body to take what it requires, itself recognising those needs, and with God's help and rest there usually can come a cure.'

'How wonderful to discover this book at your side, Dr. Ince, for it is giving me more interest than you know. I have long been fascinated by medicine.'

He was watching her with a raised eyebrow, and then turned away to write some letters and left her to it. His dark presence in the room was reassuring to

Mary. Soberly dressed in scholar's cap and gown, he was a quiet, studious companion, busy with his books and papers. Mary found she no longer wanted him to chatter – that was simply not in his character.

That night the dogs were disturbed and it woke her, but she was also aware that the dogs were not ignored as was usually the case, and there was activity in the yard and people moving about talking. Even through the shutters she could hear them but not distinctly. She quickly dozed off again, and forgot to ask about it the following morning.

Over the next two days, Mary, now up and dressed but staying in her room, would ask Dr Ince if she could see the book again for 'just an hour', so as not to be too tiring. He knew in truth she would not bother to rest if she could get a chance to look at his hip book, and she was merely soothing any likely criticism with reference to resting. However, he would sigh and hand it to her, telling her to be careful, for it was a cornerstone of his profession and gathered over his working lifetime. Her interest in the work was as much part of her healing as rest, she would say years later, and it was, for it engaged her mind on something positive and lifted her spirits. Oddly, the medical book had made her better, or certainly was the key to releasing her mind from any distress.

A routine had developed where Anne would enter with a tap on the door every two hours, carrying tiny portions of delicate and simple food. Gradually the portions grew bigger, and the gap of time between, longer.

Chapter 26

One afternoon Dr. Ince, having winkled the book from her reluctant fingers, told her to put her shoes on and take a walk outside with him in the herb garden, as it was not hot but warm and a cooling breeze was rippling the lavender.

So, outside they went, and although Mary had to sit down a couple of times on the garden seats, she felt all the better for the stroll. Ince was completely silent, as usual, but at her side.

When they returned inside, he told Mary it was time she had a bath, to wash any clinging illness from her skin, and to have her hair cut and washed.

'Although your hair has stopped falling out, and the sharp pricking on your scalp that heralded the loss has also stopped, your hair will be stronger and probably grow thicker if you have it cut quite short.'

He added, in response to her obvious dismay about her hair, 'All the fashion now in London, the queen herself has her hair short. Admittedly she often wears wigs, but they are still worn short, in tight curls.' Mary suppressed a giggle, as hearing him talk about London ladies' fashions could not be more incongruous.

He left her in the bedroom and shouted for Anne to arrange for the great, wide, wooden barrel bath to be to arrange for the great, wide, wooden barrel bath to be carried upstairs by the Loxleys, and set up in the oriel room, and for clean sheets of linen to be draped in the bath itself, 'to avoid irritation of the skin .'

Once the flurry of setting up the pitch-lined tub was done, great jugs of hot water were carried upstairs in relays, until it was half-full. Many of the younger servants came up to look at the bath tub, peeping round the corner.

John Ince put his hand in it. 'That's fine for temperature.'

Anne dared ask a question. 'If you please, doctor, is there anything to be put in the water such as oil or herbs?'

'No, just pure clean water, and I have a block of oat and rose oil soap in my bag. Use that.'

He fetched the small oatmeal-covered scented disc, wrapped in cheesecloth, and handed it to Anne along with a small bottle of soft lye soap, which sat in the bottle in golden bubbles 'for her hair.' Mary looked sadly down at her hands, where her nails had also fallen out, but small new baby nails were growing beneath. The same with her toes.

The good doctor then took up a chair outside the room, instructing that when he saw her again, he expected her to be clean, with cut hair and every bit of soap swilled off her. Large jugs of warm water were standing by for that purpose. Anne had nodded obediently and was joined by the new maid by the new maid Bess from the kitchen, happy to join in and help. When people are seriously ill, those who really care want to do something to help, anything to help, Mary had noticed over the past week.

'Oh, they're nearly gone!' cried Anne, looking at the blood blisters on Mary's chest, that were now dried up and just purple pin -pricks. Mary pushed her chin down and saw that indeed they had nearly gone.

'Wonderful! They have!' Mary was thrilled. The prickling in her fingertips had gone a couple of days earlier, and her hair had definitely stopped falling out, but she fully agreed a haircut was needed, and then she could wear a small bonnet to cover the little bald patch on the crown of her head.

'I'm more used to sheep than people,' fretted Anne, as she carefully cut off the long, odd-looking strands.

'You look after your husband's hair, don't you?'

'Aye,' agreed Anne reluctantly, 'but he doesn't mind what the sheep and cows think of how he looks, and he cares even less for what the other farmers say on market day.'

Bess chipped in, 'Well, you know what they say – it takes two weeks to make a bad haircut into a good one,' which made them all laugh out loud together - a happy sound for others in the Hall, to hear the young mistress laughing, and servants within earshot stopped work and smiled.

Anne and Bess fell silent, though, in concentration, as her locks fell and were quickly scooped up by Bess, so as not to cause distress at the sight of how much there was. At the end, Mary ran her hands through her short hair, and found she liked the feeling of freedom the close-cut hair brought. The two women had wondered if she might be reduced to tears by the loss, but her courage and pleasure at being well again made her joyful instead.

Slipping into the now warm, no longer hot, water, Mary floated happily, letting the water support her legs and then dipped her head under to come up spluttering. She started to hum to herself, seeing Anne and Bess step back, and drying their hands, they smiled down at her in her contented state.

Baths usually also involved a tent-like affair made up of a linen sheet that was supported over the bath to keep out draughts. Dr. Ince had been keen to point out that much of her difficulties were caused by her humours being too hot from the poisons, so she should be kept cooler even when her skin was wet.

There was some coaxing needed to actually get her out of the bath, as she had felt so content and relaxed. In the end she agreed, as the water was cooling, stood up and allowed jugs of more warm water to be poured over her, as instructed by Dr Ince.

Mary knew that given half the chance, Anne might have plenty to say about the doctor, but strangely she gave way for now and did precisely as she was told - an unusual reaction, Mary thought, as she was dried briskly, and a clean shift dropped over her head.

Then she was dressed in a gown that was light and soft, with buskins on her feet and hair combed into neatness as a cap of brown curls, dry already, before Dr Ince was invited back in. Mary stood waiting for him, and saw that as he entered her chamber he stopped sharply, and looked at her as if rocked.

'It'll grow back,' he muttered, and as the women started to busy themselves cleaning up the room, Mary and Dr Ince went down the main stairs to her father's study to talk. 'Hold onto the rails if you need to,' he said gruffly, and she would have done if she needed to, but discovered that her step was confident and strong.

'What now, Dr Ince?' she asked him. 'You are nearly well, but there is more to be done to have you completely recovered, so I am going to send you to hide away for a couple of weeks.' He had his back turned, looking out of the study window.

'Hide away? What an extraordinary thing to say. Do please tell me what you have in mind, and why should I hide?'

He didn't immediately respond, but went to the door and checked that no-one was about. Mary sat down. When Ince was confident no one was nearby, he sat in the chair opposite her, stretching out his long legs.

'You know that you have been poisoned and have, if I may say so, been stalwart about the matter.' Mary realised that was nearly a compliment from this sharp, dour man, so just nodded, looking down at her hands. Her left thumb wasn't sore any more.

'We must find out what you have been poisoned with, and who has done it. Most of all, in fact, at the root of all this, we must find out the motivation. I do, however, think that it is something to do with your father's work.'

'And yours…' she added, to which he didn't respond. In fact he had an annoying habit of not rising to the bait, whatever it was. 'Do you have any idea who might be doing this, doctor? It is a burden to distrust all of those around me, although I must say I suspect a woman called Alice Goodrich and her grandson, Warwick.'

She then told him the whole sorry tale, and he listened all the while as it poured out of her. He showed no emotion, but just listened.

'Well, you can stop driving yourself into an unhealthy frenzy over this woman and her grandson, because it's not them.' He summed up the twenty minutes of her speaking in one, flat, sentence.

Mary was quite offended. How could be so dismissive when she still felt bitter and distrustful about Alice?

'It's all very well you making me feel as if I am over-reacting, when from what you have just heard, you can quite see why I thought they were involved. I also cannot imagine why you might be so sure, Dr Ince.'

Her eyes shot him a hard look. 'Some of the servants even thought witchcraft was involved, and that she had taken some of my hair from a comb, and fashioned a doll that she hexed.'

John Ince scoffed. 'Really? You really think that is true? You, a woman of learning, and more keen thought than any woman I have met, think you are hexed! This superstitious claptrap is for the simple-minded and not for you. Let the fools be fools! I am telling you, but cannot at this point tell you why, that they are not involved, and this is a much more dangerous plot that you are caught up with than two thieving, malicious servants.' He was calm but a temper was rising. She rose to the challenge, just as heated.

‘Why can’t you tell me? Why?’

‘Orders,’ he said simply. ‘Orders, so that more can be done behind closed doors, from which you will not be excluded, when you are completely strong and in a safe haven. As your father would tell you himself.’

‘Father?’ she asked weakly. ‘Are there letters for me in the messenger bag?’ looking over his shoulder to the brown bag waiting on the desk.

‘I have them here in my pouch at my side,’ he answered, ‘And shall give them to you to read when we have discussed your last stage of healing.’ He then added in a much more polite tone, ‘If you would be so kind to assist in this matter, Lady?’

There was not much she could say to that, so she fell silent, resentfully.

He sat back, pressing his fingertips together. ‘Lady Mary', he said, ‘I accept that you have had some distressing experiences at the hands of this woman and her grandson. That however, is all it is, a distressing experience. These people behave in the way that has become their trading currency, how they live, wherever they go. Now let it go from your heart. They have gone and you have back, as indeed does Loxley, goods and chattels that rightly belong to you and him. What you have been subjected to is in another league of planning and delivery, and we shall get to the bottom of it.'

'Are you saying there is no such thing as evil intent?' she challenged, eyes glittering.

'Oh, there is evil, all right!' he snapped. 'There is malice aforethought, that has in it planned intent. There are some in society with a desire to cause harm and who deliberately sin for any number of reasons, from greed to a hunger for power and control. Worst of all are those who manipulate and twist the good out of people by using fear or other forms of coercion, and yet have no conscience that they have done wrong. These are the lost souls that we have to let Heaven judge, for they are by these actions less than human, whereas for our faults, man is just below the angels, we are told, and I believe that.'

Mary was astounded by this impassioned speech, that was almost longer than everything he had said to her since his arrive at Somersal put together.

He continued, 'I also believe, unless you say otherwise, that you would like to help in this investigation that has brought me here, and I know you could indeed be very helpful, because no one expects a woman to be as bright and able as you. Please do not reduce my respect for you by thinking my words are mere flattery, Mary Dudley. I am telling you what I believe to be the truth.'

That last sentence was a bit of a blow until she realised after a moment of analysis that really it was a greater praise. To think a man like this would consider her to assist was unexpected, and a delight to Mary.

'The next stage is to get you on a horse - I understand you are an adequate horsewoman - and you are to ride between Thomas Ashbourne and me the three miles to Uttoxeter, where I am going to put you in the capable hands of Agnes Picard, the apothecary. I understand you have met her, and know something of her work.'

Mary was enthusiastic. 'I shall certainly feel safe with Agnes, as I know she has a reputation as a wonderful healer, and has much good sense too.'

John Ince nodded. 'That's right, and that is why she has been chosen. I want you out of this house until I can make it more secure, and at the same time receiving therapies from Agnes, who with fortune will be able to work out by apothecary diagnosis what has been used to poison you, and that will help us further. I mean by that, not only about the healing process for you, which is the absolute priority, but also because it may lead us to clues as to who is behind this deliberate poisoning of you, and why.'

'I understand, and am happy to go, but would like to see my friend Margaret Rich. Is she is able to visit me?'

Mary was startled by his sharp reaction. 'No! I have told you, I want you to be shut away from the world in a secret place, and I mean away from everyone. No one should know where you have gone, except Ashbourne. Sometimes, I do think you are not listening. This is not, mistress, a child's game.' His eyes were glittering with anger. One moment he praised her intellect, and the next admonished her. The woman in Mary told the child in her to go away, and she apologised, knowing all was being done for her sake and the sake of her family.

'Very well. When do we leave?'

'We ride on St. Giles's day.'

'What?' Mary was astonished. 'Surely not, the entire area descends on Uttoxeter for the St. Giles's Fair. That is hardly discreet as so many people will see me.' He had the decency to give the twitch of a smile. 'I know, which is why we picked it.'

Mary was incredulous, understandably. He explained, 'The servants, neighbours and surrounding area will be in the usual bout of hysteria and excitement, all rushing about and arguing as to who should have time off. The streets will be thronged again with people crowding in, having fun, fighting and generally ignoring everything except their desire to enjoy the fair. It matters not if many people see us - the vast majority will forget in the next moment. If you go to Uttoxeter on a normal day, you will be spotted on the quiet streets and servants will whisper. This way, if you pack your own things and say nothing even to your maid, you will disappear like smoke and we shall say you have gone away for a time, which will be true.'

He leaned forward in his chair, speaking more quietly and discreetly now. 'You shall leave here in plain sight with nothing to hide, and after a few days, that will bring the wolves forward to this door to find you, as you have been their useful creature and they won't want to lose you.'

Mary's hand went instinctively to her throat, which she clasped, feeling vulnerable that people wanted her insane and sick. 'What about when I come back after healing?' she asked.

'A reasonable question, Lady Mary. By the time you come back to this house, it will be better guarded than it has ever been other than when the Vikings raided this valley.'

Mary knew Somersal meant 'summer hiding place' in Old English, and most believed it referred to be a place to hide from vicious Viking raids that plundered the area. She sat quietly, still listening intently as he continued.

'Also, we shall be much further forward in understanding what is going on, as traps will be set. And believe me, mistress, they will be sprung.'

Mary understood that she must be more discreet than ever in her life, to trust no one but a named few, not necessarily those chosen by her. She also appreciated that she was about to have a great change in her life, and a chance to be involved in some exciting work that affected security linked to the Crown, even in some small way. Her father's letters would be given to her when she arrived at Agnes's house in a few days' time, on the first day of September.

Chapter 27

The domestic life of the Hall had settled down to an efficient and happy pace. Bess and her twin daughters Matilda and Maud, had taken over Alice's cottage, with gratitude to have a chance to have a job and private lodgings. Bess was a widow, for her husband had been a sailor, and had been lost in a screaming storm on a merchant ship far away. It was not common for Midland men, so very far from the sea, to be sailors, but it did happen. Bess was glad, she told her fellow servants at the Hall, that they were living in the Midlands. 'For then I do not have to go down to the sea with cloak around me, and listen to his calling from the waves, as some of the widows do.'

A sensible, practical woman, Bess proved a great worker with a sunny disposition, and her twin girls helped out in the kitchen. Eleanor was delighted with both her new young helpers, who were well disciplined, commenting 'Those two lasses are rare for ten-year-olds. They've more sense than some I've met at forty years, and harder working too.'

The girls had beamed at each other in the odd mirroring way that twins do. Cook made them her special pets, often rewarding them with little titbits and slices of cake. Maud was the quiet twin and Matilda the comic one. Mary had heard from Anne how Matilda kept saying that she would marry Charlie the stableboy, and their descendants one day would own the Hall! Charlie didn't complain, just blushed as he was thirteen. Meanwhile, the rest of the staff chattered about going to the fair in little groups, taking turns so as not to leave the house empty. There was the usual tension about who would go with whom, but in the end they managed to sort out some kind of rota without too much bloodshed.

It seemed as if the whole area made its way to the fair, determined to capture the last warmth of summer, whilst all around the autumn leaves drifted from gold to red flame before falling quietly, caught in the winds of change.

Mary, Thomas Ashbourne and John Ince were going to join the crowds and then peel off to Agnes Picard in her apothecary shop. Agnes had seen the carnival of humanity arrive on her doorstep each year at St Giles' Fair for decades, and always spent a number of weeks preparing for it in the store room of her shop, knowing that her medicines and therapies would be required by locals and strangers throughout the celebrations. The population rose dramatically and so did the ailments and 'accidents'.

Too much drink and excitement meant the inevitable brawls, particularly if young men were competing over one of the local girls. There were also fights over faulty goods from traders or poor quality food, that often ended in hissing and swearing individuals being pulled off each other. The women could be among the worst of the combatants, often attempting a last kick, or spitting at their enemy while being held back by their friends.

Amongst the crowd were always touring actors with tragedies and comedies enough to satisfy any man or woman hungry for entertainment. They usually performed in the back yards of inns, or in upper rooms if the yard was full. It was a wonder half the time that the audiences heard anything, they were so busy joining in enthusiastically with the plot by yelling or booing. If a play was particularly bad the audience would throw rotten fruit and vegetables, forcing the actors to make a run for it. Agnes had had to treat some of the actors occasionally, but generally they just needed to jump in the river for a good clean, rotten eggs being a professional risk.

Actors were not the only catch-pennies. There were also tumblers and musicians, dancing dogs in little hats held on with string, and the inevitable quacks selling potions that were more likely to kill than cure.

Agnes joined forces with some of her other professional colleagues such as bone-setters, tooth-pullers and corn-cutters, whom she always picked with care to get the most skilled, which would enhance her reputation and ensure the local community had the best she could secure. That meant the quacks didn't last long, with so much medical talent already resident, and so they moved on to more desperate areas, never coming twice to St Giles' Fair in Uttoxeter.

Uttoxeter's was an ancient market. Scholars said that the Romans had settlements at Uttoxeter and nearby Rocester, as well as at Tutbury Castle. Uttoxeter was in the county of Stafford, as the foaming river Dove was the border between the two shires and had to be crossed. The tight bridge across the river was inevitably crowded when the Fair was on. The narrow main streets in Uttoxeter were lined with shops, and beyond spilled brightly-coloured striped booths, crowded around the people-thronged market place.

Among that throng were Mary and her two companions, who had all arrived on horse-back, weaving their way slowly through the heaving crowd. No one complained about the horses, but looked up and touched forelocks. The mood was generally very cheerful.

Mary looked at the corner of the market alehouse, where one of the town constables was arguing with a beggar, who was waving a burnt piece of wood still smoking. Mary turned to Ashbourne. 'Why is that beggar waving that bit of burnt wood around?'

Ashbourne squinted, scanning the shop fronts to see where she was looking. Having seen the arguing pair, he said, 'I am surprised, Mistress Mary, that you haven't seen that particular citizen of beggardom in London.' Mary shook her head. 'He is a glimmerer. There are plenty about. It was a particularly successful form of begging until people of recent years have realised they were being cheated. These characters turn up in crowded areas with a burnt piece of timber that is smoking, well it would be when it is constantly being re-lit, and claim their house has just burnt down and beg for money.'

Mary was irritated. 'No! What a ghastly plot, to wrench people through sympathy to part with their hard-earned pennies.' She knew that house fires were horribly frequent, particularly in the crowded streets in a tinder-dry summer, as flames would leap easily from one thatched roof to the next. Seeing these apparently poor souls begging with a smoking stick was likely to have the good townsfolk moved to open purses and pockets. The fraud was obviously lucrative and Mary could see why. These people were drawing from the best of human nature - kindness and generosity from good people - by the use of a trade in deception, the worse of human nature. Thinking of that odd balance of life - the bitter feeding off the sweet - made her wonder at the irony of life. Why did these fraudsters not have a conscience, and were they not fearful for their souls?

Meanwhile, something else had caught Mary's eye, so she gently squeezed the flanks of her mare to walk a little faster, rising up in her stirrups slightly to look over the heads of the moving crowd ahead. Yes, there, Mary had seen someone, a face she recognized but was not happy to see, and then he was gone. Ashbourne and Ince had moved quickly to keep up with her, and looked at her questioningly.

Dropping down into her saddle, Mary gave them a wry smile. 'Warwick Goodrich,' she said simply, but was flushed at the sight of him.

'Really?' snapped Ashbourne, who stared at John Ince meaningfully. Mary told herself to ask about this later, for clearly she was not being informed about something.

'There is more to be asked here,' commented Ince,

meaning Warwick being seen, and he craned over the neck of his horse, asking Ashbourne to point the boy out, as he had never seen him. Warwick had disappeared quickly, because he had seen Mary too and had frozen, before ducking down his head and dodging through the mass of humanity. He was clearly making a nuisance of himself, as people turned and complained crossly as he moved like a dog through a field of rushes.

One thing was clear, he was not nearly as cocky as he usually was, and his customary smirk had been absent. He had looked like a hunted rabbit, thought Mary, but she had not the slightest sympathy for him.

'There!' said Ince. 'They have seized him.'

Sure enough, a group of men-at-arms had grabbed Warwick by the butcher's shop. The crowd was cheering. Mary's party turned away, but she was worked up at the sight of Warwick, and angry with herself for still letting him bother her so much. 'Shall we go to the stables then, Lady?' asked Ashbourne. Mary glanced at him and tried to let go of her anger. A posy woman came to the side of Ince's horse, with a basket piled high with bright foaming blooms, tied sweet with herbs.

'Come sir, for the pretty lady, a tussymussie.'

Ince threw her a silver penny, which the wrinkled crone bit on with one of her few remaining teeth, to check its quality, and handed up a scented posy of pink and pale mauve. Ince passed it to Mary, without looking at her or making comment. Dr Ince had obviously felt under pressure to buy them, as it was unlikely that he would have done so spontaneously, decided Mary. Meanwhile, there was a distinct wave of disapproval from Ashbourne, but then again Mary knew him well.

'How lovely! Thank you, Dr Ince.'

He answered without looking at her. 'It is to ensure that in your recovering state, you do not have your humours unsettled by the stink of humanity here.'

She buried her face in the welcome scent of the flowers, as they turned their horses to the White Hart Inn on the Stafford Road. Once in the inn yard, a small gaggle of ragged stable boys dashed forward, elbowing each other competitively to take the reins and guide them to mounting blocks, prior to stabling the horses with fresh hay and water buckets. John Ince tugged and unbuckled Mary's leather bags from the horses and carried them himself. The stable boys fought for the scatter of small coins from Thomas Ashbourne's leather purse, and they left them to it.

Not every day was market day, just three days a week, and they were busy enough, but the special saints' day markets were absolutely packed. There were many hostelries in Uttoxeter, covering most needs from ale and whores to some half-decent eating establishments. Of all of them, the White Hart was the most salubrious, where at least the beds could be a private affair and not have to be shared with strangers, even of the same sex. Mary had heard of the Great Bed of Ware, which took eight couples, and that was talked about with giggles and whispers. Mary thought it sounded marvellous and even hoped she might see it one day as she could not for the life of her imagine how big it was. It was typical that she was interested in the mathematics of the arrangement, with the moral aspect passing her by!

The White Hart had no such enormous beds, she understood, but it always had wonderful roast meats, and clean kitchens and cellars and that was all she wanted. The door was wide open, as the day was warm, and they went into the dark, noisy bar and enjoyed shouting at each other just to be heard before taking a glass of wine. It took some skill actually to drink without spilling, amid the constant jostling and mumbled apologies. The large leather bags Ashbourne was carrying didn't help in the press, but it wasn't irritating, just amusing. After a short while, they had had enough of the crush, and

Ashbourne signalled politely for them to go out by another door. Still holding her posy and skirt lifted above her ankles to avoid the dust and dung of the street, Mary went out into the sunshine with her companions, and made her way to Mistress Agnes Picard's apothecary shop.

Chapter 28

The shop was situated in one of the smarter, quieter streets of Uttoxeter (and there weren't many of them), just off the main road and market square. The street was made up of half-timbered houses with decorated wooden shutters, some having leaves and flowers painted in brightly-coloured garlands on the lime plaster. There was obviously a raker at work, and a night-soil man, for dung and rubbish were nowhere to be seen. Smart indeed by provincial standards.

Mary had visited Uttoxeter on and off during her whole life, but couldn't remember having seen this street before. Agnes's shop was a particularly fine building, and above their heads a sign swung, showing a pestle and mortar piled up with herbs, one of the many symbols of an apothecary, which was needed as few could read a written sign. The locals would know only too well where she practised, but the sign was necessary for strangers to the area and there were plenty of them in the town that day.

Mary stood looking at the windows, which had small panes of thick, greenish glass in them, some of which were decorated with herbs. Agnes was clearly prosperous, as the whole property was wonderfully well kept. Mary was impressed, and looked at Ashbourne as he gestured with hat in one hand for her to enter ahead of him through the low heavy door, with John Ince following.

Once through the door, she was instantly assailed by an extraordinarily powerful spicy, herby smell that was sharp and peppery. Her eyes watered a bit for a moment, and she also had to adjust to the inside of the shop after the bright sunshine of the street. It had a calm and cool atmosphere after the hustle and bustle outside, and was surprisingly quiet. She looked around with a sense of wonder, having seen nothing like it, not even in London.

Pots of all sizes and shapes were piled on the shelves that covered the walls of the shop right up to the ceiling, while the counter had tempting displays of sweetmeats stacked high in neat cones of various colours, dependent upon the flavour. Locked cabinets with carefully marked small drawers promised the most exotic, and therefore most expensive, of all the stock.

Mary leaned across the counter to read some of the drawers, and although most were labelled in clear Latin, she knew enough to cope.

'Unicorn horn, dragon's blood and lion fat!' she read out to Ashbourne, who stood rocking slightly on his heels, which he did when he was content.

Mary was thrilled with the shop. Here she might have a chance not only to get completely well, but could also seize the opportunity to find out more about medicine and its uses. It was altogether a joyful place for her and, although she had had some slight doubts about staying with Agnes, in that moment she felt delighted it had come about. She was determined to discover as much as she could about the stock, as she realized that some would be imported from exotic places and with good fortune, she might find out about those lands and cities too.

Mary was thinking of the London docks when the shop door opened noisily behind them, as a delivery carter carried in unsteady wooden trays of fresh herbs. With the merest nod at Mary and her companions, he slammed the trays heavily on the counter, concentrating on the job in hand which was to finish this speedily, and then on to the next delivery and the next, until the tasks of the day were done. When no-one emerged he thumped his fist hard down on the polished wood top, calling for attention brightly and taking his cap off to scratch his head. Agnes hurried out from the back, wiping her hands on a cloth. She smiled and waved at Mary's party over the head of the carter and, signalling she would be with them in a moment, took out a bill of sale from layers of papers folded carefully in a drawer, and an ink pot and quill. The carter sighed, and with one hand on his hip, continued scratching his head impatiently with the other.

'Soon enough, Samuel. Soon enough,' Agnes muttered, whilst looking at the bill, and insisting that each layer of herbs be taken off by waving her quill feather, so she could see the volume and quality of the plants, including colourful flowers, lying neatly in the trays. After carefully marking each tray with a number, Agnes nodded to the man, who tugged his forelock, all forgiven, and doing the same to Mary, went out of the shop door, slamming it behind him.

Agnes came out from behind the counter, crying greetings to them all without apparently being even slightly inquisitive about the presence of John Ince. She opened her arms warmly, kissing Mary's cheek although they had only met once before, and beckoned them all through to the living area of the house. The room was comfortable and tidy, with cushions and all the dark wood polished like a mirror. None of the furniture was fashionably painted in bright colours, as was the current fad, just lots of fine wood on show. A small, cheerful female servant bobbed as they came in, and fussed about getting drinks and small sweet cakes, but the two men decided that they should go back to Somersal once Mary's bags were brought in.

They took their leave, and then Mary caught just a hint of something unspoken between John Ince and Agnes. Did they know each other, she wondered. Perhaps not so surprising, as they were both in the business of healing, but it would then be odd he did not acknowledge knowing her at this moment. Just that glance. Mary would try to find out more if she could, but discreetly, and she stored that thought away for a later time.

Although Mary didn't know Agnes well, she had seen her extraordinary work with the corpses in St. Mary's church, just a few weeks earlier. She also knew of her reputation as an outstanding healer and understood she was a widow.

Being a widow was hardly unusual but for a woman to be an apothecary trading in her own right, with only a young man for assistance, was most unusual. Her flame-haired assistant, Giles, put his head around the door. He was in his late teens, with a face covered in freckles, and wearing a cheerful smile. Having seen Agnes was with other people, he stepped back and left them alone. Before disappearing, he had waved a packet to Agnes, showing the results of an errand, and she had nodded at him.

In the past, Agnes had apparently assisted her husband, Maurice, who was also a well-respected apothecary, for all of their married life of twenty-five That meant she was able to grow in knowledge and ability for all that time. For some years now, she had been accepted fully as an apothecary in her own right, many believing she was now even better than her husband had been. He came from French stock, thus her married name, and that had given him the allure of foreign knowledge to the locals, but after a while they didn't even notice how French he was.

Agnes came to Mary and clasped her hands between hers, in a second embrace of welcome, and gave farewells to Thomas Ashbourne and John Ince for a final time before they left.

Ince, getting ready to put his hat back on his head, said in his usual measured tone, 'We shall go now, Mistress Agnes, and shall leave Lady Mary in your gentle care. I know you can take the demons out of her humours and return her to us, a content and confident Mary Dudley again.' Agnes nodded, smiling confidently at Mary, but her patient was well aware she was assessing her the whole time - her skin tone, the brightness of her eyes, and even the level of curl in her short hair, mostly tucked under her riding bonnet. Mary was glad she was being assessed, with a feeling that at last she really could relax, tucked away with Agnes. Ashbourne turned in the doorway and looked at Mary hard.

'It is not easy to part with you, mistress,' he said solemnly. 'But I know that Mistress Picard here in this place of peace will protect you from the outside world, whilst cleansing your body from what ails you. You can be sure, we will look after the Hall, and your father's work will be protected, so let that not play on your mind. You will be in our prayers, as you have been.'

'I quite agree with all of that,' added Ince. 'And next week, another bag of fresh linen and such like will be brought here, packed by Anne, but that will be left without us meeting, which means you will be able to completely cleanse yourself without interruption.'

Mary could not resist a small barb. 'Yes, and also to keep secret that I am here. I am sure, Dr Ince, that you forget that I have the wit to see what is planned. Meanwhile, I have no idea how you are going to keep the servants from finding out where I am, so good luck with that!'

She was keen to prove that though she was a woman, she was not a complete fool, and said farewell in a conciliatory and genuinely grateful tone.

'I thank you for your good offices, Thomas Ashbourne, and you, Dr Ince, and will do all I can to ensure that I am quickly back under your protection again.'

She felt a quite unexpected lurch of anxiety in her stomach as she watched the men leave, but she did see Ashbourne look over his shoulder to see if she was still looking. Seeing that she was, he waved his hat cheerfully in farewell. The doctor carried on pushing through the surging crowd at the end of the street, into which both men melted.

Agnes's voice broke into her thoughts as if she were reading them. 'No need to be sad, my dear. You are now on a firm path of recovery, and will emerge even better than before, like a flutterby from a chrysalis.' She held out her strong but work-worn hand and catching Mary's elbow, guided her upstairs. Agnes took her to a really clean, small room, with shutters closed, and a jug of scented wild flowers on the wooden chest at the end of the bed.

Looking round the room, Mary knew the way to recover was to cut herself off completely from her previous life and let Agnes do her job. In that way Mary was giving herself to the care of Agnes immediately, trusting her instinctively.

Her living quarters in the house were small but comfortable. As well as her bedroom there was also a charming panelled sitting room, where Agnes told Mary that they both could sit, plumped up with cushions, and talk whenever Agnes was not with customers or mixing potions. Agnes had a bedroom off Mary's, no doubt to listen out for any patient staying with her in this place - her tiny hospital. 'So you won't be lonely my dear. The maid and my Giles know you are here, but will say nothing, I can assure you.' Mary was somewhat intrigued by the use of the phrase 'my Giles', and felt there was a story about them to be told.

The fire was lit each day in Mary's bedroom, and in the little sitting room. Below was the kitchen which would also have a roaring fire, not only for hot water and cooking but also because some of the preparations needed to be cooked, usually by 'seething', which took a lot of heat. There was another room for Giles off the kitchen downstairs, and the maid came in each day except on her afternoon off, once a week.

Mary knew that she had been very fortunate to have been given the treatments used by John Ince, and she would also benefit from the considerable skills of Agnes Picard. Everyone dreaded a trip to a physician, unless so ill they would put up with anything to feel better. With the exception of John Ince, all the physicians she had ever heard of started the business of healing with draughts to purge the patient, often at both ends! No wonder Dr Ince did not hold with that, as the thought of all that vomiting and diarrhoea to 'cleanse' the patient of any poisonous or misbalanced cardinal humors, when the poor soul was already in a desperately weakened state, seemed particularly cruel.

To Mary's surprise, Agnes agreed, and said she too found this idea as a blanket form of treatment, as she put it, 'does more harm than good, and brings some patients to the door of death - even drags them over the threshold of death.'

Within two hours of her arrival ,when settled, Agnes had helped Mary get undressed down to her shift, and invited her to lie on the bed, which was every bit as comfortable as her own.

She was aching a bit from the short ride, as if her muscles had been strained, so she willingly accepted that she rest. Agnes pulled up a small stool and, with careful hands, looked carefully at her new patient's fingernails, eyes, and inside her mouth, and took some hair with a small set of scissors she had on a thin chain at her side. Mary did all she was told to do without question.

Some of the examination was like the first time with Dr Ince, and the overlap helped her gain confidence. Agnes also kept notes, writing carefully on a folded sheet on the small oak table nearby. Agnes then told her to get into her bed rather than lying on it, and gave Mary a hot and pleasant herbal drink, that had honey in it. 'Sip it, please. Everything in gentle moderation to give your body time to recover, and the valerian root will help you sleep.' She showed Mary the door to the privy, and told her she must use this as often as she could and should drink as much as she could too, to flush out naturally any poison left in her vital organs.

Agnes was keen to have Mary relax completely, and said,'Have no fear, for I am utterly discreet, although I have the reputation of being a chatterer. I do so for my own purposes only, and one day you will learn why my personality seems somewhat contradictory. Not a soul knows you are here other than those named, even if you were seen in that crush outside, and that is possible. No one would expect you to stay here, so we are going to keep you a secure secret, and rest assured that there is more security here and outside the building than you know.'

She started to leave the room, then added over one shoulder, 'Do not go to the window facing the street, Lady, as I don't want you seen, for a while at least.'

Mary stopped her. 'Please,' she asked quietly, 'is someone really trying to kill me, Agnes?'

Agnes turned and looked squarely at Mary. 'I believe you have been in danger, a danger designed not to kill you, but disable you and therefore in turn, your family. However, if you did die, that would also cause a distraction - which was desirable to these people.'

'A wanted distraction?' Mary was appalled. 'My death would do as second best in terms of what these people desired, but they would settle for it as an acceptable outcome?'

'I am not going to mince words with you, mistress. I feel you are bright enough and educated enough to have the truth of this, and so I am giving it to you, woman to woman, as a matter of respect.'

Agnes's face was set, and although sympathetic she was not going to simper, for from her firmness came strength that Mary could share. She added, 'Despite our determination to know the truth, the whole picture is not yet known. We can only see some of it, and I feel sure between us we can not only have you returned to full health but also to take part in discovering who is behind all this and why, and to take part in the justice. For, doubt me not, there will be justice for your pains, I am sure.'

Mary was rocked by this statement, and was starting to see that Agnes was not just a provincial apothecary with a dead Huguenot husband in her past. She was more than she appeared, and Mary reminded herself that she was sure of a knowing exchange of looks between Agnes and John Ince. She may have been overly sensitive and read into it more than existed but she was still intrigued. Agnes cut into her thoughts. ‘Now, please don’t ask any more, for I do not want your head full of ideas, most of which will be guessed, and therefore probably wrong and a waste of vitality. We will get to the bottom of all this and you are absolutely safe here with me and Giles and those that guard.’

She smiled a good-night and left Mary alone. Mary lay on her back with eyes wide open, and repeated to herself out loud part of what Agnes had just said: ‘Those that guard’. What, by Heaven, could she mean by that, except the obvious, that I have guards discreetly watching this place to ensure my safety?' That knowledge gave her even more comfort, and her breath started to rise and fall regularly.

She slept that night deeply with no dreams, or none she could remember. The next day she was told to stay in bed and rest, or put on her robe and buskins and move from room to room, upstairs only for the first day, and then gradually to take more exercise. It was a return to the regimen of Dr Ince. Starting again did not frustrate her, as she knew it had a purpose, so she did not argue.

The food she was given was at first very simple: home-baked bread (with fresh butter), cold meats and jug upon jug of sweet water drawn from Agnes's own well, which was capped and locked between use. Agnes watched Mary's reaction when given food, particularly, for some reason best known to Agnes, how she reacted to the smell of different dishes.

One day, a week or so after her arrival, she gave her patient a cup of apple juice, and Mary pulled back in horror at the smell. Agnes watched this as she sat with her, taking the cup and putting it to one side on the table. 'Does the smell of apples revolt you of late, sweetheart?' she asked. Mary nodded, answering, 'Yes, and I do not know why, for I have always loved apples, both sharp and sweet'.

Agnes then asked her a number of questions about the nature of her nightmares, if her heart pounded, and if she had ever been sick for no reason. Did her fingertips tingle, and did she have a red rash or blisters anywhere on her body? Had she lost her hair, or nails? All of these questions, Mary was able to answer with a firm 'yes', as her eyes searched Agnes's face, for she could see that she was onto something, and excited by Mary's answers.

'Got it!' said Agnes victoriously, and went off downstairs, returning with a tight jar and a cloth.

'What is it?' Mary called, but Agnes didn't answer, and

instead opened the jar, and with the cloth fetched out a strange hairy root that looked like a little person with body, head, arms and legs, about eight inches long and pale in colour.

'There,' said Agnes, 'is the source of your problems. This is mandrake, which has been used in medical treatment, magic and wanton poisoning, back to Adam'.

Mary interrupted, 'Oh, I've heard of mandrake. Don't they use dogs with special collars and chains to harvest it from the ground, as when it's pulled up, it gives a high pitched scream, that can kill a person stone-dead, and then the devil comes and takes the dead person away?'

'That's the tradition, Mistress Mary, but I use mine in small traces only, bought from a wholesaler coming up with a cart from many miles away. It's a popular medical ingredient, but has to be handled with great care. Interestingly, Mary, this mandrake is also called the Devil's apple, because it smells of apple, and its flavour can be hidden in real apples – such as in a pie or juice - for those acting on the dark-side.'

Instead of being appalled, Mary was thrilled. 'So!' she said victoriously, 'Dr Ince told me I was being poisoned and now you confirm that. All these horrible visions, vomiting and terrible fears, can all be accounted for because I have been given this mandrake.'

'That's right,' said Agnes, putting the root back in to the jar and taking it downstairs, before returning quickly. 'Now we must be thankful, Lady Mary, for we know what ails you and why, and all can be treated and you will completely recover. You are on your way now, and can go home in a week or so if you feel ready. What we still don't know, however,' she frowned, 'is who, or, indeed, why.'

Mary was sure in her heart that she knew the answer and shared it with Agnes.'This is the work of Alice Goodrich, who many have called a witch, and her grandson, Warwick. They were cast out by Ashbourne and myself from Somersal Hall some weeks ago, having indulged in theft, blackmail, and intimidation of staff. Her reach is long and I am sure somehow she has poisoned me through one of her agents, in revenge.'

Agnes sat down again and took Mary's hand, and looked into her eyes with compassion. 'No,' she said, 'for they are both dead, swinging on the gibbet, only half a mile from here, and have been dead since the day you arrived at my door. They had been in custody and unable to meddle in your life or anyone else's for a fortnight or more before that, awaiting public execution at the Fair. They are now food for the crows, and a warning to all.'

Chapter 29

Mary was reeling with shock. As wicked as Alice and Warwick were, to be hanged publicly and bodies left on the open gibbet to rot – surely not?

'It can't be so,' cried Mary, sitting up sharply, 'For I saw Warwick the very afternoon I arrived. Dead? I just can't believe it! What, both of them?' Mary knew the answer, for she had already been told it was so, but like many people who have had a shock, they ask the same questions over and over until it sinks in.

'They are, my dear, as I have told you.' Mary stood up and paced the floor. 'But I saw Warwick! I am sure I saw him when I arrived here on horseback, and he certainly saw me, but instead of his usual insolence, he looked wild-eyed, and fled as if the hounds of Hell were after him'.

'No wonder,' said Agnes darkly, 'For I have been told he had managed to escape at the hanging, by wiggling through the ropes that tied his wrists, and was on the run. His grandmother did not escape and was hanged. They caught up with him too within the hour, and he will have had a last memory of the roar of the crowd, as the trap was opened below his feet.'

Mary knew well that part of the expected entertainment of St Giles' Fair was to hang criminals as a public spectacle, supposedly to act as a deterrent, and there was no doubt the crowds looked forward to a good hanging. Agnes apparently felt no horror in reporting this. She just told the simple truth of the matter, brutal as it was. She was a woman of the world and accepted more than most in human nature.

'How did they come to this Agnes? Do you know?'

'Oh, I know all right, along with everyone else in the district. It's been a matter for gossip all around, as you can imagine.' She looked at Mary and answered the unasked question. 'I know you will be surprised that all this was kept from you, but you must understand that despite all the servants at the Hall knowing about it, you were in an intensely fragile state and unfit to receive this knowledge. Once dark news is given, it cannot be ungiven, and innocence of this matter would protect you until you were fit to know. I consider you fit now, not least so you are able to put away the idea that they were behind your illness, for they could not have been, from the lock-up.' The lock-up was a tight little prison off the market-place, that flooded in times of rain, and was a source of interest to those passing, who would stop to look through the bars and jeer at those caught inside.

Mary looked down into her lap, trying to take in what she had just heard. She now understood why Ashbourne and Ince had exchanged glances when they arrived in Uttoxeter, those meaningful, questioning glances when Mary cried she had spied Warwick in the crowd. The next urgency on her mind was that she desperately wanted to know what had happened to bring Alice and Warwick to the hangman's noose. Agnes poured them both some wine, and invited Mary to sit near her to hear the tale of the fall of Alice and Warwick Goodrich.

'When they were thrown out of their cottage they had to act quickly, so Warwick and Alice went around various farms outside the boundaries of Somersal, knocking on doors and offering their experienced services. Alice carefully picked farms where they knew Somersal had little or no contact.'

'They took a risk not leaving the area completely,' Agnes continued, 'but decided as they had so many useful contacts in the area, that to make a bit of extra money,or in their case, a lot of extra money, they would stay in the district, and make themselves as willing and useful as possible where they gained employment, albeit at a lower rate, and with no cottage, but sleeping in the barn.'

Mary interjected sharply, 'Alice and Warwick wouldn't like that, but I can see what they were up to. They would take time to gradually feed in nonsense about me and Ashbourne, and the Hall, undermining confidence in our reputations, to help them wriggle out of any evil spoken of them at Somersal being believed.' Mary put down her cup angrily. 'You have it, young mistress. I am pleased your senses are all recovered.' Mary was grim. 'Agnes, is it not a shame that so many criminal types are able and bright, but just weave lies, and involve themselves with criminal acts that could cost their lives?'

Agnes agreed heartily. 'Absolutely. If that energy would be put to better things, then they would not be dodging the law and creditors queued up to seek revenge. Peace is never in their hearts or the hearts of their families either.'

'So, what happened at the farm, whose was it?'

'A widower called Bird. His wife died some years ago. She was a kind and pleasant woman, and I've no idea what she was doing with him.'

Mary had never even heard his name mentioned before. 'Why?' she asked. 'Is he a cruel man?'

Agnes pulled back some stray grey hair that had dropped across her face.

'Farmer Bird is a large, brutal man with no softness in his nature. He treats animals and servants the same. Whip and stick for all, which is why he always has jobs for people, because not many stay, and yet despite all, some of his servants are loyal to him.'

Mary was astonished. 'Really? Why?'

'Yes, Mary, some people are loyal, and not only because they know which side their bread is buttered. Some decent souls want to do the right thing, believe it or not.' Mary looked hard at Agnes as she was starting to get a sense of clarity about why Alice would choose Farmer Bird.

'As a known widower, she was lining him up for marriage, wasn't she?' and although incredulous, Mary was not at all surprised to see Agnes smile in acknowledgement.

'So how did events turn dark for her with such clever plans in place? She is, she was, a wily creature, Agnes, and her true nature not easy to spot at first.' 'Over-confidence and poor timing did for them both. Apparently, Alice had not spent enough effort grooming the servants to do her will, or follow her. They couldn't care less about her or Warwick, except she was sharp- tongued almost as soon as she got on the farm. A bit too soon in fact. Anyway, one of the other women, a milkmaid, had already got the farmer lined up for marriage and was watchful of Alice and Warwick, as she wanted the prize herself.'

'A taste of her own medicine, then?'

Agnes continued 'So, when the pair of them started on a simple lad, bullying him and aping him to the other servants for a cheap laugh, it all backfired. The other servants were protective of the lad, and so no one laughed, leaving Alice stinging.' Agnes described things wonderfully, so Mary could see these dramas in her imagination, as she knew only too well how two of the protagonists would react.

Agnes went on, 'Incredible as it may sound, three of the servants, including the ambitious milk maid, set her up in such a way that she had an opportunity to steal, but they were watching them, to be able to give damning evidence against her. The stealing was a rather larger matter than the other servants had realized, which had been a revelation. Both Alice and Warwick were stealing food, wine and money from the dairy sales at the local market.' Agnes sat looking into her cup.

Mary wasn't surprised about what they had done, of course, but she was astonished as to how they went about it and so quickly after arriving at the Bird farm.

‘Wasn’t she careless? Not so bright, then, and no doubt the milkmaid gave evidence at the trial. Did many come to watch?’ ‘I was there. You could hardly get into the chamber it was so crowded. Plenty of people came forward to give evidence from other places too. She had a number of enemies built up over the years, Mary. They were all waiting for a chance to get their own back…. and they did.’

‘Was the magistrate…?'

‘Yes, Ashbourne had told me much outside of the courtroom, and he acknowledges that the magistrate knew all about the Somersal connection, and the pair’s behaviour at the Hall. There was talk, you know, about the case being heard at Tutbury Castle, but it was thought it would raise too much interest in your family.’

Mary raised her eyebrows questioningly.

Agnes bent forward, and said comfortingly, ‘You see, there are many who will protect you from cruel and vengeful tongues.’

‘Why was I particularly protected from all this?’

‘It is pretty straightforward. The magistrate had been asked by Ashbourne, speaking on behalf of Sir Edmund Dudley, not to pursue Alice Goodrich over the Somersal thefts, as you would have had to give evidence. As the death sentence was inevitable, it was thought to be too much for you, so everyone waited for her to do it again.

Which she did. You can see why Ashbourne and your father would be shy of you as a witness. There was another point of discretion, that you and the Hall should not be a matter of gossip, that could be heard at the Castle, and elsewhere!'

Mary understood, and was not offended, for although keen to take her place in the world and do some things usually only men did, she admitted she would have been distressed to appear at such a hearing. She always wanted to be merciful if she could be. She also understood that gossip could be damaging to the family. Although they had done no wrong, even having their name mentioned in a criminal trial was undesirable.

'Were Alice and Warwick petrified in court?'

Agnes shrugged. 'I got the impression she had been there before. Not him, of course. He arrived at Somersal as a babe, didn't he?'

'Yes, but I was young too, so don't remember much about them arriving.'

Agnes stabbed the table by her with her forefinger to make a point. 'Alice had her chin out, defiant, her arms would have been crossed if not roped in front of her. Oh yes, she is a hard customer, that one - was, I mean,' she corrected herself, adding 'He was snivelling throughout the proceedings, like all cowards.'

'Alice had enough conceit to be hopeful that her smart mouth would talk them out of real trouble. Well, it didn't work, that mouth, and to see her turn almost green when they were told they would be hanged was worth seeing. Warwick turned on her in the dock at that point, and started screaming abuse, saying it was all her fault. He had been made to do it, and he could tell them a lot more if they would just let him live.'

Mary went and looked out of the window and remembered his haunted face again as he dashed through the crowds, trying desperately to make his escape.

Behind her Agnes had a caveat to the tale. 'Your name came into all this, you may be surprised to hear.'

'Not at all,' replied Mary sadly. 'I should imagine there is plenty of gossip already about the thefts from Somersal, despite our best efforts.' 'No,' Agnes shook her head. 'Your name came into this trial in another way.'

Mary felt a sense of alarm about what might be said next. She had had enough shocks for one day, she felt. Equally, she was keen to know the whole truth. Agnes gave her that truth in her clear voice.

'Alice was able to write a little, as I am sure you know, Mistress, and begged for pen and paper so that she could write a letter to you, asking for you to intercede, if not for her, then for Warwick, who had his whole life ahead of him.'

This was unpleasant news indeed for Mary, but she was also very concerned that the letter addressed to her, had been kept from her. She also understood perfectly well why, as she might well have crumbled, having read it. Deep down she knew Alice was a wicked person, and Warwick was showing to the world that he, in time, was likely to become even worse than his grandmother. 'Alice clearly misunderstood that my influence was not nearly as great as she might have thought or hoped, and my view was neither here nor there. Any amount of letters and undertakings on my part would make no difference to their sentences.'

'I know, but she thought it worth a try. Which is extraordinary, because presumably by then she knew you would have seen the content of her cottage, and found out about Loxley…'

'So you know about the affair, Agnes?' 'Yes, I know and a sad story, with no blame on Loxley.' Agnes got up and put another log on the fire, which was dimming.

The two women carried on talking for another hour or so, Agnes making it perfectly clear that Mary should accept the logic of taking such people out of the world, when they are irredeemable on Earth, and letting God, the ever merciful, redeem them in Heaven. Then she added, 'After about two hundred years in Purgatory - of course.'

Mary smiled, as she realised Agnes was deliberately being subversive, for the Church of England no longer recognised the existence of Purgatory, but Mary reflected that it was a difficult thing to ban a belief. Moreover, she appreciated that Agnes spoke sense, but she still couldn't bear the thought of those black, tarred corpses swinging in cages at the crossroads for all to see as a stark reminder of the strength of English law. That night, in view of discovery of the nature of Alice and Warwick's deaths and the later conversation, Mary fully expected to have nightmares again, but she did not, and instead as a gift she discovered that her spirit was freed, along with the bitterness she felt about Alice and Warwick. It was over.

Only one question lingered unanswered in the air, delivered by a dark shape that melted into shadows.

If it's not Alice – then who is it?'

Chapter 30

Mary spent four more happy days at the apothecary shop, during which time she had learned that the room she slept in, and the little solar room – where she and Agnes would sit – were for assisting those in childbirth or individuals who had fallen ill and could not be cared for at home.

Mary had ventured into the garden by the covered well, where all was completely private and almost every inch was stuffed with flowers and herbs both planted out and in pot, always using the back stairs, so she did not have to go into the shop. She would sit on a little stool in the still warm September sunshine, face turned towards the golden sunlight, and tell herself how wonderfully well she felt. Giles would be pottering about, always working hard, and checking every now and again with Agnes. He was clearly full of respect for her and there was a close bond between them.

The following day, she was given somewhat of a revelation, as Agnes told her quietly that Giles was adopted. 'Oh, he is not my son in terms of my body, but in every other sense he is,' she had said, perched on a stool, deftly pulling leaves off a pile of plants in the drying and preparation room. Mary stood by her quietly, realising this was a moment of good faith on the part of Agnes and so had said nothing but merely dropped her eyes and waited. Agnes, when she had put down her leaves, looked up at her. 'You are an unusual creature, if I may say so, Lady Mary, not poking and prying. You know how to be quiet when others would not be, and more to the point would be keen to go and gossip this abroad.'

Agnes explained that it had been at another St Giles' Fair some fifteen years earlier that a little red-haired boy had been found abandoned when all of the visitors had gone, with no trace of who his parents were. Agnes had taken him in, and with no children of her own, had come to love him like the son she had never had. She had also trained him in her trade and in time, she said, he would inherit the shop.

That shop became Mary's only world during these days. A world populated by Agnes, her maid and the quiet but always busy Giles. It was a world of safety, and Mary knew she was growing in strength, but her mind was still leaping from one question to another. She had whole hours of peace and contentment, but that would be undone by a single thought that unsettled her. It was as if her mind was knocking on many doors in her imagination, looking to see if what lay beyond the door was the answer. She visited earlier griefs over and over again, such as the memory of her mother's death, as well as the apparently endless need to think again about the dark boy and the hallucinations she had suffered.

'Suffered' was the right word. Despite her now knowing the reason she had the visions was because she was being poisoned with mandrake, a drug that was known to have that effect, she still felt deep down that the dark boy was real, whilst accepting that other things she saw were not. She didn't know why, except to say she thought she could smell his body, which was unwashed and very much alive.

'Now, Mistress Mary,' chivvied Agnes one day. 'I want you to fill that enquiring mind of yours by looking at people for me.' Mary looked nonplussed.

'What I mean by that is you should start to learn a great deal more about human nature. Even though you are perceptive now, you will need more understanding. This is necessary if you want more than anything else to fulfil your ambition to be a healer. By observing people from all walks of life of all ages, after a while you learn that the hopes and desires of people are largely the same in different forms.'

‘Will that really help me with healing skills?’ Mary sounded doubtful.

‘Of course,’ Agnes laughed. ‘Many, many sicknesses are from the mind, and I don’t mean lunacy or idiocy, I mean the mind turning in on itself and making the body ill.’

Mary was amazed. ‘Really?’

‘Yes, really! There is also a sobering attachment to this learning process, which is that it never stops throughout your life, and sometimes even the most experienced healer can be fooled occasionally.’

Agnes led Mary to the shuttered window, and deftly removed a long thin slat of wood. She then told Mary to pull up a stool, as the slat was low down, and to look out of the window through the gap. ‘See, the whole street is visible as far as possible, and no one knows you are looking, so you can get a real sense of people that way. You see most people put on a front when speaking to others - that is human nature - but this way you can see the real life of people unfolding before you.’

Mary thought this spying was somewhat distasteful, and was not at all sure she approved, which showed on her face, much as she liked and trusted Agnes. Of course the apothecary had spotted it.

'Treat it as a study in the nature of mankind, Lady Mary.' Mary shrugged but nodded. Then Agnes showed her another secret window that looked down from that room into the shop below. The shop was double height so it was easy to look down.

'Now, this is even more interesting, as you will see. Start off with the road view, and then move on to here in the shop. I will sit with you when Giles is working down at the counter and you will learn a great deal about medicine. Don't worry, I will tell Giles you may be watching at any time and he will quite understand.'

Mary felt better about that, so, perched on her stool she looked out of the window to the street, and towards the edge of the market place with the Stafford Road beyond.

It had been raining, which was welcome, but it had made a mess of the St. Giles' Fair. Rubbish was being gathered up in great sloppy piles by gloomy labourers, who then shovelled it into waiting carts, with patient heavy horses harnessed to them. The rakers had been out in the night to clean up the dung, and the night-soil men to empty the privies.

'Some people have awful jobs' breathed Mary, who, despite her reticence, was quite enjoying the scene playing out before her. One or two drunks were wandering around in the light rain, and shopkeepers with folded arms were bellowing pleasantly to each other. It seemed, under the grey glowering sky as if the summer had gone with the Fair, had packed its bags and left.

Horses were picking their way down the streets and occasionally riders would stop and chat. Amongst them was the magistrate, Roger Bartholomew, who Mary saw leaning down from his saddle and talking to some of the town constables. Enquiries about the murders, Mary guessed. It was all terribly odd. She must remind herself to ask Agnes what she thought about the fine strand of blue in the rope used to tie up the murder victims before death.

Then, happily, she saw William Loxley in his cart. The vast farmer appeared to have a matching vast wife, squeezed in next to him on the bench seat, with her cloak hood almost falling off her head. They were laughing about something together as they turned the cart onto the Stafford Road, both plump bodies swaying with the cart.

Mary then saw a sight that really affected her, as it made her heart race uncomfortably. She saw Gregory and James from Woodroffe's, on big cobs without saddle bags ,going from street to street, talking to people occasionally but not stopping for any errand that she could see. Then again, she accepted she couldn't see everywhere, just her bit of Uttoxeter. She found herself straining to see them, rather breathlessly, and then to her horror the horses turned down Agnes' street, and tying the horses outside, the two men came into the shop. Mary sprang through to Agnes, moving as quietly as possible, hoping she was still upstairs. She was, and Giles was downstairs.

Mary whispered urgently, 'Agnes, Agnes… quickly.'

Agnes frowned, and came though straight away, also whispering. 'What is it? What have you seen? Your face is the colour of new milk.'

Mary was holding her hand against her chest to quieten her racing heart. 'Gregory Rich from Woodroffe's, and the servant James. You know, I told you about Margaret's horrible brother and the ghastly James. They are downstairs.'

Agnes caught Mary's hand and they went to the tiny window looking down into the shop. Giles was talking to them, and they were able to hear every word.

Agnes caught Mary's hand and they went to the tiny window looking down into the shop. Giles was talking to them, and they were able to hear every word.

The two men were looking around and slightly beyond Giles, but there was nothing to see, as the door into the private part of the house was closed. Giles was leaning attentively on the counter. The conversation was part-way through when Agnes and Mary were able to listen in. It was slightly muffled, but clear enough.

'No,' Giles was saying, 'I haven't seen Mistress Mary Dudley for as long as I can remember. Why are you asking? Is she missing?'

Gregory was all bluster. 'No, not at all. My sister is a friend of hers and hasn't heard from her for a while, despite sending messages. As you are a local medical person, or someone is in this building,' he added insultingly, looking at Giles's youthful face which did not flicker, 'I wondered if you knew if she was ill. I care not for myself, but for my sister.'

Giles shook his head and smiled apologetically. James meanwhile was lifting up pots and looking at them, but as usual remained silent. Gregory looked irritated.

Giles decided to have his money's worth. 'So gentlemen, can I offer you any goods from the shop? Sweetmeats? Spices?'

Gregory took up a small bar of Castile soap and sniffing it, paid for it and left without another word. James, following him, hesitated in the doorway and looked round again as if they were being tricked, and Mary was going to pop up behind the counter. On the doorstep they met two women with baskets, who were offended as the men rudely barged past them. 'Manners!' one shrieked after the men.

Mary looked wild-eyed at Agnes. Meanwhile Giles had come upstairs to join them, having told the ladies he would return in a moment if they would care to look round. He knew very well what to do when anyone asked for Lady Mary, but he had thought it was odd they were going to so much trouble, especially since, as Mary had pointed out, Gregory treated his sister so badly, he wouldn't give a fig for helping her in their relationship.

'Thank you, Giles,' smiled Agnes. 'We saw it all, and you were quite right to alert us.' Giles nodded, and set off back down the stairs.

'Be calm, Mary,' Agnes caught her hand. 'You may be reading too much into this visit, you may not. You are perfectly well hidden here, and safe, so relax. Later this evening I will send a note with Giles to the Hall for John Ince and Thomas Ashbourne, to inform them. Put it out of your mind for now. You are doing so well, don't let those two put you off course.'

Chapter 31

After the shock of seeing Gregory and James, Mary recovered quickly and got on with watching the customers to the shop. This engaged her for a couple of days, despite her original misgivings. Sometimes Agnes was nearby but if a woman wanted to speak to her privately, rather than Giles, then down she went and Giles busied himself out the back.

One day, a giant of a man with a huge waistline and voice to match and a large purple-veined nose came into the premises. He was dressed in green and wearing a giant jerkin and a thick brown belt, with a pewter tankard, a spoon and a fat purse dangling from it. He didn't mind who heard him. 'I'm a widower, tha knows,' he told Giles with his booming voice, 'and I 'ave me a fancy for the baker's widow. She is a comely wench, and our silver together would make a grand statement in this town.'

Giles listened politely to the man, who, Alice whispered, was a farmer with two butcher's shops. Giles winced, as the man bellowed, 'So, I want a fine smelling thing to draw her to me, and a pot of something she might like as a gift. What more could a woman want, young man?', he askedc onfidently.

Giles did not comment, but just produced some perfumed creams and oils, which pleased the man, who paid up without complaint and left, whistling loudly. Mary thought this entertaining as did Agnes, who sat by Mary watching, but little did she know it would soon get even more entertaining, as Agnes flashed upstairs about an hour later. 'Watch below, Mary' she hissed. In the shop was a neat, slim, well-dressed woman, with a pretty face. Her linen was fresh and her cloak of good quality rust-coloured wool, with the hood lined in blue. Calm and confident, she asked to speak to Agnes privately and Giles withdrew to fetch her. Agnes was already on her way downstairs from Mary's side, and appeared in the shop, asking modestly how she might help.

Mary decided she didn't want to miss this enquiry.

'Mistress Agnes Picard, you are a woman of the world. I am Mistress Baker.'

It was a common practice to name a person to their trade and this was the baker's widow the purple-faced butcher was after. The woman looked around to see if anyone was about, before clearing her throat discreetly.

'I have… what might be called a hankering,' - she hesitated, then it came out in a rush, - 'For my young work-hand, and wish him to have a hankering for me.'

The woman was fidgeting with a hip purse, showing subconsciously that she wanted to pay and get out of the shop with all speed. Mary was learning, she told herself, to spot the signs of inner feelings, as they can be given away in the smallest of movements. The woman then looked back to where her horse was tethered.

Mary went quietly over to the secret window in the shutter, and saw that there were in fact two horses tethered outside and being soothed by a striking young man who had a head of golden curls and honey-coloured skin. He was dressed finely in dark blue leather, edged with red. It was certainly not the dress of a servant, but that of the kept lover of a rich older woman.

Mary was fascinated by this intrigue, and the young man was as about as far away in looks as one could be from Master Purple Nose. The butcher would have to interest himself in another chop, for this lady was taken, and Mary didn't blame her. Money was not everything and Mary understood the baker's widow had enough to sustain her and her love. A small bottle exchanged hands in the shop, and Mary heard the door of the shop close, and saw the woman approach the young man with a smile on her lips.

Despite the romance Mary could not help being caught up in the farce that she was seeing, as the woman in the shop had secured a potion for her beauty, and the butcher had no idea that his gift would be wasted.

Agnes rushed upstairs to laugh with Mary, knowing how entertained she would be. 'Don't tell me,' said Mary, catching Agnes's arm, 'That he will be in later seeking a gift for another young lover. I couldn't take the tension.'

Agnes enjoyed the joke, but blowing out her cheeks said, 'Not he. He has more sense, that one, and years of joy and security for them both lie ahead – and I mean lie!'

'Would you not be fearful, Agnes, that some might say that the potion you just sold the baker's widow might smack of … magic?'

'You mean witchcraft, Lady Mary, but I like your tact,' laughed Agnes. 'No, I sold her a bottle of spiced wine, heavily sugared, that will give them both a lift, although I suspect he doesn't need help in that department. The potion will work because they think it will work. If I had sold someone a potion to murder, or wrote them a hex to curse, then I would rightly hang for doing damage against God's will, and the law of this land.'

Agnes was not slightly annoyed that Mary had posed such a question, for she understood why she had asked it and it was reasonable to ask. Agnes really was a wise old bird.

The two windows continued to engage Mary, and she did indeed learn a great deal about human nature in a way she couldn't have learned in any other way, or with such speed. One day she saw that while Giles was making up an extensive order for a well-dressed woman accompanied by a man-servant, the woman quietly slipped an expensive soap into her basket, glaring at the servant not to say anything.

However, when she went to tell Agnes urgently what had happened, Agnes told her calmly that the woman was Mistress Parnham, a regular customer. Apparently she stole something every time she entered the shop, and every time the cost of what she had taken was simply added to her next bill without comment, and without her noticing, so it balanced out without the need to make a fuss.

On another occasion, a woman came to the shop seeking a cure for the fact that her moon courses would not come. Agnes asked carefully if the woman could be carrying a a child, as it was forbidden by law to give her anything to bring on her flowers if so, but the woman said sharply that she would know if that was the case, as she had nine children already. Agnes nodded and gave the woman a mixture of mugwort and pennyroyal, with stern advice that the woman should not be impatient and not under any circumstances take too much. The woman nodded, snatching at the bottle, and produced some coins. Agnes had closed the woman's hands around the coins, saying softly 'Keep this money, but keep my orders in your heart and come and see me in a few days if all is not well.' The woman looked astonished at this kindness and mumbled thanks, then was gone. Agnes carried on leaning on the counter, deep in thought as the door closed behind her, but then clearly remembered Mary might be watching and looked up expressionless, before tidying the counter.

Mary saw the woman again three days later, in the street outside the shop, looking cheerful and well with her brood gathered around her like ducklings. She came to the shop window and, tapping on it, nodded to Agnes, who waved at her. That was that. Another drama, another healing, another intensely feminine sharing.

The time Mary spent watching the apothecaries helped her to understand why assessing the patient, and not just depending on their word, was so important. Day after day, Agnes and Giles were busy boiling up potions, or making herbal pastes on a cold slab. Agnes rarely looked at a book but made her receipts up from memory, and could subtly change the formula, dependent on any one patient's needs.

The drawers and cupboards were full of packets or covered bowls of ingredients, and Mary realised that there were hundreds of different receipts and ingredients, and felt that she could never learn them all.

When she mentioned this to Agnes, she simply replied that it came with years of working with the ingredients, and was a matter of learning how to use the whole of God's creation for its healing purposes, whether the ingredients were familiar or exotic. She mentioned that she used many imported goods, and had to learn how they would react with English bodies. One of these was the plant called rhubarb, which she and others were trying to grow in England to meet demand. It relieved stoppage of the bowel, but the challenge was to avoid an excessive dose, which might then cause the opposite problem, requiring another treatment in turn.

Other receipts used familiar things, but in unfamiliar ways. Somewhat to Mary's distaste, Agnes told her that one receipt involved seething a live male fox in six gallons of olive oil, and once the fox was dead, gradually removing its remains, while slowly reducing the mixture down to an ointment, mixed with spices. Fox oil was used for rheumatics and any other type of painful joints. It worked on the principle that heat was good for joints, and the fox represented heat because of its fiery colour and hot-blooded instincts, while males, as with humans, were thought to be naturally hotter than females.

These properties were captured by dropping the fox in the boiling oil, and the sense of heat increased still further by the use of a brass pot, a hot fire without smoke, and hot spices. This combination of heats helped to counter the effects of the damp which often led to the joint problems in the first place.

It all sounded logical in a way, but it was surprising that inanimate objects such as the type of pots used made any difference. Mary also knew animals were used in medicine such as bear and lion fat, and cobwebs for some wounds, but she was still rather disconcerted by the poor fox's death. It sounded appalling. Seeking to change the subject, Mary commented that such a large amount of oil must be expensive, but Agnes replied drily that it balanced out, because she could get the foxes for free.

The brilliance of Agnes meant that her medicines and mixtures seemed to take on a life of their own as they were often able to transform men, women and children.

Some patients were lost, but not many during Mary's time there, and there were even receipts for the dying, to ease pain with sweetened poppy syrup, as well as perfumed balms to rub their hands as they waited for the collecting angel. Mary, as her own health was restored in this apothecary shop, had also started her journey as an apprentice apothecary, and more than ever wished to carry on and learn to cure others.

The days turned into weeks, although it felt like a lot longer to Mary. During that time Mary was able to eat heartily, rest well and felt both her confidence and her sense of humour return. The two murders played on her mind though, as she understood from Agnes and Giles that there was still considerable agitation in the area about those tragic deaths. The magistrate had not stopped asking questions, if anything stepping up his enquiries, and searches were still under way.

About four days after the St. Giles' Fair, there was great consternation when a dead body was found near Uttoxeter in a ditch, battered and bruised. It was not, however, in any way linked to the previous murders, according to Agnes, who was called in to examine the body. There were no similarities, no caved-in head or rope with blue threads to bind the victim. The death was instead linked to ale - a lot of ale, and a lost card game and an empty purse. There had been a noisy fight over all these matters in a local inn the night before, but no-one had dreamed the local drunk was so badly injured he would end up dead in a ditch. Four were arrested, some whipped publicly, but none would hang.

Mary, on hearing this news, had watched two cats fighting in the street, yowling enough to wake the devil, and wondered if slinky black Hope was being well looked after at the Hall while she was away. Mary would be glad to feel the cat curled up against her feet in bed again. Time to be away, she told herself, as she had been far too long from home and now she was in fine fettle, as Anne would say.

It was time to return to Somersal, she felt, so she told Agnes, who agreed. Mary sent a note to Ashbourne and Ince, carried by the ever-useful Giles, who set off at a pace that evening. She had asked in the note if she could be collected the following evening.

'I shall miss you my dear,' said Agnes taking her hand, 'But I know my job is done for now with you, and it is time for you to take your place in the world, stronger and brighter than ever before.'

'And better educated about people!' joked Mary, with shining eyes that also told of tears near the surface. I am sure we shall stay friends for ever, Agnes,' she added sincerely. 'I have so much to learn about medicine still, to come anywhere near your standard. I want to come back here again and again – if you will have me!'

Agnes most certainly would, she told Mary warmly, still holding her hand, but for now a chapter in both their lives had come to the end.

Chapter 32

John Ince, in his black gown and cap, was looking out over the beautiful gardens at the Hall in the evening light. the leaves were licked with orange and yellow flame on the trees and hedges. Mary stood by him quietly, also looking at the long pale streak on the horizon. She had arrived home only that day from the apothecary shop, which now felt a bit like a dreamy interlude in her life. They had spent a good hour talking solidly about the risks to Mary. Access to her person was, according to him, too easy, and something was going to be done about it. John Ince had something up his black sleeve, Mary could tell, as she looked at him waiting for what he was going to say next.

'I have pulled into service two of my most trusted agents from London. I arranged all this while you were staying with Agnes Picard.'

'Are they good?' asked Mary, who did not want to show how relieved she was at this news, as deep down she felt she could not stand it if attacks on her started again, and might take a different form, so no one would necessarily know what to look out for. Somehow, whoever was doing this would get at her now she was back at the Hall. She had considered moving to London again, but that journey might not be safe, and even with outriders she would be too exposed on the roads and in the inns on the way.

Ince looked down at her with arms folded. 'Oh yes,' he said. 'These two are the best I have ever met: nothing gets past them, and I trust them utterly not to speak a word of what is happening here, and that is crucial. Messengers back and forth have suggested they would arrive today or tomorrow. Ideally, I would have preferred the day before you came back home, but I know the journey will be long for them.'

'Why? Are they coming from far shores? Two weeks is a long time.'

He shook his head. 'You will see why, when they arrive. Just hold your peace, mistress, if you can.'

He looked sideways at her. She ignored that snipe. Then she tried again for more information, quite liking the fact that it might irritate him.

'What are their names, can you tell me that at least? What is all this secrecy about, as I will soon meet them anyway?' Ince did not respond. He just kept staring ahead, but there was a little twitch at the corner of his mouth. Yes, thought Mary, he is stifling a smile. She could hardly believe it. Then he answered her.

'Clench and Holdfast,' he said solemnly, without a further flicker of amusement. He was apparently speaking the truth.

Mary winced. 'Well I am glad they will be on my side with names like that!' she retorted, before turning on her heels and heading back to her room to write a letter to her father.

She trotted up the stairs with a lightness in her step. She was now often wary about using her father's study, which was a shame, as she had loved that room. The memory of that dark shape in the corner, and the abject terror she had felt that night, made her avoid it now, especially if she was on her own, even in the day. She told herself that part of her recovery should be gradually getting into the habit of going back to the study, even for a few minutes at a time, and then stretching the visit.

An hour later, she heard what sounded like a great cart rumbling into the yard in the last of the evening light. There were voices too and, unexpectedly, laughter for some reason. Ince's and Ashbourne's voices were clear, booming away, as were both Loxleys, despite usually being quiet souls. She could not make out what was being said, though.

She hurried downstairs, gathering her skirts, and out of the main door, and then across the circle of lawn, and dipped through the little door set in the gate to the horse yard - and there was an astonishing sight.

A massive flat-backed cart with vast wheels was being unloaded and a messenger with strapped leather bag was alongside the cart on his black cob. On the back of the cart was a huge barred iron cage about eight feet high by six wide.

Mary gasped at the sight, for the cargo in the cage was quite a shock. Inside, hunched ready to jump down, were two giant English mastiffs, fawn in colour and black of face. The cage was piled with cleanish hay, and Mary could see bones and water in bowls for these esteemed passengers. Meanwhile, the two dogs showed their impatience, and were roaring and snarling like Cerberus at the gateway to Hell.

The men in the yard all turned at the sight of Mary, with laughter in their eyes. John Ince held out an arm, which was unusually dramatic for him.

'Behold, Mistress Mary, two of my finest agents: Clench and Holdfast.' At the sound of their names from their beloved master they howled, bringing out other servants from the kitchens with hands on hips, or peering round doors nervously, while the Hall terriers barked nervously from the safety of the barn.

John Ince signalled for the cage gate to be opened. With some understandable trepidation, young Loxley did so, and the dogs bounded down rushing towards Ince at speed. He did not move, but held up a hand as they approached, and like tame lambs they sat down in front of him, watching his face with absolute concentration.

'Mistress Mary, don't be frightened, please. Do come here, as I have to make some introductions, to ensure key people are safe from these agents.'

Mary, trusting him, came forward and stood beside him. John Ince lifted his finger and said 'Friend… seek.' They looked at Mary, and Ince took her wrist and let the dogs smell her hand.' Forgive the familiarity, Lady Mary, but this is necessary.' She nodded dumbly.

The dogs looked away from her and back to him. He then followed the same pattern with Ashbourne, who had looked terribly anxious when Mary had put out her hand.

Both Loxleys were also formally introduced. 'What about the other staff?' Mary nodded at the staff, gathered about but at what they hoped was a safe distance.

'No,' said Ince simply. 'They will learn to stay in their rooms at night, and only in the house in the daytime. I will tell these dogs precisely what I want them to do, and they will do it.'

Mary said teasingly, 'Some might call you a magician.'

He raised one eyebrow at her. 'And some might be wrong. Although I must say that Dr John Dee at the court of her Majesty is not hard done by with the same title.'

Mary had actually seen the famous magician Dr Dee once, when she was about ten. He had been all in black and bearded, with hair topped with a scholar's cap like John Ince. Dr Dee, it was said, picked all the auspicious dates for the queen, by examining a great chart in a gloomy chamber deep in Whitehall Palace.

That thought gave her nightmares for a couple of weeks.

'No,' said Ince. 'There is no magic in mercy.' He went on to explain that he had rescued the two magnificent animals from a bear-baiting ring one autumn, not far from where the old Savoy Palace had been. Like many others, including Mary, he found baiting innocent animals repugnant.

'They were in a terrible state, covered in great bleeding wounds, and the bear screaming. So I stepped in and risked being mobbed by an angry crowd, because bets were placed. In the event, the bets were moved to the next bait and I bought both dogs and trained them to be the best agents in London.' He added, 'As you will see.'

Mary put a hand of approval on his arm and looked up into his face with a smile. He looked down at her and then, to Mary's astonishment he too smiled, very briefly, but it was definitely a smile.

Meanwhile, Ashbourne and the Loxleys were chatting enthusiastically about the new Somersal guards. Phrases like 'I'd like to see someone try and get in here now!' drifted across from them on a light wind which had struck up, rustling the leaves above.

They all watched both dogs sniffing around and slobbering water out of the horse trough. Mary gathered that the dogs had run about eight miles a day alongside the cart on the journey from London, but would bark loudly when they wanted a ride in the cage. It was, she decided, probably a lot more comfortable in that hay than the rattling front bench for the driver and assistant. The younger man who had travelled with the dogs, Mary would discover, worked for John Ince and would help care for the mastiffs when at Somersal.

Mary called to Edward Loxley, 'Could you find this man a place to stay please, and the driver? They will not be going back to London without the dogs.'

'Aye, I will, mistress.' He touched his forelock, and gestured for the two men to follow. They raised their hats and gave a small bow of gratitude before following Loxley.

'Now, there is more work to be done with them,' John Ince said to Mary, who had been enjoying all the excitement, and was quietly pleased to learn of Ince's compassion for animals. The servants, who had been enjoying themselves hugely, muttered sulkily as Ashbourne shooed them back indoors to their duties.

Ince called the dogs by name and they came to him immediately, sitting again obediently. He didn't even have to speak very loudly as they were so acutely aware of their surroundings and his commands. They owed him their life, and acted as if they knew it. He raised a finger, and the dogs listened intently. 'Search!' he commanded, and pointed to the Hall.

The dogs bounded away, sniffing around the building. On they went round the Hall to her father's study windows. Suddenly one of the dogs bayed, and Ince signalled with his hand for Mary to stay, as he headed off at a run to join the dogs. She had never seen him run before and was surprised to see he was a fast and athletic runner. Mary saw him stop, move some herbage and then pick something up, with the dogs sitting to mark they had found something.

He showed it to both dogs and said something she couldn't quite hear, but it was enough to put them into a barking frenzy. After this he put whatever he had found carefully in his leather bag, almost always held across his body and lying on his hip. Then he and the dogs set off round the corner of the Hall. Mary could hear him giving further commands as he ran with them to the borders of the Hall.

On he ran, along the long avenue of trees by the churchyard that had high, disused gates at the far end. Again he dipped into his bag, again the dogs roared. All this was repeated at every boundary, every gate, every ground floor window and every door. Mary trotted round to see what was happening at the kitchen door, where he stopped, and called out Eleanor the cook to join him in the garden. He then formally introduced her to the dogs.

She looked as if she really didn't want to be introduced to Clench and Holdfast, but they looked delighted with her – Cook, as one might expect, smelt of delicious food. Mary was amused to see her backing off from the two drooling mastiffs.

‘So, Dr Ince,’ said Mary formally, as she met him on the way back to join her. ‘You have included Cook in the honour of meeting your agents.'

‘I have reason to trust her,’ was his reply.

He had also offered to introduce Anne to the dogs.

‘What is in the bag please?' asked Mary, as she walked alongside him. ‘A key,’ he said simply. ‘In fact,’ he added, 'the key to almost everything.’ He ended off her request to see it by adding, ‘You will see it in time. Please be patient.’

He then bent down and gave both dogs a really good scratch in appreciation of their skills. They clearly adored him. Mary was not going to insist he show her the key, because if he had wanted to, he would have done so.

She felt piqued by this but felt in such good spirits with the arrival of the dogs, the feeling soon passed.

That night, when Mary went to bed, she decided to get up and have a look out in the garden, where a light fog was sitting eerily on the lawns, shifting like ghosts. The moon was quite bright as the fog was low. She watched as the dogs wove backwards and forwards across the grounds, sometimes together and sometimes one alone for a while before the brother hove into view. The Hall dogs were as silent as if foxes were about, and Mary felt that if she were one of the Hall dogs, she would be quiet, with these two abroad.

Just as dawn approached, she got up again, as she was once more sleeping lightly now she was no longer with Agnes and her spirit was on guard. Again the dogs were on the move. It seemed they did not sleep the night through, and she felt a rush of gratitude to those monsters.

This became the routine of life at the Hall at night as he great guardians patrolled. One night, after a couple of weeks, she thought she could see a figure in the field which jumped into the garden. The dogs must have seen it too, for they bounded furiously across the grass towards the figure and it disappeared again.

'Could be anyone,' Mary told herself. 'It doesn't have to be someone after me.' Using good sense to calm herself worked only moderately well, for she was unnerved by the sight of any unidentified figure in the grounds.

Interestingly, John Ince came out with a lantern at that moment. Although the dogs had only barked once, it was enough, it seemed, to rouse Ince from his bed.

Mary then fell into a deep sleep, and continued to sleep deeply in her own bed, safe and sound with Hope curled up upon her feet or stretched out like a long sausage along her arm, holding on with her paws.

There were some amusing moments with Clench and Holdfast over the following weeks as, although they were on watch day and night, they could rest a little in the day, and one of them (Mary never could tell the difference between them had taken a fancy to Cook. Mary would often come upon them, with Cook twisting off the ends of beans and constantly talking to the dog next to her, as his face was level with hers when he was sitting down and he was usually drooling. It was comedy fit for the finest playwright, as the dog seemed to be listening to every word, and now and again would put his head to one side as she reinforced some point by wagging her finger. Mary even took to hiding behind an arbour to watch, even when it was a little cold, for it was worth it and she would giggle into her cloak collar.

There was also a slightly unpleasant side-effect to having the dogs nearby, as they were given not only water, but small beer from the brewing shed. Every now and again the dog would give a monumental beer-scented belch straight in the face of Cook, who would take out her waist cloth and flap it, shouting abuse at him. He would just look up at her with melting love, drooling with pleasure. Then she would settle down again and carry on doing whatever she was doing in her lap. Now and again, she would even pat him on the head, and was that a small kiss when no one was watching? Yes, it was.

'Oh, yes, I have the measure of you, Cook,' laughed Mary quietly to herself from her hiding place. She was particularly happy because she could see that Cook was over her constant desire for that highly addictive drink that Alice Goodrich had brewed. Everyone, it seemed was recovering.

All Mary needed now was answers.

Chapter 34

One unseasonally cold afternoon at Somersal Hall, the world could see Mary Dudley on a frantic mission, and that mission was to catch the Dark Boy, who had reappeared.

She had just seen him on the main stairs, and indeed smelt his unwashed body. That is what had convinced her in the middle of it all that he was real: he stank to high Heaven, and she had noticed that, even at a distance both previously and now.

Heart racing, Mary tore around the side of the house, looking feverishly left and right. That figure was definitely real flesh and blood, and the yowl of fury from Hope as he trod on her had proved it! Mary had always in her heart known the figure she now called the Dark Boy was real, and here was her chance to prove it. Vindication, at long last.

He had darted in front of her from the shadows and was almost within her grasp in the upstairs hall, but he had swerved aside and darted away.

After the initial shock, a growing rage gave her great strength. She had frozen for a moment, heart racing and feeling violently sick, but that passed almost immediately. He had darted in front of her from the shadows and was almost within her grasp in the upstairs hall, but he had swerved aside and darted away. After the initial shock, a growing rage gave her great strength. She had frozen for a moment, heart racing and feeling violently sick, but that passed almost immediately. Skirts hoisted, she headed at speed down the stairs. She looked around in the hall and on through the main door and outside into the chilly air. Looking around, she ran to the left, hoping it was in the right direction, past the bare branches of the sleeping rose gardens before coming to a sharp breathless halt.

There, sitting on a wall, was the cheeky stable boy, Charlie. The cold didn't seem to bother him as he sat in a cloud of frozen breath, for he was in shirt sleeves and he had one leg cocked up on the low wall, with his breeches rolled up to the knee and a thick woollen stocking pooled round his ankle. Biting his bottom lip, he was intent on picking off a big scab from his knee. As Mary stopped by him, he didn't leap to his feet and pull a forelock, and didn't even bother to look up, as he was at a crucial point of being able to rip off the scab. 'I suppose you want me to stop doing this,' he said, still looking at the scab.

'Yes, I do,' snapped Mary. 'You are being disgusting, and I want to ask you something now so just stop and look at me. It's terribly urgent!'

'Is it to do with yon dark lad?' he asked slowly. Mary was absolutely rocked by this answer. No-one else had ever given a whisper that they had seen him. Maybe it was the first time for Charlie just now, as the figure ran past.

'Get up, Charlie!' she cried. 'Tell me, have you seen him just now? Where did he go?'

At this, Charlie ripped off the scab with a wince of triumph and having flicked it away in disgust, he pulled up his stocking and carefully pulled the breech leg down over the now bleeding wound. He stood up, hopping a bit as he straightened his leg, and looked Mary straight in the face. Charlie was not in a hurry.

'Course I have,' he said simply. 'On my patch. I don't like people on my patch and I saw him back and forwards all hours until I got fed up of him, buggering about, climbing through windows, and creeping about like a loon.'

There was no sign of the Dark Boy now as he had melted away, probably through the trees on the right of the Hall, thought Mary sadly, but at least she had this precious witness. Bending forward, she caught hold of Charlie's shoulder and shook him gently. 'Why didn't you tell someone he was here when you saw him? It was cruel, Charlie, not to tell someone like the Loxleys. You know I and others at one time thought I was ill, and had lost my wits, as no one else has seen him here.'

'No point,' he protested, with his bottom lip sticking out. 'Who's going to listen to a stable lad?' Those bright dark eyes with such a steady stare were right of course. He was teased quite a bit, Mary remembered. The other servants had once sent the boy to Loxley in the stables, to ask him for a long weight. Loxley had him sit down for an hour and then told the boy, 'You have waited long enough now!', and the lad had slunk off to the sound of laughter.

It was a kind of bullying but apprentices expected such treatment, and they would do it to others in time as they rose up the servant ladder. These can be the invisible people who move in and out of the lives of those in the great house but are hardly seen, hardly there. He would probably have been accused of trying to draw attention to himself if he had said he had seen the Dark Boy - no one would have believed him: he was right, Mary thought.

'Anyway,' he added cheekily with a broad grin, 'You ain't mazed, and you ain't dreaming. I've got him in the store shed by the brook.' Mary didn't know whether to laugh or cry. There was this lad, with the life philosophy and quick-wittedness of a grown man.

'No, really Charlie? Tell me the truth. He is over there in the shed – really?' Charlie puffed out his chest. 'I just netted him from up that low branch.' He pointed to an evergreen by the shed. 'You'll see, I've got the bugger!'

Mary caught Charlie's shoulder again, as he led her towards the shed. She hoped this wasn't some dreadful prank, and feared that no-one would be in the shed, but she couldn't miss the sight of Charlie's little chest, puffed out like a pigeon in the mating season. She was also anxious that the boy of shadows might have found a way to escape, but for all Charlie's pretending not to be in a rush and busy with his leg, Mary felt sure he was keeping one eye on the shed until he was able to reveal his captive in triumph.

He waved her on as he might a kitchen maid, and she walking quickly alongside him as if he were master. 'That's how I got that cracking scab on me knee,' he said proudly. 'Chasing 'im one night last week, and I nearly caught 'im, but I fell down and scraped me leg, but now I've got 'im.' He nodded hard with a jutted chin. 'Got him good!'

Across the lawns near the grove walked both Loxleys, Edward and Will in animated conversation, tools over shoulders. Mary called out sharply, and the men started, seeing her for the first time, as they had been so engrossed. She beckoned them across urgently, so they dropped their tools and ran towards them at great speed, skimming across the cold grass. They were surprised that the young mistress was with Charlie, but asked no questions.

Charlie led the way proudly to the small stone and wooden building, grown over with ivy which he then pulled back like a green curtain. He lifted the wooden bar and victoriously threw open the door.

The three adults bent down in the low doorway and peered inside, and their eyes gradually became accustomed to the darkness, smelling of hemp and earth.

There in the far left corner was a dark shape, a shape that Mary had once dreaded, but although her mouth was dry and her heart thumped violently, she was notbacking down now. There was a small glint - the whites of his eyes - and he was glaring insolently at Mary.

'Well I never!' whispered Edward Loxley, shaking his head. 'You were right, mistress - this nasty piece of work breathes.' His voice was growing fiercer with temper by the second.

'Aye, it's him, all right,' interposed Charlie, not wishing to be back of the queue for attention now the Loxleys had arrived. 'He's a reet nuisance too, dancing about like a fool and running about in the dark, so I got him. It took a bit, but I got him.' Edward Loxley clumped Charlie on the back. 'Proud of you, ma boy – this'll not be forgotten for many a long year.' Charlie preened, and smiled broadly at the prospect of being the hero of the hour.

The younger Loxley went in and grabbed the boy roughly round the back of the neck and by the arm. 'All right,' the Dark Boy hissed. 'No need to break my bloody neck,' as he was hauled reluctantly into the daylight. 'No,' said young Loxley, 'I'll let another with the hangman's noose do that job.'

As for Mary, the moment she heard the boy speak, the spell was properly broken. He was just a slit-eyed boy of about fourteen, with a knowing look on his face. He was dressed in a strange, tight-fitting, black garment, with a black hood over his head, with folds near the forehead. The sleeves were turned back at the wrist, and again were in folds. He could not move easily, as he was wrapped about with the bird net that Charlie had dropped over him from the tree, before bundling him into his temporary prison. This bird from Hell could no longer fly.

The boy spat at Charlie as he was dragged past. Charlie managed to dodge the spittle, cheerfully crying out

‘Missed!’ That earned the boy a hard thump in the ear from Loxley, which made the lobe bleed, and the boy gasped with the pain. Mary felt no sympathy as he winced up at her sullenly.

‘Why?’ she raged at him. ‘Just tell me why?’ He just sneered at her, as Loxley held the back of his neck in a tight grip, but she was no longer frightened of him and he could see it, and it was no longer a thrill to see the fear in this young woman’s face. He would never again have a chance to see her blind panic, and the power he had enjoyed over her was broken. Now the tables had turned, and he had reason to be frightened of her and the young stable lad at her side who had hunted him down and caught him, without Mary or anyone else even having known he had been trying to catch himfor weeks. The hunter had become the hunted, and now captive.

Will Loxley thumped him again, this time in the guts, and he doubled over in pain.

‘Well done, Charlie,’ Mary said. ‘I am so grateful to you, and you shall be rewarded.’ Charlie puffed out his skinny chest again. Mary turned to the men, giving a firm instruction. ‘Bind him tight,’ she said grimly, 'and take him to Roger Bartholomew. I will give no mercy plea for him: he gave no mercy to me.’

All bravado left the boy as he realised that a hangman's noose was likely waiting for him. Will Loxley growled at him, and hauled him away in his ropes, accompanied by his father. The boy, desperate to escape, swore and struggled hopelessly.

'Don't you go feeling sorry for him, mistress,' said Charlie firmly. 'He would 'ave kept this up until he was stopped.'

'And you stopped him, Charlie. Wonderful, just wonderful.' She bent down and kissed his dirty cheek. He blushed furiously, scrubbing his cheek with his hand in disgust.

'Don't get too carried away,' he muttered, and then set off, hands deep in his pockets, knowing that his place as a hero was set in the household memory, and he would be able to tell the tale for decades of how he trapped and caught the Dark Boy. He would receive two silver shillings for his fine work that day.

Mary just had one thing to say, as a parting shot to Charlie. 'Charlie!' He looked round hopefully. 'Stop saying "bugger!"' She struggled to stop herself laughing, as he said 'Whatever you bloody say, mistress.' Then he strode away, whistling in the thin cold air, without a care in the world.

In the far distance, a small group piled into the open cart, the two Loxleys on the front seat, with the boy thrown into the back like a bundle of laundry. Mary was struck by the thought that he looked like a giant moth chrysalis as he was roped on the floor of the cart, heading for whatever the law would throw at him. That of course would depend upon what would be revealed over the next days. Was he the one poisoning her food? Was he working alone, or had some individual or group put him up to this cruel trickery, and if so, why? She knew that the catching of the Dark Boy was just the beginning of the end. Meanwhile, Ashbourne had emerged from the Hall to see what the noise was about, and after a brief explanation from Mary, swiftly ordered up his own horse. Asking Mary to give instructions for John Ince to follow him, he rode after the cart.

Chapter 35

Thomas Ashbourne returned to Somersal that evening. Mary was sitting in the great hall before a good fire, with leaping yellow and orange sparks dancing up the chimney. When the cart had set off that afternoon, she had felt victorious, and rightly so, but then needed to rest her body and clear her mind from its endless questions, so had sat with a sense of drowsy peace drifting over her in the past few hours. She turned her head towards the sound of the horse cantering in, and the muttered voices from the yard. Ashbourne's heavy, long leather boots came purposefully up the stone-flagged corridor to the great hall. At the sound of that familiar tread, she found that her mouth was dry as she stood to receive her steward with his news.

Mary waved away one of the maids who had come to attend, and instead fetched him a glass of wine herself from on top of the court cupboard, as much to give herself something to do as to care for him, as she had become very agitated at what he might tell her. She poured one for herself too, and made ready to hear Thomas, who discarded his cloak, gloves and hat, then shook himself like a dog to gather his wits before sitting opposite Mary.

This was a time not for courtly formality, but to get on with finding out what this boy had said under interrogation. Mary was aware it wouldn't have been pleasant. She said nothing to Ashbourne, but waited patiently for him to gather his thoughts. Now she was going to know the whole truth, she hoped, or at least part of it.

'Mistress Mary,' he said, gently looking straight at her. 'You have been much wronged, and many people, including me, must offer you apologies for not having believed you about the Dark Boy.' He looked down at his hands, embarrassed. 'What I mean by that is that I have known you since you were a little girl, and knew that lying was simply not part of your soul. You have been terribly frightened, and there was no reason on this earth for you to lie, as you were clearly distressed, and so it is was unforgivable that I did not believe you were seeing a real person.' He stumbled his words, flushing. 'I wondered... if you were ill.' He looked at her, then dropped his eyes, shaking his head, ashamed. 'Forgive me!'

Mary leaned forward towards him and smiled sweetly. 'Thomas Ashbourne,' she said, 'You have done no wrong, and neither have the others who doubted me, for I too believed I was sick or going mad. That is past.

Speak on, my friend, and tell me all you know. Let us have the truth of this boy and his motivation.'

Thomas told her all that had happened, that both he and Ince had arrived at Roger Bartholomew's grand house in nearby Doveridge at a canter, well before the cart, which they had passed on the way. They had found the magistrate and his guards in the house, by great good fortune. Bartholomew had received them immediately, and listened carefully to what had happened with concentrated brow, and resolved to address such criminality immediately. He had said to Ashbourne, 'Come then, for Lady Mary's sake let us have the truth of this boy. It sounds to me as though there is great wickedness here.' He had spoken with anger.

The cart had arrived at that point with its cargo, and the boy had been bundled into the magistrate's meeting room by his guards. It sounded as though the Somersal men had handed him over reluctantly but not without one of them giving the boy another sharp punch in the back, which had winded him, causing him to wheeze painfully.

'There was no need for that, Ashbourne,' complained Mary. 'He is the brutal one, with cruelty in his very veins, but I would rather one of our men had not been so uncivilised when the captive is just that – a captive!'

'I agree, mistress, but you should understand that there is fury in this place for your sake. First Alice Goodrich, then Warwick, and now this young rogue. The treachery rolls on and those loyal to you will lash out.'

'I understand that,' muttered Mary, for she also knew instinctively that the fury was also born out of guilt for not having believed her. At that point there were loud voices outside the Great Hall, and much stamping about.

'John Ince returns, I think,' said Mary wryly, as there was no denying he was an expert on making all aware of his presence, rather like the first time he arrived at Somersal, bellowing and throwing the trembling local midwife out of her chamber. She was used to him now. Ashbourne craned round in his chair as the door opened and both men nodded to each other. Ashbourne looked strained, and Ince looked irritated. He often did, thought Mary.

Instead of taking a chair, he perched, arms folded and ankles crossed, leaning on a window sill.

'Go on then, Ashbourne,' he ordered, waving his arm. 'Let's put Mistress Mary out of some of her misery, if not all.' Mary frowned – so there was a caveat to the explanation of what had happened at the magistrate's house.

Rather than start again for Ince's benefit, Ashbourne simply carried on where he had left off. The Dark Boy had stood sullenly before the magistrate Roger Bartholomew, not so much sorry for his deeds, as sorry to have been caught, according to Ashbourne.

'The ropes wound around his body were untied, with only those on the boy's wrists left tight. The magistrate, along with me and Dr Ince here, questioned him, with a secretary present to record what the boy said. He was sly, as you might expect, but watchful too.'

'Was he used to being in trouble then, do you think? He sounds in charge of his wits.'

'Yes, mistress,' agreed Ince. 'You could tell he had been bred to take part in a criminal life, and was not only used to being in trouble, but adept at squeezing out of it too.'

Thomas Ashbourne continued, 'At first he was reluctant to speak, and insolent when he did, but the punch in the stomach had made him think again about playing up too much. Doctor Ince, with permission from the magistrate,' - Mary looked at John Ince who just kept frowning while looking at Ashbourne - 'examined the boy's unusual clothes before questioning started. He discovered that the wrinkle of black cloth over the forehead meant the boy could could pull it down over his face, and look through the cloth, which was not so thick as to blind the wearer but allowed vision. All the boy could do was glare at Dr Ince, and even more so when he went round behind him and realised the wrist folds were so his hands could be covered. Both the hood and the hand covers could be pushed up and down really quickly, a clever design with a particular purpose. Upon his feet were soft leather ankle boots used by performing acrobats at festivals, and mummers. The dark clothing was made for the purpose of 'disappearing' in the dark.

Mary gasped, leaping to her feet, looking at the stretched-out figure on the window sill. 'I understand now, John. When one moment I saw him with his hand over his face, in the next moment he had apparently disappeared by pulling down the hood and sleeves, then slipping silently into shadows until I left the room, and then he could creep out and away.'

Ashbourne and Ince both nodded, and the latter added, 'Precisely. Simple as a concept, but effective and well-designed. He admitted that he only visited in daylight today because he had twice been scared off by the dogs at night.' Ince looked with the merest hint of sympathy at Mary, but she was elated by this news.

'Well, it makes sense, John,' she exclaimed. 'It makes sense. And don't you see how important that is for me?'

'Of course,' said Ince. 'You were right all along. It was not madness, it was not witchcraft, but it was poisoning, coupled with this boy as the physical aspect of this planned attack. There may be more physical aspects here at the Hall too, but we are working on that.' He looked pensive, and Ashbourne turned away from him, to listen to Mary's response.

'There is rhythm and planning in this.' She stopped briefly, looking at each man, both listening quietly. 'But by whom?' She had absolutely no idea who would plan such an arrangement, or indeed to what purpose. 'Ashbourne, John Ince, who is behind all this? What did he say when questioned?'

Ince got up from his narrow perch, and stood by the fireplace with his arm resting on the small stone ledge that was the mantel. He looked down into the fire for a moment before replying.

'I am afraid we are none the wiser, Lady Mary, for we are content that we have squeezed all from him that he knows. I am sure of that.' Mary didn't ask how, and didn't particularly want to know the methods of interrogation used. 'What we do know is the boy, named Elijah Jones, was part of a performing troupe working

working the area, and I do mean in the most immoral sense.' He frowned.

'Is it his real name?'

Ince raised a corner of his mouth. 'Who knows?

Mary cried out to thin air, 'A mummer and acrobat! Elijah Jones, why did you do this to me?' Ashbourne nodded, as if it was a fair enough question.

Mary burst out with frustration, 'That explains why he was able to move so silently, and knows how to shift into shadows using trickery, and the stealth and certain movements of a trained acrobat! But, why did he do it?' she asked again, somehow not accepting that they knew no more. 'You must know something, he must have said something, even the tiniest thing to give a hint.' She couldn't believe how fruitless this capture appeared to be.

'Usual reason.' Ince shrugged. 'Money. A lot of money, would you believe? We actually found a coin on him. Not just any coin.'

Mary held her breath, as she could tell a surprise lay ahead by the way Ashbourne was looking under his eyebrows at her. 'A half-angel!'

Mary could not believe her ears, as a gold half-angel was a significant sum, and never seen in the hands of ordinary people.

'Who paid him? Did he say?'

Ashbourne continued. 'That is much less clear, I am afraid, mistress. He claims a cloaked and hooded stranger approached him in a crowd when the mummers were performing in the marketplace in the summer, and told him if he kept his mouth shut and told no one, he could be richer than his wildest dreams for a small task or two, and he was given a silver sixpence for his silence until the next time they met. The boy had never held a silver sixpence before, he told us grudgingly, and that coin was all his, so it turned his head.'

Elijah Jones had admitted that he agreed, knowing it would be something illegal. Illegality was not a problem in the society of mummers and performers, for it was known that when they were in an area, there was a good chance that there would be a rush of burglaries and petty theft just before they left the area, and cleared off to another, unknown, destination. At Christmas, as many as five or six different groups would appear at a door, dressed in bright streaming rags with hobby horses and musicians and commonly, whilst the family and servants had gathered in the largest room of a house, and were entranced by their performance, young, lithe members of the group in black were stealing from other rooms with speed and alacrity.

They tended not to waste time with small houses, for obvious reasons, as they knew the pickings were almost non-existent. The boy was a perfect choice for the job of entering the Hall and terrifying Mary, making her weak and distressed about the balance of her mind, so that those who paid him could take advantage of the distraction. Agitated, Mary chewed at the side of her nail, tearing at the skin without realising she was doing it, before making a good point. 'Payment must have been after each break-in to the Hall, or else he would have disappeared if they paid him in advance.' She was working it through, trying to snatch at least some evidence from the wreckage of the interrogation.

John Ince cut in. 'Yes, he admitted that without problem, because he knew his answer would be vague. He just said it was someone in a hooded cloak, he thought it was a man, but it was a low whispering voice so difficult to tell. The person, his client effectively, left money in a bowl on top of a turnstile and stood way back from Elijah when he collected it. He admitted, however, that he thought the person who first approached him was not the person who paid him and gave instructions thereafter.'

'Why? What was it about the first and second that was different?'

Ashbourne replied, 'He just said the first was taller and stockier, and the second was quite short in height. Not exactly strong evidence about who might be behind it.' He sounded frustrated too. They all were.

'Elijah knew it was wrong,' Ashbourne added. 'The cocky little devil was enjoying not being able to tell us anything much, part of the fun as his last bit of power, and being the centre of attention. By the sound of things, the plot was all very anonymous and well-organised. A professional hand is behind this, perhaps more than one.

'And before you ask, Lady, we did ask him if he was asked to take anything from the Hall, and leave that in the turnstile bowl but he said not. He is a professional thief and liar, though, and he would continue to deny it.'

'Presumably he doesn't want his family, if he has one, to suffer too?'

Ince replied, 'The criminals on the edge of our society tend to see being caught as a professional hazard. However, it is likely to be true he probably is nervous that anything he might say could involve his circle in some way if they are involved. Too much of all this is supposition, as we grope around in the fog for answers.' Ince was vexed by the vagueness of it all, and tapped his foot in irritation, crossing his arms again, as if restraining himself from the desire to slam about. Mary suspected that in his own home, he did a lot of slamming about.

She was in that moment struck by how often his obviously brilliant mind was swamped with anger. He saw her looking at him, and flashed her a challenging look back as if he knew what she was thinking, then gave a small nod as if in apology.

A silence fell on them for a while as they thought through what they had just talked about. Just quiet thought, as if reason edged into the room and drove out frustration.

'Will he hang?' Mary broke the silence, but really in her heart she knew the answer to her question. Ince answered her in a now calm manner.

'Yes, almost certainly, Lady, for conspiracy and breaking in, and whether or not he administered the poison himself, he was clearly involved in some way. He is old enough and not a useful creature in this world, for he has the morals of an animal. I know as a physician that I have a duty to treat all as equal and indeed I would him, if he needed such treatment from me, and to the best of my ability without judgement. That is part of a physician's oath. I also know he would spend his life causing harm and trouble. It is a way of life for those such as him, and I have not so much time for miracles these days. I have seen too much.'

Mary attempted to sum matters up as she saw them, as no one else was doing it, or saying what needed to be said. She stood up, saying firmly, 'Meanwhile, whilst we debate his lack of morals, two individuals, or a group out there, have caused me great harm for some unknown reason and these two cloaked and hooded figures are involved. It strikes me as a plot from a cheap play, except this is not theatre and it nearly cost me my life. All three of us must now push harder to find out who and why, not just for me, but for my father's sake and almost certainly for the work he is engaged in.'

She went to one of the far windows, from which she saw what looked remarkably like the figure of the magistrate, Roger Bartholomew, leaving the grounds. She said nothing but stored it away for when things were more developed, in case it was relevant.

Chapter 36

'What moon, is it, Anne?' asked Mary, knowing very well what moon is was, for it had risen like a great bronze shield dropped by an ancient warrior in heaven.

'Time for Harvest Moon, of course, Lady Mary.'

'Tell me of it, Anne.'

' 'Tis a time for thanksgiving for the riches of food from the orchard, the fields and the butcher's block. A time to pay attention to the old rituals, so that there will continue to be great harvests and Heaven does not punish with famine. The moon watches over all of this.'

'Thank you, Anne' said Mary, with her chin cupped in her hands as she leaned on the small table in her room. She was content and loved to listen to Anne. This was especially precious now she was well again, for she took nothing for granted. The calendar was filled with colourful festivals and traditions at this time, as the icy breath of the winter gods was close. Wheat and barley dollies were carefully twisted into shape, with designs born from different family traditions. Hundreds of them could be seen hanging from door frames, windows, trees and in every nook and cranny of the church. When the very last clump was gathered from the field it was called 'necking', and it would be held up to great cheering and then, when decorated with ribbons, 'the neck' would be carried at the front of a parade of the harvest gatherers, with great scythes over their shoulders as the sun set. Then there would be singing and dancing in the landowners' barn until dawn. All safely gathered in, all feeling safe for another winter.

There was also the traditional harvest time tradition of 'clipping the church', where after the service the church congregation and some outsiders would come, join hands and dance round the building, moving in and out around its walls, touching the church with their toes on the inward movement. Those throwing themselves into the fun, both men and women, would wear head wreaths of leaves and berries, with ribbons tumbling down to their shoulders. It was great fun watching people trying not to fall over and some of the much older residents sat it out, cheering and calling out rude remarks. Mary had absolutely no idea how the tradition started, and she had asked about it from learned types in London, only to discover that quite a number of counties did this at harvest time, and even if its meaning was lost in the mists of forgotten years, it was still a much-loved tradition.

As she left the Hall, crossing with the household for the harvest service, she had Thomas Ashbourne on her right, and John Ince on her mind – why didn't he join them for services? She wondered whether he was a secret Catholic, or just on guard, for anyone knowing the family might know the house would be virtually empty at service time. She gave him the benefit of the doubt, and disliked the new suspicious nature she had developed, that made her question everyone's motives.

She turned her mind to more cheerful, safe things, for she had guessed what the morning would smell of and sure enough, the air did smell of wet leaves and wood-smoke, such a nostalgic smell of autumn and early winter, reminding her of every year of her life.

The noisy, chattering line of the Hall's household was soon joined by the villagers pouring through the lych gate, most of them nut-brown from their time in the fields. The church wardens and their helpers had evidently been busy for days, as the doorway and porch were elegantly wreathed in greenery, as well as a blaze of barley, wheat and flowers. There were gasps of appreciation and praise to the wardens and their helpers, who shook hands and nodded cheerfully.

That morning there were a lot more attending the service than usual, and no wonder, for it was well known that the Hall was thrown open every Harvest Festival morning to all worshippers. After the service, drinks would be served, with delicious things to eat, both savoury and sweet. Music and dancing were essential features too. With this in prospect, it was hardly surprising the tiny church was packed, with many standing right to the back, and crammed around the walls, peering round the garlanded pillars. It was a legal requirement to attend all Sunday services and great feasts, but there was more than one service and indeed church to attend. On this day all could come to Somersal from the surrounding area, and did so knowing they would be treated like grand visitors at 'the 'all'. The congregation called out greetings and best wishes to the new arrivals, as the service had not started yet. The youngsters were nudging and elbowing each other, hardly able to contain their excitement. The altar steps were also heavily decorated with a cascade of autumn's riches as well as wheaten loaves, bottles and jars of preserves, given up to be blessed and then given to the poor. The candles were bright and so were everyone's spirits.

Thomas Ashbourne and some of the servants joined Mary in the carved box pew as the household had done for over one hundred and fifty years. There was a definite pecking order as to who could come into the family pew, and woe betide any servant who tried to push in. All around them in the tiny church, the rest of the congregation were standing, while the narrow ledges of stone on the windowsills were all taken by the elderly or infirm, where they could perch like little birds. Many of them had sensibly brought cushions with them.

'Or they'll get piles,' Anne had announced loudly, when Mary asked some years ago about the cushions. 'All that sitting on cold stone – it draws you, you-know?' Mary did indeed know, as apparently did most of the rest of the congregation, who had been listening intently to everything said. Mary remembered blushing furiously, and the more she was aware of it, the more her face burned. Those days of blushing were not over for her, but were a lot less frequent.

The floor of the church had been sweetened with fresh rushes and strewing herbs for the festivities. Just as well, for in autumn and winter, the rush floor could be a stinking affair, with an eye-watering smell of urine, as animals were sometimes driven into the church for warmth and protection from wild beasts. Mary looked up at the ceiling, thinking that the wolves that surrounded her now were human, and a lot more dangerous, in that it was not always easy to see them clearly.

The priest arrived at last, a little late and beaming all over his round, red, shining face. He was an obviously enthusiastic trencherman and the Somersal family privately felt that if he stumbled and fell at any time, he would remain unhurt, as he would roll – gently. His pink hands were clasped before him holding his green and gold stole together as he came down the nave and made his way to the chancel. Down past the ancient christening font, which some said was there when the Vikings came. They had not smashed it up for the angels had made it invisible. It had been a miracle!

Father said it was more likely to have been left because it was not made of gold or silver, and therefore not of interest to the marauders

Mary had been christened in that font, and so had every member of father's side of the family for as long as anyone could remember. For a christening, warm water was poured in on a cold day, and daisies and moss from the brook arranged around the top of the font so it looked like the river Jordan. Mary doubted if anyone knew what the edge of the Jordan looked like, except for her ancestors who had gone on the Crusades to the Holy Land. Sometimes Father would get a little fed up with all the old wives' tales and make up his own. 'Noah filled that font,' he would say seriously. 'After the great flood had withdrawn, he kept some of the flood waters in a leather bucket, like the one in the stable, and that font miraculously has never had to be filled again.'

Mary, aged eight, had looked at him amazed, then frowned. 'That's not true, is it Father?' 'No,' he agreed. 'That is a load of rubbish, along with fairies and ghosts, so don't you forget it next time you are falling for that nonsense by the kitchen fire.' Father had told her not so long ago that her face had been full of wonder when listening to his tales, and how much he missed his little girl. Mary pointed out that his ittle girl was a big girl now, but she was definitely still his.

She blinked and pulled herself back to the present time, as the choir of little boys in white passed by, singing a glorious anthem of thanksgiving. The chief altar boy was proudly swinging the best silver thurible, used for high days and holidays. The clink of the long chains, and the lid rising and falling a little as it was swinging, announced the arrival of the procession whilst a waft of perfumed smoke was so thick drifting up before him that the priest could hardly be seen for a moment. His thin white hair stood up at the back like a bird's tail, revealing he had clearly been dozing off, no doubt leaning back comfortably on a bolster after a good breakfast, and rushed from his house upon waking in a startled state, so as not to be late.

At the altar steps the boy accidently tipped the thurible, and a few red, glowing chunks of charcoal fell out onto the fine rug stretched in the sacred place. This caused much consternation as the carpet was usually proudly hung over a great oak chest, and was allowed to be on the floor only for such occasions. The Dudley family had given the church the blue and black carpet which was considered a rare treasure. The priest and altar boy hopped about vigorously, to the delight of all who watched, open-mouthed. Eventually the hopping pair did actually manage to kick off the red coals so as not to burn the rug or indeed set fire to the rushes.

There was a pause with much suppressed giggling, and then it was impossible to hold back, and laughter rose to the smoke-filled rafters. The priest was in such a good humour, he could not be bothered to clip the boy around the ear, but just ruffled his hair. That meant both of them had hair on end.

How memorable that service was, and although she missed the usual presence of her father by her side, squeezing her gloved hand, she had the replacement of Ashbourne, who made sure he was just the right distance apart from her to ensure he didn't encroach. Mary realised that soon, in past years, she and her father would be preparing to go back to London to spend Christmas and winter there, only returning to Somersal in the summer. This year would be different. She looked around her, and although lacking sophistication,the beautifully decorated church,bright with the handiwork of the locals was delightful. In that moment she felt a rush of love and affection for this place and the people around her, many from her own household, for it was as if they really were one family.

Ashbourne tapped the back of her hand discreetly, as a hint that the service was over, as he had seen Mary was staring straight ahead, and was somewhere else in her mind. Now it was time to stand for those sitting, as the choir sang a closing psalm of thanksgiving, and the priest left with his hand held high in blessing. Some bowed their heads and made the sign of the cross devoutly, whilst others just looked straight ahead. It was not difficult to see the Protestant reformers and pick them out amongst those who still harboured Catholic thoughts and longings in their hearts and souls.

Fortunately, the queen had once said, 'I will not have windows in men's souls,' and only those who openly challenged the current position of the English Church were likely to find themselves in trouble.

Spilling outside, the congregation joined hands for the clipping. Mary took the hand of Bess one side, and Anne on the other. On the way round, Mary saw a handsome, well-dressed couple talking animatedly to the priest, who was clearly enjoying their company. The second time round, getting more breathless all the time, she saw the handsome man pass the priest a leather purse that looked fat and the priest received it happily. It was indeed a joyful day for the church of St. Peter and St. Blaise.

Then the rowdy clipping was over, and some threw themselves, panting and whooping, upon the churchyard grass, which was mercifully dry. Then they were up and going through the Christening Gate to the great green circle in front of the Hall. Tents had been erected, full of benches to accommodate the large number of broad bottoms, of both sexes. As well as sweet cider, perry and ale, there was spiced wine for the gentry, and hippocras for the grand. Most people of all backgrounds made for the perry, as they were parched from dancing. The Hall produced a particularly fine cloudy perry from the packed pear orchards in the next field, running in neat lines alongside the apple orchard.

Food was being passed round by both inside and outside staff, and the front door of the Hall was wide open to welcome the local community and beyond at this happy time. 'This happy time indeed,' said Mary to herself.

Then she was saddened and a little guilty to have forgotten those murdered souls in Tutbury churchyard, and wondered if there was any progress in finding the perpetrators. She reminded herself to ask the magistrate, as he was drinking away nearby, with his pinch-faced wife at his side. She looked miserable, and who could blame her? Her husband was, as usual, chatting to any woman there he considered might be beddable, which in his view was almost anyone with a heartbeat, and ignoring her.

A touch on Mary's arm made her jump, putting her hand to her heart. It was John Ince.

'You startled me!' she complained.

'Good, that was my intention. I want you to have your wits about you, please, and not be caught off guard in this throng.' In his hand was a pewter plate, with delicious-looking pastries on. 'Please take this, mistress, and do not under any circumstances eat anything else, unless I give it to you. The same applies to drink. Here is pear juice, for I know that apple juice still makes you queasy, but watch your cup.' Mary didn't complain as this great care seemed necessary.'

‘What else, Dr Ince, to please you, sir?’ She was only being a tinge sarcastic, and her eyes showed him she wasn’t really being ungrateful for his good care. ‘Humph,’ he grunted. ‘Agnes will be at your side all the time, and I shall be occasionally, or Thomas Ashbourne. We shall all be watching, for not only do we wish you to remain well, and give no one the chance to poison you, we also want to see who is acting suspiciously. I am not a gambling man but I suspect whoever is attacking you, is here today.’

Agnes came and kissed Mary on the cheek, as John Ince walked off to keep up his watching vigil at a distance. Agnes pointed out a pleasant looking country girl hanging adoringly on the arm of Giles at the far side of the garden.

‘Do you mind, Agnes?’ Agnes shook her head. ‘It looks as if you are going to lose him to yonder maid.’ Agnes looked at Mary with knowing eyes. ‘They will live with me when the time comes, and I couldn’t be happier than to have both those loving souls under my roof.’

‘Look,’ hissed Mary out of the corner of her mouth. ‘It’s the purple-nosed butcher. I’m surprised he is not clipping the church in Uttoxeter.’ His great shape was swaggering around in good humour, bellowing as a matter of course, even in normal conversation.

Agnes chortled. 'Well, you don't know him. His fat purse and belly come from being tight-fisted. He would skin a flea if there was anything in it for him. There is free food and drink here, which is enough to bring him.'

Mary looked at her. 'Has he caught the fair baker widow in his net yet?' 'No chance of that! He tries, but he is stingy when it comes to courting presents. She is receiving a different sort of present from her handsome servant, and it is difficult to wrap that present up.' Mary laughed, knowing that at one time she would have been shocked by such a ribald comment, but now she was enjoying the sense of understanding real life she had learned at the apothecary shop with Agnes.

Later, Mary was cheerfully talking to some old tenants when Margaret Rich came rushing across the grass towards her, with face alight with pleasure. Unfortunately, with her was the ghastly Gregory, who was sauntering about arrogantly, drink in hand, and didn't bother to come across to greet Mary. She was peeved, and wondered what the courteous and highly-educated scholars of Oxford thought of this rude man in their midst.

'My dearest friend!' squealed Margaret, causing some folk to look round. John Ince frowned, standing once more alongside Mary, staring at this apparently brainless woman. Margaret ignored him, if she even saw him. Instead she embraced Mary tightly, kissing her cheek over and over.

Mary giggled. 'Why Margaret, do not be afeared. You see I am quite well, with no bad effects from my illness that laid me so low for so long.'

Margaret became serious ' I know how ill you were the first time you were struck, and when I came to you I know I gave you comfort, so was astonished they would not let me see you, or send gifts or even letters. I was so distressed not to see you.' Her blue eyes had filled briefly with tears, which she dashed away, looking embarrassed. 'What in Heaven has happened to you, my dear?'

Mary looked lovingly at her friend. 'What I suffered was nothing to do with Heaven, but a great deal to do with Hell,' she said.. 'It is behind me now, although I have to be very careful what I eat or drink.'

'What a shame,' pouted Margaret. 'Oh look, the rain's coming Shall we go inside please?' Mary looked up into what had been a clear blue sky, and sure enough drops were coming softly, but it would soon gather force if those grey clouds were anything to go by.

'Quick, indoors! called Mary, and the servants hurried everyone who wanted to take shelter into the great hall while others made their way to the kitchens. Breathless and laughing, the crowds came in, the music continued and there was even some dancing. Mary moved around her guests as she should, and then lost Margaret from view for a while, but saw the obnoxious brother standing in front of the door which led to her father's study and the great stairs, talking in what looked like an irritated tone to a local farmer, who in turn looked offended.

'The Hauling,' came a shout from outside. Mary looked at Agnes at her side, as they spilled out of the Hall, along with everyone else, chattering excitedly. Fortunately, the rain had stopped again. 'I didn't know there was to be a bed-hauling! Who is it for?' asked Mary. 'Can't you tell from the heat of their blushes?', replied Agnes.

One of the herdsmen and his new young wife stood on the grass circle outside, looking abashed, and she holding his arm. There was a surge of people who swept them up like trinkets as they made their way towards the cottage. Mary saw even the priest had joined in, laughing along with the rest, and his hair was still on end.

Into the couple's cottage they went, and after some good-natured shoving and shouting, out came the bed into the small front garden, where their herbs grew.

This ceremony was all about the Harvest Moon, as couples seeking to conceive would sleep in their own bed outside under the moon on a clear night, as this now promised to be. The belief was that the moon's light that gave fruitfulness to the crops also did so to mankind. Mixing God and moon-magic in the outside bedchamber, the priest said prayers over the bed as the couple lay upon it, fully dressed, and holy water was sprinkled on them as a blessing. 'Eh oop! It's raining again!' cried out the purple-nosed butcher, and everyone laughed. Women then came forward and decorated the bed with pre-prepared flowers, and garlands of wheat and barley. Then the crowd left them, arm in arm and chattering happily.

'Such sweetness,' said Mary, entranced by the first time she had witnessed a bed-hauling.

'Aye,' said Agnes, 'And one day your bed will be decorated too,' as she twinkled up at Mary.

'I pray for peace now, Agnes.'

'So do all, and may the blessings of God through this Harvest Moon fall on us all.'

That night Mary went to her father's study, still humming some tune she had heard played that day, and she made a discovery. She had gone in to check something, and found her suspicions were founded. At some point during the celebrations, with the house flooded by people, someone had been into the study, broken the seal on the messenger's bag and removed a letter that was on the top.

Mary had deliberately set this trap earlier, when she re-sealed the bag, having counted every letter. She had also noted the contents of each letter before re-sealing it. Her father told her little except he was on the move on the queen's business in the North. It was the only letter in the bag with her father's handwriting on the outside, addressed to her. The other letters to Ince and Ashbourne were from other people.

'So,' said Mary, gritting her teeth. 'Now I know someone has been coming here to read or steal these letters. Someone has poisoned me to distract from the stealing and reading of these letters.' It was a relief, strangely. Just as much a relief as being told she was wasn't going mad or dying. There was a plot afoot, and she knew the face behind it or had met them, she didn't know which, but they had been in the house that day. Now she would deal with it.

Chapter 37

Two weeks later, Mary was preparing for her birthday celebration on November 1st, All Saints Day. She would make the most of the event, even if her father would not be present. Ashbourne and Ince were with her in her father's study, talking about enquiries into the two murders and how they were progressing. All three hoped that the investigations, if fruitful, would have a link to the Mary mystery but none of them had any idea at all if that were true.

'Where did those gloves come from?' asked John Ince sharply, pointing at some dark blue gloves that had fallen from the pile of loosely cloth-wrapped presents 'hidden' under her father's desk. They had arrived as a big saddle roll from her father. The messenger was ordered to drop off the bundle a few weeks earlier, so as to be in plenty of time for her celebrations. The messenger had been moaning slightly about the weight of the bundle when they arrived, Anne told her, until he saw Bess in the kitchen with a piece of custard pie in her hand for him. The buxom glory of Bess was enough to make any man temperate when he saw her, and the custard pie was a bonus.

Mary had been tempted to open the bundle, held in a large linen cloth but did not poke about in the pile until the day itself came, for otherwise the surprise would be gone. Mary went to pick up the gloves to look at them more closely.

'No,' ordered Ince, but Mary knew his abruptness was born of concern. Leaning down he picked them up himself with a small piece of cloth that he took from his purse. He laid them on the table, looking at them curiously. Mary and Ashbourne drew alongside him looking down at the mystery gift. They were midnight blue and of the fashionable gauntlet style, embroidered with curled green leaves and fruit. The fruit looked like a quince at a glance. They looked stylish and, unusually, made of some type of closely woven wool instead of calf leather, which might have been expected of gloves of such quality. They would still have been expensive though, Mary thought.

What's the matter with them, John Ince?' she asked, looking at his frowning face. Ashbourne had now gone down on one elbow on the table top to look more closely at them.

'I know precisely what gifts your father gave the messenger to bring to you, and what is in each wrapping, and not one package contained gloves.' He looked up.

'Where did they come from, Mistress Mary, have you any idea at all?'

Mary went over the past weeks in her mind. Since that pile of gifts had first been placed under her father's desk, nothing had changed that she had noticed. Someone working against her had been there though, stealing letters, so at some point whoever it was had found an opportunity to gain access. She lifted her hands, opening them to show she knew nothing, and shrugged. John Ince carried on staring at her guardedly.

'Think, please,' he urged.

Mary glanced at Ashbourne, expecting him to disapprove this questioning but instead, he just looked worried. That vein was pulsing in his temple again. The room had gone quiet so Mary broke the silence.

'They are probably from Anne. It's easy to ask,' she suggested.

'Too expensive,' said Ashbourne simply, 'And too fashionable to buy in the area.'

John Ince, without a word, simply took the gloves out of the room and away to the room that he had made his own study, off the kitchen garden. Mary turned to Ashbourne. 'What does this mean, Ashbourne?'

'I don't know, Lady Mary,' he replied, 'But there is something going on with those gloves for John Ince to behave as he just did, and so I feel it would be judicious to let him do what he must do to protect you.'

Mary said nothing in reply, and then decided there were far too many mysteries in this house. As she had been so bright and cheerful earlier, she wished to be so again, and ran upstairs to try on her birthday gown.

Upstairs, Anne and Bess were together laying out Mary's clothes of bright violet velvet, slashed with crimson silk and decorated with embroidery of tiny pansies in bright silks and pearls. There was a creamy ruff and her best silken shift. Even the stomacher was decorated although no one would see it, except Anne and Bess, until a husband came along. Mary tried not to think of that possibility as the spotty ex-betrothed haunted her memories. Bess and Anne were crying out with pleasure at the sight of the glorious, puffed sleeves, shaken out and twinkling in the candlelight. The tiny silver buttons shaped like acorns held in loops intrigued them both, as they were so minute, and the sleeve points had silver bells on.

'It is all so lovely, mistress' said Bess, her eyes full of pleasure, and not a hint of jealousy.

‘So different from Alice,’ thought Mary. Bess had unwrapped another padded bundle, exclaiming ‘And these shoes!’

Even Mary had not seen the shoes, only the glorious gown wrapped in linen, which she had peeled back in child-like excitement, for they were chosen and sent by her father with Ince in advance of her gifts. His birthday gift to her had within the folds a short letter that spoke of love. The shoes were scarlet leather and had silver ribbons to accompany the gown, and carved wooden heels. Father had taken a great deal of trouble and laid out a deal of gold to make sure that the most feminine and beautiful gown and shoes were with his daughter on this special night.

A bowl of warm, perfumed water was brought and a soft natural sponge, and she was washed and dressed. As they worked their feminine magic, all three women sang in the round, laughing as they tripped over the words and had to start again. Finally, tiny wooden pots were brought forward carefully, and just a smudge of blush-pink cream added on her cheeks and lips. The other two women stepped back, clasping their hands together as Mary rose from her chair smiling, and turned towards them.

'Oh mistress,' they murmured. 'You look so lovely as to be a fairy.' Mary laughed with pleasure, for she could see from her reflection that although she would never be a beauty like Bess, this was as near as she was going to get to it. She noticed that the little silver bells tinkled like frosted stars as she moved. To her delight, she also found there were tiny pockets set inside the gown, that held small perfumed blocks so that there was music and sweet scent drifting from her like a cloud. It was an enchanting gown and in that moment she felt its magic.

This night was a dress rehearsal for her birthday celebrations, to make sure all fitted well and her hair, still short, was curled and pinned in a way to flatter the style of the gown. There was even a small hairpiece to pin on to give the style bulk. It had been sent up from Silver Street in London and set on a web of linen. It made all the difference, she decided, and was happy.

That early evening, together with Bess and Anne, was just as it was before, when she was rather light headed, trusting and frivolous. Now she realised that Alice, Warwick and the poisoning had in some ways killed the young Mary Dudley for now, although she was entirely herself she was older, more watchful and although she mourned the carefree days, at least now she was using her intellect, and growing up into a thinking woman. She undressed again, and put away the womanly glories of silk and pearls, and set herself in pale grey homespun.

When she had finished dressing, she asked Anne to stay with her for a moment while Bess returned to the kitchen. Mary had enjoyed the interlude from her worries, but knew that the mystery of the gloves needed to be resolved, so she asked Anne whether they had indeed been a gift from her, although she was careful not to give away the fact that Ince and Ashbourne thought that there was anything amiss. Anne assured Mary that she knew nothing of any gloves, but told her that she would have to wait until her birthday before she would know what her gift would be.

She needed all the courage and all the common sense she could muster, for later that evening she and Ashbourne stood together with John Ince in his room just off the kitchen. On the work table, with its scattered papers under the yellow candlelight, lay a large dead rat, screwed up in the agony of its last moment on earth. It had been poisoned, and nearby floated a pair of dark blue woollen gloves in a shallow bowl of water. All three looked at the gloves and Ince turned one over, palm side down, with a stick.

'There's a pomegranate!' Mary cried out. Both men squinted down to look, and sure enough, part of the embroidery showed not a quince as Mary had previously thought, but a small pomegranate burst open to reveal the jewelled red seeds inside.

'A Spanish symbol, isn't it, Ashbourne?' Mary was quite feverish at this discovery,

Ince answered for him. 'Yes,' he said shortly.

'Well spotted, mistress. This is indeed a sign of Spain, and the device of Katherine of Aragon.' They all looked at each other, wondering if this really was a clue to what had been happening.

Ince threw a bit of a damper on the excitement by pointing out, 'Do remember that the Spanish Tudor was also Queen of England, and her device can be found woven in many cloths. Not fashionable and many would frown at the sight of it, but it is still around in society in many forms.'

'Not in commissioned new pieces like these said Mary sharply. 'I can't hope to know many things, Dr Ince, but I know a new piece of embroidery when I see one, even on sodden gloves. These are new, so specially commissioned or bought in Spain, as this glove style can be seen in many courts in Europe. I have seen people from such places in London'.

The gloves just ignored the conversation, and floated like small blue corpses. The water was milky and deadly, and if Mary had drawn those gloves onto her hands, she would have been dead within hours. They were all silent, absorbing what they saw before them.

'How did the rat come to take it? asked Mary.

John Ince looked sideways at her. 'I mixed some of the soaking water with minced meat, and the rat ate it eagerly.' The other rats that John Ince had in cages were usually scampering about and squeaking when people were there. Now they were silent, watching their brother dead on the table, and now Mary knew why he kept these creatures, prisoners waiting to be poisoned. Mary felt similarly some days not so long ago. On a table by the cages, Mary's eyes turned to a small strange shaped object that looked dark and knobbly. Inquisitive, and seeing John Ince start towards her, she beat him to it, and picked it up.

'What's this, John Ince?' He took it off her gently, and held it up between his long fingers so Ashbourne could see too.

'Well, what is it?' asked Ashbourne.

'This, Mr Ashbourne is the heart of a lamb, stabbed through with nails.' The impact of these words was not lost, as Mary and Ashbourne both gasped.

Ince continued, 'Yes, you are right to gasp, and I don't doubt you both know that such a thing is used in witchcraft. It is packed with dark magic, and made purely to cause harm to a known person. Malice aforethought, and even if it is all superstitious nonsense it can kill, because it plays on the mind.'

Mary gaze fixed on it. 'That heart is meant to be me, isn't it?'

Bile was rising in her throat. Then she had a flashback and remembered something about the day that Clench and Holdfast had first come to the house. She swivelled on her heels, looking directly into John Ince's eyes to ensure there was no deceit. 'This,' she said victoriously, 'was what you found in the undergrowth under the study window, isn't it? The dogs found it, and you scooped something up. I saw you. It was this – answer me, please.'

John Ince leaned back on the table. 'Yes, it was, and that is why when you asked me then, I told you it was a key. That heart told me that not all was your imagination, and someone was physically coming here and intended to leave that in your bedroom to further frighten the lights out of you. His aim (and I am sure it was Elijah) was to leave it in your room. He was disturbed in his task and he must have dropped it as he fled through the study window.' His voice was getting louder, showing he was angry too, and Thomas Ashbourne looked disgusted.

'Does that not mean, Dr Ince, that we should have realised that someone was linked with the study, and that the form that Lady Mary saw was Elijah?' The guilt of not believing her had flooded back to him, and he was keen for a scapegoat to ease his conscience. Ince knew what he was doing, and had some sympathy for his slightly aggressive stance in this matter.

'Not at all,' he said calmly. 'It does not implicate the Dark Boy *per se*, just that someone was near the study window at some point recently with this, for it was not decayed when I first found it. It did prove irrevocably, however, that a terror campaign directly against Lady Mary here existed, for whatever reason. Now, this night, because of sharp eyes and a good well-founded argument, we now know Spain is behind it all, but to what end, and why here at Somersal?'

'They could have killed me this time, then?' Mary asked unnecessarily, and both men looked at her, but she showed no signs of trembling or fear, just a cold resolve.

‘Time to be more careful, then, as to who and what comes into this house.’ It was an obvious comment that didn’t need an answer, and then Mary added slowly, ‘Unless we set them a trap.’ Both men looked at her nonplussed.

She shrugged ‘Well, I for one, my dear friends, am rather tired of being a sitting target for their arrows. I intend to fight back now, with a trap we shall set and which we shall spring. On our terms. Let us turn the tables and make them the victims, and like this creature have them dead before us – in time.’

It was quite a speech for a young gentlewoman to make, with its masculine overtones of vengeance, and both men frowned at each other, but they understood. Oh yes, they understood and straightened up, staring at her. She didn’t really care if they thought her shocking, as it was time to change tack

Mary turned to leave the room before saying, ‘Haven’t you heard, good sirs? I have grown up!’

Chapter 38

Mary woke in the dead of the night. Despite having been desperately ill not so long before, her routine had returned to what was normal for her, which was her night vigil when all others slept. She sat up, looking at the pale blue moonlight cutting shadows on the panelling. Frequently recently, she had slept with the shutters wide open to let the moonlight in and comfort her. Now, she had grown used to the changing fortunes of the moon goddess Diana, and could sleep even when the feminine deity peered into every corner of her room.

Sitting up, Mary could not see any misty white figures or mouthing spectres. All she felt was a soft warmth and confidence in her own bedroom. No longer a stranger in a far land that had looked familiar, but had become dangerous. All was well, all manner of things were well. The Dark Boy was in his own dark place now, from which he would not escape.

She pulled her knees up in her customary style and clasped her hands around them, giving her balance as she thought through the recent months. Such an odd pattern of events, and whilst Mary fully appreciated she was not mad, or indeed mentally ill, someone had sought to harm her, and in doing so put her in danger of dying.

'Why? Why me, why now?' asked Mary, of a silent, empty room.

Although she had no hard evidence, it was clearly something to do with her father. He had sent John Ince to protect her. It was important, the work Edmund Dudley was engaged in, and so serious that her father could not leave it to return to her, even as close to death as she had come. That didn't sting Mary, as she was certain of her father's love for her, but it did tell her that she was in the middle of some kind of web ,designed by a brilliant mind or minds, to get access to her father's work, whatever that was. Somehow she must try to understand. After deep thought and concentration she said out loud to herself. 'I'm the stepping stone. I have been made ill as a distraction, or to lure my father back here.' She absent-mindedly stroked Hope, who was curled in a warm ball near her. 'What on earth is this all about?'

She reached into the recesses of her mind, and said to herself, 'Chess – human chess,' which was one way of looking at this conundrum, and so she continued with that thought process. 'Chess means not merely the move about to be made, but a more strategic mind is manyjust moves ahead.'

Mary instinctively knew this concept was important, so started to go carefully through the names and faces of all the people she knew in the immediate area. The Castle kept appearing as important, but she could not work out why, and realised it came from an old memory. Her mind had recognised something relevant and there was a truth in the mist of confusion. If only she could grab at that truth, and shake away all the other fragments of possibility that clung to it, like flotsam after a shipwreck.

One face after another rose in her imagination, as can happen with the mind wandering in the middle of the night, sometimes being gripped with wild ideas, and then discarding them as quickly as they appear.

She decided to try and sleep, and then just as quickly decided to give up and get a robe on and downstairs she must go to her father's study. She set off purposefully down the great stairs.

Crossing the study Mary made sure all the shutters were closed tightly, and in moving one she saw that that Clench and Holdfast were on patrol, with ghostly, pale blue bodies rolling massively as they paced around. One had stopped and listened, turning his head from left to right before setting off again. The ever-watchful presence of the dogs was a formidable security.

Mary then set about lighting candles on her father's desk from the dying red embers of the fire, before settling down with a quill, having smoothed out a few sheets of blank paper and, seating herself comfortably, she set to work. By now, she was wide awake and her concentration was honed like a knife, for she had a purpose. Reaching into a drawer on her right, she fetched out a pile of letters and, taking the top one off the pile, she laid it by the side of the blank paper. Tongue in the corner of her lips in concentration, she started to write.

Hour after hour, checking carefully the shape and form of her father's handwriting, she repeated it onto the blank paper. Part of her task had involved her in checking a map of England. It wasn't easy to read, but tilted at an angle by the candle, she could see what she needed to see. Her eyes started to stream and itch after an hour, but she just wiped them with the back of her hand and carried on. When she finished one letter, she picked up the sander and sprinkled it on, letting the excess ink soak up before shaking the loose sand onto the last of the burning ashes in the fireplace, where it crackled and hissed.

Before dawn, she had completed three letters, perfect in detail and totally false in content, except that last one, which she folded as carefully as the others. It was, in its truth, the most important of them all. As always, she tidied up everything carefully. She had noted, when she came to open the drawer where her father had his seal and red wax, that the lock had been tampered with but had held firm. The scratch marks on the wood gave the game away. Whoever had tried to open that drawer had been interrupted.

Instead of being alarmed at the sight of this, she felt victorious, for those scratches made her all the more certain she was right in her analysis of what was going on.

'Almost done,' she told herself, as she dripped the red wax on to the letters and sealed them. She then stopped her busyness, which had consumed her for the last few hours, and stared at her family crest.

When the seal was cold and hard, she slit open the letters and set them in order, but left only one out on the top of the desk with the messenger's bag open next to it as if it had just arrived.

Pleased, but incredibly stiff, she stretched her arms high above her head, and fanned open her aching fingers.

Blowing out the candles, she made her way up to her room at speed, as the servants would be stirring. Foxglove had woken by the fire as the kitchen door opened, and the spaniel looked up adoringly at her young Hope had come down from her bed, and sat fearlessly next to Foxglove, showing how lovely the dog was, as she merely pushed the cat gently with her nose. Mary, watching them, celebrated her work by breaking the rules, and took them both to her bedchamber with her, Hope in her arms and Foxglove making her way slowly up the unfamiliar stairs.

Mary lifted them both onto the bed and, taking off her robe and throwing it on the floor, jumped in and let the pets settled down at her feet. Hope was quite used to this but Foxglove was in heaven, and rolled around on the warm softness.

Mary knew Anne would be astonished to see the spaniel as well as the cat in her mistress's bedroom, but in some ways that appealed to her: it was her new life, where she could take control of her own choices and maybe, just maybe, do extraordinary things now and again.

The morning was indeed a noisy affair, with Anne mid-morning trying to drive the dog off the bed, but Mary woke up enough to say 'Leave her, please,' in a sleepy, thick voice, and then went back to sleep for another couple of hours.

When Anne came in for the fourth time, she found Mary talking to Foxglove, who looked for all the world as if she was listening intently, while Hope was sleeping by her on the bolster.

‘Very well, Anne,’ she smiled. ‘You can take them out now, but gently please, no scolding .’

Anne seemed relieved to see her mistress bright after sleeping so deeply, so didn’t mutter or moan, but carried out Hope, with Foxglove following obediently when called.

When Anne came back with breakfast, she put it down and looked closely into Mary’s face and tutted. ‘I know you are well now, mistress, but I don’t like those shadows under your eyes.’ She added, ‘After all these hours’ sleep, too.’

Mary tried to look innocent ,as she discreetly slipped her right hand under the covers, for her second finger was stained with tell-tale ink.

Chapter 39

Mary decided she would check her father's study straight after breakfast, to ensure there were no clues to lead to her night-time activities. That must at all costs be kept a secret. It was just as well she did check, for there were small drips of red wax dried firm on the desk, so she quickly scraped them off with her fingernail. Then, taking the end of a candle, she rubbed the mark, before buffing it to a bright shine with a patch of leather used to roll the quills in. Finally, she picked up the folded map of England and, opening it, looked closely at the main cities and towns, running her finger from one place to another, ending at Tutbury. Satisfied she was not mistaken in what she had written the night before, she folded the map carefully again, and put it back in the drawer.

The next stage of her plan must now be put in place, so she went to the kitchens and waved her hand at the servants. who stopped chattering at the sight of her, some rising to their feet and touching foreheads or bobbing a brief curtsy. The kitchens and drying room were absolutely stuffed with baskets of fruit and vegetables, with more herbs than usual hanging from the rafters above.

'Please ,' she said, 'Don't let me disturb you about your tasks. I am here to speak to Cook'.

As the chatter resumed at a quieter level, Eleanor left her work and sat by Mary at the far end of the kitchen for privacy. A fat chance of that, thought Mary, with every ear in the place seemingly being turned in their direction.

'How can I be of service, mistress ?' Cook asked, with her head on one side. Mary knew what she was about to say would cause a sensation.

'I have a fancy, Eleanor, to throw not just a party for dinner on my birthday, but a glamorous feast.'

Cook's eyebrows shot up. 'A feast, mistress?' adding, 'And would that include a banquet by any chance?'

'Yes, Eleanor, it would.' Cook put her hands to her cheeks for although she was capable of producing a really high standard of food, building the extraordinary sugar and marchpane figures and flowers, even plates and goblets, was not something she had ever attempted before, and no wonder, for training to be a sugar mistress could take years (this skill was very often that of a woman servant).

Cook eyed Mary sideways. 'I will need some help, mind.'

Mary put her hand on Eleanor's arm and smiled.

‘Of course you will, but now you have Bess to help you, and her girls Matilda and Maud are talented with their small hands, and may have a go at the marchpane flowers’.

‘Marchpane flowers,’ breathed Cook, with a sense of wonder.

‘I also have a gift for you, Eleanor, which I am sure your considerable talents will make the most of.’ Mary reached behind her back and fetched out a small bound printed book, within which were receipts and ideas for meal-planning that would please any cook’s heart. She placed it on the great table and Cook jumped up to look at it and, although her hands were clean, still rubbed them on her apron before picking up the precious book and looking at it with wonder. The other servants crowded round, their eager faces peering over shoulders. Some called for Bess to come over and read it to them. Bess could read, and even write her name, albeit with a shaky hand.

‘Read it out, Bess, so we can all hear.’

Bess cleared her throat importantly, aware of her rapt audience, and ran her finger under the words, narrowing her eyes in concentration.

‘To make a pippin pie,’ she announced victoriously, then reading on slowly and clearly, ‘Take good pippins, cutting small and lay in a coffin of sweet butter pastry.’

She looked around for approval, as some of the servants repeated everything she said to each other. 'Scatter with sugar, rosewater and mace, and dot with butter before putting to a hot fire'. The storeroom was well acquainted with these ingredients.

'How long shall the coffin be set by the fire?' asked the timid voice of a kitchen maid.

Mary answered, 'It is a book for those who are already able cooks like ours, and know such details without having to be told.' Cook tried, unsuccessfully, to look modest, then she suddenly had a thought. 'Mistress, I may not have all these wonders to work with. Some recipes may demand ingredients from far shores, not heard of hereabouts.' She was absentmindedly stroking the book, as if it were a pet.

'Quite right, Cook,' agreed her mistress. 'There is s plentiful supply of rare and exotic goods at the Castle for feasts, including dried foods and spices. I can make polite enquiries, and acquire some if not all of what you want, and then simply replace what is loaned. It is quite in order. Just ask.'

That evening, she asked Anne, 'What moon is it, Anne?' and Anne said, 'The Hunter's Moon, mistress.'

Mary nodded. 'It's time for the farmyard killing too.

'I care not for this time, for the sound of the screaming of the pigs above all other slayings turns my blood cold.'

Anne was not keen either but, as the wife and daughter of farmers, much more accepting of the necessity of the slaughter. 'Just think though, mistress, soon the house will be filled with the smell of smoked bacon, spiced pies and herby sausages packed with flavour.'

As a traditional time of giving, some of these delicious foods would be given to the poorest in the community whilst the rest of the excess was sold at the market, alongside the cheese and beer also produced at the Hall. The cloudy perry was usually kept for the Hall family and servants, with its sharp, dry, flavour.

'How is man influenced by the Hunter Moon, Anne?'

'All desire to pick up their spears, daggers, bows and arrows, and hunt not just food, but other prey they seek, which can be other people.'

Mary went to the window. 'It is calling me too,' she thought.

Chapter 40

A couple of days later on a bitterly cold afternoon, Mary was ready to set the next stage of her plan in place. She wanted to see John Ince, so made her way to the small door of his rooms, just off the drying kitchen. It was not permitted for the servants to enter under any circumstances, but they must knock if they wished to see him. As a number of the staff were wary of Ince, such a restriction did not pose a problem. She knocked, and when she had no answer, she went in and found him bent over some papers spread out over a polished table. The cages of rats were quiet, and watching her every move. So engrossed was he, that he hadn't heard the knock. As might be expected, he was startled at the sound of her coming into the room be-cloaked, and he straightened up sharply with a frown, which cleared when he saw who his visitor was. 'Lady Mary, forgive me, I was about the detail of my paper. Is all well?'

'Doctor Ince, I wonder if you might favour me with some of your knowledge on a particular matter.'

He looked surprised, and straightened up. 'Of course, if I can be of service.'

There was then silence between them as Ince waited patiently for Mary to speak, but she was struggling somewhat to find the words she wanted.

'Doctor Ince.' There was a pause as she twisted a ring on her finger. 'I would like you to teach me how to whistle through my fingers as you do, to call Clench and Holdfast.'

She swallowed with embarrassment, looking steadily at him chin high and daring him to laugh. Instead, Ince looked at his table, and proceeded to shuffle papers, saying 'Of course,' as if it were the most natural question to be asked by a young gentlewoman.

The burning desire to whistle at all was unlikely, never mind whistling for two muscle-bound, flatulent mastiffs. Mary was watching Ince suspiciously, and had an unpleasant sensation that she could see his shoulders going up and down as he carefully rolled and tied scrolls with his back to her.

However, when he turned to look at her, his face was perfectly composed, and with a small nod he pointed the way with an open hand to the back door that led to the gardens, snatching up a thick cloak on the way.

Over by the holly hedges, two dark figures could be seen blowing clouds of white from their mouths in the icy air. 'Do you think me mad, Doctor Ince?' smiled

Mary, but half meaning it and challenging him to take her seriously, although she suspected that was a lost battle.

'No, Lady,' said Ince with serious air. 'I think it is an interesting idea, and a useful skill, as you never know when you might need it.'

He gave a small bow, and Mary narrowed her eyes, just in case he gave the slightest snigger. He did not and so then the serious business of learning how to whistle like a street urchin began. Fortunately, at such a quiet time of the year in the gardens, there were few servants abroad to witness their efforts except Charlie the garden boy, whose distinctive lean and leggy shape could be seen darting over to the churchyard for some reason. They both stopped the lesson to watch him.

'Acting oddly, that boy,' said Ince, as the shape ran from sight.

'Why do you say that?'

'Have you not noticed? I think it was him up the tree, the day I arrived.'

Mary shook her head. 'I can't imagine why.' John Ince was muttering. 'Darting about, hiding up trees and generally, well, acting oddly.' He shook himself from his thoughts, and then proceeded with the technique of achieving sound in a particular way.

'It's all in the tongue shape,' he explained, 'and forcing the air tightly through your fingers. If your fingers are too far apart, it doesn't work. Equally, if your tongue is held in the wrong shape, it doesn't work. Do try, with concentration on what I have said, then we shall have this battle won.'

Mary took a deep breath, before setting her tongue in a curl, and then putting two fingers between her lips and giving a blast which was hopeless, and no more than a pathetic squeak. After ten minutes or so of practice, at last one or two efforts sounded quite hopeful, but fell into disarray at the end of the note with a raspberry effect.

John Ince did not laugh. In fact, Mary was full of admiration for his gathering gravity at her attempts. She was not at all sure she wasn't going to burst out laughing herself, and every time she sucked in breath, wanted to laugh.

'Like this,' he demonstrated yet again his curled tongue for Mary to look at, and then two fingers. 'Then like thus,' and he blew such a strident note, the rooks took off shrieking from the bare high trees nearby. The terriers set off barking, of course. Ince lifted his hand for Mary to listen, and sure enough there was immediately a terrific thundering sound and around the corner of the house came the two massive mastiffs, shoulder to shoulder and coming straight for them. The speed and aggression of their approach was breathtaking, but she stilled herself, having confidence in John Ince which was not ill-founded, as he lifted his hand, palm towards them, and they came to a grinding halt at his feet. The concentration on their faces was absolute as they waited for an instruction from their master and saviour.

'Good! Quiet!' and having praised them, he said 'Lie down,' so they flopped over with great sighs. 'They have been sleeping in the stable, no doubt.' She was filled with admiration at the way he managed those brutes.

'Do you think, Doctor, that I really may be able to achieve such obedience?'

'I can assure you, you can,' answered Ince, solemnly. Then out of the blue Mary produced a perfect sound, and then another. The dogs sat up immediately, looking at her in rather a bewildered manner. Ince clapped a little. 'You see! Well done, Lady, well done.'

He then set off at speed calling the dogs to heel as he turned the corner of the house, shouting, 'Count to ten and then whistle.'

Mary got to eight but couldn't wait any longer, so curled her tongue, put in her two fingers and whistled brightly and sharply. She was delighted when sure enough the dogs thundered around the corner of the house, followed hotly by John Ince with his cloak flapping. As the dogs approached, Mary stood firm and put up her hand, palm out, saying clearly 'Good! Quiet!' and couldn't remember the next bit, but it didn't matter for John Ince had arrived, panting a little with the cold air tightening his chest.

He beamed at Mary such a smile as would part storm clouds, and took her hand in congratulation. They both laughed, and Mary realised it was the first time she had ever heard him laugh. The dogs were sent back to bed and they strolled off, but not before Mary had bent down and patted them affectionately, making them drool with pleasure.

'How do I make them attack?' asked Mary, as they crossed the grass alone with the sun dipping golden.

He frowned, but didn't argue. 'It's simple,' he said. 'Just say "Stand!" which makes them stand ready to attack, and then "Kill."'

Mary looked at him sharply. 'Well, that is certainly clear.'

John Ince said firmly, 'You forget, Lady Mary, that

the dogs were gladiators in the pit against the most ferocious bears you have ever seen.'

'How do I call them off after an attack, Dctor?' He carried on walking, looking ahead. 'Well, I hope you will never need it, but the word is simply "Leave!", and they will return to your feet for further instructions, hurt or otherwise. They will defend you to death, literally." Now it was time for mistress and tutor to part.

'Thank you, Doctor Ince,' she said warmly, and they clasped hands briefly again, courteously. It had been the oddest hour she had ever spent in her life, tucked away in a hedge in the winter, learning how to whistle killer dogs - but she had enjoyed it.

Chapter 41

The next day, Mary called a war council in her father's study, asking John Ince and Thomas Ashbourne to give her an hour of their time. She also wisely arranged for Edward Loxley to position himself outside the study door on a chair, to ensure that they were not overheard.

The men arrived at the same time, and took chairs near the fire, ready to listen to Mary.

'I know who is behind it all,' she began. 'I don't know why, but I do know who.'

Both men looked astonished. Ashbourne said, 'Mistress Mary, you did think Alice Goodrich…' His voice tailed off, for fear he might seem insolent or jeering to his young mistress.

'Yes,' she answered firmly, '… and I was wrong. Now I am right, and I shall set out for you how I have reached this conclusion.' Both men leaned forward, listening intently.

'First, let us consider opportunity. Who had the opportunity to come to this house frequently to poison me? Who paid and briefed the Dark Boy to terrify me and gather information by stealing my father's letters? Those letters are the key to all of this, I have no doubt of that.' Both men nodded, and Mary continued.

'The magistrate, Bartholomew, was a suspect in my head for a while, as he kept coming here, sitting in the kitchen unannounced, talking to the servants. I have seen him myself dodging round the garden, and all without announcing himself to me or Ashbourne, which was odd. Particularly as a murder enquiry was under way, that was odd.'

Both men agreed, but Ince interrupted, 'I can explain that.' Mary was all ears, as the magistrate had thrown her ideas for weeks.

'It's Bess,' he said simply, adding, 'Bartholomew loves a pretty woman, and the good widow Bess is very pretty, and warm and kind. She has, unwittingly, stolen his heart, so he is hanging around and bringing gifts in the hope she might allow a kiss or two.'

Thomas Ashbourne looked prim. 'Well, the servants should have reported this to me, I am steward after all. He is a married man and I care not to have the servants picked off like ripe cherries. If you knew this, why did you not inform me, Doctor Ince? I would have dealt with the matter discreetly.'

Ince shrugged 'Does it really matter? The longer he was about, the less likely the attacks would take place, since, believe me, they would have seen him here.'

Both Mary and a reluctant Ashbourne saw the sense of that, and Mary said, 'That, my dear Thomas, is life, with all its unexpected turns, and I am a fool for not realising it earlier. Let me continue, then, for I am eager to share this with you.' The men fell silent.

'So, I realised after a while it was not Bartholomew. But it might have been the unknown rich couple I saw at the Harvest Festival in the churchyard, giving a bag of money to the delighted priest.'

'No,' said Thomas Ashbourne. 'They are a brother and sister from Kent who also have property near here. I don't know them well, but I do know they arrived only the day before, having been away for months, so not them. Or the vicar,' he added, appreciating after a moment that might be a natural link.

'That clears that up, but they were not truly at the front of my mind as real possibilities, I was just curious at a time when I was suspicious of everyone. Well, almost,' she added politely. 'I trust Agnes, because you trust Agnes, and I feel there is more to you and Agnes, Doctor Ince, than you have revealed, sir!' He did not respond, but just carried on silently looking at Mary.

'So,' she went on, 'I am sorry to have been so dumb-witted not to see it earlier, for now I know that the person responsible for my being poisoned was involved in the murders.' Ince looked as if he knew who Mary was going to say, but Ashbourne was on the edge of his seat. Mary left a brief dramatic pause and then blurted out, 'It's Margaret Rich, and her cronies Gregory and James.'

Ashbourne leapt to his feet. 'She is a friend of yours, Lady Mary. She comforted you, and you must have had complete trust in her!'

Mary looked up at him, anger flashing in her face. 'That's so, Thomas: she appeared a close and kind friend, who was also poisoning me, and would have killed me as she did those other poor souls, without compunction.' Thomas sat down again, and the three sat silently for a while.

'Tell us' urged Ince.

Mary explained that she had during the last few nights gone over and over the sequence of events that led her to her belief. She explained how Margaret had pushed herself forward at Tutbury Castle to meet her without introduction, and how what she thought was anger in Gregory's eyes when the discovery of the murders was announced by the captain was not anger, but panic that the bodies had been found so quickly.

Margaret's cry of pain outside the Great Hall door was faked, so Mary could feel sympathy towards her and that was developed further with all sorts of untrue tales.

Margaret had had ample opportunity to drop poison in Mary's pot of rose cream, and had brought suckets for Mary, and had Mary close her eyes so she could guess what flavour they were. This apparently childish game enabled Margaret to avoid taking any herself and Mary would not know, as her eyes were closed. She reminded Ashbourne of how they had met them unexpectedly, on the way to the church, and how they had tried to find out what Ashbourne and Mary knew about the murders. Ashbourne nodded.

'I remember, and you were careful, Lady. I remember that too.' Mary continued at a great pace, the information pouring out of her.

'When I was ill, she came to visit, and in my poorest state asked where my father was and what he was doing. She also made a thorough job of looking over the whole house, out of every window to see opportunities for the Dark Boy. Meanwhile she was feeding my mind with doubt and anxiety about madness, appearing to be sympathetic but actually damaging me.'

Mary was becoming increasingly agitated as she spoke, so she paused for a moment. She stood up and stabbed at the fire, which was not needed, but helped her to compose herself, before she sat down again and resumed her story.

'After I recovered from her poison a little, I went to Woodroffe's and there ate her food, and was desperately ill again over the next few days, despite thinking she was making me better. Amongst other things, she gave me apple juice, which I know now would be ideal for concealing the taste of mandrake. What is more, there were jars there with labels in Spanish, which I found surprising, although Margaret did her best to explain that away, and I accepted her explanations at the time.

Gregory was at the house the whole time, and his bursting in on me in his study was set up. Also, did you not notice that she came to visit me by great co-incidence when the messenger bag was due, and Anne told me that once she had caught her in the study and although she pretended as an excuse that she thought I was there, Anne didn't trust her. Even after the Harvest Festival service (which they didn't attend, they appeared in the grounds, and I saw Gregory blocking the door to the corridor between the great hall and the study, no doubt while she was inside.' She had only just remembered that.

John Ince's voice was gentle. 'Go on, this will do you good.'

'I knew someone had been in my father's messenger bag, and I knew that the interest Margaret had in the study was beyond usual. When I was away with Agnes, I knew that I had been got out of the way, and was interested that Gregory and James were looking for me. The little poisoned blue gloves indicate Spain to me, and that indicates Catholic spies!'

Thomas Ashborne gasped, but Mary ignored him, as she was in her stride. 'Those poor, innocent people were murdered by them, so they could take their place. There has been planning in Oxford, London and here for all this to take place.' John Ince looked at her. 'How do you know that?'

Mary's sense of victory was apparent in her answer. 'I took the liberty of writing to a friend of Father's at Oxford University – as he went there – and asked for a description of Margaret and Gregory Rich, explaining that his discretion was essential. I think the old boy was rather thrilled by this mysterious enquiry, and answered promptly.' Mary sat back with a smile. 'I can show you his reply, and I can tell you that the murder victims were the real Margaret and Gregory Rich. She was red-haired, and he had two fingers missing on his left hand and was tall.'

'Brilliant, Madam!' said Ince. 'But I wish you had told me all this earlier, for I have reached the same conclusion but using a different path. The Oxford contact was a master-stroke if I may say so.'

Mary was rather pleased with herself and that gave her confidence that her mind was fully returned.

Thomas Ashbourne, meanwhile, was rather left out as this tale unfolded, and looked aghast that he had not seen all this himself.

'What now then?' he asked. 'We must take action before anyone else is harmed.'

Mary said, 'My tale is not entirely over, my friends. I have over the past days not only learned how to protect myself with the dogs.'

Thomas looked mystified, so John Ince told him, 'I have taught this lady to whistle them,' which was not helpful to Thomas, as he looked slightly shocked.

'Whistle?'

Mary nodded, and wanted to laugh at his face. 'I have also forged some letters in my father's handwriting, that give false information as to where he is, and what he is doing.'

John Ince wasn't smiling any more. 'But what have you put in the letters, where did you say your father was?' he asked urgently.

'Knaresborough Castle, in Yorkshire and then on to Ludlow, in the first.' she said coolly.

'The others?' he asked.

'Knaresborough again, then Sheffield.'

John Ince interrupted sharply. 'When did you say Sheffield?'

Mary's face burned, suddenly aware that she might unwittingly have been right. 'That letter has not been taken yet, but the first one has.' She suddenly felt less victorious and more alarmed.

'Show me,' he snapped, so Mary went across to the bag and showed them there were two left. The top one mentioned Sheffield, she told him. John Ince and Thomas Ashbourne, who had joined them, stared owlishly down at the handwriting. Ince uncharacteristically gave a little whistle. 'You have written these…?'

She was defensive. 'I have.

He suddenly smiled again. 'Well, they are brilliant, wonderful forgeries. There is more to you, Lady Mary, than meets the eye!'

Ashbourne agreed, but Mary knew he would not approve of the forgeries, although he couldn't help but admire her investigation and spirit.

'Are you going to tell us, John Ince, what business my father is about, now we have earned trust?'

His answer was simple. 'No, Lady, I will not tell ,but all will be revealed soon and Sheffield may have a part in it. That is all I will say now, but you will be in at the kill. Now we must have a tight plan to ensure we catch them red-handed'. They poured wine, stoked the dimming fire and talked and talked. At one point Edward Loxley begged brief release so he could go to the privy, but he quickly returned. Food was served in the room and that night as they parted, all was clear. The last battle had begun.

Chapter 42

Anne was laying out Mary's clothes for the next evening, which was to be the occasion for her birthday celebrations But this night was All-Hallows-Eve. As Anne put it, 'The time of the year when the veil between the living and the dead is at its thinnest. Man must light fires outside tonight, for those in Purgatory to find comfort by seeing the flames below, so the dead can find their way home to where they used to live. Food and drink should be left out for those family spirits, for tonight they join the living. Fear comes to man like a cold cloak, unless his soul be free of sin. He will feel it more as his ancestors come to stare into his face as he sleeps.'

Anne was getting into the swing of this gruesome tale and Mary was smiling to herself, for she was not afraid. The church had been full for the service and most houses had candles and ugly carved vegetable faces in their windows. This was so that, if evil spirits came to the door, they would see the ugly face and realise the house already had its own spirit, and would leave it alone.

Food was left out for fairies in the cowshed so they would not sour the milk in revenge for not being fed. People would snuggle into their beds, as witches were out this night, dancing with demons or the Devil himself.

Having frightened herself senseless, Anne made the sign of the cross, and left for the evening. Mary had an idea that she would ask Loxley to walk her home, and he would, as he often did, with a lantern.

Dinner was a quiet affair, and afterwards Mary spent further time talking to John Ince and Thomas Ashbourne about the following night. The detailed planning was all in place and all was ready. Mary thought how fitting it was to be discussing it this night, for it was the eve of when they would root out their own evil spirits.

The following day, the air was full of the smell of bonfires burnt out from the night before. The Great Hall was full of servants fetching and carrying flower and berry displays, dried flowers, and yellow beeswax candles, as all the candles must be replaced for the evening, and the stumps burned elsewhere in the house. The silver gilt was polished, linen whitened and carefully pressed, and the great family salt of silver and crystal in the shape of a ship was produced to stand in front of Mary.

Vessels of Tutbury glass, fashioned into curious shapes, were wiped carefully and servants were told over and over again about the etiquette of serving: napkins to be placed over the shoulder of the guests, ewers and bowls of water with dried rose petals prepared for the washing of hands between courses, and the showmanship that was the arrival of each course were drummed into the nervous-looking servers.

'I am sure I'm going to drop mine!' Mary overheard one say with a trembling voice.

'Bugger that,' came the response, in a voice that Mary recognised. She looked around the door of the kitchen, which was in a frenzy, and winkled out Charlie, who must have just said that. He wasn't a server, but was interested in everything that was going on.

'Come here please, Charlie,' she asked, and the kitchen went silent, but he swaggered after her confidently. Mary hauled him to one side and told him the importance of secrets, and how later he was going to be given a job to do that involved a bell, and hiding inside the door on the top corridor that led to the female servants' attics, the one with the big crack in the door to look through. He was thrilled, and promised he would keep absolutely quiet because there was a silver shilling in it. Mary didn't remember making that offer, but took the hint, and promised it.

He sat cheerfully, as in the background the minstrels warmed up enthusiastically.

‘Pastance in Good Company’ was the cheerful sound echoing around the corridors at that moment.

As dusk drew in, Mary was dressed in the outfit that she had tried on a fortnight before. For this night she was not only wearing a new gown, she was also wearing a certainty that tonight she would have her revenge.

The carriages and guests arrived, one after another. The Deputy Constable of the Castle and his wife, the magistrate and his, poor soul, a prosperous local farmer who came alone, Margaret and Gregory Rich, and many more. At table, John Ince and Thomas Ashbourne sat either side of Mary. She had had to put up with Margaret kissing her on each cheek, but the temptation to pull away had been strong. She noted that Margaret seemed dizzy and happy to speak to all and sundry about how lucky she was to have such a close friend. Gregory was as miserable and watchful as ever.

The meal was a huge success: fowl, beef, venison and dipping sauces, salat, and sweet and salty fish dishes cooked with wine and herbs, all carried in to a fanfare from the musicians, and much cheering and drumming of the table by the merry guests. Except some of them were nothing of the sort. Mary chatted away loudly, talking of how sad she was that her father was still away from her, but mentioned that two letters had arrived just before the feast, and he would tell her where he was and what he was doing, she was sure! She acknowledged the glasses raised in a toast, and when a second toast was proposed to the queen, she joined in happily.

The candles were bright and the outside of the Hall was lit by flares at the stables. Then the marchpane conceits arrived with great ceremony, and Cook was called in with Bess for the guests to applaud their skill. Bess called her twins and they too had a clap, with Matilda and Maud tight with excitement. Along with pink and gold marchpane flowers, the centrepiece was a lovely peacock all made of sugar, surrounded by little puddings, tarts of honey, nuts and rosewater to please the sweetest tooth. Sweet wine was served, and people started to get up to walk around a bit or perhaps go to the privy.

In that moment, Mary and Ince and Ashbourne were keeping an eye on the door, and sure enough at a particularly noisy moment, off went Margaret slipping through the door, and Gregory took up his guarding position. Mary gave it one minute and then signalled the minstrels to be silent. She saw

Gregory narrow his eyes, as he wondered what was going on. He was jumpy, and no wonder.

Mary asked for quiet and many of the guests thought she was going to make a speech, but no, she was listening for something. There, there it was – a bell ringing, and then it stopped.

'Seize him!' was the instruction from Mary, and some of the male servants on that command grabbed Gregory, and held him fast despite his struggles. Ashbourne hurried past to the study, and called out 'The letters are gone, and she has left by the back stairs!'

'Bring him along to watch,' said Mary, pointing at Gregory. While some of the guests were alarmed, others knew only too well what was happening and surged after Mary, who had Ince and Ashbourne on either side of her as she walked rapidly to the stables and the flaming torches.

As the stables came into sight so did Margaret Rich, who had her horse being led to her and was snapping for them to hurry so she could mount. Then Mary heard a noise she had been listening out for, and it came, a shrill bird-like cry and there was the simple boy Toby from Tutbury Castle, with his brother, coming out of the stable and pointing to Margaret.

'Her!' Toby cried. 'Her whipped me, and it hurt.'

He put his hand to his cheek, and Mary nodded at his brother, who led Toby away gently.

'Hold that horse and take it back,' ordered Ashbourne fiercely, and the stable boy led it away without question.

Mary strode up to Margaret who started gibbering, 'Oh Mary, Gregory has been so brutal to me of late. I must escape him tonight. Will you help me?' Then her words froze on her lips, for she saw Gregory who was weeping like a child with fright, held firm by two burly men. Suddenly, Mary struck her with the back of her hand with such force that Margaret staggered, and from her fingers fell two letters. She gasped, and her hand flew to her burning face as Mary scooped up the letters.

'Mine, I believe, Margaret, or whatever your name really is'. She chose the second letter in her hand and opening it first, passed the other to John Ince. She read the letter out in a clear voice to the assembled crowd, who were agog as this drama played out.

'The carrier of this letter is a murderer, thief, liar and has committed High Treason against Her Majesty and this land.' She had signed the letter with her own name in her own handwriting. Her eyes were bright with fury. Then she put two fingers in her mouth, and gave a sharp whistle. The people crowding round were astonished, but not so astonished as when they saw two mastiffs of huge proportions rush to Mary's feet, and sit at her command.

Margaret started to run but Mary gave the command to attack, and the dogs felled her like a tree before she had gone a dozen paces. Mary called the dogs off the screaming woman, and had them come to heel as Margaret was roughly lifted and held under arrest. Behind her, she could hear Gregory whimpering, 'It wasn't me, it was her. I had to do everything she said or she would have killed me like she did that man and woman.' That was a bit of a revelation.

Margaret was taken to the cart, with her arms pinioned. As she passed, Mary realised that Margaret's features didn't look like her anymore. She was brutal and cold as ice. Mary held up her hand to stop them. Looking Margaret in the eyes, she said, 'Now you can go mad, for I have had enough of it.' Mary and Margaret both knew that a traitor's death lay ahead, a thought enough to send anyone mad. The magistrate came up, breathless, speaking to Ince particularly. 'We have their servant, he was up the road waiting. He is obviously the one who has been watching the roads for the messenger, and tipping the woman off. We have also secured Woodroffe's, and will search it in the morning for more evidence.'

Mary thanked him, and also gave thanks to William Agard from Tutbury Castle for allowing Toby, along with his brother, to accompany them to the Hall. She didn't forget to give a silver sixpence to Toby, via Thomas Ashbourne.

Before he left, the magistrate added, 'We may have a number of these traitors from this night's work. We may break a large web.' He bowed briefly to Mary, and then the party broke up, but no one was disappointed as it had been an unforgettable night. Or almost no one, for back in the great hall Mary found Eleanor looking sadly at her uneaten sugar peacock. 'All that work,' she said, but then she brightened. 'Well, at least they have eaten the tarts,' and then she was off, humming to herself.

Chapter 43

The next day reports came in by dusk about what had been found at Woodroffe's, although some of the magistrate's men remained there to search for additional hiding places. The traitors meanwhile were on their way under guard to London to be questioned by subtle, dangerous men who sought to know who else was involved in this treacherous plot. The evidence against them was irrefutable, and would be fatal.

'What was behind this treachery?' asked Mary of John Ince, who had passed on this message from the magistrate. 'Can you still not tell me?'

He shook his head. 'I am sorry, Lady, I can tell you nothing at this point, but I will later, I promise. You will know everything.'

Then, oddly, Mary jumped to her feet as if in shock, and walked round the room. Ince, who was slightly startled, asked 'What ails you, have you just remembered something?' Mary nodded, opening her arms. 'Something extraordinary has just occurred to me, which is that death would have knocked on Alice Goodrich's door this year even without the hanging!'

Ince sighed, as if he was sick of hearing about this woman and her grandson. 'How so?'

Mary smiled at him. 'Why? Because, my friend, she would have stolen the suckets that Margaret left me – all of which were poisoned - and she would have also lathered my rose cream on her hands because she wanted whatever was mine. It is likely she would have taken the suckets for Warwick too, and he would have gulped them down in one.'

Mary had been tapping her fingers into her palm at each point. Ince looked hard at her. 'You are right, and not content with that deduction you have also succeeded in misdirecting the traitors' efforts to Ludlow. We discovered your forged letter ruse worked like a charm, and it would have caused great cost in terms of time, as well as difficulties in putting their plot into action.'

Mary cheered, and was then embarrassed, but he twinkled at her as she said, 'Oh, just a wonder, John, that I might with my simple plan have caused such disruption.' He got up from his chair, saying, 'You certainly have, and I am pleased to be able to show you something discovered this morning that will explain much.'

He called for a servant to fetch Thomas Ashbourne, who arrived calm and again in charge of the house.

Ince beckoned them both to the desk. 'Come and see,' he said, fetching a long box from outside the door, and laying it on the table, opened it. There were astonished cries from Ashbourne and Mary, for inside the box was a long whip with strands of twisted rope with knotted ends, and through the rope ran a bright blue thread that stood out starkly. Only three of the nine rope strands were still attached to the handle. The other six were missing.

'They cut them off to bind their victims.' Ashbourne sounded solemn and no wonder.

'Why?' asked Mary.

John Ince replied 'This whip is used for self-flagellation by the more fanatical Catholics, and the blue thread shows a devotion to the Virgin Mary. I believe by using these rope strands, the murderers in some way treated their crimes, not as murder, but as some reasonable sacrifice for their treacherous ideology.'

It was a sobering thought, and Mary added 'The means justifying the end.' She spoke softly. 'Does my father know of all this?'

Ince replied, 'He knows much of it, and this latest news is on its way to him. In mid-January he returns to Somersal to complete his task.'

That was the best news of the day.

For Mary, the days and weeks after this, moved quickly. Roger Batholomew and William Agard from the Castle visited fairly frequently, updating Ince and Ashbourne on developments. The three prisoners in London had revealed six others in their conspiracy, and all three of those who had lived at Woodroffe's were in the pay of Spain as well as being religious zealots. They were all found guilty on a number of counts, including murder of the brother and sister, before going to their own appalling deaths. 'To know you are going to be hanged, drawn and quartered must be a terrible burden,' said Mary to Anne one day. 'The woman may be spared the worst of that, for public decency, but she will still be executed.' Anne simply replied, 'They deserved it and the world is better without them.'

One day in early December, Mary asked Ince something that was nagging her. 'Did you not say that you also suspected them? Why so?' He looked up from the leather-bound book in which he was writing and said, 'Yes. Frankly, she was far too honey-coated, and he didn't know the first thing about star-gazing. All those objects such as star charts in Woodroofe's, the false Gregory had taken from the baggage of the real star-gazer when he was murdered. I studied star-gazing at university, and I know a fake when I meet one.' He carried on writing, and Mary carried on being happy.

Christmas came and went with a suitable flurry of romantic snow, and the children from the village at dawn ringing little bells and running around excitedly. There were garlands throughout the house, slightly drunken servants, and feast upon feast, joy upon joy. A normal Christmas, with loving letters from her father and on Twelfth Night, she received a jewel, sent in the messenger bag from her father. A lovely pearl set in gold, with the note 'For you, a pearl amongst women, and I am immensely proud of you.' That reduced her to tears, and John Ince tutted, saying, 'Women,' as he walked away, shaking his head.

Thomas Ashbourne was rushing around the estate, ensuring the tenants' cottages were in a fit state of repair and no one was starving or freezing to death. Pretty Bess announced her engagement to Edward Loxley and the happy couple, plus twins and Will Loxley all moved into one of the estate cottages. The magistrate didn't call any more.

Then January came and Mary asked Anne 'Remind me what moon it is.' Anne answered, 'The Wolf Moon, Lady Mary. A dreadful time for those that leave their hearth, as the wolf has grown hungry, and many of its prey sleep deep in the ground. So, it seeks man, and any other living creature. It is hungry for blood and it is an ill fortune, often, for those who travel at this time, and men take on the viciousness of the wolf in their nature.'

Chapter 44

There came a particularly breathless winter morning for Mary, and a great deal of activity in preparation for it. The servants, headed by Thomas Ashbourne, had for two whole weeks been carrying bundles of fresh linen, polishing wood and sweetening. Somersal Hall must look its finest for the arrival of Sir Edmund Dudley and the person who was considered the greatest mind in the country - the Secretary of State for the Kingdom of England, Sir William Cecil, although the servants could not know in advance that he was in the party. Even Thomas Ashbourne looked a bit flustered, unusual for him, as the sound of the horses and outriders clattered into the frosty stable yard, and through to the front of the house, causing the dogs to bark.

Mary was watching from her bedroom window, which was the oriel room these days, as she was reluctant to give up her healing nest. Her old panelled room was where Mr. Secretary would sleep. A good quality table had been lugged in with much groaning - it was large, as a special request from Cecil's household, so he could work in private and quiet. Mary had dressed modestly for her rank, and Anne was all fingers and thumbs, dropping pins and the ivory comb.

Mary was smiling to herself, for the house was so excited at the master's return, you could feel it in the very timbers. Her hair had grown into a fine halo of brown curls, and her eyes were bright with good health.

She hadn't seen much of the good Doctor Ince of late, as he was caught up with his little leather-bound book which, he had confided to her, he hoped soon to have ready for publication. They had occasionally strolled in the garden over the winter mornings, bound up with thick woollen cloaks and talking of what had been.

There were men's voices, and doors opening and closing, as Mary made her way down the main stairs to go into her father's study, with heart racing. The fire was bright and watery sunshine washed the room.

'Mary, my dear,' said her father, rushing forward and taking her hands. He seemed to have aged about ten years, no doubt from worry about her, and his eyes were bagged with lack of sleep. In this moment,however, he was joyful.

'Let me look at you.' Then her father slipped one hand around her waist, and holding the other hand took her to William Cecil, who had stood respectfully on her arrival, along with John Ince and Thomas Ashbourne.

'Master Secretary, may I have the honour of presenting my daughter Mary?'

Cecil's thin hand took hers as he bowed, and she gave a curtsy. He was tall, hair going from dark to silver, with a long beard, a long thin nose and silver grey eyes that seemed to miss nothing. He was dressed in a plain fashion, but cut in the finest cloth, his gown lined and edged with shining brown fur. 'We have much to thank you for, Lady Mary, and we were all concerned to hear of your illness, and indeed how you came to be cured.' He added, 'May I say your master-stroke of those forged letters caused our enemies much wasted time and harm.'

Beside her, Mary could hear her father almost buzzing with pride, and he smiled at her broadly.

'Come, stay in here with us,' invited Cecil, 'for there is much to discuss, and all we need is our local agent to join us.' Mary looked sideways at Ince, who looked back but gave nothing away except that merest twitch in the corner of his mouth.

She hissed at Ashbourne nearby, 'It's not the dogs, is it?' He looked as if she had lost her wits. 'No!' was all he said, and then servants were moving about to bring in another visitor.

It was Agnes, who came in beaming, and William Cecil took her hand as if he had known her for years. Mary must have looked amazed, and her father smiled quietly.

'Agnes Picard is one of the best intelligence gatherers we have, and the fact that you are so astonished rather proves the point as to why. Her fluency in the French language and being based here in the heart of England is all helpful. As a trained apothecary she is able to move in and out of places without being questioned. She is, in short, remarkable.' Mary stared at her father and back at Agnes, and then to John Ince and Thomas Ashbourne, all of whom looked amused.

'You will get used to it, Lady Mary,' said Ince.

'Did you know about this, Ashbourne?' whispered Mary accusingly, and he looked shifty and answered quietly, 'Only recently in full. I knew your father had business with Agnes that was state business, but no more than that.' Mary narrowed her eyes at her steward.

'You're not a crown agent as well are you?'

He shook his head. 'Sadly not. I merely help when I can, and taking care of you was a priority, which is why John Ince had to come to protect you, and to discover the truth of what was going on in the area.'

Suddenly Mary was aware that William Cecil had stopped talking to Agnes, and that they were looking at her. In fact everyone was, so she dropped her eyes and fell silent.

Cecil spoke. 'Come now. Mary Dudley has the right to hear what this is all about, as she nearly lost her life, so make sure the room is guarded, please, Thomas Ashbourne, by a trusted servant. Preferably a man: women talk too much.' Mary flushed, but held her tongue at this comment, for she knew plenty of men who gossiped. Ashbourne soon returned, telling that a Loxley was perched outside.

William Cecil sat before the stocked up fire with a wine cup in his hand, and sighed deeply before speaking. 'If I may, without interruption, for all shall be revealed.' Mary was a bit peeved at this comment but no one else was, apparently. He continued, 'Mary Stuart, latterly queen of Scots and dowager queen of France, crossed into England last year and asked our Queen Elizabeth, her cousin, to assist her. She had been widowed from the king of France who died at seventeen. After his death she had gone to Scotland and then married a brutal man with royal blood in his veins, Lord Darnley, who was murdered. Then within weeks she married James Hepburn, the earl of Bothwell, and there was an uprising, for the people of Scotland believed she was implicated in the death of Darnley in order to marry Bothwell.'

Cecil sniffed, and spoke in a deeply disapproving manner. 'This queen was taken at Carberry Hill, locked up, miscarried twins, and then escaped from her prison in the middle of a lake. She went on to lose the battle of Langside and then escaped into England, Carlisle to be precise, with a small entourage.'

Mary felt William Cecil with those cool eyes was always precise.

'This woman, who draws darkness to her wherever she goes, thought she could displace our queen, and claim the crown for herself. For she is a papist, like much of Europe; she has never been declared illegitimate; she is prepared to marry; and she has a son, James, with Tudor blood in his veins. Much that our own queen has not. However, our queen is much loved by her subjects, is highly educated and seeks to grow and unite her people, not cause schisms like Mary Stuart. Our queen has great wisdom, by God she has, and the Scottish queen has none, and acts like a spoilt child.'

Mary Dudley had throughout her lifetime heard snippets of information about Mary Queen of Scots. In recent years she had been spoken of in whispers because of her scandalous behaviour. She remembered the gossip about her at Tutbury Castle the night the murders were announced, and realised now that the gossip was well-founded.

Sir William was quietly spoken, and measured. He spoke much less than her father and John Ince, but took in every word, correcting only if necessary, or adding more detail for a fuller picture. When asked by Thomas Ashbourne what the Scottish queen expected from 'our queen', Cecil looked long and hard into his glass before looking up.

'This cast-out queen must have expected an invitation would come rapidly from London, where she would be fêted and applauded, and given troops and gold to win back Scotland. She was a fool to expect it. At her coronation in France she described Elizabeth publicly as a "protestant whore" - pardon me, Lady Mary. That comment was laying down a defiant challenge to the English thronc that she, a Catholic queen, would take it from Her Majesty, a protestant. These last months there has been a commission to investigate the facts, and letters have been produced that prove that she was guilty of plotting her husband's murder, along with her lover, Bothwell.'

This made sense so far, but Mary was still puzzled. 'What has this to do with what happened here, and my father's letters?' she asked.

Ince leaned forward and, receiving a nod from Cecil, replied 'Mary Stuart is coming here to Tutbury Castle at the end of this month, all being well. She is to be held there, far from London, Scotland and the sea, with the earl of Shrewsbury, the Constable of the Castle, as her gaoler. Until now she has been held awaiting judgement, but Tutbury will be her prison.' Mary restrained herself from whistling like a schoolboy, but just waited for what would come next.

Your father has been accompanying her virtually all the way, staying at first at Carlisle, then at Bolton Castle, and has helped to plan her journey from Bolton to Tutbury, stopping at Rotherham, Sheffield, and Chesterfield.'

Mary cried out 'Sheffield!' and William Cecil responded.

'Yes, Lady Mary, that is why there was such consternation about your letter saying your father would be in Sheffield. Unwittingly, you were right, and that could have led to her being rescued, with a serious risk of an uprising and releasing her to lay waste on this land.'

Mary was aghast, and John Ince answered again, 'Have no fear. As you know, we seized that letter before the spies at Woodroffe's had the chance to pass it on, so no harm was done. For added safety, the journey will now bypass Sheffield, for all that Shrewsbury may wish a night in his own castle.' There was no tension in the room over this, but Mary started to realise how terribly dangerous it could have been if the letter had been seen by enemies.

'I am desperately sorry. It was not my intent to cause harm, quite the opposite, but I do fully understand what they were after from my father's messenger. Presumably they must have known about the Scots queen coming to Tutbury, or they would not be concentrating on the area so.'

'Not necessarily,' said William Cecil. 'They were focussed on your father, having learned somehow he was with Mary Stuart, and therefore wanted to draw him home to cause disruption, or better still, find out our plans.'

'If I may ask, sir,' urged Mary, 'To what end? What could they do?'

Cecil looked hard at her. 'They intend to try and rescue her, put her in a safe place, and then cause an uprising amongst the English Catholics to put her on the throne of England. It's a foolish plan in many ways, but it could cause great trouble with her free as a figurehead.'

Mary replied gravely,'We must keep her close, then.'

A silence fell on the room, before Agnes spoke, having held her peace so far. 'Forgive me, Sir William, if I may say that Lady Mary Dudley here showed immense courage in the face of the treachery that surrounded her.' Edmund Dudley looked across at his daughter and leaning over, patted her hand.

Over the next couple of weeks, with Sir William a quiet house guest, the messengers were arriving twice a day and the house was awash with letter-writing. He was mostly in his room at his desk, and although a few strangers came to the house, he saw them in the privacy of his chamber. Mary didn't know who they were and didn't need to know, she understood that. The servants had no idea who the important guest was, and were told not to speculate, so they didn't, at least not where they could be heard. Just as well, for Cook and Bess would have had what Anne called 'a purple fit.'

Mary, meanwhile, carried on as if life had never changed although it had. For her, the events of the last few months had changed her life forever, and above her in the heavens, the wolf moon was ascending.

Chapter 45

At the beginning of February 1569, Mary Dudley was seated on her chestnut mare by the great inner gatehouse of Tutbury Castle. Four men sat on horses alongside her. All the group were heavily cloaked, muffled and hooded against the winds and injuries of heaven which raged down upon them. The horses stamped their feet, jangling at their harnesses impatiently, causing the leather saddles and straps to creak with their shifting weight. John Ince and Thomas Ashbourne sat on her right, her father on her left and beyond him, the mighty William Cecil steadily staring ahead, the unsleeping, ever-watchful guardian of the nation. Ashbourne, beyond Ince, gripped his reins tightly with tension. They were a silent group, all aware of the solemn nature of the vigil.

Now,' said Cecil simply, 'Let it be done.'

Ahead, a group of about forty riders approached the Castle gates, as a gale tunnelled through the streets of Tutbury. Bare trees lining the road waved dark arms against the morbid grey sky. The riders were grouped carefully around one particular horse at the front. Mary could see that men and women made up the party, which also included soldiers. There was a purposeful pace about them, and no wonder, for they were about the business of Queen Elizabeth of England, and the safety of the nation lay in their offices that early February day.

As they drew close, Mary stiffened at the sight of the face of the prisoner, for that is what she was. For the past months the exiled queen of had been held on 'house-keep' further north and after a lengthy journey down to the heart of England, she was now arriving at Tutbury Castle, her first official prison.

There was the sound of whimpering from some of the queen's ladies, which the wind caught and snatched away. None of the group looked at the silent riders at the gate, but the captive looked up in terror at the great dark gates, and then started to vomit black before collapsing across the neck of her horse.

She was, as could be seen even in the saddle, immensely tall and slim. Long, red hair tumbled from beneath her now lost riding bonnet. She was carried bodily down from her horse by her attendants and then steadied upon her feet to walk through the gate, but held under her elbows. One woman had an arm around the prisoner's waist to support her further. They were not allowed to carry her, she must walk.

Mary was dismayed at this scene, for it seemed brutal and cruel. She looked sharply to her left at her father, but

Sir Edmund did not look back at her, and gave the slightest movement of his head in warning that Mary must be still and remain silent, and so she did. Her group continued staring coldly at the lonely scene before them as if they were ghosts watching from the wings of Heaven at this tragic daughter of debate. This Mary, Queen of the Scots and Dowager Queen of France and Heir Apparent to the English throne, entered Tutbury Castle.

All was now revealed, all was now understood. Minutes passed as the pathetic retreating figure wove unsteadily between the narrow streets of packed buildings in the inner bailey, moving towards what would be her residence in the South Tower.

Mary and her companions all waited some minutes and without a word or glance backwards rode away. They all but one turned their horses towards the London Road. Sir William would only go part of the way, as he intended to go east to his golden house of Burleigh, just outside Stamford.

The night before at Somersal, he had by candlelight written a note to Queen Elizabeth of all that would happen. The letter could not leave until the deed was done, in case changes to the letter had to be made, but now the sooner it left, the better. He looked towards the crossroads, where there were two figures, one on a large strong horse, carrying a leather messenger bag across his body, waiting for the signal. William Cecil gave that signal, raising his right hand, and the horse leapt away at a great pace.

A solid cob remained where the messenger had been. On it was a slight figure with a jaunty air. It was the garden boy from Somersal, Charlie, who was going to 'make himself useful' as Mary had explained to Ashbourne and Ince. Both men had exchanged doubtful glances, but Mary was determined to give the boy a chance of adventure, and he had taken it with unrestrained joy. He would be part of their merry band in the years to come, and now was a start.

Only one man would look back, as they were joined by armed guards to protect the group on their long journey south: Thomas Ashbourne, who was to return to Somersal to close up, and who waited until their figures were almost out of sight, and then turned his face into the biting wind.

Lightning Source UK Ltd.
Milton Keynes UK
UKHW041925220621
385992UK00002B/48

9 780905 98595